ASYLUM

A STAR KINGDOM NOVEL

LINDSAY BUROKER

1

Mari Moonrazor adjusted her ocular implants to simulate normal human eyesight as she gazed over the forest of evergreens toward the rising sun. Pinks and oranges burnished the blue sky, the sight gorgeous and still novel to someone who'd spent most of her life on spaceships and habitats. She couldn't, however, help but wonder if she was truly seeing the sky as unaltered humans would. Her mother had surgically installed numerous chips and cybernetic implants in her before she'd been a year old, and Mari couldn't remember what it was like to be fully human.

As she watched the sky slowly change colors, an increasingly familiar sense of hiraeth crept over her. Why did she keep coming up to this clifftop to look at the sunrises when they kept stirring up emotions that could only get her in trouble? Emotions that prompted her to take action. To *leave*.

With her mother's plans to assemble an ancient wormhole gate and lead their people to another system recently thwarted, Mari's life's work seemed insignificant. What need did the astroshamans have for a terraforming scientist, or the technology she made, now that they were hunkered in an underground base on a planet that already had the rich atmosphere, soils, and climates of Old Earth?

Behind her, heavy feet crunched through the foliage on the clifftop. Her augmented hearing had no trouble picking up the noise over the hum of the generator that kept a camouflaging shield over their base to hide it from the network of satellites that orbited Odin. It was her mother's crusher, a huge tarry-black combat robot that could liquefy and re-form into any shape. Its approach had to mean that her mother was also coming.

Concern stirred in Mari's gut, though she wasn't doing anything wrong. Not yet. Surely, even beings who longed to integrate themselves with machines, if not eventually give up their biological bodies entirely, could appreciate the aesthetical appeal of a sunrise.

"It is not the worst view one could have for a secret base," her mother said, stepping around the crusher and up to the edge of the cliff to join her. Her short white hair stuck up in all directions, as if she'd just roused from bed, though it always looked like that, and implants made her eyes appear the same whitish-blue as Mari's. Her skin was bronze, a few shades darker than Mari's, who had the coloring and slim build of the father she couldn't remember, a father long gone. "I should know. I've spent much of the last twenty years hiding in one place or another."

"It's an improvement over the ice base on Xolas Moon," Mari said, "but can we truly consider it secret? The land was a gift, right? At least one person in the Star Kingdom government knows we're here."

"It was not a *gift* but a *prize* acquired through negotiations. And it is only temporary, until we can build a gate from scratch with the data we gathered—" her mother waved to the ground, indicating the complex engineering project their people had started in the freshly excavated base built under the cliff, "—and resume our quest to travel beyond the Twelve Systems and find a new home, one not impinged upon by humanity's spread. A place where we will not be judged for seeking the next logical evolution."

Mari didn't point out that astroshamans were as apt to judge normal humans as vice versa. "When? Shall I continue my research?"

"Of course. Our allies in System Geryon are manufacturing an automated ship that will take our finished gate to the new system we've chosen, install it, and link it to the existing network, so we can quickly travel there ourselves. If you've completed work on your prototype terraformer, we can build more of them and send them along on the ship to create a world suitable for biological matter. Since our people have not yet been able to agree collectively to give up our original forms—" Mother waved at her mostly human body, "—for entirely machine-based bodies, that will be necessary."

Mari grimaced. She hadn't yet told her mother that she'd lost the terraforming device. It had been in her lab on the *Celestial Dart*, one of the spaceships that had battled the Kingdom Fleet in their Arctic Islands and crashed. She'd had instructions to grab everything valuable before transferring to a transport vessel that wouldn't go into combat, but there had been too much to take and not much time. She'd forgotten her prototype.

"Do you think it's necessary for us to leave now that the Kingdom is under more progressive rule?" Mari asked to change the subject. "Perhaps we could stay here and be..."

"What? Welcomed with open arms?" Mother snorted.

Mari knew that was unlikely, but she couldn't help but think of the list she'd made on her eighteenth birthday. The Human List.

It was full of things she had never experienced and only read about in books, things that were frowned upon in the astroshaman community because they appealed to "base human emotions." Drinking caffeinated and alcoholic substances, air-bike racing, hang-gliding, kissing, having sex, eating chocolate, even walking barefoot on a beach with sand squishing between her toes. They were all things she was curious about but had never been permitted to do.

"Even if we hadn't gone along with high shamans Chatelain and Cometrunner," Mother continued, "and attacked this world, the Kingdom never would have accepted us. They never did before. Even those in progressive systems call us freaks and weirdos, always making it clear that we do not belong. If you doubt that, all you have to do is go out among them and walk in their streets with your implants visible."

"Can I?" Mari smiled to make it a joke, but that sense of longing returned. Her mother had never given her or her siblings the opportunity to go out among normal humans. But it would be easy now that they were living on this world. Even though she couldn't see the distant capital of Zamek City, not even with the binocular setting on her implants, she knew it was there, a mere two hundred miles to the east. Mari envisioned Glasnax-windowed skyscrapers glinting pink in the rising sun.

"No." Her mother turned a horrified expression on her. "Especially not now. They're still repairing their cities from the bombings. They would kill you on sight."

That would be unfair. Mari hadn't had anything to do with the bombings, nor would she threaten any humans if she went among them. All she wanted was to experience the items on her Human List.

"Give up such notions," her mother said, as if reading her mind, "and focus on perfecting the terraformer so we can make more of them."

It struck Mari that if she confessed to having lost it, she might have the excuse to leave. If their lost ships hadn't been salvaged, someone could fly up and retrieve the device. *She* could volunteer. Oh, the frigid Arctic Islands weren't anything she longed to see, but while she was out, maybe she could also visit one of the cities on the mainland. Since her people had few working transport devices, maybe she would even need to go to a city first to acquire a small craft to fly up there.

"I should have told you earlier," Mari said, "the prototype was on the *Celestial Dart.*"

Her mother grimaced. "You didn't take it with you when we left?"

"There wasn't much time, and I didn't even think of it. I left it in a cabinet in my lab."

Her mother radiated displeasure.

"I hadn't truly believed our ships would be defeated."

"They *shouldn't* have been," her mother growled. "If *I* had been in charge, I wouldn't have underestimated Casmir Dabrowski and his pesky clone."

"Perhaps I could go up to the crash site and see if the terraformer survived. I had it tucked away in an insulated box."

Her mother squinted at her. A suspicious squint?

Mari raised her eyebrows, turning her expression into what she hoped looked like a desire to be helpful, not a scheme to escape.

"It would be easy to find it," Mari added. "I know you prompted the other ships to self-destruct when you and the survivors fled, so that the Kingdom wouldn't get our technology, but I found the *Celestial Dart* on their satellite imagery."

"It was *also* supposed to self-destruct, but the program failed, or the equipment was too damaged by the crash. The rest of us were too injured and concerned about surviving and escaping to go back to finish the job. By then, their troops were crawling all over those mountains."

"The terraformer was locked in a cabinet. Scavengers might not have found it. I can—"

"No. It is too dangerous. They have a military outpost near the crash site, and unscrupulous salvagers are likely still fighting over

the pieces." Her mother's mouth twisted in distaste. "I assume you
have the schematics. You can build it again."

"The raw materials—"

"Make a list. I'll find a way to acquire whatever you need."

"But Mother. Shouldn't we at least check?"

"It's too dangerous," her mother repeated, her voice hard. "You
may not go."

Mari clenched her jaw. She was twenty-four. Had she been a
normal human born into a human household on almost any
planet or habitat in the Twelve Systems, she would have been
considered an adult, free to make her own decisions. Free to go
where she wished.

"It is for your own good, Mari," her mother said, her voice
softer. "They would see you as a spy if not a saboteur, and they
would kill you. If I thought you merely wanted to sneak in and out
of the crash site without being seen, perhaps I would say yes, but I
believe you want more than that. As you've admitted before, you
want to walk among them, a scientist experiencing the culture and
curiosities of the indigenous people."

Mari's cheeks warmed, and she looked out upon the forest
instead of meeting her mother's gaze. She shouldn't have been so
frank about her desires in the past.

"Perhaps they would not kill us," Mari said. "Perhaps one
could prove that one had no ill intent and might be permitted to
explore their world."

Just proving she didn't have ill intent might not be enough.
What if she was willing to share her knowledge about
terraforming with the Kingdom? Her prototype was far more
advanced and faster working than the equipment they used. If she
could find it and show it to them, maybe they would want to hire
her. Or even grant her asylum.

"Just because Minister Dabrowski is willing to turn enemies
into allies doesn't mean the rest of them will see us as anything

but threats to be destroyed. He is not in charge of their people. The very fact that we must remain hidden—" Mother pointed upward toward the camouflaging shield over the base, though it was only visible when Mari shifted the setting of her implants to detect energy instead of light waves, "—is a testament to that. Their military would *destroy* us if they knew we were here. You will stay here in hiding, as we all will, until it's time to leave the Twelve Systems forever."

Mother glanced toward the rising sun, then turned her back on it and headed to the tunnel that led into their base. A temporary base on a temporary planet.

Forever. The word haunted Mari. If she didn't go out soon and experience humanity and what it was like to be one of them... she would never get a chance.

For her entire life, she'd obeyed her mother and the elders. But as she looked toward the rising sun, she decided she'd had enough. She would take her chances and trust she could keep herself alive among potential enemies. It was time to leave her people.

"I never thought I would rob a greenhouse."

"These buildings are experimental seed and plant germination centers," K-45 said in his robotic voice.

"I never thought I would rob a germination center."

"Are you having misgivings about this mission?"

"You might say that." Kenji Chisaka—who went by Kenji Backer, in the vain hope that neither the Kingdom Guard nor Zamek City Police would find out he was the son of a terrorist—pushed his hands through his hair hard enough to dislodge strands. "When we were robbing from the corrupt nobility, who are hell-bent on keeping commoners enslaved in a backward system, it seemed right and just. But these are Queen Oku's greenhouses, and *she's* in charge now. By all accounts, she's a progressive academic who remembers the names of the little people, and she's dating a commoner."

Kenji didn't want to rob anyone at *all*. For the last eight years, he'd been doing honest work, whatever jobs he could find without being chipped and in the system. Just when he'd eked together enough physical currency to bribe a spaceship captain to take him out of the Kingdom so he could start a new life, not one but *two* invading forces had come to Odin. They'd dropped bombs all over the planet, including onto the apartment building where he'd been squatting in the basement. He'd lost all of his meager belongings; he'd almost lost his life.

"Minister of External Affairs Casmir Dabrowski was cloned from the legendary war hero Admiral Mikita," Kay said, "and, in the aftermath of King Jager's death, was awarded a position in the nobility."

"Yeah, but he was born a commoner and raised in an apartment in the Brodskiburg District. That's as common as it gets."

"I was born in Refuse Collection Bin Thirty-Seven," Kay said, "but I am uncommon."

"That is true. I used to take classes from Minister Dabrowski. He was *Professor* Dabrowski back then."

"You were accepted into an institute of higher learning?" Why did his robot companion sound surprised?

Kenji wished he could legitimately say yes, but... "I squatted on campus for a while and sneaked into classes in the huge lecture halls where nobody took attendance."

It was unlikely Dabrowski had known he existed.

"Backer!" one of the thieves standing guard outside the greenhouse whispered harshly. "Quit yapping with your junkyard of a robot. This isn't the coffee house. You're supposed to be standing guard. *Alertly*."

Kenji sighed and focused on the parking lot across the field from the greenhouses. He was stationed next to an irrigation shed halfway to the lot, and his duty was to delay the authorities if any shuttles or ground vehicles flew or drove in.

His stomach growled, a reminder that he had few crowns in his pocket, and it had been more than a day since his last meal. He didn't want to rob anyone, but he needed to eat.

"I am also having misgivings about this mission," Kay said in a lower tone of voice. "My materials may have been *acquired* in a junkyard, but like human beings, I am worth more than the sum of my parts."

"Yes, you are." Since Kenji had assembled Kay, he wouldn't disagree, though even he admitted his multi-metaled bipedal companion wasn't the most state-of-the-art robot in existence. None of his parts were dented or rusted, but the service panel on his back that allowed access to his internal wiring did not look like anything other than the toaster door that it was. "I'm sorry I let myself get talked into this. If I had money to rent a shuttle, we'd be up in the Arctic Islands, scavenging the wrecks from the big battle there. It's rumored that some of them were astroshaman ships. Even if they've mostly been picked over by now, can you imagine how much we could get for even a few smidgens of their technology?"

Kenji picked up his borrowed DEW-Tek rifle, prepared to do his duty if police or the Kingdom Guard showed up. He tried to hand a pistol to Kay, but the robot closed his mechanical fist, refusing to accept it.

"You're not willing to help out?" Kenji asked.

"You know what my foundational programming is."

Yes, when Kenji had been building the robot, there hadn't been many free options for embedded operating systems. He'd wanted Kay to be able to help him with the mechanic job he'd been holding down at the time, but the only foundational

programs that had been available were Kitchen Assistant and
Academic Tutor. Figuring the kitchen-assistant operating system
would have left Kay prone to chopping and roasting everything in
sight, Kenji had opted for Academic Tutor. For the most part, it
worked fine, and he'd been able to add numerous engineering and
repair programs afterward, but Kay did have a tendency toward
lecturing. Even worse, he often opined on philosophical and
moral matters. Such as robbing greenhouses.

"I am incapable of acting in a violent manner toward human
beings," Kay added.

"You could shoot out their tires."

"I am incapable of acting in a violent manner toward tires."

"I had no idea tutor robots weren't allowed to do that."

"We are programmed to be serene role models for impression-
able young humans."

"Will you at least wave a wrench menacingly if someone
threatens me?" Kenji asked.

"I will consider this."

A police shuttle flew along the border of the park, its distinc-
tive green and blue lights identifying it even on the dark cloudy
night.

Kenji leaned into the shadows of the irrigation shed. Against
his advice, the gang of thieves had shot out the lights around the
shed and the four big greenhouses before sneaking in, but their
flashlight beams were visible through the glass walls as they
searched for the "special seeds that would go for a fortune to the
right buyer," as the leader had put it.

Kenji held his breath until the police shuttle flew out of view
beyond the trees edging the grassy fields. Maybe they hadn't seen
anything. Maybe this would work.

So long as shooting out the lights hadn't activated an alarm
somewhere. Even though the greenhouses had been secured by
nothing more than padlocks on the doors, Kenji had a hard time

believing there wasn't an alarm system, not if the contents were as valuable as the gang thought.

"If we make as much as the guys think, our five percent could be enough to finally get us passage out of the Kingdom—and away from my father's inimical legacy." Kenji wiped a hand on his trousers, as if he could wipe away the blood that had once been there, blood of the people he'd been forced, as a boy, to help his father kill. If the authorities ever found him and ran a DNA test...

Two police vehicles swung into the parking lot, lights flashing. Damn it.

"Police," Kenji whispered into his comm unit. "Everyone out."

"We've almost got the seeds. Lay down cover!"

The police vehicle doors flew open, and officers in gray combat armor leaped out. Kenji grimaced. That meant that even if he dared shoot them, they would be protected.

His teammate at the greenhouse door fired at the police and their vehicles, crimson DEW-Tek bolts lighting up the night. As expected, the energy blasts bounced ineffectively off the armor and the armored vehicles.

As Kenji pulled out one of the three grenades he'd been given, the police shuttle flew back into view.

"Abort," he whispered into the comm. "There are more coming. Abort *now*."

"We only need thirty seconds! Keep them busy!"

The fearless police officers charged across the grassy field toward the greenhouse. Kenji threw one of the grenades, aiming well in front of them. He wanted to deter them, not hurt anyone.

The grenade blew a crater, the boom echoing across the park, hurling grass and dirt in all directions. Unfortunately, the officers ran into the smoke, navigating the smoking crater easily in their armor, and kept coming. They would soon pass his shed on the way to the greenhouses.

"This is unacceptably violent." Soft clanks sounded as Kay did the robot equivalent of wringing his hands. "I do not approve, Kenji. You should not have involved yourself in such a scheme."

"No kidding. You need to run. Get a head start. Meet beyond those trees over there."

The robot didn't need to be told twice. He clanked away from the shed and the parking area. One of the officers must have noticed his movement, for he shifted his rifle in that direction.

Kenji stepped away from the shed and lobbed the second grenade in the officer's path.

Shots fired from another direction, and glass shattered as one of the thieves blew a hole in the back of the greenhouse they were in. Four members of the gang sprang out through it, some carrying sacks of seeds, two carrying what looked like potted ferns with huge balls of fruit dangling from the fronds.

They would have to run hundreds of yards across a field to the trees and the getaway vehicle parked on the road on the other side. Kenji was even farther away from that escape.

Though instincts told him to flee, Kenji knew the thieves wouldn't be able to outrun the authorities, not when the officers' armor gave them greater strength and speed than typical. He had to try to delay them further. They'd gotten out with hopefully valuable goods. This job could still be worth it—if they could escape.

As the second grenade blew, Kenji lifted his rifle and fired at the police officers. He targeted the seams in their armor at their knees, shoulders, and ankles, keeping his aim steady though his heart pounded. If he got caught, he'd be screwed for more reasons than shooting at the police and robbing a greenhouse.

His aim was pinpoint, thanks to his father's training and a few not-quite-legal enhancements his parents had made to his genes before he'd been born, and one of the police yelped and grabbed his shoulder. He stumbled to the side and out of the formation, but two other officers spotted Kenji in the shadows.

"Get that one!"

Two men veered toward him as the others continued after the rest of the gang. As Kenji sprinted away in the opposite direction, he threw his last grenade over his shoulder. It landed by the shed, blowing it to pieces and pelting the men with wood and metal.

Doubting that would slow them for long, Kenji raced across the field, not toward the getaway car but in the direction Kay had gone. Trees loomed up ahead. If he could reach them, maybe he could lose his pursuers and escape.

He *had* to. He couldn't be captured, couldn't take the chance of being identified and linked to his father. If that happened, he would be charged not with a misdemeanor but with murder, and spend the rest of his short life in the penal asteroid mines.

Kay, who clearly had no objections to fleeing, kept running, his mismatched legs propelling him with impressive speed. Kenji glanced back, worried about the lack of cover as they raced across the open field. But his grenade had either deterred the pair of men pursuing him, or they'd realized the main group was the bigger threat. Maybe Kenji *could* get away.

As he neared the trees, a dark figure in black armor leaped out of the branches.

What the hell? This wasn't one of the policemen.

A silver logo above the faceplate on the man's helmet gleamed in the night, the letters ME standing out against the surrounding black. Kenji groaned. He'd heard of this guy.

Kay halted so fast that he clattered, his bulbous head jerking forward. He flung up his arms in surrender, but the armored figure grabbed him and hurled him twenty feet through the air.

Kenji pointed his rifle at the man, but he couldn't keep from gaping. Even with strength-accentuating armor, that was an incredible feat. Kay wasn't light.

With a thunderous crash, the robot struck a trunk hard. Kenji gritted his teeth as anger surged up in him. Kay wasn't indestructible either.

"You bastard," Kenji snarled, firing at the man's armored chest. "That's my *friend*."

He kept himself from saying his *only* friend, since that was pathetic. Even if it was true.

The armored man focused on him, his face too shadowed to make out behind his helmet's faceplate. As they had with the police, the energy bolts bounced uselessly off him. Kenji shifted his aim to the neck, again hoping to find a seam, but that looked like much more expensive—and higher quality—armor than the police had.

He should have run, but where? His genetic enhancements were modest; he couldn't escape this man. Kenji's only hope was to damage that armor enough to deter him.

But the man sprang at him, powerful legs taking him through the air as if he'd leapt off a trampoline. Kenji jumped to the side, turning his rifle into a club at the last second, hoping vainly to smash through his foe's faceplate.

A hand snatched the rifle out of the air, tearing it from his grip. So fast Kenji didn't know what was happening, he found his legs knocked out from under him. He hit the ground hard, landing on his back, his head thudding against the earth. A weight landed on his chest, pinning him. The armored man's knee.

"I surrender!" Kenji jerked his hands up.

He had no idea if the capital's new self-proclaimed superhero known only as the Main Event killed criminals, but with all the weight on his chest, and his ribcage creaking, Kenji worried the guy would crush him to death by accident. The Main Event was reputedly cybernetically enhanced, giving him strength and agility even beyond what the armor offered, and it would be easy for someone like that to carelessly snap a rib—or a spine.

The man paused, looking toward the police and the other

thieves. The leader and someone else had been captured before they reached the getaway vehicle.

"I didn't seriously hurt anyone." Kenji struggled not to panic at the crushing weight on his chest, and the fear that he'd scraped by his whole life only to die helping thugs steal *seeds*. "I didn't want to do this mission, but I've got no job and can barely buy food. My home and everything I have was destroyed in the bombings."

He doubted the Main Event cared.

But Kenji's captor kneeled back, the painful weight coming off his ribs. He hefted Kenji to his feet, a steel grip not letting him go.

"The city has shelters and offers jobs to those who need them," the Main Event said in a passionless but surprisingly cultured voice. He sounded like a noble.

"Only if you're chipped and in the system."

The Main Event looked at him, his face still too shadowed by the night—or was he wearing a mask?—to see. "You can *get* chipped and get into the system."

"No, I can't. Uhm, family troubles. That would be a really bad idea for me. I have a father who's, ah, he didn't treat us well." Why was he babbling and explaining this to some justice-fighter? "A real scum. Mom's dead because of him. I don't suppose you know what it's like to come from a bad family?"

Surprisingly, the man barked what might have been a laugh. It also might have been coughing up of phlegm. Something that was hard to spit out when one was in combat armor.

"I also *really* don't want to have a blood test done by the police," Kenji went on, hoping he could somehow talk his way out of this. "You're into anonymity, right? You've got to get it."

Another firefight broke out in the trees across the park. A couple of the thieves had made it to the getaway car and grabbed bigger weapons. One turned a hand cannon on the police officers. That might be powerful enough to cut through their armor. Kenji willed his captor to go help the police and leave him alone.

An alarmed yell came from the firefight. One of the police? That was the first hint that the encounter might be going poorly for them.

The Main Event released Kenji but only to pick up his fallen rifle. He flexed his armored arms and snapped it in half. All right, that was impressive. Kenji's thoughts of having his spine snapped returned.

A faint rattle came from the other direction—Kay trying to get to his feet. The Main Event glanced at him but only tossed the pieces of rifle to the ground.

"I've dedicated myself to protecting this city, boy," the Main Event said.

Kenji bristled at being called a boy—he'd just turned twenty-four—but if his youth might lead this guy to be more lenient, he would keep his mouth shut.

"I'm watching out for it. Thieves who shoot at police officers aren't welcome. If I come across you in Zamek City again, I'll drop you off at Police Headquarters, and you can burble tales of family woes to them." Without waiting for a response, he took off across the field toward the fighting.

Not questioning his good luck, Kenji ran to Kay and helped him up. His robot buddy was a whiz at repairing everything from kitchen appliances to vehicles to spaceship engines, but his junk-yard body, as one of the thieves had called it, wasn't evenly weighted, and he struggled with things like standing up and climbing stairs.

"Are you badly damaged?" In the dark, Kenji couldn't tell how smashed Kay was after being hurled against a tree.

"My housing is dented in numerous places, but my circuitry and skeletal framework appear sufficient for fleeing this odious place, which I dearly hope is next on our agenda. I will do a full diagnostic scan shortly."

"Yes." Kenji helped him through the trees and away from the

park, frowning at the robot's lopsided gait, though his hip ached, and he was also limping after being hurled to the ground. "When I get some money, I'll buy you better parts."

Whenever that would be.

"Most thoughtful, but unless I am mistaken, you will not be receiving a five-percent stake from tonight's mission."

"I know, but there's something else I've been thinking about. Something that could be more lucrative."

"You are not going to sell me, are you?"

"No. Friends don't sell friends." Kenji didn't point out that he would have had to *pay* a junkyard owner to take an ancient K-45 off his hands, especially one with toaster parts.

"Excellent. I concur. What is your new plan?"

"Since we can't stay in the city..." Kenji glanced back, but neither the police nor the Main Event were in sight. "Maybe it's time for that salvage mission in the Arctic Islands that I've been dreaming about."

"You said you couldn't afford to rent a craft to take us up there."

"We'll borrow one."

"From a friend?"

"From a shuttle-rental service with lax lending standards."

Kay rotated his bulbous head, his oval-shaped optical sensors looking at him. "I am concerned for your future, Kenji."

"It'll work out."

"Who will I converse with if you end up in a detention center?"

Kenji didn't mention that, as his personal property, Kay would end up deactivated and stuffed in a storage locker in the same detention center. "We're going to make it work this time, Kay. We're going to make enough money to get out of the Kingdom and start new lives. You'll see."

"I do hope so. I believe one of my toes just fell off."

"I'll build you a new foot. Once we're on the way to the Arctic."

2

The wan sun did nothing to warm Mari as she sped over ice fields and away from the military outpost on a rented air bike, the wind needling her even through multiple layers of clothing. Her fingers were numb inside her gloves, and she could barely feel her toes, but she didn't care. She had done it.

She'd sneaked away from her mother's base, sabotaging the security system long enough to slip out without leaving a trace. After a few miles of walking, she'd found and taken over an automated logging vehicle, altering its programming to give her a ride to a mill on the outskirts of Zamek City. Once in the capital, she'd located a rental shop with a clerk willing to take her money without asking for identification. She'd checked out a bike from him, ridden to a military base near the city, and used a couple of her hacking programs to unlock a hatch on a cargo ship heading to the Kingdom outpost in the Arctic.

Mari smirked as she imagined what her mother would think of her using the engineering and computer knowledge all of her people were educated with to become a serial stowaway. It had been easier than she'd expected. Oh, she'd expected to be caught at any point along the way, but after dealing with her people's ultra-secure networks, getting into and navigating the Kingdom networks, even the private ones, hadn't been that difficult.

The harder part had been avoiding scrutinizing stares from people in the city who'd noticed her implants and must have wondered if she was an astroshaman. Normal humans sometimes got cybernetic upgrades, and most of them had embedded banking and network chips, but few people had their working eyes replaced with implants or the equivalent of a circuit board with ports and an extra bank of chips stuck in the side of their head. Mari had kept her shoulder-length blonde hair combed over that the best she could, but it was noticeable.

She hadn't dared shop for food or to experiment with any of the items on her Human List. Once she had her terraforming prototype and could offer it and her knowledge in exchange for asylum, she could explore the world. She just had to hope it was still in the wrecked ship and that it hadn't been destroyed. And that the Kingdom government would want what she offered enough to overlook that her people were their enemies.

Jagged white mountains rose up ahead of her, the sun glinting on their frosty slopes. According to the satellite imagery, the *Celestial Dart* had crashed on a cliff on this side of them.

She increased the magnification of her ocular implants, looking for any hint of a ship's hull amid the snow and ice. Also searching for signs of people—especially the soldiers from that outpost. Hopefully, they didn't run patrols out here, but she didn't know.

Even though her mother had negotiated something of a truce with Minister Dabrowski, and he apparently owned the land they'd constructed their new base on, Mari doubted the planet's military had instructions to leave astroshamans alone if they saw them. More likely, they would try to capture and interrogate her.

As she tilted back on the handlebars to lift the nose of her air bike and climb up into the mountains, an alert blinked in her vision, a silent ding sounding in her mind. Her implants had detected an anomaly in the terrain. It was atop a cliff, as she'd expected. The wreck.

She sped up. This was it.

An unexpected tangle of emotions filled her as she came upon the wreck, what had once been a great spaceship capable of housing hundreds of engineers and researchers now buried under numerous feet of snow. The *Celestial Dart* hadn't been her only home, but it had been the ship she traveled on when her people were not staying on one base or another, doing their best to avoid human civilizations. She'd studied and researched aboard that ship, been raised with her siblings, and learned the religious and secular ways of her people. It had been a more permanent part of her life than most of the homes they'd fleetingly lived in.

Loss and regret and sadness made her slow down as she surveyed the mess. Moisture filmed her eyes and dampened her lashes until they froze, little crystals battering her cheeks every time she blinked. Since her tear ducts had never been altered, she had no trouble crying, but she rarely did. As her mother and others had told her so often, intense human emotion was a reminder of their biological evolution and a sign that one was regressing toward a more primitive state. Rational computer-like beings did not cry.

"Just be glad you weren't on board when it crashed," she muttered, navigating around the snow-covered wreck and looking for a spot where she might gain access to the interior.

In addition to a few weapons for protection, she'd brought a toolbox that included a plasma cutter, but as she eyed the white drifts piled atop the mangled remains of the hull, she wondered if it would be enough. She navigated toward a spot on the windward side of the cliff where the mounds of snow were less substantial and lucked across a hatch. Scorch marks marred the hull around it, as if some scavenger had tried to force his way in but failed.

"Open," she told the hatch and wasn't surprised when it didn't budge. There wasn't likely any power left to run the computer system.

Mari removed a glove and rested her hand on a panel, resisting the urge to jerk it back at the icy chill. The hatch hissed open with the breaking of a seal. At least the battery-powered mechanisms still worked.

The hatchway led into a corridor near the crew cabins. Would she be able to find an intact route to the laboratories? And would *they* be intact? They were in the interior of the ship, next to sickbay, and well-protected, so maybe. But finding a navigable route to them would be difficult.

After putting her glove back on, Mari pulled out her plasma cutter and nodded to herself. She could handle difficulties. If she wanted asylum here in the Kingdom, she had to have something valuable to offer in exchange. She would find her terraformer and also take any other valuable technology she came across that she might be able to trade. At least, unlike the scavengers who had already been here, she had a rightful claim to the devices inside the ship.

The wind howled across the cliff, tossing snow over the side. Before climbing through the warped hatchway, Mari scanned her surroundings to make sure no soldiers or other craft were nearby. She also guessed that her mother had found out she was missing by now and might have sent someone after her. Hopefully not that crusher. With her tools and weapons, Mari believed she could defend herself against most humans, but a nearly indestructible combat robot was another matter.

Fortunately, the barren landscape was empty. Good.

Mari climbed inside, grunting in annoyance when a collapsed

ceiling and caved-in bulkheads stopped her right away. She ignited the plasma cutter. This was going to take a while.

"Have you previously been educated on how to fly aircraft?" Kay asked from the copilot's seat of the shuttle.

It was Kenji's first time traveling out of Zamek City in years—and his first time taking Kay anywhere. He assumed the robot's skepticism had more to do with their conveyance than his piloting skills. As they'd entered their seventh hour of flight, an ominous rattle and a puff of black smoke had come from one of their thruster housings. A readout next to a flashing yellow light on the navigation console kept insisting they service the engine. Earlier, Kenji had commed the rental place about the alert. The man working there had said it was fine and to ignore it.

"My father taught me how to pilot everything from a flyer to a galaxy charger spaceship. I'm a little rusty, but if we crash, *I* won't be the reason for it."

Per the man's instructions, Kenji tried to ignore another puff of smoke wafting from the thruster. Since they were flying over an iceberg-filled sea, there was no place to stop and do maintenance.

He'd been so pleased to find a rental service clerk who would wheel and deal with him that he hadn't questioned his luck. He'd promised to pay after he got back and sold some of the salvage he was determined to find. Surprisingly, the man had agreed, so long as he brought double the usual fee. Maybe he'd only agreed because he'd known the shuttle would crash, and he hoped to make an insurance claim.

"You have not spoken of a father," Kay said. "Are you close?"

"No."

"If he taught you to pilot, that suggests an interest in your education and ability to care for yourself as an adult."

"He wanted me to be able to fly the getaway craft after he bombed buildings, stations, or habitats."

Kay's bulbous head rotated toward him. "Did you say *bombed*?"

"Yes. He's a terrorist. He wanted me to be his little acolyte." Kenji didn't mention that he *had* been his father's acolyte, or at least his assistant in his vile endeavors, until he'd turned sixteen and mustered the courage to stage his death and run away. To this day, he didn't know if his father truly believed he was dead or simply hadn't cared enough to track down a son who didn't want to serve him and therefore had no purpose.

"I thought you said you came from a noble family."

Had he told Kay that? Maybe one night when he'd been drunk. Drinking took the edge off. "My mother did, but she's been gone since I was eight. *He* might have done it. I never had any proof, but she kept trying to keep him away from me. He didn't like that. I'd been his idea, you see, the gene cleaning and enhancements and everything. A little scion to the business. You want to know the funny part?"

"This is a funny part? I am not an expert on human emotions, but your tale appears to lack in humor."

"No kidding. But he hated King Jager and having a senate comprised of nobles. He always railed about all that, and how the common man had no power, and also the idiocy of genetic engineering being outlawed in the Kingdom. He was trying to make statements, blowing things up as a way of fighting the system." Kenji eyed another puff of black smoke and checked to see how far they were from land. "That was how it was in the beginning anyway, at least according to my mother. I guess she silently supported him back then. Even though she was a noble, she didn't approve of the system. But later..." Kenji shook his head, memories popping up of dead people—*murdered* people—and blood everywhere, including on his own hands. "I think he liked it. *Likes* it. He's still alive out there somewhere, but not in System Lion, I think. He had a couple of close calls with knights who'd been sent to hunt him down, and it's been a few years since anyone saw him here. He's reputedly a thief, bounty hunter, and who knows what in another system now, but the Kingdom hasn't forgotten his crimes. They want him dead."

And they would happily take out the son who'd assisted him too. Kenji *had* to get out of System Lion. He couldn't keep flirting with the authorities. And now that damn self-proclaimed superhero.

When Kenji had checked the news, he hadn't been surprised that the rest of the greenhouse-incursion party had been arrested. He was still shocked that the Main Event had let him go. He wouldn't press his luck and return to the capital longer than it took to drop off the shuttle. Even though he'd lived in Zamek City for years and knew it well, Kenji could make the money he needed to charter a space flight elsewhere.

"Such as right here," he murmured, spotting white land coming into view on the horizon. "We're going to make it."

"I am most relieved," Kay said.

"Me too."

The trip back might be dicier, but while he searched for valuables, Kenji would have Kay perform any repairs that might be possible without spare parts. Earlier, he'd seen a toolbox in the back.

"There is a military outpost on this island," Kay said as they flew over a glacier, a herd of walruses near the water, startled by the shuttle's passing—or the plumes of smoke. "Will they not object to salvage operations taking place near their compound?"

"We're not going to ask for their permission. And we're one man and a robot, not a salvage operation."

"Do you seek to acquire more trouble for yourself?"

"No. We'll be circumspect."

"I have concerns."

"If anyone asks, we'll say we came up here to hike," Kenji said.

"Robots do not participate in recreational physical activity."

"You can fix the shuttle while *I* recreate. Don't worry. I think the wrecks are several miles from the outpost and in the mountains." Kenji banked to head toward the snowy peaks on the horizon.

He had been doing research on the network, learning everything he could about the battle and the likely locations of wrecks. Too bad there wasn't more information. Reports that Military Intelligence and Royal Intelligence had filed about the conflict had been classified, leaving the media outlets to share only opinions and guesses. Kenji hoped what he'd gathered from those sources would be enough.

He fished his glasses out of his pocket and put them on, activating the network interface and display to bring up the maps and data he'd bookmarked. The research would have been easier if he'd had a chip in his temple wired directly into his brain, as was typical for people in the Kingdom and most of the Twelve Systems, but the government could use such devices to locate a person, so his father had never had Kenji embedded with one. And after Kenji had run away from the old man, it had seemed wise to continue to stay off the grid.

"Watch the scanners, will you?" Kenji asked. "Let me know if any other ships are in the area."

"Certainly." Kay tilted his body forward at the hip to peruse the limited instrumentation. They would be lucky if the dilapidated shuttle could detect obstacles in their flight path, much less other ships in the area, but maybe the scanners were more advanced than they looked. Kay scraped at something brownish and gunky on a display with a finger. "I believe this is food detritus."

"Looks like mustard. The last copilot may have been into ham sandwiches."

"Did he not grasp the merits of cleaning up after himself? This is a societal courtesy that those of us in the tutoring industry are programmed to impart to our charges."

"Not everybody has a robot tutor when they're growing up."

"Very unfortunate. Still, one would think that sanitation protocols would be implemented between one rental party and the next."

"Not when one doesn't pay in advance or share his identity with the clerk."

"I do hope you will succeed with this mission and achieve your goal to reach a more financially elevated rung of society."

"So you don't have to scrape week-old mustard off the consoles of future aircraft that we rent?"

"Precisely."

Kenji piloted them past the small military outpost, staying well south of it, and continued west until they reached the mountains. The chain ran roughly north-south, and he turned them north, assuming most of the fighting had been near the outpost. The shuttle hiccuped and spat another plume of black smoke.

"Another aircraft is entering the local airspace," Kay said.

"Military?"

"This equipment is not sophisticated enough to differentiate between military and civilian vessels, but it is coming from the southwest rather than the outpost. It is possible it is flying to the outpost."

"What's off to the southwest?" Kenji mentally retraced their route. They'd come up the coast from Zamek City and flown northwest over the sea. There were a few towns in the inland mountains of the northern continent, but the majority of the population centers were along the eastern and southern coasts. The far distant western coast was prone to tsunamis and had few towns of size.

"Little," Kay said.

"Hm."

They flew over a snow-blanketed cliff with a lumpy surface that might have been rock or might have indicated something buried under the snow. The scanners were ineffective at determining if wreckage lay underneath, but the equipment did detect one anomaly. Kenji squinted over at Kay's console.

"Is that an air bike parked on top of that cliff?"

"Actually, that is a large mountain directly ahead of us." Kay pointed at the forward display.

"Don't tell me someone else has already been here scavenging."

"I will *tell* you that you must veer to the side promptly." Kay's hands twitched toward the navigation controls, as if he meant to take over.

"I see it. We've got plenty of time." Kenji adjusted their course to swing around the mountain, so he could come back and check on the air bike.

"Few humans would consider 4.3 seconds until impact *plenty* of time."

"And few robots, apparently."

"Indeed."

As the shuttle flew around the mountain peak, the scanners detected the air bike flaring to life behind them. Kenji adjusted the display to bring up a visual off the shuttle's rear. A white-cloaked figure who almost blended in with his or her surroundings jumped onto the air bike and flew down a steep slope and toward the east.

Toward the military outpost? To report *him*?

No, that cloak wasn't a part of any military uniforms he'd seen. It looked like it had been chosen specifically for camouflage. The white backpack the figure wore also blended in but not so much that he couldn't see it bulging. As if with choice scavenged parts plucked from a crashed astroshaman ship.

"Someone beat us here," Kenji grumbled.

"Given that the battle was weeks ago, it is likely that *many* people—or salvage operations—beat us here."

Kenji sighed. Well, he wouldn't chase someone off across the ice to mug him. Just in case it mattered later, he used his glasses display to record a video of the bike, including stickers on the back that read *Lease to own!* and *Blazing engines!* Someone else was making use of rental vehicles for the trip up here.

"I'm going to see if I can find a stable place to set us down." Kenji flew toward the clifftop, activating the shuttle's hover feature. The craft shuddered and bucked before obeying. "Let me know if that other ship you detected comes this way. I hope it doesn't. It's hard to believe this place is so delightful that everyone is visiting it at once."

"If the wreckage contains a plethora of valuable materials to salvage, would that not cause a human to find it delightful?"

"I suppose it might." Kenji frowned as they descended, noticing a lot of boot prints and evidence of landing skids from numerous types of vehicles in the snow. "It definitely might."

Had he been delusional to think that this was an original idea? Maybe a steady stream of salvagers had been up here since the battle.

"There might not be anything left inside," he admitted, guiding the shuttle gingerly down next to the snow-covered wreck. There wasn't a lot of space between it and the edge. "Let's hope they overlooked something, and we'll get lucky. If we even found enough to cover the rental cost and the supplies we bought for the trip up here..."

He wouldn't say that would be enough. It wouldn't. Why couldn't he catch a lucky break?

Wherever his father was skulking these days, Kenji hoped some Kingdom agent would soon capture him and deliver him to a penal asteroid for years of arduous mining by hand. Possibly while being beaten up by prison toughs who didn't like terrorists.

"You may wish to hurry," Kay said. "The other aircraft is continuing in this direction."

"Wonderful. While you wait, see if you can give the shuttle a tune-up, will you?"

As soon as Kenji stepped outside of the climate-controlled interior, he realized how ill-prepared he was for an arctic excursion. The sun was bright, almost blinding as it glinted off the snow all around him, but the air wasn't remotely warm.

He should have brought cold-weather clothing and emergency camping gear, but he didn't *own* either of those things, nor would his meager funds have covered their purchase. He would have to work quickly and hope the shuttle didn't break down fully and lose power. If it did, he would be forced to trek to the outpost and beg for shelter.

"This is why I'm a city boy," he said, teeth chattering as he walked along the wreckage. "A city boy from a temperate climate zone."

His boots crunched on detritus in the snow as he walked around the area. Pieces of warped metal from a spaceship hull. This was the place.

The snow was packed from other people's feet, so Kenji didn't need special shoes to get around, but he grimaced at this further evidence that this spot had already been thoroughly scavenged. He stopped at a hole in the hull, the dark interior warped and broken with pieces torn from the ceiling to dangle down. It reminded him of a stalactite-filled cavern he'd once seen on a vid.

Most of the boot prints led to this spot. Kenji continued around the wreck, hoping to find a less obvious place where he might enter and find choice items that hadn't yet been looted.

His comm beeped.

"Already?" he answered.

"If you wish to know if that aircraft is *already* approaching," Kay said, "the answer is yes. It is coming here, not to the outpost."

The breeze shifted, carrying the distant roar of an engine. Frustration bubbled up inside Kenji as he glowered at the southern sky where an unremarkable gray shuttle had grown visible. It *did* appear to be heading for this clifftop.

"Do you wish to flee?" Kay asked.

"No, damn it. We just got here, and this is Kingdom land, a park open to the public. We're hikers exploring an interesting wreck in the middle of these geologically interesting mountains that naturally draw tourists such as ourselves. We're not doing anything wrong." His self-righteousness might have been less pronounced if that had been a military or Kingdom Guard shuttle approaching.

"Do you want to know if *I* wish to flee?"

"Not really."

"Your disregard for the feelings of robots is noted."

"Just watch my back if a bunch of thugs in combat armor spring out of it and attack me."

"Do you wish me to wave my wrench menacingly at them?"

"Yes." Kenji continued to tramp around the wreck, but he tugged a rifle off his shoulder, an old-fashioned firearm full of gunpowder cartridges. It had been all he could scrounge up after the Main Event snapped his previous rifle like a stale breadstick. "And then pilot the shuttle over to land on them."

There were fewer footprints on the back side of the wreck. Only one set, small and maybe belonging to a woman. They appeared fresh, and he looked in the direction the air bike had gone, but it had disappeared from view.

The shuttle continued its inexorable approach. Kenji hoped he wasn't being an idiot for staying, but the incoming craft didn't have weapons or appear that threatening. It might even be another rental shuttle. If it carried another scavenger—or hiker—maybe they could share the wreck.

Kenji spotted an open hatch and climbed up a drift toward it. A gust of wind kicked up snow—the shuttle was hovering right over the wreck now. He eyed it warily, hoping it didn't have weapons that he'd missed on first glance.

In case the pilot was looking down at him via a display, Kenji smiled up and waved. "Might as well be friendly with the competition, right?"

"Was that question for me?" Kay asked, reminding Kenji that their comm link was open.

"No, but I trust you agree."

As he scrambled up to the hatch, the gray shuttle landed not far from Kenji's rented craft. It was about the same size, its sides dented and its paint faded with age. The name of a competing rental company stamped the side above a picture of a shuttle flying toward a sun with a comet streaming from its backside.

Kenji had reached the hatch and thought about flinging himself inside, but the twisted mess of a corridor promised that he wouldn't be able to advance into the interior quickly. Fresh snow prints dotted the tilted deck—from the woman? He was surprised drifts of snow hadn't made their way in. Maybe the hatch had only recently been opened.

"The limited scanners of this vessel are not allowing me to determine how many people are aboard that shuttle," Kay said.

"So it could be an entire mercenary company, or it could be an old man with a divining rod?"

"That is correct."

The new shuttle powered down, and its hatch opened. Kenji shifted his rifle so it wouldn't be visible and waited to see who or what would come out.

Two people in civilian parkas with the hoods pulled up stood on the threshold. If they carried weapons, they weren't as obvious as a rifle. Steps unfolded from the craft and lowered to the ground. The pair descended in tandem, stopped, and peered straight at him.

"Hello." Kenji offered his best friendly wave again. "Are you here to explore this fine mountainous park?"

They looked at each other without speaking. He trusted they were communicating chip-to-chip. Even if he'd avoided the technology all of his life, he was familiar with it. His glasses replicated it, for the most part, though he had to speak queries or laboriously enter them via the eye movement reader. He couldn't simply *think* commands into a chip attached to his brain.

"What are you doing here?" one of the figures finally spoke, looking at him again. It was a woman. She sounded young.

He supposed women could lead scavenging careers too. He'd certainly come across female thieves.

"Exploring," he said.

"You seek to steal from the *Celestial Dart*?" the other one asked, another woman with a young voice.

Kenji could make out a wisp of blonde hair escaping from her hood.

"The *Celestial Dart*?" He pointed at the wreck. "I don't know if that was its name, but I think it's just a hunk of metal now."

"It belongs to our people." One of the women pushed back her hood, revealing fingernails that looked like chips of metal, cold mechanical eyes, and a strange implant at her temple that ran halfway down the side of her face.

Astroshaman.

A chill ran through Kenji as the other woman also pushed back her hood, both of them oblivious to the cold, and gazed at him with the same inhuman eyes. The astroshamans had been responsible for the second invasion fleet that had bombed Odin.

Kenji swallowed. He would rather have dealt with soldiers or the police.

One woman drew a small metal box from a pocket. Kenji started to swing his rifle toward them, but astroshamans or not, he couldn't shoot women his age. Instead, he sprang through the hatchway so he wouldn't be in their line of sight.

But whatever that box was sent a blue beam of energy arching around the hull of the ship and through the hatchway. It slammed into his chest like a lightning bolt.

Pain ricocheted through his body as he lost control of his limbs and almost his bladder. His heart throbbed, threatening to explode in his chest. Terror clenched him, but he couldn't run away. He couldn't do anything at all except drop to the deck and flop around like a dying fish.

The beam winked out, but his body kept twitching, his heart beating hard and erratically against his ribs. The pain faded slowly, but many long seconds passed before his spastic tremors subsided. He gasped in air, only realizing then that his lungs hadn't been working, and he hadn't been breathing. A headache pulsed behind his eyes.

"I take it back," he groaned, rolling onto his side and hunting for his rifle. "I *can* shoot women."

As he wrapped his hand around the barrel, a shadow fell across him. One of the women had climbed up and stood in the hatchway. With that little metal box in her hand, her thumb on the button. Hell.

Kenji had little doubt that it could kill him.

"I think there's been a misunderstanding," he said.

"You are not a lowlife opportunist attempting to capitalize on our people's misfortune by scavenging what your kind may deem valuable technology from our ship?"

"No, *noooo*. Of course not. Is *that* what you thought?" Kenji clutched a hand to his chest, in part to feign innocence, and in part to massage his heart back into a normal rhythm. He didn't have the medical background to know if that would work, but soothing rubbing seemed like a good idea. "This is a misunderstanding."

"What *is* your purpose here?" She eyed his rifle.

Kenji crossed hiker and tourist off his list of possible answers. They would never fall for it.

"I'm a bounty hunter." That would explain his rifle, anyway. "I'm up here after a fugitive. *He's* a lowlife opportunist scavenger. Very bad man. You should appreciate that I'm trying to capture him and turn him over to the law."

She squinted suspiciously at him. "What is his name?"

Uh, good question.

"Tenebris Rache." Kenji used the name of the first criminal who wasn't his father that popped into his mind. "I trust you've heard of him? He used to be a pirate captain loathed by the Kingdom, but now he's lost his ship and his crew. He supposedly died in the very battle that crashed these ships, but rumors suggest that he may have survived. Lots of people are willing to pay for his head." All that was true, at least according to the news and all the press coverage there had been after the battle. Kenji had no idea what had happened of late to the infamous pirate, but he wagered the astroshamans didn't know either. "I believe that he's out here and has resorted to scavenging. Opportunistically. Like the lowlife that he is."

She kept squinting at him. Was she buying any of this?

Maybe he should have chosen someone who wasn't known and detested in all of the Twelve Systems. Someone that a young guy like him could reasonably capture. Given that she'd taken him down with a button, she probably doubted his ability as a bounty hunter.

The silence stretched. Her metallic irises appeared glazed and unfocused, but she was likely communicating with her twin out there. Why astroshamans didn't get implants and prosthetics that looked like normal human bits and bobs, he didn't know, but it was like they *wanted* to appear freaky.

"You seek out and capture people?" she finally asked. "For a living?"

"Absolutely. I'm not a veteran, admittedly." As in, he'd never collected a single bounty. His father had trained him well enough that he probably *could* become a bounty hunter—so long as he could avoid people with metal boxes of death—but it wasn't a career he'd ever longed to pursue. "I'm out to make a name for myself by getting Rache."

He kept an eye on her as he sat up.

A *clink-clunk* came from somewhere in the depths of the wreck. Kenji hoped that was an icicle falling or the ship settling and not another scavenger to deal with. There weren't any more ships or air bikes parked out there, so it *shouldn't* be, but well-off people sometimes had slydar hulls that camouflaged their craft, so he couldn't assume that they were alone. And where was Kay? He hadn't spoken for some time, despite their comm line being open. Was he waving a wrench at the other woman, or had she pressed a button and zapped him?

"It is unlikely you will find Tenebris Rache," the woman said. "If you do find him, he will kill you. The Kingdom and countless bounty hunters have attempted to capture or slay him for many years. However, should you succeed, our people would reward you. He has vexed us."

"He's vexed a lot of people."

"Yes, but we believe he is dead. There is no need for you to seek him. But *we* are seeking someone. How much do you charge to find a person? This person must be captured alive."

"Er, what?"

"One of our kind has escaped with knowledge that is important to us. It is, however, difficult for us to go among your people. In other systems, humanity lets astroshamans pass with only wary

glances and snide comments. Here, in the xenophobic Star Kingdom, it is a different matter, and we find it difficult to enter your
population centers without costumes. If you are a bounty hunter,
you must have ways to track people down and find them."

"Yes, of course." Kenji pushed himself to his feet, slowly
picking up his rifle so she wouldn't find the movement threatening. He was careful not to aim it in her direction. "But I'm already
on a mission."

"A suicidal mission that you will fail."

"But if I succeed, I'll make a *lot* of money and, even more
important, make a name for myself."

"You will not succeed."

Kenji opened his mouth to argue further, but what was the
point of defending his fictitious story to death?

"Despite the recent thwarting of our plans, we are not financially insolvent or without means," the woman said. "What
payment do you require for finding a fugitive?"

"Some guy has committed a crime against your people?"

"Some *woman*. As I said, she has escaped with knowledge."

"Epically criminal."

She squinted at him again. "It is considered so among our
people. She had no right to take the knowledge. It is also possible
she means to betray us in some way. We must have her back. We
will pay fifty thousand of your Kingdom crowns for her to be
returned to us alive."

"Fif—" Kenji choked on the amount. "Fifty thousand, you
said?" He'd never had even fifty *hundred* crowns. Right now, his net
worth was closer to *fifty*.

"Yes. We will pay you five percent up front and ninety-five
when you return her to us. I assume physical currency is
acceptable?"

Hell, yes, it was. That would be enough to pay the shuttle
owner back with plenty to spare.

Once more, she delved into her pocket. He tensed, hopeful that she was pulling out money and didn't intend to zap him again. She withdrew a wad of Kingdom crown bills and a compact comm device.

"We must have her back within the month. If you agree to the terms, you will take this and contact us when you have captured her. We will meet you at a designated area to pay the remainder of your fee and pick her up. Do you agree to the terms?"

Uh, did he?

He'd never bounty hunted before, and these astroshamans were no slouches, but what if their missing person was the woman he'd seen flying away on the air bike? He might be able to find and capture her before sunset. It could be the easiest money he'd ever earned, and it wasn't as if he cared one way or another about astroshamans hunting other astroshamans. For all he knew, these people had been the ones to bomb his last home.

"You came up here looking for her?" Kenji asked. "Was she in the battle?"

"She was in one of our ships in orbit, as were the rest of us siblings, during the fighting on your planet, but..." The woman glanced at her twin, who was doing who knew what outside—Kenji couldn't see her from the corridor. "Our leader thought she might come here. This ship has meaning to us."

Kenji thought about telling them he'd seen her, but he didn't know that he truly had. That could have been *any* woman on an air bike. This was clearly the hot spot of the Arctic Islands. Besides, it would be better to catch her himself. And collect the bounty. With fifty thousand crowns, he could finally buy passage on a ship heading out of the Kingdom. A *luxury* ship. He and Kay could head off to a new life, to a system where nobody had heard of his loathsome father.

"I can find her," Kenji said. "What's her name, what's she look like, and I'll take any other information you can give me."

"Her name is Mari, and she looks like us. We are sisters, all born of genetic material from the same mother and father."

"Bunch of test-tube twins, huh?"

"There are more than two of us, so that term is inaccurate, but as I said, we share identical genetic material. We are, however, all very different." She sniffed. "Tari and I would never *leave* our people."

"I'm sure your parents appreciate your loyalty."

She stepped outside, waving for him to follow. "Loyalty is expected among our people."

Before Kenji could step out of the corridor, a clatter-clank came from behind him, followed by a buzz. He whirled as he sprang out of the hatchway, anticipating weapons fire.

Four drones flew around obstacles in the corridor toward the exit. Kenji raised his rifle but hesitated. Were these astroshaman devices? Drones made from the very technology he sought to find and sell?

No, they looked like typical Kingdom drones, and each one was carrying either a bag or some device clutched in mechanical graspers. They had to be someone's remote scavenging tools. Which meant that he and the astroshamans weren't alone out here.

As the drones buzzed out the hatchway, the sister, who hadn't yet given a name, ducking, Kenji lifted his rifle to fire at one of them. But his brain caught up with his reflexes and reminded him that he had a new gig. He didn't *need* to worry about another scavenger taking things from the wreck. Besides, someone in a nearby ship would be irked if he fired at their drones.

But it didn't matter. The astroshaman produced a pistol and shot.

"Those are our belongings!" she yelled, pelting the rearmost offender with energy blasts similar to but different from DEW-Tek bolts. The drone exploded like a grenade going off.

The other sister was at the base of Kenji's shuttle—with Kay flat on his back at her feet.

Kenji cursed and ran down the snow drift, hardly caring about the drones. "That's my robot. Back away from him!"

The three remaining drones flew past the shuttles, then over the cliff where they descended out of sight.

The astroshaman woman next to Kay frowned and faced him, one of the metal boxes in her hand.

Kenji ground his teeth, lifted his hands, and made himself politely say, "I would prefer it if you not damage my robot, ma'am."

Was it too late? Kay wasn't moving. Maybe he'd also been zapped with that current, and it had fried his chip.

"Especially if I'm going to be working for you," he finished.

"The robot was going to attack me," the woman said.

"That's not in his programming. I assure you it was a bluff, that he waved nothing more menacing than a wrench, and only because he thought it would protect me."

The astroshaman he'd been making deals with ran past Kenji to peer over the side of the cliff. She was still clenching her pistol, her mouth twisted in righteous anger. Kenji was glad she'd believed him when he'd said he wasn't a scavenger.

"Repairing him will be a simple matter," the closer woman said.

Kenji shook his head, lifted the inert but heavy Kay, and dragged him into the shuttle. The roar of an engine came from somewhere below the edge of the cliff. The drones' owner? And his ship?

As Kenji settled Kay on the deck, the faint buzzes of weapons fire came from outside. Something slammed into the side of his shuttle, knocking him into a wall.

Cursing, he ran to the hatchway, though he wasn't foolish enough to go back outside. A huge black vulture-shaped ship hovered over the cliff, casting a winged shadow. A railgun mounted on its belly swiveled toward them. It fired at the astroshamans' shuttle, blowing a hole in the side.

The women ran for cover by the wreck, but the railgun swiveled to follow them. It fired again, blasting a blizzard's worth of ice and snow into the air.

Kenji had no idea whose ship that was, but he felt it his duty to try to protect the women, astroshamans or not. He fired at the hull, realized his bullets would do nothing against the armored vessel, and targeted the railgun. Maybe he would get lucky and blow *it* off.

But it was one of the twins who came up with an effective attack. She dipped into that pocket of endless wonders, threw something at the ship hovering over them, and dove away before a railgun blast slammed into her.

The projectile she'd thrown looked like little more than a large marble, but it splatted against the hull instead of clanging off. A field of sizzling blue energy spread from the device like wildfire ripping across a prairie. The railgun stopped firing, nothing but popping and crackling noises coming from its barrel.

The winged ship wheeled away, soaring over the cliff. Kenji stood on tiptoe, hoping to see it crash in the foothills far below, but after a few wobbles from its wings, it recovered and gained altitude. Before it had gone far, it disappeared from sight. He blinked. He knew about slydar hulls, and their ability to camouflage spaceships except from very close up, but he'd never witnessed such a craft before, never watched a ship disappear before his eyes.

He tensed, afraid it would bank and come back to attack again. But the clifftop grew silent.

The astroshamans tugged at the hems of their parkas, then smoothed them, the gestures so similar that Kenji was sure the word twins applied just fine to them. Even if there were more than two. They weren't quite identical, but they were very similar. If this Mari looked like them, identifying her wouldn't be a problem.

"Is the woman you want to catch armed as well as you two are?" Kenji asked.

"She did not leave our base without resources."

He'd been afraid of that.

3

From the icy tundra behind the military aircraft hangar, Mari sat on her air bike and contemplated the gray smoke rising from the mountains. Unless she was mistaken, it originated from the clifftop she had just searched. Was someone *bombing* the wreck? Whoever had been approaching in a shuttle as she'd left?

When she'd heard the craft flying in, she'd hurried to leave, not wanting anyone to spot her up there. She had no idea if the Kingdom military had placed some claim on the wreck and would drive off—or shoot—trespassers. *Someone* had spent a lot of time up there, scavenging and looting the remains.

Fortunately, they hadn't thought of the science labs as places that held valuables. Mari had found some of her equipment, including her prototype terraformer. The compact spherical device didn't look like much from the outside, but it held a tiny fusion reactor and had the power to break down the surface layers on a hundred square miles of land, creating rich fertile soil and depositing seeds and growth-enhancing enzymes. Essentially, it could turn a portion of the inhospitable surface of a moon or planet into a thriving garden in a much shorter time period than traditional terraforming technologies.

She was proud of the work she'd done on it and relieved she'd found it still tucked in a cabinet in her lab. By offering this technology to the Kingdom, maybe she truly had a shot at winning asylum. A place in their world and protection from her family, who would doubtless prefer Mari shared nothing with humanity.

The hangar door rattled and started rolling open.

Mari hit reverse on her air bike and nudged it back around the corner. She pulled out a device that activated the same astroshaman stealth technology that hid their base in the Kingdom forest. The air shimmered faintly to her energy-detecting implants as a flexible camouflaging shield enrobed her and the bike. Unless someone came very close, they shouldn't see her.

Though the technology was powerful, it was good not to move when it was activated, so Mari put the bike on idle as the first of two aircraft roared out of the hangar. Their hulls were painted gray and blue, Kingdom military colors.

As soon as they took off, heading to the mountains to check out the smoke, Mari rode her bike into the hangar. Two aircraft remained parked inside, with voices coming from the other side of them.

She nudged her bike into a corner near stacks of supply crates so she could wait for her opportunity to catch a ride back to the mainland. Earlier, she'd spied on the soldiers and read their schedule, so she knew the same cargo ship that had flown up here to deliver supplies should have been emptied and would be heading back soon.

The voices, both belonging to women, continued on, talking about a mess needing to be cleaned up. At first, Mari took it literally and assumed some chemical spill might be endangering the hangar, but she didn't smell anything, nor did the women or any cleaning robots come out to attend to messes.

She nudged the bike forward, glad the battery-powered craft ran silently, and found the women—two soldiers in parkas and uniforms—pointing at a wall display. It showed the gray smoke wafting from the snowy clifftop.

The feed had to be coming from the camera of one of the aircraft flying closer, for it was a much better view than Mari had gotten from outside the hangar. Now, she could make out a gray shuttle perched on the cliff—surprisingly, not the one she'd seen arriving as she'd taken off on the bike. It was smoking, recently damaged by weapons fire. More damage appeared to have been done to the *Celestial Dart* too, though she couldn't imagine why.

Two figures in parkas came into view. They were working inside an open panel on the back of the shuttle, probably trying to repair it for flight. An uneasy feeling came over Mari. Even though she couldn't see their faces, they oozed familiarity.

One turned toward the camera, a pale face coming into view for a second, before poking the other. They ran inside, closing the hatch, and an instant later, the shuttle took off.

Mari sank low on her bike. That had been one of her sisters. No, *two* of her sisters.

How had they known she would come here? Mother must have sent them—and mentioned their sunrise conversation. If their shuttle—that was some rented Kingdom craft, not astroshaman technology—hadn't been damaged, would they have already found her?

Mari closed her eyes. Her escape had barely begun. She *couldn't* let them drag her back.

Now that her mother knew she wanted to leave the community, she wouldn't let Mari out of her sight again. She would never get another chance at freedom. She hadn't even done anything on her list yet.

She'd meant to acquire chocolate for her trip up here, or some other delectable human pastry or dessert she'd read about, but she'd received so many odd looks from people in Zamek City that she hadn't dared do something as prosaic as grocery shopping. On top of that, there were so many *people* in the Kingdom's capital. Millions of them in the streets, on the magtrains, in the subways, walking along sidewalks, shopping in stores. And all *speaking.* So few had communicated with each other via their chips. It had been overwhelming to her senses.

"Didn't know this duty station would have so much action," one of the women said, still watching the display.

"The only action I've gotten is in Sander's bunk."

"Lucky you. He's a cutie. So earnest, so handsome."

"He's earnest in bed too. If I had to get stuck up here in this armpit of an outpost, at least it was with someone with a squeez-able ass."

They shared snickers.

It took Mari a moment to realize they were talking about sex. Even though she'd read books and seen vids, she hadn't been around people in sexual relationships very much. There were others like her in their teens and twenties who'd been birthed and raised in the astroshaman community and had an interest in such things, but far more were oldsters who'd been born into a normal human existence and come to the Advanced Path later in life. None of them seemed like promising partners, and most of them considered themselves above human biological needs now that they were ascending up the Path. They were experts at frowning with disapproval when any of the youths experimented with amorous activities.

"Be glad you've got a bed buddy. All I've got are my Moon Melters, and I'll have to ration my stash." The soldier rattled a bag of what must have been a food item, for she dug out a piece to toss into her mouth. "If what we unloaded from the supply ship is any indication, we're not getting anything good for our entire tour of duty."

"You don't think the crate labeled *firm cakes* sounded promising?"

"Not when I dropped it on my foot and it weighed fifty pounds. No good cake could be that heavy."

"Military rations are meant to be filling. And firm."

"Like cement bricks."

The ding of a comm unit came from another room, and the women trooped through a doorway and into a corridor of offices. They'd left something on a table under the display. A package. The aforementioned *Moon Melters*? What was that? Candy? *Chocolate*?

Mari eyed the cargo ship she needed to sneak into with her bike. The hatch was closed and likely locked. Her software for thwarting electronic locks would take a minute or so to run, and the soldiers might come back any second, so she shouldn't dawdle. She knew that, but her curiosity turned that package of candy into a neodymium super magnet.

With great willpower, she made herself ride over to the cargo ship first. She rested her hand against the lock while running a program to find the right combination of electronic signals to order it to open.

From her spot, she could see the label on the candy bag. It *was* the package of Moon Melters.

The women hadn't returned yet. Maybe she could—

A breeze whispered through the hangar door, bringing the distant sound of an engine. The soldiers returning?

The lock thunked open, the hatch unsealing and rising as a ramp lowered. She drove her bike inside, a much easier feat than it had been when the cargo area had been full of crates. Only a few crates remained to be unloaded—or maybe they were going back to the mainland for some reason.

Mari tucked her bike against the wall beside them, stepped off, and trotted to the open hatch. She paused on the ramp to look back.

Since she was carrying her cloaking device with her, the bike was now visible. Visible and blatantly out of place in the cargo hold. Any soldier peeking inside would be puzzled about where it had come from. And the sound of an approaching engine was getting louder. The aircraft had to be angling for the hangar.

"This will just take a second," she whispered, trusting her cloaking technology would continue to make her hard to detect.

As Mari hopped to the ground and ran across the hangar to the table, the display continued to show footage of the cliff. At least one of the military aircraft remained there, recording the area around the wreck. Her sisters must have repaired their shuttle well enough, for it had successfully taken off. Was it possible they knew where she was and were heading here?

"Can't dawdle," she whispered.

Mari picked up the package of Moon Melters. It was nearly full. Another reason not to linger. The soldiers would surely return soon for their prize.

She dumped several of the items into her palm. They were brown lumps and didn't look as appealing as she had expected. They reminded her of animal droppings more than moon rocks. She sniffed the open package, debating if the faintly waxy scent promised something delicious. The contents *did* smell sweet. Wasn't there a human expression about appearances—and perhaps scents—being deceiving?

The engine roared closer, and she spun, about to run back into the shuttle with her prize, but she realized she was stealing candies without paying for them. A twinge of guilt came over her. It was a small theft, but...

As she fished into her pockets, depositing the candies and seeking some barter of equal value that she could leave, the pitch of the engine changed. It was landing outside instead of flying into the hangar. Maybe she had a couple more seconds.

She couldn't leave any of her weapons or various tools behind as payment. They had far more value than lumpy brown candies, and she would need them in her adventures. Her fingers brushed a wrapped rectangular item. Ah ha.

She laid a ration bar on the table. Her people made them out of the edible mushrooms and algae they could easily grow on their spaceships. They weren't particularly appealing, but they were nutritionally substantive. A soldier would appreciate such a gift.

Mari turned to run back but spotted someone standing in the hangar doorway, someone with a rifle pointing at her. The young man with bronze skin, short black hair, and intent brown eyes wasn't what she'd expected. He definitely wasn't an astroshaman or anyone her sisters or mother would have sent. Judging by his mishmash of clothing, none of it appearing warm enough for this climate, he wasn't a soldier either.

With her camouflage activated, he should have struggled to see her, but that didn't seem to be the case. He was looking *right* at her.

Only then did she realize she was standing in front of the display. Her technology could hide her effectively against stationary objects, but the movement on the display had to be a challenge for it to match itself to. He was squinting, so she doubted he could see her well. She risked sliding to the side.

His eyebrows flew up, and the rifle followed her, but its aim was less certain once she was out from in front of the display.

"Stop right there!" It was a whisper instead of a shout, immediately making her positive that he'd sneaked into the area too—and that the soldiers would object to his presence. "I need to... talk to you."

Sure, he did. With a firearm.

Was this another scavenger who wanted some astroshaman

technology? Mari had the urge to sprint toward the cargo ship, but fast movement would also make it difficult for her cloaking technology to compensate. She made herself ease soundlessly toward the open hatch.

He glanced at the door leading to the offices, frowned briefly at the bar on the table next to the rest of the candies, and stepped warily into the hangar. He murmured something into a comm link too quietly for her to hear the words, then trotted in her direction. Though he kept his rifle up, he didn't fire at her.

She pulled out a compact stunner, opting for that instead of the more painful—and potentially deadly—arc blaster, one of her people's favored defensive weapons. Thus far, she didn't know who this man was, but if she started killing Kingdom citizens, the probability of her gaining asylum on their world would plummet.

Unfortunately, he headed straight for the cargo ship and the open hatch. She picked up her pace, but he got there first, springing lightly onto the ramp and glancing inside. His glance turned into a second look, and she knew he'd spotted her air bike. She had no choice but to stun him.

But a second before she squeezed the trigger, he stepped inside. She was off to the side and couldn't see into the hold yet.

The sound of another engine grew audible. The display on the wall had turned off. The aircraft that had been recording the clifftop had to be flying back. Had the second one chased off her sisters? Mari hoped so.

She hesitated beside the cargo ramp, debating if she wanted to leap inside and stun the man or simply wait for him to come out. If the soldiers returned and found an unconscious body in their ship, they might start searching for her. Her cloaking technology fooled human eyes well, but it wouldn't stand up well to a hangar full of soldiers with scanners.

A soft clack came from inside. Was he messing with her bike?

Mari leaned around the corner of the hatchway, finger on the trigger, but he startled her both by being *right* inside and by throwing something at her. A gritty brown powdery substance struck her full in the face and plastered her open eyes and mouth. Whatever it was surprised her with a sweet taste, but that didn't keep her from stumbling back.

She heard a thump as he leaped down from the ramp, and she fired at him. But with the gritty stuff tearing her eyes, she missed and hit the side of the cargo ship. Her attacker bowled into her, probably seeing her easily in the middle of a brown cloud of powder that hadn't yet dissipated. Before she could shoot again, he caught her around the waist and knocked her to the ground.

A strong hand tore the stunner from her grip and flung it across the hangar. It clattered far out of her reach as it bounced across the cement floor. He wasn't a huge hulk of a man, and Mari tried to buck him free, but he was strong, tenacious, and had the body weight advantage, so he succeeded in pinning her to the floor. As she squirmed, she maneuvered her hand toward a pocket, not the one with the candy but the one with her arc blaster.

"I don't want to hurt you," he whispered, squeezing her tightly as he tried to flip her over and pull her arms behind her back. He managed to get her onto her side, but she fought mightily. She needed to free a hand to grab her weapon. "But your sisters hired me," he added. "They said you went rogue with their information."

"I don't know what that means," Mari growled, jerking her arm free, "but it's not true."

"They said you're a fugitive. They're paying to get you back."

"I'm not a *fugitive*. You don't know anything about it. Let me *go*."

Mari managed to clip him in the stomach with her elbow. Judging by his gasp and pained grunt, that might have been lower than his stomach. His grip loosened enough for her to grab her arc blaster.

She spun onto her back, startling him, and for a moment, they were face to face in some parody of a lovers' embrace. He must have realized she'd pulled her weapon free, for he grabbed her wrist. But she fired first, the burst of energy slamming into him like an electrical current and knocking him back.

"Not *again!*" he gasped around jaws spasming open and closed.

Mari scrambled away as he rolled on the floor, his entire body jerking and flopping about, his face contorted in pain. If he hadn't just tackled her, she might have felt sympathy for him, but anyone willing to hunt someone down for money, not knowing if they were innocent or guilty, deserved some pain.

Aware of the roar of the engine growing ever louder, Mari sprinted for her stunner. She released the button on her arc blaster as she picked up the less lethal weapon.

The spasms of his body lessened, and from flat on his back, he managed to say, "Thank God. That thing is horrible."

She stepped into his view and pointed the stunner at his face. "I am *not* rogue."

"Uh." His bleary eyes focused on the muzzle of the weapon. "You didn't run away from your people with top-secret valuable information?"

"I did not *run*. I walked away with only the information in my brain."

"Is it top-secret and valuable?"

She opened her mouth to deliver an indignant answer, but Mother and her siblings might genuinely feel that way. It had been almost ten years since she'd finished her schooling and moved from the derivative work of replicating others' experiments to running her own and creating devices such as the prototype terraformer.

He must have found her pause condemning, for his wary gaze turned into a suspicious squint, and she could see him trying to figure out how to relieve her of her weapon. She stunned him.

He only had time to get half a curse out before losing consciousness.

"Of course the information in my brain is valuable, you idiot." She should have said that *before* she shot him.

Alas, there wasn't time to pin a note with the message to his chest. The engine was roaring closer, and she had no doubt that the aircraft would swing into the hangar. And find the stunned man and start a search unless she could hide his inert form quickly.

Mari grabbed him under the armpits and leaned her body weight into pulling him across the floor. The upgrades to her skeletal system and a few muscular enhancements that Mother had given all of her children helped, but she was not some cybernetically enhanced supersoldier. With much grunting, under-her-breath swearing, and straining of muscles, she dragged him toward the closest stack of crates. As she got him tucked out of sight, the aircraft she had expected roared into the hangar.

Only one flew in, hopefully meaning the other was indeed chasing her sisters out of the area. Mari didn't want them to be harmed, but if they were driven all the way back to their forest base on the mainland, it might give her time to reach Zamek City again and speak with people who could grant her asylum. And if they refused... she could leave the Kingdom and try another system. Somewhere far away from bounty hunters, or whatever this man was, and her oppressive family.

Mari made sure her camouflaging device was active again and crept out from behind the crates. The pilot was hopping out of his aircraft, and she grimaced. He'd landed close to the cargo ship with its suspiciously open hatch and the also suspicious pile of brown powder that had settled to the floor.

The pilot glanced at the cargo ship, but he must have assumed that one of his fellow soldiers had left it open. Without checking inside to see her damning air bike, he trotted toward the offices.

Just as she thought she was in the clear, he paused at the table and stared down at the ration bar and the package of candies. Mari slumped against a crate. Would her guilt and need to deliver a fair trade result in the search she'd been trying so hard to avoid?

He reached for the goods but grabbed the package of candies instead of the bar. He tilted his head back, dumped the brown Moon Melters into his mouth, shoved the now-empty package in his pocket, and continued toward the offices.

Not questioning her luck, Mari made sure the bounty hunter was still unconscious, then ran toward the cargo ship. She hoped he was a *criminal* bounty hunter and that the soldiers would find him and have a *lot* of questions for him. No, maybe she didn't. That could lead them to realizing she was stowing away on their cargo ship.

The thought made her halt, run back, and find a tarp. She draped it over him like a blanket. Better they not find him at all.

With that accomplished, she hid in the cargo ship and closed the hatch. One of the crates was open that hadn't been before, and she peeked inside. The bounty hunter must have done that. A canister was open with a label that read *cocoa drink mix powder*.

Was *that* what he'd thrown at her? She wiped her face, finding some of the gritty stuff still on her nose and in her eyelashes. Someone had written *past the expiration date* on the top of it and several other food containers in the crate.

As minutes passed, Mari debated what she would do if the bounty hunter woke up from the stun before a pilot came back to fly the cargo ship to the mainland. But the engine soon reverberated through the deck, letting her know that it was being made ready to fly. Another minute, and it navigated out of the hangar and took to the air. Nobody had checked the cargo hold.

Thankful, Mari leaned against her air bike and pulled off her pack. She hoped the bounty hunter hadn't damaged any of her equipment, especially the terraformer.

A couple of the favorite tools she'd collected from the lab had been bent in the skirmish, and she frowned. It didn't seem right that they had survived a crash only to come to a bad end in her backpack. Hopefully, she could fix them. At least the terraformer was in an insulated box. She let out a relieved breath when she pulled out the dormant sphere, flicked it on, and the glowing indicators came to life. It was ready to terraform a planet, or at least a hundred square miles of a planet.

Who in this planet's government would appreciate such technology? Mari had been reading about the new Kingdom queen, Oku, and knew she was a scientist. A botanist by training who engineered seeds to grow plants that thrived on space stations. *She* would appreciate terraforming technology; Mari was certain of it. But how to get it to her?

The queen would be in her castle, guarded by hundreds of trained men and security robots who would forbid an astroshaman—or even an unknown Kingdom subject—from entering the premises. She highly doubted she could send a contact request direct to Queen Oku's chip and that she would accept it.

As she put away her device, she pulled up a digital copy of the recent bestselling novel by Kim Sato, wondering if it might have any clues as to how she could get an audience with the queen. Mari had already read it, since it was the Kingdom's rendition of the events that had led up to the battle between the Kingdom Fleet and the astroshamans, but it was mostly about Sato, Casmir Dabrowski, a couple of knights, genetically engineered cat women, and a crazy bounty hunter lady from another system. The mercenary Tenebris Rache had also featured in it. A strange collection of characters. Her mother had called it propagandistic drivel and forbidden Mari to read it. Naturally, she'd read it three times.

It occurred to her that the author was good friends with

Minister Dabrowski, the man who was now dating the queen. Could he be a possible route to Oku?

No, Dabrowski also knew Mari's mother. They might have started as enemies, but now they had a truce—he'd even given her that crusher—so he might tell Mother that Mari was in his city.

Maybe Kim Sato was a better option. The novel had mentioned her home, a cottage on the Zamek University campus. Was it possible she still lived there? The book hadn't been written that long ago. A university campus would be easier to gain access to than a heavily guarded castle. And this Kim Sato was also a scientist, perhaps someone who would see the merits of a terraforming device... and an astroshaman looking to defect.

"That's the plan," Mari whispered. "Find Kim Sato, show her my equipment, show her my earnestness, and see if she can get me an audience with the queen."

Nerves tangled in her belly. It was quite possible this path would lead her to an audience with a dungeon—or a torture chamber. What if neither the queen, Sato, nor anyone else in the Kingdom believed Mari was what she said she was?

She poked into her pocket, determined to put the worries out of her mind. It would be hours before she got back to the capital, and she had a plan to follow. There was little point in fretting.

Most of the Moon Melters had fallen out during her skirmish, and she found only two sad brown nuggets with lint attached to them. She wiped them off and stuck her tongue out to taste one. The coating wasn't that appealing—she remembered the waxy scent she'd detected—and if she hadn't seen the soldier scarf down the entire bag, she might have tossed the candies away, but she plopped one into her mouth and chewed with determination. She had left her people to experience life as a human, and humans ate Moon Melters.

The candy was sweeter than the scent led her to expect, and under the layer of coating, there were crunchy pieces mixed into a gooey substance that pleased her taste buds. It took a few seconds of analysis before she decided she liked the combination.

She ate the second candy slowly, knowing it was her last. When it was gone, she was disappointed that she hadn't managed to keep more of them. If she ran into that bounty hunter again, she would let him know how inconsiderate he'd been to tackle her and send her Moon Melters flying. And then she would shoot him again. Possibly not with the stunner.

4

Kenji woke on his back, his vision blocked by something blue. He was shaking—no, shivering. The chill from cold hard cement seeped through his clothing and into his stiff body.

Before he figured out where he was, someone lifted the blue blanket off him. A *tarp*, he realized, feeling like a pile of lumber covered in someone's backyard.

He lifted his hands protectively, expecting soldiers with rifles or the woman—Mari—with her horrible astroshaman weapons. Kay stood looking down at him, the tarp in his metal hand, the open hangar door behind him.

"Where are the soldiers?" Kenji rolled gingerly onto his side, his entire body aching, both from the aftereffects of the stun and because he'd been left lying on a freezing floor. "And who repaired you?"

Since he'd been hoping to catch up with his prey, Kenji hadn't taken the time to run a diagnostic on Kay. When last he'd seen his robot buddy, Kay had been dented and offline, lying on the deck of their rented shuttle. He'd had a hunch Mari might plan to stow away on a military vessel heading back to the mainland—the only other place on the island where one might find a ship was a harbor that supported only ocean-going ships—and he'd been right. For all the good it had done him. He was lucky she hadn't killed him.

Some bounty hunter. Less than an hour into his mission, and his target had electrocuted him *and* stunned him. His father would have been so proud to see the results of Kenji's childhood training and gene enhancements.

"I waited until none of them were present in the hangar," Kay replied, "but they left the rolling door open, so it is likely they expect another aircraft, which could arrive at any time. I suggest you move swiftly and we retreat before they come out to investigate the shuttle that you opted to land distressingly close to their base."

"I didn't realize my parking spot caused you discomfort. I thought it was clever feigning mechanical failure and landing behind their satellite dish. It's about the only cover out there." Kenji stood up, wobbled, and caught himself on a nearby crate. Had Mari dragged him back here all by herself? Strong woman. He'd been foolish to take her on without more of a plan than, *Stop! I want to talk!* But he'd been afraid she would get out of the Arctic and be much harder to track if he didn't act quickly.

"It was not clever," Kay said. "It was brazen."

"In some contexts, the word brazen would be considered complimentary."

"Not in this context. You can imagine my alarm when I came out of my repair cycle and noticed I had not only been left on the deck of a shuttle by myself but that said shuttle was parked less than a quarter mile from the military outpost we have been seeking to avoid. Of course, as an innocent robot, I should have nothing to fear from Kingdom soldiers, but since I have been associating with a thief of late, one never knows what kind of retribution might be in store."

"I doubt they'd zap you worse than the astroshamans did." Kenji hadn't seen Kay's zapping but trusted it had been as unpleasant as the not one but *two* zappings he'd now received. He rubbed his aching chest at the memory.

Kay's head swiveled on its neck mount. "An aircraft has come within range of my auditory detectors."

"We should leave then." Kenji hobbled toward the door, his legs like jelly. If he had to run before the effects of the stun wore off, he would end up face-planting.

"Precisely what I've been saying. You are fortunate the soldiers have not come out to investigate our shuttle. Perhaps they have been distracted by the winged ship at the wreckage."

"Let's hope."

As they left the hangar, hustling across the packed snow and around the corner of the building, Kenji also picked up the sound of an approaching aircraft. Probably one of the two that had flown up to investigate the skirmish atop the cliff. He and Kay needed to get to the shuttle, but he worried about being spotted by the incoming pilot.

"As for repairs," Kay continued, "it is within my base-level programming to run a diagnostic via my backup CPU, should my main CPU ever be knocked offline, and issue any repairs necessary to my software and operating system before attempting to come back online. Unfortunately, I must rely on humans to hammer out dents and repair wiring."

Kenji could hear the aircraft getting closer, so he tugged Kay to the side of the hangar. They could run for the shuttle after the military craft landed inside.

"I trust you will repair me fully on the way back to civilization," Kay said. "As if being electrocuted by a crabby astroshaman wasn't bad enough, this cold is gnawing away my lubrication like a flesh-eating bacteria."

"Thank you for the imagery." Kenji pressed his back against

the hangar as the aircraft flew inside. He noticed a camera on the wall above them and wondered anew how the soldiers hadn't spotted them—or their shuttle.

"Did I mention the snow? When the wind blows, the tiny crystals embed themselves in my seams. This is particularly noticeable on my left side where the gaps between my shoulder, arm, and torso panels are greater than on my right. I am not ungrateful to you, since you did bring me to life from scrap, but I do admit to a longing for a slightly more refined body."

"Many humans long for that. Join the support group."

Soft clanks sounded as the hangar door rolled closed.

"Is there a network address you can refer me to?" Kay sounded serious.

Kenji imagined an online forum where robots bitched to each other about their assembly deficits. "I'll look it up later. Come on."

He pointed toward the satellite dish and their shuttle parked behind it, hoping he could take off again without being noticed.

He and Kay made it to the dish without anyone running out of the hangar to ask who they were, and he was almost laughing at how easy it had been to get in and out—given that two different women had kicked his ass today, he decided smugness wasn't called for—when they rounded the shuttle and came face to face with two soldiers in parkas. One of them, a man, had forced open the hatch and was about to step inside, and his cohort, a woman, was pointing a rifle right at Kenji.

Kenji halted so quickly that Kay bumped into him. The armed woman scowled at them.

Panic flashed through Kenji, and he jerked his hands up as he groped for a way to save himself.

"Oh, *there* you are," he blurted loudly over the woman's demand to know who they were. Kenji pretended he hadn't heard her question and pointed to the hangar. "We were looking for someone in there. I was hoping one of you fine soldiers might be

able to help us. We came up for some sightseeing, but the shuttle
we rented in the capital is flying terribly. All the way here, it was
making noises and spitting plumes of black smoke like the Castle
Tower geyser on its hourly eruption."

The soldiers blinked and looked at each other. Whatever
they'd expected him to say, that wasn't it.

"This is one of the shuttles that was at the wreck," the woman
told the man. "*Sightseeing.*"

"Yes." Kenji could hardly deny it when they'd likely been
caught on camera by the military aircraft. "But I barely got it
back in the air. It's just a rental, you see. Not reliable. I'm
concerned it won't make it back to the capital. Is there any
chance you have a mechanic or someone here who can look at it?
I can pay."

"This isn't a service station," the male soldier snapped.

"We *are* the only facility for a hundred miles in every direction," the woman said.

"If people wouldn't fly up here, they wouldn't *need* the use of
facilities."

"I didn't intend to bother you," Kenji said. "As I said, I'll pay of
course."

"I could use some more Moon Melters," the woman grumbled.
"Someone slurped up all of mine like a vacuum robot with its
nozzle stuck on turbo-suck."

Kenji was familiar with the candy—he remembered finagling
some from an elderly vendor in one of the public markets when
he'd been a boy—but he'd been thinking more along the lines of
the crowns the astroshamans had given him for his five percent. It
also crossed his mind to bribe them to let him go. Would that
work?

"Let's see the problem," the man said, eyeing Kenji suspiciously.

"It'll be apparent if you turn it on. And you're welcome to do

---

that. You know the old saying. He who has the biggest gun does whatever the hell he pleases."

"If only that were true." The man climbed inside, leaving the woman still pointing her weapon at Kenji.

He kept his hands up and attempted to look innocent.

A gust of wind sent snow skidding across the tundra. Kay sighed.

"Uneven gaps?" Kenji asked.

"You know my difficulties well."

"Especially since you've been so kind as to make me aware of them. Repeatedly."

The shuttle started up with a hiccup, two shudders, and an uneven rumble. A vent spat enough black smoke that the woman stepped back, as if afraid the craft would explode. It did seem to be a possibility.

"You flew here in this thing?" She pointed her rifle at it. "You must have really wanted to *sightsee.*"

"I find astroshaman technology fascinating. They're a strange but interesting people, don't you agree?"

"They can all go to hell," the man called from inside the shuttle. "They demolished entire blocks in several of our cities while trying to steal an artifact that was rightfully ours. If I ever see one of their kind again, I'll shoot 'em between the eyes."

"You might want to be careful calling them interesting." The woman was less vitriolic, but her eyes were cold, their focus back on Kenji.

"Yes, of course. It's really more their technology that calls to me than *them* per se." Though one was calling to him now. The one worth fifty thousand crowns.

More plumes of black smoke came out of the exhaust vent. The male soldier leaned out to look at it. "Guess the kid isn't lying after all."

"We believe in being forthright and honest and doing the right thing," Kay said.

Kenji nodded. "It's true."

"Uh huh. Bunch of scavengers." The man hopped out with a toolkit and scanner, and opened the engine panel in the back of the craft.

"You're lucky," the woman said. "In addition to being an expert candy thief and a mediocre pilot, Corporal Sock is our aircraft mechanic."

"I don't know how you're so sure it was me," Sock said, his voice losing the frostiness from the astroshaman discussion. "There aren't even any working cameras in the hangar."

"You'll eat anything sweet. Even the rock-hard and rock-heavy military *firm cakes* that keep coming with our rations."

"The chocolate chunk cakes aren't so bad."

"True. I used one to squash an arctic wolf spider in my shower the other day. Loathsome thing. You wouldn't think the original colonists would have felt the need to bring the embryos of so *many* of Old Earth's species to Odin."

"I'm sure arctic wolf spiders fulfill an important ecological niche," Sock said.

"The niche under my five-pound firm cake, yes."

Kenji looked at Kay, amazed at how chatty these soldiers were —and that the corporal was actually doing some repairs to the shuttle. He'd been certain they would throw him in whatever the tiny outpost's equivalent of a jail was. Probably a storage closet full of these dubious firm cakes.

If they truly helped him and let him go, he would have to reassess his opinion of the military. As someone who'd grown up on the wrong side of the law—thanks, Father—he was predisposed to mistrust and dislike anyone in a uniform.

"They shouldn't be renting this thing out to anyone. The parts are older than I am." Sock pulled out an air filter choked with black particles and crud. "Possibly older than *anyone* is."

"The life-extension treatments available in other systems mean there are some pretty old people out there," the woman said.

Sock blew off the filter the best he could and inserted it again. "I stand by my statement."

He tweaked a few more things, grumbling about the lack of replacement parts, then closed the panel. "It might get you back to the capital. Fly slow. Don't stop to sightsee along the way."

"Did he steal anything from the wreckage?" the woman asked, cocking an eyebrow toward Kenji.

"Not that I saw," Sock said.

Only then did it occur to Kenji that his invitation to have the soldier repair the shuttle had also allowed him to snoop inside.

"All right. You and your dilapidated robot can go." The woman pointed toward the hatch.

"*Dilapidated*?" Kay protested. "I am a perfectly serviceable robotic companion. The dents I have received while assisting my human creator in battle are badges of honor."

"Is that corrosion?" She waved at the piece of copper that made up his abdomen.

"It is a patina that adds character to my housing that other robots lack."

"Uh huh."

Kenji patted Kay, whispered a low, "Sh," then told the soldiers, "Thank you for your help."

"You're lucky it was a slow day," the woman said. "We only had four scavenger ships to chase off. I recommend you don't come back. It can be dangerous up here."

"Just ask the spiders." Sock winked at Kenji before putting away the toolkit and walking toward the hangar with his colleague.

"We got lucky today," Kenji said when he and Kay were back in the shuttle and taking off.

"That is an interesting statement from a man I recently found unconscious under a tarp."

"You didn't find me *dead* under the tarp. I consider that lucky." Kenji rubbed his achy chest again. "I may have underestimated this Mari. Given the reputation astroshamans have, it's surprising she didn't kill me."

"Will you continue to pursue her?"

"For fifty thousand crowns? You better believe it. That's life-changing money for someone like me." And, dear God, how he wanted his life to change. "We *are* going to have to get some better weapons before confronting her again." He wondered how much it would cost him to get a stunner, energy nets, and whatever might be out there for thwarting the fancy astroshaman technology that could make her invisible to the naked eye. Had he truly been a bounty hunter, he would have had all of those things and more. "It was rash of me to try to capture her without even a stunner."

"Some would even say foolish."

"But my loyal robot companion wouldn't be so insulting."

"Hm."

Kenji set course for the mainland and eventually Zamek City. Maybe it was his imagination, but the shuttle seemed to jerk and wobble less after the mechanic's brief tinkering.

He wondered what the soldiers would have done if his story about needing repairs hadn't been as convincing. Or if they'd caught him and Mari fighting in their hangar. Their frostiness toward astroshamans might have made them shoot her outright and not with a stunner. Since she'd had the opportunity to kill him and hadn't, he wasn't inclined to want her dead. Also, her sister had stipulated that she be brought back alive for the knowledge in her head. If Kenji wanted his reward money, he couldn't let anyone kill Mari.

"You have set course for Zamek City," Kay said. "Do you believe she will go there?"

"I'm guessing the military cargo ship she's stowing away on is going back there. They have a huge base north of the city, between the urban area and the launch loop. I think most of the military supplies for the continent—and the arctic outpost—are distributed from there."

"Since she has an air bike, could she not open the hatch and let herself out at any point along the way? There are numerous cities along the coast north of the capital, as well as towns inland."

"That's a good point."

Kenji thought of her rental bike and the stickers he'd seen on the back. He'd gotten a picture of them, so he brought them up on his glasses display and murmured a search query to look for matches on the public network.

"That blazing-engines sticker is from Rent the Stars." Kenji laughed. "She got her air bike from the same place we got our shuttle."

Maybe, when he turned in his shuttle, he would see if he could ask—or bribe—the clerk for the ident chip of Mari's air bike. With the right software, he might be able to track her down with that.

"An interesting coincidence," Kay said.

"I think it's just that we both found the only place in the city that would rent vehicles to people without banking chips or proper identification. That's implied by the sign out front. *We take gold, silver, jewelry, and trade. No questions asked!*"

"Yes, but why do you think an astroshaman would have traveled to such a populated place as Zamek City? It is as likely that the police will apprehend her as they would you."

"Maybe she planned all along to get a ride on a military cargo ship leaving from Zamek City. Also, the police shouldn't have gotten a good look at me at the greenhouses. There *shouldn't* be a warrant out for my arrest." Or so he hoped.

"The Main Event got a good look at you."

"True, but I think he's an independent, not someone who works alongside the police. His methods are unorthodox. Meaning often illegal. They should be trying to arrest *him*."

Kenji rubbed his hip. Though he had bigger bruises elsewhere now, he hadn't forgotten being knocked to the ground by the over-muscled superhero. It worried him that he was heading back to the city the Main Event had told him to leave.

Only long enough to capture Mari, he told himself.

"Perhaps the police do not wish to be thrown against trees." Kay mirrored his gesture and rubbed one of the dents in his metal torso.

"We'll use some of the money the astroshaman gave me to pick up weapons and supplies so that such things will be less likely to happen in the future." Kenji started some new searches, specifically for energy nets and other tools useful for bounty hunters who didn't like to be bested by their prey.

"Are there supplies that can keep one's robot from being smashed against dendritic obstacles?"

"I think so. This catalog I dug up on the network has everything from caltrops to stunners to police flex-cuffs to armored tanks and drones to historically accurate landmines from the era of the World Wars on Old Earth."

"I believe tanks and landmines would be *more* likely to result in robots being smashed into dendritic obstacles than less."

"That's true. We'll stick with the stunners and flex-cuffs. Besides, tanks and landmines are out of my price range."

"As a robotic tutor designed to encourage good social development and acceptable law-abiding behavior from his charges, I won't mention my concern at the chagrin in your voice."

"I'm your creator, not your charge, so I don't think you need to feel responsible for my social development."

"That's a relief."

5

Mari did not find it difficult to locate Kim Sato's address in the directory of Zamek University's student and faculty housing, nor was there a security checkpoint that she had to navigate through to get onto the campus. But as she drove the air bike through the streets to the residential area, she noticed law-enforcement drones with cameras flying about in threes and fours.

Were they on the hunt for a criminal? Mari pulled the hood of her parka up to hide her face.

The night air wasn't as cold here as in the Arctic Islands, but it was damp and misty, so she didn't think her disguise was that out of place. Perhaps the drones disagreed. A group of four of them started following her, having no trouble keeping up with the air bike.

Maybe she was exceeding the speed limit. She forced herself to slow down, though she had the urge to crank it to top speed to evade them.

A teenage girl peddling a wheeled bicycle came from the opposite direction, several boxes and bags from shopping destinations piled precariously on a perch behind the seat. The drones buzzed off to follow her.

Odd but fortunate. Mari's plans would be seriously derailed if she were captured by the authorities. If she had any chance at being believed as someone who wanted to help the Kingdom, she had to approach the government first.

Queen Oku would never believe her story if she shared it from behind bars, even if she volunteered to be questioned with truth drugs. Judging by the general opinion on their public networks about astroshamans, they would think she had some technological—or magical and mystical—ability to thwart drugs. Which was silly, since her biological body worked the same as that of a normal human.

A scream came from behind her, and Mari halted her bike to look back. A few other students were out walking or riding in the rain, and they also froze to peer toward the noise. The girl had fallen off her bicycle, and the drones were buzzing away from her, carrying the boxes and bags that had been stacked behind her seat. How strange.

The girl sprang to her feet, shouting that the drones were stealing from her, and rode her bicycle after them, yelling for help. For a second, Mari was tempted to lend assistance—with her faster air bike, she might be able to catch up with the drones, and she did have weapons that could knock them out of the air—but that would draw attention to her. Besides, for all she knew, the girl had stolen those items, and the drones were returning them to their owners. Given that they had *Campus Security* written on the sides, that seemed more likely than a random theft by robots.

"I've got to stop drinking after classes," a young man nearby muttered and continued his trek to wherever he'd been going.

Once the bicyclist and the drones were out of sight, the rest of the pedestrians returned to their business. Mari brought up the campus map on her ocular implants again, the information feeding through her cranial nerves to form the image in her mind. Only six blocks to Sato's house. Good.

She rehearsed what she would say when she arrived. *Greetings, I'm Mari Moonrazor*—no, she had better not mention her surname. The Kingdom soldiers who'd battled the astroshamans had interacted with High Shaman Moonrazor and might not think favorably of her.

Greetings, I'm Mari, an agronomist researcher and terraforming expert who wants to defect from her people and seeks asylum in the Kingdom.

That was better. Agronomists were unthreatening and had no link specifically to high shamans. Should she tell everything to Kim Sato? She was the only conduit Mari could imagine that might lead her to the queen, but Mari suspected she would have to convince her of a lot before Sato would consider making that introduction.

Another pair of drones whizzed down the street as Mari was about to turn onto the dead-end road that led to Sato's cottage. They slowed down and hovered in the intersection. They had cameras at four points on their disc-shaped bodies, so it was only her imagination that they were watching her specifically.

Or was it? The pedestrian traffic had diminished as she'd moved into the residential area, and nobody else was around.

Reluctant to have them track her to the house, Mari drove the bike past the turnoff. They spun to follow her.

She grimaced and kept driving, hoping they would find some other more interesting target to stalk. They couldn't be after her because of her backpack, could they? She'd passed a lot of students with such packs. Granted, hers bulged with the box, tools, and equipment she had jammed inside, but it didn't look anything like a stolen shopping bag.

But the drones continued to pursue her, even as she drove down a side street. Maybe they had scanners more sophisticated than the simple visual recording cameras she'd noticed. If so, they might know she had more cybernetic parts than the typical human. But that wasn't a crime. Even here in the somewhat backward Kingdom, a place that frowned on mechanical enhancements to the body outside of prescribed medical uses, people had cybernetic parts.

Two more drones flew out of a side street ahead. They turned and flew straight toward her. Not sure if they would try to halt her or fly past, she veered into the parking lot of an apartment complex. All four drones followed her.

What *was* this? Mari had picked Kim Sato as a first point of contact because she'd assumed it would be easier to get onto a campus than into the queen's castle. Maybe that had been a mistake.

As she drove under trees with leafy branches extending over the sidewalk and pavement, she hoped the drones would be deterred, but she doubted it. She braced herself for them to voice orders for her to halt for a search or some such. With one hand, she surreptitiously drew her arc blaster from her pocket. It was designed to work on humans, but the electrical shock could short-circuit robots as well. And drones.

But they all had cameras, with footage that could likely be recovered even if they were wrecked, and what were the chances of her making it through a skirmish without her hood falling back?

She sped back out of the parking lot. Her bike was meant to be steered with hands on both handlebars, and it wobbled as she tried to follow a bend in the road while holding her weapon.

Without warning, all four drones zipped at her. They dove under tree branches or around the trunks like dire wolves attacking prey in the forests of Algar Nine.

Ready for them, Mari fired at the closest two. Her first shot connected, blasting the drone across the street with a satisfying zap of electricity, but her bike wobbled again, and she missed the second one. Something thumped her in the back—one of the other drones. She spun to shoot at it but pitched sideways, almost falling out of her seat.

Cursing, she halted the bike and jumped off, crouching beside it for cover as she fired again. She'd caught the first drone by surprise, but the remaining three had enough intelligence to be ready for her attacks. Her target anticipated her and zipped sideways as her blast sizzled through the air, hitting a tree branch instead. The branch cracked and fell to the street, twigs snapping and leaves flying. The scent of burning wood stung her nostrils.

Two drones flew at her from the front while the third circled behind her. She crouched low, putting her back to the bike, bumping her pack against it, and fired at that one. For some reason, they wanted to hit her from behind. She was surprised they didn't have stunner technology to deal with people they wanted to arrest. Maybe they did and they just hadn't used it yet.

She fired, her target too close to evade her in time. Her shot only clipped the drone, but that was enough to knock it ten feet. It crashed into a block of mailboxes and fell lifeless to the ground.

While she was distracted, the two others swept in again. They bumped her, one thudding against her shoulder and one the back of her head. It was so puzzling that she didn't react for a moment. Was this truly the arrest protocol here? She knocked one aside with her elbow, though striking its hard carapace hurt her more than it deterred the drone.

"Cease and desist," came a call from farther up the street.

"They're attacking me!" she blurted, bewildered as she imagined some scenario where she got in trouble for being a victim.

The two drones backed off as two wheeled security robots with humanoid torsos, heads, and arms whirred down the street.

"You are malfunctioning," one stated, speaking not to her but to her flying assailants. "Return to the drone depository."

From behind her bike, Mari watched the robots approach. The drones flew off between the trees and then over the rooftops of houses, but she wasn't convinced she would be safe from these new robots. She gripped her arc blaster, then realized they might be sophisticated enough to recognize it as astroshaman technology. She stuffed it in her pocket and groped for a story to explain what she couldn't begin to explain.

But the robots were focused on the retreating drones rather than Mari. Once they disappeared, they wheeled around and rolled back toward the main street.

Mari's mouth dangled open as she watched them go. A breeze blew the mist onto her cheeks, making her realize that her hood was down. She swore, yanking it back up. Had the robots identified her as anything other than a typical human? Had the drones?

She glanced around, hoping there weren't any pedestrians on the street. It was night, but copious street lamps illuminated the neighborhood. She didn't see anyone outside, but lights were on in several houses, and a couple of faces peered through curtains at her.

"Great."

She climbed on the air bike and drove slowly back to the main street, not wanting to catch up to the robots. With her ears straining to detect the whir of more drones, she returned to the intersection that led to Sato's cottage. It was clear of drones. Warily, she turned down the street toward the home at the end. A giant zindi tree in the yard partially blocked the cottage, but she could tell that the lights were on inside. She could also tell that a hulking black robot stood in front of the door.

No... She squinted. That wasn't a robot. It was a *crusher*.

It was identical to the one her mother had and, knowing how formidable the constructs were, Mari had no idea how to bypass it. The arc blaster wouldn't work, nor did she have anything else that could damage one. Even if she'd had a grenade and could blow it up, the nearly impervious crushers were capable of reassembling themselves within seconds. Not that she would have hurled explosives at the door guardian of someone she hoped to befriend. But what *was* she supposed to do?

Mari stopped her air bike on the sidewalk several houses away.

Since she'd read Sato's novel, she knew that a crusher was a constant companion for Minister Dabrowski, but Sato hadn't mentioned having one of her own in their adventures. She'd given the vibe, through the text, that she wasn't enamored with the killing machines, even though Dabrowski's apparently had personality and had been programmed to be a bodyguard rather than an aggressive killer. That didn't mean the one at the door was his. In the months since the book had been published, Sato might have gotten one of her own. An aggressive one.

Mari rubbed her face, wondering if this was worth it. Maybe there was someone else connected to the queen who would be easier to visit. Such as the knights that had also been a part of the events depicted in the book. Or even the genetically engineered cat woman or bounty-hunting pilot. But she had no idea if any of those people were on the planet right now. Besides, Sato was a scientist, like her, and Mari thought they would be more likely to form a kinship. Or at least an understanding. And a scientist should be rational and not as prone to jump to conclusions about astroshamans.

But this scientist was under the protection of a crusher. Mari stared glumly at the black robot, its face indistinct, only vague orifices where a human's eyes, nose, and mouth would be. She didn't know how to proceed.

~

The shuttle was smoking again by the time Kenji flew over the rental shop toward the landing and parking area behind the building. A crater—damage from the attacks on the capital that hadn't yet been repaired—ensured nobody parked out front. The bomb that had left it had also taken out what had once been a house-cleaning service on the same property. The sign out front had survived, but the building was missing. Meanwhile, a vehicle maintenance facility at the far end of the property had been left unscathed. The vicissitudes of the universe.

With the front parking area out of commission, the rear lot was packed. Kenji landed gingerly, setting the shuttle down among other aircraft, ground vehicles, racks of air bikes, and a random bratwurst vending cart. He eschewed the auto-park and guided them into a narrow slot, glad for his piloting skills even if he resented the man who'd instructed him. He'd only been nine or ten when he'd learned to fly, but he well remembered his father watching from the copilot's seat with his disapproving nothing-is-ever-good-enough glower firmly affixed.

"It is fortunate the shuttle is handling better," Kay said.

"If you don't mind the smoke billowing out of the back."

"Robots are indifferent to airborne particulates and gases."

"Unless they signal a swift and rapid hurtling to the ground from great heights?"

"They are concerning when they lead to that, yes," Kay said, "but our flight back to the city was without difficulty. I was able to run further diagnostics and download software updates over the network."

"It's good to be updated."

"It is. I trust you'll need my assistance to locate the astroshaman woman."

"I will." Kenji turned off the shuttle, looked for belongings to unload, and remembered that he had none. At least the wad of bills in his pocket ensured that he could buy the gear he needed to finish his task. "I'm prepared to bribe the clerk, if necessary, but the advance the astroshamans gave me won't last forever. The less

I spend on bribes, the better. Let's plan for me to distract the clerk while you sidle around the counter, plug into his computer, and find out if Mari's air bike has been returned. If it hasn't, get the ident for its locator chip."

"Do you not think we could simply ask the clerk for that information?"

"The guy didn't even let me use the lavatory the last time we were here."

Kay looked over at him. "This indicates an unwillingness to share data?"

"If you're not willing to share your toilet, you're definitely not going to share data. Come on."

Kenji led Kay to the cracked and pitted walkway that took them past the crater and to the front entrance of the rental shop. One would have thought the owner would have put some caution tape around the great hole to keep customers from falling in, but other than an amusing orange cone ten feet down in the center, there were no warnings.

The buzzes and whirs of drills and other shop equipment came from the repair shop on the other side of the crater, and a surly-looking man in coveralls stood in an open side door, glaring at Kenji and Kay.

Kenji faltered, wondering if the man somehow recognized him —he lived in fear that he would come across some of the people his father had tormented in the past—but the glare seemed to be for the building behind them. Maybe the clerk had also rented him a faulty shuttle.

When Kenji stepped inside, two other people were waiting in front of the chipped counter, their shiny black combat boots contrasting with the stained and cracked floor tiles. Their backs were to him, leaving him a view of utility belts bristling with weapons that ranged from DEW-Tek pistols to stunners to knives, and each had flex-cuffs dangling in between the armament. Despite the combat boots, they didn't look like soldiers or police officers, not with their distinctly civilian attire, the oddest combination of camouflage and... was that purple fur trim? And were those... sequins?

Even though they had long black hair, one with it in a ponytail and one in a braid, it took him a moment to realize they were women. Maybe because they were significantly taller than he—at least six-feet-two—and had the powerful builds and broad shoulders of bears.

The clerk wasn't behind the counter. Maybe they'd scared him off.

One of the women glanced back at him, and Kenji nearly fell over. They had *pointed ears* and... was that *fur*? Not on the trim for their clothing but on *them*.

He gripped the doorjamb for support, inadvertently blocking Kay, who bumped into his back. The woman smiled at him, which was almost as alarming as the fur—she had *fangs*—and turned back to the counter. That was good, because he realized he was gawking. Rudely.

Kenji closed his dangling jaw and swallowed. She wasn't *entirely* furry. Her face was mostly normal, aside from the fangs, and feminine despite the large muscular frame. And her hands only had a light dusting of fur on the backs. The rest appeared almost normal except for...

He swallowed again. They had claws. The other one was tapping a rhythm on the counter with a claw painted purple to match the fur trim on her jacket. Kenji caught his jaw dropping again.

Maybe they'd *eaten* the clerk.

No, they wouldn't be standing there impatiently if they had recently been sated by a tasty meal. Kenji resisted the urge to flee and stepped into the lobby. They were obviously genetically engineered women from another system. He'd read all about such creations after he'd learned that *his* genes had been altered before his birth. Maybe he should be relieved that his father hadn't made him fanged and furry.

He reminded himself that the Kingdom was turning more progressive and allowing foreigners of all types to visit, so he should expect to see more beings—people—like this. The queen had even put out some incentives, giving bonuses to tourist businesses that brought in foreign crowns and Union dollars. Since Zamek City was the capital, and the closest major city to the launch loop, it made sense that these foreigners would be popping up here.

Kenji glanced at Kay as he clanked in behind him, wondering if this might be their opportunity to snoop in the computer system. Would the large women object if they ambled behind the counter and helped themselves to some data?

But he must have stepped inside far enough to trigger the door chime, for a soft bing echoed through the building. The same clerk Kenji had dealt with before—wearing the same grease-stained shirt with a hole under the armpit—walked out of an office. He jerked in surprise when he saw the women.

"You're still here," he blurted, stepping back, his shoulder clunking against the doorjamb.

Kenji imagined a lot of people ran into doors when they saw these women.

"Yes," the one who'd smiled at Kenji said. "You said you would let us know what you found."

"I meant in general. At some future date. Actually, that was a brush off. I thought you would take the hint and leave."

"At least he's honest," the other one said. They had pleasant voices, though they would definitely be singing alto in the cat-woman choir, should such a thing exist.

"I'd be happy to help you if you want to rent something," the clerk said. "We'll rent to anyone. No questions asked. As long as you've got money."

"As we said, we're interested in buying the lot next door, not renting a shuttle. Our real-estate developer friend did some research and learned that you own this building, the now-empty lot, and the repair shop on the other side of it. All the taxes have been paid, and you seem to be doing well despite the disrepair here."

She eyed the floor tiles and then the armpit hole in his shirt. His hand was up to scratch his head, so it was easy to see.

"I don't waste needless money on frivolous things. Look, I don't know if you noticed, but the lot next door is now a *crater*. I'm still waiting for the insurance money. There have been a lot of claims, and they're backed up. Do you... *women* need air bikes? A way to get around town? Like I said, I don't discriminate." He eyed their pointed ears with the same dubiousness that they were eyeing his armpit.

"We know that it's a crater. That's why we're interested. Our friend said we could get a good deal, fill it in, and build on it."

"What do you want to build? A cat cafe?" He snickered at his wit.

The women did not.

Kenji groped for a way to butt in to the conversation. For his distraction, he planned to ask the clerk to come outside to see the repairs needed on the shuttle. Before Kenji got a word out, the rumble of a hover van came from out front. Instead of parking in the back, it floated a couple of feet over the crater, not far from the front door.

"This isn't a very good part of town," one of the women said. "We understand there's a lot of crime. We plan to open up an office so people can visit us and inquire about our services. We're bounty hunters, and we're going to branch out into private investigations and possibly hiring ourselves out as bouncers. There are quite a few of us, and my captain doesn't need all of us all the time when she flies."

"Bounty hunters?" Kenji asked, considering their weapons again. Maybe they knew where to get good deals on the right kind of gear.

Both women turned to face him and smiled, one hiding her fangs with her lips, the other revealing them and the rest of her teeth. Hers was a brazen smile, and she looked him up and down with a speculative gaze. It took him a long moment to realize she was checking him out.

"Yes," she said.

"Are you in need of our services?" the more subtle one asked. "I'm Liangyu Qin Three. You can call me Qin."

"Or you can call her Squirt." The flirty one winked.

"That doesn't seem like a bounty-hunter name," Kenji said.

"We gave it to her when she was six. She was a runt."

Kenji eyed Qin's substantial height and muscles and found that hard to believe.

"*I'm* Tigress. I was *never* a runt."

"This is true," Qin said. "She was always a big brute."

"A big sexy brute." Tigress looked Kenji up and down again. "What's your name, Cutie? For select customers, I might be willing to throw in certain bonus services alongside the bounty hunting."

"Uh, I was actually going to ask where you got your weapons or if you have any used gear for sale. I'm getting into the business myself, but I don't have a lot of start-up funds yet."

"That female is looking at you with the alarming mien of a predator," Kay whispered. "Perhaps you shouldn't engage them in conversation."

"It's all right." Kenji hoped.

"You're going to be a bounty hunter?" Tigress raised her eyebrows. "You look like a Squirt yourself."

Qin elbowed her. "Don't assume that. Kim isn't very big, and she kicked Rache's mercenaries across a submarine."

"Rache?" Kenji mouthed as the clerk did the same thing.

"The lot isn't for sale," the clerk said firmly.

A clank came from out front—the sliding door on the hover van being thrown open. Six men in camouflage uniforms with masks covering their faces sprang out, landing at the edge of the crater. They carried DEW-Tek rifles and charged straight for the front door of the rental shop.

"Move, Kay." Kenji grabbed the robot and tugged him over to a corner as the men charged inside.

"No freaks!" They yelled and opened fire at the counter—no, at the *women.*

But Qin and Tigress had leaped into action before the men made it through the door. Instead of running away, like the clerk did, they charged their assailants, knocking aside rifles and bowling them over.

Energy bolts hit the ceiling and the walls as the women put themselves back to back, kicking and punching rather than drawing their weapons. That didn't keep the attackers from using *their* weapons, but the women were close enough—and fast enough—to knock aside the men's arms and the barrels of the rifles, sending the shots flying.

Kenji, afraid random fire would take him down, looked for something to hide behind. The only thing in the lobby was a fake rubber-tree plant in a cracked plastic pot. He ducked behind it, intending to drag Kay with him, but Kay headed for the counter. A stray bolt clipped his metal shoulder, burning a hole in his housing and almost knocking him over.

"Get down, Kay! Or run into the back with the clerk." Kenji wished *he'd* done that.

But Kay went behind the counter as the fight escalated, more energy bolts slamming into walls—and people. Yelps of pain sounded amid the thuds of fists hitting flesh. Kay disappeared with a clank, and Kenji worried he'd been struck with a more damaging attack.

Something slammed into the base of the potted tree. A rifle that had been ripped from someone's hands. One of the men followed, flying through the air and slamming into the wall a few feet from Kenji. He thudded down with a groan.

One of the women grunted in pain. Kenji wondered if he should help them, but he had no idea what this was about. If he got involved, it would only be in the hope of stopping the fight so innocent bystanders wouldn't be killed.

An energy bolt blasted through the trunk of the faux tree, dropping plastic leaves on his head. He also wanted to stop the fight so innocent *lobby decorations* wouldn't be killed.

The man crumpled next to him grabbed his rifle, rose to his knees, and aimed at one of the women. They were busy dealing with the other attackers and didn't seem to see him.

"Look out!" Kenji barked and lunged over to kick the man's rifle aside.

He was in the nick of time, and the man's shot went wide. The women glanced over. Unfortunately, the attacker growled and swung the rifle toward Kenji.

Kenji jumped up, fear making his second kick lightning fast. His toe connected with the barrel an instant before the man fired. The rifle flew out of his hands and struck the ceiling.

Before Kenji had to defend himself further, one of the women sprang over, landing beside the man. She hefted him from his feet as if he weighed twenty pounds instead of two hundred, lifted him over her head, and threw him across the lobby.

Kenji glanced around, afraid someone else might be targeting him now that he'd picked a side, but the battle was winding down. Four men lay groaning or unconscious—hopefully not dead—on the floor. The other two, realizing the odds had rapidly gone out of their favor, glanced at each other and sprinted out the door. They leaped into the van, and it took off, not waiting for the other four.

The women dropped their fists to their hips.

"As we said," Tigress said, "this isn't the best of neighborhoods."

"But that makes it the perfect place to start a business for hunting criminals," Qin said. "We'll have to set up a network site, so people who are afraid to visit the area can reserve our services online."

"Good idea. Maybe Casmir would help."

If the clerk was listening from the back, he didn't reply. Kenji eased along the wall, stepping over one of the crumpled men, to check on Kay.

Other than the melted blast hole in his shoulder, Kay didn't appear damaged from the battle. He had tilted over at his trunk crease and was accessing the shop's computer, which was tucked into a nook below the counter.

"Are you almost done?" Kenji whispered.

"There was a passcode to bypass that delayed me, as well as weapons fire squealing over my head, but I have almost achieved the objective."

"Good work." Kenji turned and leaned an elbow casually on the counter to hide Kay from view if the clerk walked in.

One of the downed men tried to belly-crawl toward the door. Tigress plucked him up and shoved him against the wall, his boots dangling six inches above the floor.

"Why did you attack us?" She pinned him in place with one hand against his chest while she searched him with the other.

"Because you're freaks." He tried to kick her, but she lifted a knee and blocked the attack while removing laser cutters, pistols, and even a grenade from his pockets. "Nobody wants you here."

"That's not true." Qin picked up one of the rifles and held it on the other three men. "No fewer than seven people are quite tickled to have us on this planet. Did someone pay you to attack us? How'd you know we would be here?"

The clerk stepped into the doorway and peered warily around. Kenji put a hand on his hip to take up more room and block his view of Kay. The clerk looked at the women and the men on the floor and barely noticed Kenji. He didn't seem to see Kay at all. Good.

A boom and a flash of light came from outside. It startled everyone, and Qin stepped outside to peer down the street.

"That's unexpected," she said. "I believe that's their getaway van. It *was* their getaway van."

"What happened?" Tigress asked.

"I'm not certain, but the remaining pieces are scattered up and down the street out there for a block."

Kenji didn't know what was happening either, but he couldn't have hoped for a better distraction. So long as the clerk didn't glance over and notice Kay.

"Maybe whoever hired them turned on them when they failed," Tigress said.

"That's *murder*." The man she'd pinned craned his neck to peer out the door.

"You needn't sound so affronted," Tigress said. "Weren't you going to murder us?"

"Yes, but you're *freaks*. We're Kingdom subjects."

"This planet is so backward, Squirt. Are you sure you want to set up a shop here?"

"You said yourself that it has nice trees."

"It does, and like you said, your captain doesn't have enough work for *all* of us, so it makes sense for half of our sisters to find work here, but..."

"The Kingdom will get better for people like us. Queen Oku is making improvements." Qin smiled brightly. "Casmir is advising her."

"I thought they were just snogging on the sofa."

"I'm sure he's taking his duties more seriously than that."

"While snogging."

"Ha ha."

Kenji ignored the bewildering conversation and resisted the urge to look over his shoulder to check on Kay. He didn't want to risk bringing the clerk's attention to him.

Qin picked up another man trying to crawl for the exit. "Look, you can leave if you tell us who hired you. You didn't kill anyone, so we're not terribly upset with you. We just want to know."

"*I'm* terribly upset," Kay muttered. "I lost my shoulder plating."

His words drew the clerk's attention. "What are you doing back there?"

"Hiding from deadly weapons fire." Kenji shifted to further block Kay's activities as the clerk tried to peer around him. "I started out behind that fake tree over there, but it was a frequent target. You can see that it's been terribly defiled." He pointed emphatically at the topless tree, willing the man to look at it. To look at anything except the robot fiddling with his computer. "You may need to order a new one. Perhaps an entire forest of potted trees, thus to provide cover for innocent patrons needing to hide from firefights in the lobby."

Frowning, the clerk stepped toward him and lifted a hand.

"Were there any injuries in here?" a new voice said, a man in black armor and a mask striding through the front door.

Kenji barely kept from shouting a curse. It was the Main Event again.

He crouched so quickly he cracked a knee on the floor. Kay was now visible to the clerk, but Kenji couldn't do anything about it. If the Main Event recognized him after warning him to stay out of the city...

"These men are somewhat battered," Tigress said, not sounding even minutely surprised by the appearance of the would-be superhero. "And that plastic plant has taken grievous damage."

Kenji eyed the corridor leading to the offices and maybe a back door, but the clerk blocked it. He was looking at the Main Event instead of Kenji cowering behind his counter, but how long would that last?

"Their getaway van also took grievous damage," the Main Event said dryly.

"That was you?" Qin asked.

"It may have been."

"Where did you come from?"

"The nightmares of criminals hell-bent on mayhem and violence."

"Did Casmir give you that line?"

"He's been advising me in the ways of superhero speak. Apparently, one must have memorable one-liners available to trot out in case reporters are within earshot."

"You want reporters to... report you?"

"I need the populace of Odin, preferably of the entire Kingdom, to realize that I am on their side. A protector of the average citizen. An inexorable force for justice in the city. Then one day when Queen Oku pardons me, there will be no question that it was the right thing to do."

"You're a strange man."

"*I'm* strange? Did you know that your pointed ears twitched when you said that?"

"They do that."

Even *more* bewildered by the conversation and the odd assortment of people in the lobby, Kenji looked back at Kay. They had to get out of here.

Kay withdrew from the computer and turned without lifting his upper body into view. This time, he kept from speaking and drawing attention to himself. Maybe he remembered his recent encounter with the Main Event—and that tree.

"Where did you come from?" the clerk asked. "And who *are* you?"

"A concerned citizen across the street called the police," the Main Event said. "I was in the area and arrived sooner than they, though I suspect they'll toddle along soon. I saw that these two warriors had the attack under control but noticed that a man in the repair shop over there was watching the goings on with binoculars while getting updated by someone on the comm. I have enhanced hearing and heard the van driver *delivering* the updates." He looked at Qin. "It seems that your inquiries into buying the adjacent real estate alarmed the mechanic enough to take matters into his own hands."

"He hired thugs to attack us so we wouldn't buy the crater next to his shop?" Qin asked.

"That is what I gathered from my eavesdropping. You're welcome to question him yourself."

"We didn't even make an offer," Qin said in a sad, hurt tone.

Kenji would have felt for her if the hard floor hadn't been grinding into his knees and he hadn't been afraid of being caught.

"We were just trying to get some information," Qin added.

"Kingdom subjects sleep with their prejudices cuddled close at night," the Main Event said. "You may have difficulty finding neighbors hospitable to a pack of feline bounty hunters."

"Are you done?" Kenji mouthed to Kay, hoping the robot had a program downloaded for lip-reading.

Kay's metal fingers curled into a fist, and he poked his thumb up.

"We're not *felines*," Qin said. "We're genetically engineered women with dreams, goals, and feelings."

"We're also not properly called a pack," Tigress said. "Viggo calls us an ambush."

"You know that's a gathering of cats, right?" the Main Event asked.

"Of *tigers*," Tigress said.

The clerk cleared his throat. "I have a business to run here. And a mess to clean up. I believe I hear police sirens. Maybe you'd all like to leave the premises. And take those creeps with you." He waved at the remaining attackers.

Kenji nodded firmly, though he expected the Main Event to object. He *worked* with the police, didn't he?

"The police can gather the rest of these miscreants," the Main Event said. From his voice, it sounded like he was turning to leave. Dare Kenji hope? "My work here is done."

"Maybe we can find another crater to buy," Tigress said. It sounded like they were leaving too.

"They are proliferating this city currently," Qin said, "and I've got another week before the captain plans to leave again. We can keep shopping."

"Or maybe we could save money by setting up an office by the street on Asger's property. He's your boyfriend. Boyfriends are supposed to let you use their property for the dreams and ambitions of you and your sisters."

"I don't think you can have a bounty-hunting office on a nobleman's estate."

"Why not?" Tigress asked, their voices growing quieter as they walked farther away.

"Zoning rules."

"Huh."

Kenji carefully poked his head over the counter, worried the Main Event might still be standing there with his arms folded across his chest. But he and the fearsome women had departed. They had neglected to take their assailants with them, but the men had recovered enough to crawl to the door by themselves.

Kenji grew aware of the clerk frowning down at him.

"Sorry." Kenji straightened and put the key fob for the shuttle on the counter with the money he owed. "I came to return that, pay you, and thank you for the shuttle. It served its purpose, and I believe we're done here." He waved for Kay to follow him around the counter and to the exit.

"Hold on." The clerk grabbed his arm.

Kenji tensed, prepared to rip his arm free and sprint for the door.

"You owe me another hundred crowns," the clerk said.

"For what?" Kenji glanced at the holes in the walls and the broken rubber-tree plant. "I didn't engage in the fight."

"Mileage charge." The clerk tapped the spot on his temple where people's chips were embedded. He must have already gotten a report from the odometer system in the shuttle. "You flew *way* more than the two-hundred-and-fifty miles allowed for a one-day rental."

"Was a mileage allotment in the contract?"

"It was in the fine print." The clerk released him but held out his hand and rested his other hand on a bulge under his shirt. A weapon?

Kenji didn't think the very brief and indifferent digital contract he'd signed had mentioned miles, but since he'd just stolen information from the man, and his shop had taken more than a hundred crowns' worth of damage, he decided to pay without argument. As soon as he captured Mari and returned her to her people, he wouldn't have to worry about such small amounts of money.

Once he and Kay stepped outside, finding—to their vast relief—no sign of the Main Event, they headed off the property and toward the nearest public transportation system.

"You got the locator chip number?" Kenji asked.

"I did, and I have already downloaded a program to tap into the vehicular database to make use of it."

"That's amazing. Where's her air bike?"

"It *is* amazing, especially given the trying and bizarre circumstances I had to endure while working."

"Tell me about it."

"I am. The air bike is currently parked in a residential area on the Zamek University campus."

"That's less than ten miles away." Kenji clenched his fist. "This is it. We can capture her tonight."

"Do not forget to purchase used bounty-hunting supplies on the way."

"I won't. We can find a weapons shop easily in this neighborhood."

Youths in black leather scurried around, scavenging valuables from the van that had blown up, even as a police vehicle descended into the rental shop's parking lot.

"I believe we'll easily find ten or twenty weapons shops in this neighborhood," Kay said.

"Good." Kenji thumped him on the back. "Let's do this, my metal friend."

6

While Mari was debating if the crusher would allow her to stroll up and knock on the door, it surprised her by leaving its post on the single step that led up to the cottage. It walked across the grass and around the home to a fenced backyard. She leaned off to the side to see it spring over the fence and disappear into the yard.

"Hm." Mari waited a minute to see if it would return, but it did not.

A faint whir sounded behind her at the turn-off for the street, and she glanced back in time to see a drone buzz past. It wasn't safe to stay outside on the sidewalk.

Taking a deep breath, Mari drove the bike to the yard, parked it, and walked up to the door. She lifted a finger to press the chime but hesitated. After being attacked by drones, Mari was flustered and struggled to remember the words she'd been rehearsing.

"I came to see if you are in need of protection," a male voice floated out an open window. "I did not know you would have a crusher poised to protect you from campus hooligans."

"Zee is here to protect *Casmir* from campus hooligans," a woman said, "though I suppose he is programmed to protect me from danger as well. Also, according to the news, the crimes have been committed by drones that are malfunctioning, not hooligans. Are you allowed to use your superhero crime-fighting powers to thwart one-foot-wide drones primarily used for pizza delivery purposes?"

"I fight crime wherever it originates and in whatever shape it appears, but I'm sure someone is behind the drones' actions. Probably a younger, less rectitude-conscious version of Casmir."

"That seems likely." The woman had a flat almost monotone voice. Was this Kim Sato?

Mari shouldn't eavesdrop, but she had hoped to speak with Sato alone and was hesitant to ring her chime when an unknown man was present. Perhaps it was one of Sato's brothers. Mari's research revealed that she had half-siblings that lived in the city. Or perhaps a lover? No mention of marriage was listed on her network profile.

"And since when do the campus-security drones deliver pizzas?" the man asked.

"Casmir reprogrammed one to be at his beck and call for deliveries."

"I withdraw my statement about his dedication to rectitude."

"Pizza delivery isn't immoral. Where is *your* crusher?"

Mari glanced back, worried that a second one might show up.

"Ordering more flex-cuffs and a new stunner for me," the man said, "while wallowing in depression over the execrable state of my soul."

"Did you revert to your old ways and do something villainous?"

"I was in fact delivering miscreants to the police headquarters in the Temple District. A gang of youths were stealing from the offering boxes in one of the churches. They *deserved* to be dropped on the lawn in front of the police building."

"What was Amit's objection?"

"That the dropping was literal. And from a height of twenty or thirty feet. Bones may have broken."

"Ouch."

"I would find it easier to assist with crime fighting if the police weren't attempting to arrest me themselves to find out who I am. I'm forced to fly past swiftly when dropping off criminals. Can you believe that they and some of the crusts on the senate object to my tactics for halting crimes?"

"Your *tactics* aren't always legal."

"But they are effective. I employed similar methodologies as a mercenary."

"Yes, I believe that's the problem. Just be glad nobody seems to have associated you with—"

Someone grabbed Mari under her armpits and hefted her off her feet. She couldn't stop herself from blurting a startled squawk, and the conversation in the house halted.

She tried to wrench herself free, but her captor's grip was like steel. When she kicked backward, her boot connecting with something solid, she only hurt herself. Her captor didn't budge.

As she tried to wriggle a hand into the pocket with her arc blaster, she glimpsed the tarry black body of the figure behind her and groaned. There was no point in using her weapon. The crusher had her.

It hadn't made a noise while sneaking up on her. She would have expected it to stomp around with the subtleness of an elephant.

The crusher extended a finger to reach past her shoulder. If she hadn't been aware that it could liquefy and reshape itself, she would have found that disturbing, since the two hands gripping her hadn't let go. The finger rang the chime.

The door opened promptly, making Mari suspect the people in the cottage had already been on their way to check on the situation.

Surprisingly, only Kim Sato stood inside. Given human cultural customs, and beliefs that men were more capable of dealing with dangerous threats than women, Mari would have expected the man to answer.

Sato regarded Mari calmly, her face surprisingly non-emotive given the stranger dangling a foot above the ground in front of her, though her dark eyes were curious. She wore exercise clothing, with her black hair back in a ponytail, and had come to the door without a weapon.

Wonderful scents wafted out of the house from a meal cooking in the kitchen. It smelled far more appealing than the chocolate candies, though Mari had enjoyed those. This was exactly the kind of exotic human fare she'd hoped to sample. She supposed, given the circumstances, Sato would not invite her in for dinner.

"I have apprehended an eavesdropper, Kim Sato," the crusher said in a monotone even flatter than hers.

"I was about to ring the door chime," Mari said, though she couldn't legitimately deny that she'd been eavesdropping. It wasn't her fault that a window had been open. It was chilly and drizzling. Who left windows open in such conditions?

"You are not a reporter," Sato said.

Had she *expected* reporters? Maybe the success of her novel had made her a Kingdom celebrity.

"Uhm, no. I'm a scientist."

"She was studying the house for several minutes before she approached," the crusher said. "I saw her but could not legally constrain her before she stepped onto the property. I believed she would approach, if not for my formidable presence, so I hid in the backyard, thus to lure her closer. My ruse was successful." Did the crusher sound... *smug*?

"You are an effective crime fighter, Zee. And the legality of your tactics is admirable." Sato glanced back into the house—at the man she'd been speaking with?—but he didn't comment.

"Yes. I am an admirable crusher." It was *definitely* smug.

"I'm not a criminal." This introduction wasn't going at all how Mari had rehearsed it. "As I said, I'm a scientist. I admit I was deterred by the crusher's, ah, formidable presence, and that is why I paused. I didn't have anything criminal in mind, Scholar Sato. I came here hoping to speak to you about a private matter."

"Are you an astroshaman?"

Mari squirmed as much as she could. The steel—no, that was an alloy much stronger than simple steel—hands holding up her weight from under her armpits were not comfortable. "Yes."

"Did High Shaman Moonrazor send you?"

"No." Not even close...

"Do you wish to speak to *me*?" Sato touched her chest. "Or Casmir?"

"Uhm, I had thought you might be most interested in my work." And least likely to turn Mari over to her mother. "I've come to offer my services, and also my prototype terraforming device, to your queen, or whoever in your government might deal in such matters, in exchange for asylum."

"Terraforming device?"

Mari had assumed Sato would ask first what she had done and why she wanted asylum, but perhaps because she was also a scientist, the promise of useful technology interested her more. Mari *hoped* that was the case.

"Yes, I'm an agronomist and also have some modest engineering capabilities. The terraformer is in my backpack. I can show it to you if you like." Mari gestured over her shoulder at the pack, inasmuch as she could while she dangled in the air. "If your door guardian will set me down."

"I object to releasing the intruder," the crusher said. "The humans Kim Sato and Casmir Dabrowski, as is the case with many others of their kind, have had numerous hostile interactions with astroshamans. The eavesdropping nature of this astroshaman suggests inimical intent."

"I wasn't eavesdropping."

"Please put her down, Zee. She looks like she's in pain."

"This prisoner should be held captive while she is searched. If my grip is painful, I can modulate the surface tension of my hands so that they have a cushioning aspect to them. I have grown quite skilled at this."

"Yes, I've seen you become a couch for Queen Oku's dog. Put her down, please. You know Casmir likes to give people the benefit of the doubt."

Did he? Maybe Mari *should* talk to him.

"This is true, but I am a bodyguard. I must regard all strangers from enemy nations warily." Despite his objection, the crusher set Mari's feet on the ground. Unfortunately, it didn't let her go. The crusher did soften its grip, but it remained in place, as unyielding as before. "Casmir Dabrowski is returning now from the carbohydrate retrieval mission. Perhaps he will search the prisoner."

"Casmir's too shy and polite to pat down a strange woman," Sato said. "What did you say your name is?"

"Mari." She didn't know whether to be relieved or not that Sato didn't want to search her. She had nothing to hide, but she *was* armed. Only because she'd believed she might have to deal with situations exactly like the one with the strange bounty hunter in the Arctic. It hadn't occurred to her to remove her weapons and stash them somewhere before coming to Sato's home.

"Just Mari?" Sato frowned slightly. Indicating suspicion?

"Yes. Since I am leaving my people, I have no need of a surname that indicates astroshaman origins."

"You mentioned wanting asylum." Sato's gaze shifted past Zee toward the street. Someone was riding up on an air bike. "Have you committed a crime among your kind?"

"No, but it is not encouraged to leave our society, especially if you are young and were born into it. It's possible they will send someone to retrieve me." Not just *possible*; that man who'd attacked her ensured people were hunting her right now. She trusted her sisters hadn't given any bounty hunters orders to kill her, but what if she inadvertently caused Sato or some other ally of the queen's to be injured? Her chances of being offered asylum would plummet.

"Are you saying you ran away from home?" Sato asked.

"Who ran away from home?" the newcomer asked, parking the air bike on the walkway and trotting up to join them.

He carried a long narrow loaf of bread in a brown bag, the fresh scent of warm sourdough filling the air. It was so enticing, especially compared to an algae ration bar, that it momentarily distracted Mari from answering.

"I perpetrated a ruse to capture an eavesdropping astroshaman who may have inimical intent," Zee said.

"Good work, Zee." The newcomer patted the crusher on the shoulder and looked curiously at Mari.

"I do not have inimical intent. I am seeking asylum." Mari, assuming this was Minister Dabrowski, looked at him with equal curiosity.

Even though she'd seen pictures of him, she'd expected him to be taller and more physically formidable. She wasn't sure *why*, since he'd earned her mother's respect by hacking into a highly secure astroshaman network, designing the crushers, and somehow winning the trust of the AIs that had settled Verloren Moon, but it startled her that he was no taller than she, with skinny arms and shaggy brown hair that hung to his eyebrows. He wore a T-shirt with a cartoon character on it. She'd envisioned someone with a title like Minister of External Affairs wearing expensive and fashionable clothing when running errands.

"Apparently, she left the cult," Sato said.

Mari frowned. "We are not some strange religious sect.

Astroshamans believe in using advanced biotechnology to meld our bodies and consciousnesses with computers to allow us to achieve greater intellectual feats. We seek to live in a state less reliant on and motivated by biological frailties while we partake in the journey to humanity's ultimate fate, becoming one with the machine."

"Cult," Sato mouthed to Dabrowski.

"I know," he mouthed back.

Mari resisted the urge to argue further. After all, hadn't she left because she wanted to experience more than her people's strict lifestyle within a community that frowned upon any experimentation that wasn't in line with its goals?

"Perhaps I can show you my prototype terraforming device," Mari said, "as an example of what I can offer. I do not expect anyone to grant me asylum without a reason. I am prepared to trade my knowledge and my abilities for a place where I can work and experience your Kingdom culture."

"Wait, are you looking for asylum with *us*?" Dabrowski pointed the tip of his bread loaf at himself, then at Sato. "It's only a two-bedroom cottage, and the couch isn't that comfortable."

"Or typically uncluttered and available to sit on," Sato murmured.

"My tools aren't clutter," Dabrowski said.

"What about the comic books and dolls?"

"Those are limited edition collectible action heroes, not dolls. I'm waiting for someone to make one of the Main Event. That's when he'll know he's made it."

"Hm."

Mari didn't know what to make of these two. They weren't at all what she had expected, nor did they seem to be taking her offer seriously.

"I am not looking for refuge *here*," she said, "but perhaps in a secure location unknown to my people where I could pursue meaningful work that would help *your* people. I have much to offer, and I believe this would make the exchange equitable."

"Let's see this device," Sato said.

Mari attempted to pull her backpack off, but she couldn't manage with Zee still holding her. As she shifted, something clunked to the ground—a pistol that had been in her pack. Strange. That shouldn't have been able to fall out.

Sato and Dabrowski looked down at it.

"That's not it." Mari hoped they didn't recognize the astroshaman pistol as a weapon. It didn't look much like their DEW-Tek pistols. "I can't reach it."

"Zee." Dabrowski wiggled a finger in what might have been a let-her-go gesture.

"That is a weapon," the crusher said. "She may have other weapons on her person. I have not performed a body search yet."

"Let's save that fun for later. I trust you can stop her if she tries to shoot us."

The crusher gazed at him. Since it took Zee a moment to comply, Mari suspected a text exchange over the network. Finally, the crusher released her, though it remained nearby, blocking her escape should she wish to run.

But running wasn't her intent. She slung the pack off, alarmed at how light it felt. She patted the bottom and found a hole ripped in the fabric. Her shoulders slumped as she looked down at the weapon and back toward the street, hoping to spot not only the case for the terraformer but the other laboratory tools she'd taken from the ship. Almost everything had fallen out of her pack. She poked her hand inside, as if she might be mistaken, but only small items stored in inner pockets remained.

"The drones." Mari looked back toward the intersection, half expecting to see the pack of four hovering there, her items dangling in their mechanical grips as they taunted her. "I was attacked by drones. They must have cut my pack and taken my device."

That sounded ludicrous as soon as it came out, and she wished she could explain further.

Dabrowski's eyebrows rose. "They usually deliver pizza when they visit me."

Sato lifted a hand. "There *has* been a rash of drone attacks and thefts on campus today. It's in the news. Ra— someone came over to protect me tonight."

"Is *someone* here now? Should I have brought more bread?"

"Yes, but you know he rarely eats anything as devoid of nutrients as bread."

"Right, only superfoods for a superhero."

"Who controls the drones?" Mari asked. "My device represents a great deal of work and is valuable." Not to mention it was her bargaining chip.

"Usually some nerd in the computer lab," Sato said.

Red lights flashed at the intersection, and a municipal police van rolled down the street.

Mari tensed, afraid the authorities were here for her. *She* wasn't the one mugging people, but as long as the Kingdom considered astroshamans to be enemies, she was in danger of being reported for her mere existence in their city. Her hood had fallen back more than once since she'd arrived on campus—it dangled around her shoulders again now.

Zee, who'd released her so she could search her pack, clamped down on her shoulder again. Mari caught herself before reaching for a weapon but barely.

"Kim?" Dabrowski asked.

"I have not messaged campus security or the police, but it is possible someone else did, especially if they saw Zee apprehend our visitor." Sato looked toward other houses on the cul-de-sac, lights on in the homes. More than one face was pressed curiously to a window, and at one property, a couple stood outside, openly watching the exchange.

"I haven't done anything wrong," Mari said.

"As High Shaman Moonrazor was told," Dabrowski said, "her people have free reign of the thirty-thousand-acre parcel in the forest two hundred miles to the west of the capital, and they—you —are welcome to have deliveries made for projects, but I haven't yet been able to finagle the senate into giving astroshamans permission to walk freely on the rest of the planet. Relatively few people even know you're there, and it's probably a good idea to keep it that way for now. For your own safety more than anything. There are a lot of people who lost family in the bombings. *I* know your people had nothing to do with the first set of bombings, and you even helped me deal with the person responsible, but... our people are kind of fuzzy on who to blame, and there's a lot of blanket hatred toward astroshamans right now."

"That means you believe I *have* done something wrong?" Mari asked. "By leaving the forest?"

The police van stopped in front of the cottage, the doors slid open, and two policemen jumped out. They carried flex-cuffs and stunners instead of deadly weapons and wore uniforms instead of combat armor, but Mari didn't know if she could overpower them, especially now that many of her tools and weapons were missing.

"*I* don't think so." Dabrowski touched his chest. "But the police may insist on questioning you. I wish you'd gone through High Shaman Moonrazor. Maybe she could have messaged me, and we could have worked out permission for you to visit other places on the planet with some kind of diplomatic passport."

Mari looked bleakly at him as the policemen walked up with their stunners drawn. "She wouldn't give me permission to leave. She's the person I'm seeking asylum from."

"Oh," Dabrowski said. "Why?"

"She's my mother."

He mouthed another, "Oh."

"Minister Dabrowski?" One of the policemen stopped, looking warily at the crusher. "I'm Sergeant Schutze. Are you all right? An astroshaman spy on campus was reported. It's possible she's here gathering intelligence that may be used in a raid." He eyed Mari darkly. "Military Intelligence has warned our department to watch out for their kind. They may be angry that we thwarted their plans and could be plotting vengeance against our people."

Mari shook her head. Her mother *had* been annoyed to be defeated, but she hadn't been the high shaman behind the attack on Odin. She'd never wanted to kill people, only to seek technology that could help the astroshamans further their goals of leaving the Twelve Systems and finding a new home, one where they wouldn't be shunted off as kooky *cult* members by the rest of humanity. The two high shaman leaders who had pressured her into the invasion had died in the attack. None of the astroshamans who'd settled in the forest here wished the Kingdom ill will. Few of them had warm, adoring feelings for the locals, but Mari didn't think any of her people were plotting against the Kingdom. That would be a foolish thing to do while they were living on the planet that was the seat of the Kingdom.

"That's what Military Intelligence is warning?" Dabrowski scratched his jaw.

"Yes, my lord. We have orders to apprehend any astroshamans and question them under the influence of truth drugs."

Mari's insides knotted. She *personally* didn't have anything to hide, but what if they took the opportunity to ask all about her people? About their command structure and their technology? And what they were up to on the land they'd been given? Nothing *Mari* would consider nefarious, but would the Kingdom military agree? And what would her mother and sisters think if she allowed herself to be questioned in such a way?

"Is there any chance I can override those orders and send you off to find the drones that are robbing people on campus?" Dabrowski offered an easy smile, but his eyes were intent.

"Ah, no, my lord. It's my understanding that the Minister of External Affairs is a diplomatic position. You can only order diplomats around."

"Which has indeed been satisfying, but..." Dabrowski gestured at Mari. "I don't suppose you'd like to change up your story and say you're here on a diplomatic mission for High Shaman Moonrazor, thus falling more into my domain?"

"I..." Mari couldn't tell if he was serious—would that actually work?—or if he was humoring her. Surely, he had to be on the same side as his law enforcers, not trying to work against them for her sake. "I would rather not get her involved."

"If only you knew someone with broader authority," Sato murmured to Dabrowski.

"She's on one of the lunar bases, currently in a meeting with several of the nobles who rule over the habitats. They're discussing the crown's authority over them and how much leeway they have to set trade tariffs and the like. These meetings tend not to be short. Much to her consternation."

"Ah."

The sergeant cleared his throat. "Minister, if we may take the prisoner?" He eyed the crusher again, as if he didn't want to tangle with it. "For your safety and that of your neighbors. And for Kingdom security."

Dabrowski hesitated, and Mari held her breath, thinking he might object and that the crusher would keep the policemen from hauling her away. Maybe it wasn't too late for her to feign diplomatic status and hope that would protect her. But no, that would only end up with them contacting her mother to verify it—and thus letting her mother know where she was.

"Of course," Dabrowski said. "But be nice, eh? We have a treaty with the astroshamans, and we're not at war with them right now."

"Certainly, my lord. We are not brutes."

"Good to know. Mari, ah, it's probably best if you cooperate with the police. If nothing untoward comes up, maybe I can get you a diplomatic passport, and then you can make your proposal when the queen returns."

Mari feared whatever help he could offer—if he truly meant to follow up on her case—would come too late. Soon, she would be questioned under those drugs and would blab all of her people's secrets to government agents with recording devices. Mari also worried that Dabrowski would let her mother know she was here and that she would mount a rescue mission to retrieve her before any such secrets could be sucked from her brain. Such an action, especially if it couldn't be done without violence, might start a war.

"Thank you," Mari made herself say, but bleakness filled her as the crusher stepped aside, allowing the policemen to snap flex-cuffs around her wrists.

7

Kenji crouched in the shadows behind a tree several houses down from the cottage of Professor Dabrowski—now Minister Dabrowski, though from what the news said, he still taught a couple of classes on campus. Kenji watched as a crusher released Mari into the hands of two policemen. A third officer sat in the driver's seat of their van, waiting while the others trundled her toward an open sliding door in the back.

"This isn't good," Kenji whispered, trusting Kay's auditory receptors would pick up his words, though the robot stood behind a different tree several feet back. "How am I supposed to capture her, return her to her people, and collect the bounty if she's in a jail cell?"

"It will be more difficult," Kay said. "It was *already* difficult obtaining the code for her air bike and tracking her here."

Tracking her hadn't been that hard once they'd had the locator code—Kenji glanced toward where she'd parked her air bike—but he agreed that the situation at the rental shop had been unexpectedly fraught. If he didn't get off the planet, or at least permanently out of the capital soon, he worried he would end up in the Main Event's sights again. Fate kept thrusting him in that man's path.

Kenji chewed on his lip as Mari disappeared into the van. "It would be foolish to risk the ire of the police and other local authorities by rescuing her, right?"

"Rescuing her in order to capture her?"

"Yeah. I doubt the police want to collect her bounty. They probably don't even know about it. They just came because..." Kenji wasn't close enough to the cottage to have heard the whole conversation, but he'd arrived in time to see the crusher restraining Mari, with Dabrowski and Scholar Sato—a figure almost as renowned as the professor after publishing that book—questioning her. "Probably because Dabrowski commed them. He must have felt threatened. Maybe the crusher caught Mari spying on them for nefarious purposes. Her people could want her back not just because she has their top-secret information but because she's a threat to the tenuous peace between the astroshamans and the Kingdom."

The sliding door shut, and the police van started up.

"Stay there," Kenji whispered to Kay.

He left his tree and hugged the shadows of the sidewalk to hurry back to the intersection before the police van rolled down the street. A harebrained idea popped into his mind, one that might work, since he'd purchased a stunner on the way over. The police weren't in armor, so they would have no defense against a stun blast. Not that stunning them was a *good* idea—it certainly wasn't a legal one—but if Kenji could do it without being identified, maybe he could get Mari. The police might figure out his identity later, but if he first collected her bounty and could get out of the Kingdom before they caught up to him, maybe it wouldn't matter.

He cut through a yard to run around a house on the corner,

then jumped out into the main street. Fortunately, the evening had grown late, and there was no other traffic on it.

As the van drove toward the intersection, Kenji grabbed his side, started limping dramatically, and shambled toward it. He feigned being gravely injured, hoping the drone muggings on campus would give him a plausible reason for being wounded.

The van slowed as it reached the intersection, the driver spotting him.

Kenji crumpled to his knees, then flopped onto his side directly in the police vehicle's path. The driver could navigate around him, but he was counting on policemen feeling obligated to help a poor injured student.

The van halted. It wasn't the driver that got out but one of the men in the back. Even better.

Kenji prepared to draw upon all of his meager thespian talents. His father had insisted he learn to fight, pick locks, and pilot, but acting lessons hadn't been in the mix.

"What happened, kid?" The policeman stopped beside him and looked down. His hand rested on the butt of his stunner, and there was wariness in his eyes.

Kenji groaned and slurred, "I dunno... was walking back home... got attacked... by drones." He turned puzzled eyes toward the police sergeant, working pain into his wince. "Why? I didn't... do anything. They took... took my bag."

He resisted the urge to elaborate on a story of purchases he'd made and was bringing home, both because he was supposed to be in terrible pain and because his father had always told him that people who were lying tended to blurt out way too many details for their made-up stories. Kenji had no idea what was going on with the drones and was only aware of the problem because the news had popped up when he'd been researching events on campus, trying to figure out why Mari had headed here.

"Yeah, we've got a team checking on the security station to find out what's going on with them. You need a ride back to your dorm?" The policeman sounded sympathetic, but he hadn't taken his hand off his stunner.

"Hospital?" Kenji asked hopefully, still gripping his side. That was farther away and would give him more time, and he didn't know the campus well enough to make up a fake address. "I think they... broke some ribs."

"All right." The policeman held up a finger to the driver. "Can you get up? Or do you need a hover gurney? I can call an ambulance."

"I can get up." Kenji rolled to his knees without letting go of his ribs. He didn't want to risk being carted away in a different vehicle from Mari. "Just need a little help."

The policeman offered him a hand. How solicitous. Kenji hoped he wouldn't ask to read the chip that Kenji didn't have or ask for proof that he was a student.

Limping dramatically, Kenji tried to guide the policeman to where he wished to go while seeming to appear that *he* was being guided. He could already tell the man wanted to maneuver him toward the passenger seat next to the driver instead of into the back of the van with their dubious astroshaman prisoner.

"Just need to lie down for a few," Kenji muttered, limping toward the sliding door in the back.

He glimpsed Kay watching from his spot in the shadows of an oak tree. At the end of the cul-de-sac, Dabrowski and Sato had disappeared into their house. That was good. The odds of Dabrowski recognizing him were extremely low, especially since Kenji had never officially been on the roster, but it was possible Dabrowski would think him familiar and look him up. Of all the people he didn't want researching him on the network, Dabrowski topped the list. Anyone who could hack into astroshaman networks could easily find old photos linking Kenji to his father.

"It would be better if you sat up front," the officer said.

Not for Kenji.

"The floor is all right. Don't need any... special treatment." Kenji feigned a stumble that happened to take him toward the open sliding door, and he tumbled into the van.

The other policeman sat on a bench across from Mari, sipping from a coffee cup with a Beans and Brews logo on the side. Kenji had no trouble seeing it since, unfortunately, the lights were on in the van. He'd hoped for a dark identity-hiding interior.

He tried to hide his face so Mari wouldn't recognize him until he was ready to enact his plan. Flex-cuffs bound her wrists in her lap, and her pack and weapons had been taken, but she wasn't gagged and could blurt out that she recognized him.

Sighing, the policeman who'd helped him to his feet climbed into the back and maneuvered him onto a bench before shutting the door. Still hoping Mari wouldn't recognize him, Kenji slumped down and kept his chin to his chest, but he was now across from her and worried that wouldn't be enough.

"Go ahead, Anzhong," the officer said, presumably to the driver, for the van lurched into motion.

"Hospital first?" the driver asked.

There was a wall separating the cab from the back of the van, and the voice came over a speaker. That potentially meant Kenji only had to stun the two policemen in back with him, and one was drinking coffee, so he might not be that attentive. After they were knocked out, Kenji could stun Mari, throw her over his shoulder, and slip out while the van was idling at a traffic signal.

"Yeah. Hospital, then headquarters. We'll make sure the astroshaman doesn't try to get out along the way."

"She's not going anywhere." The coffee drinker had a stunner in his other hand, and he kept it pointed at her.

The other one also aimed a stunner in her direction. That she had their full attention was good, but Kenji was slumped on the bench between them. He thought he could get his stunner out of his pocket without them noticing, but he didn't know if he could stun one to either side of him before anyone stunned *him*. He imagined a scenario where he knocked out the policemen even as they got him, and Mari was free to escape *all* of their clutches, leaving him to wake up later in jail. That would not be ideal.

If having the weapons pointed at Mari concerned her, she didn't show it. She was eyeing the Beans and Brews cup.

"Your beverage smells sweet," she said. "It contains something other than black coffee?"

The officer's eyebrows went up. "Cinnamon. It's a horchata latte."

"Cinnamon is a spice obtained from the inner bark of numerous tree species from the genus *Cinnamomum*." Mari's head tilted. "Its scent and flavor come from its principal component cinnamaldehyde as well as the allyl chain-substituted guaiacol eugenol."

"Thanks for the encyclopedia entry." The officer rolled his eyes and mumbled something about being sent to arrest computers.

"I do not believe I have had cinnamon," Mari said. "Or a *latte*."

"Maybe Kovacs will let you try his." The other policeman smirked.

"May I?" Mari asked.

Kenji almost laughed. It seemed a genuine request, and he imagined her guzzling the man's drink if given the chance.

"*No*." Kovacs glared at his colleague, then gave Mari an even more hostile look. "There's no way I'm letting some astroshaman freak leave saliva on my cup."

Even though Mari's ocular implants made her eyes seem more robot than human, Kenji didn't have any trouble reading the wince of discomfort—or shame?—as she looked away from them. Her cheeks turned pink, and she appeared far more affected by the glare and the insult than she had been from having weapons pointed at her.

Kenji shifted uneasily in his seat, questioning for the first time if he was doing the right thing. When he'd accepted the bounty-hunting gig, having one astroshaman pay him to capture another astroshaman hadn't *seemed* morally ambiguous. They were *all* enemies to his people, after all. But Mari asking to try someone's latte because she'd never had cinnamon before didn't seem very... enemy-ish.

A message from Kay popped up on his glasses display. *You are coming back for me, are you not?*

Yes. I'll get out with Mari as soon as I can. Kenji used eye movements to type the response—a slower and kludgier way to enter commands than by voice, but it worked in a pinch. As he replied, he groaned, keeping up his ruse. *If you can, follow the van so you're not far away when we slip out.*

Follow the van? It is moving at more than twenty-five miles per hour. I did not know robot calisthenics would be required tonight.

The mention of speed reminded Kenji that he didn't have much time. He was fairly certain they were still on campus, but they wouldn't be for long, and the hospital wasn't far away.

Just give me a minute, and I'll let you know where we end up. Kenji pretended to adjust his grip on his ribs while slipping his other hand into his pocket. Since he was an injured and innocent bystander, the police hadn't searched him. He wrapped his fingers around his stunner.

Mari must have noticed his movement, for she was scrutinizing him openly. Kenji suspected she'd recognized him as soon as he tumbled into the van. She hadn't tried to out him as something other than an injured student. Was that promising?

He widened his eyes, shifting his pupils to the left and the right to try to hint at what he meant to do, in case she was willing to distract them, but he didn't dare do anything as obvious as pulling out the stunner before he intended to use it. Mari might be the officers' focus, but since Kenji was shoulder to shoulder with them, they would notice anything he did.

What are you doing, bounty hunter? A message scrolled down his display.

From... her? How had she known the ident chip in his glasses to contact him? For that matter, how had she messaged him without sending one of the ubiquitous requests for permission to contact him that were designed to keep away spammers?

Questions for later.

Rescuing you. Work with me, eh?

Her eyes narrowed with suspicion, and she didn't do anything helpful. If anything, she kept staring at him, which he worried would lead the *policemen* to stare at him.

Maybe she didn't *want* to be rescued. Or, more likely, she didn't believe that was his intent.

The van drove through a pothole, jostling everyone, and Kenji took his chance. He tugged out his stunner, fired at the man on his right, and whipped it toward the coffee drinker, firing again.

But the second policeman had the split second he needed to react. He dropped his cup and knocked Kenji's arm away. The stunner blast struck the wall. The policeman tried to smack the weapon from Kenji's grip, but Kenji jerked his arm back in time to avoid the blow. He sprang from his seat, giving himself room so he couldn't be blocked again.

As the policeman surged to his feet and opened his mouth to shout a warning to his driver, Mari kicked him in the groin. His warning shifted to a pained grunt as he staggered back a step. That gave Kenji time to fire again. The stunner blast struck the policeman in the chest, and he crumpled to the floor.

Mari sank down and dug into his pockets, pulling out a fob and tapping the button to unlock her flex-cuffs. They clanked to the floor.

"Come on." Kenji pointed his stunner toward Mari to ensure she didn't kick *him* as he opened the sliding door.

He'd planned to stun her, but he didn't think he could jump out of a moving vehicle with her slung over his shoulder.

No sooner had he had the thought than the van halted abruptly, not bothering to pull over. The driver must have figured out what was going on.

The door opened automatically. Kenji leaped to the side of it for cover as the driver got out and ran back. He sprang into view, a stunner in each hand, and fired into the van before he could have gotten a look inside. Mari had grabbed a fallen stunner and also jumped for cover, taking up a position on the other side of the door. The twin blasts hit the back wall, the edge of the nimbus buzzing against Kenji's skin as they passed but not catching him fully enough to knock him out.

As if they'd planned it, he and Mari leaned out together and fired. The policeman saw her first and jumped to the side in time to avoid her blast, but Kenji's caught him in the chest. He pitched backward into the street.

Kenji jumped down, spotting the headlights of other vehicles heading in their direction. Though he was tempted to pause and drag the policeman out of the street, there wasn't time, not if he wanted to get away. Someone else would come along and help the men.

Besides, Mari leaped out and raced into a parking lot, not glancing back. Kenji cursed. A woman was supposed to stop and say *thank you* after being rescued.

He rushed after her, relieved that his longer legs let him gain on her. He raised his weapon to stun her, but before he got the shot off, she glanced back, then darted sideways onto a walkway between two buildings.

Instincts warned him that charging around the corner after her might be dangerous. Instead, he threw himself into a roll, the pavement pummeling his shoulder and back as his momentum carried him across the walkway and to the building on the other side. His instincts had been correct: a blue stun bolt zipped past above him. It would have hit him if he'd been standing upright.

He jumped up, firing at her from around the corner of the building. Mari had ducked behind a lamppost, but it wasn't wide enough to hide her fully. His blast caught her in the side, and he held his breath, waiting to see if that would be enough to knock her out.

When he poked his head around the corner, she'd dropped to her knees and slumped against the lamppost, but she wasn't fully out. She scowled at him and fired again. He jerked back a split second before the shot blasted past, the skin on his cheeks instantly going numb. As much as he cursed his father, he knew he had his better-than-average reflexes to thank for still being conscious.

Kenji squatted low and leaned around the corner, prepared to fire again before springing back, but she'd crumpled the rest of the way to the ground, her fingers open with the stunner falling out of her grip. Though he half expected it to be a trap, he risked trotting closer.

Shouts came from the street, and the flashes of police lights reflected off building windows in the parking lot. Kenji didn't have much time.

He snatched Mari's weapon, and her fingers twitched. Her eyes were half-open and glassy, but she didn't otherwise react. He'd only stunned her partially, meaning she would rouse soon.

"My apologies for the manhandling," he said, rolling her over enough to fasten his set of flex-cuffs to her wrists.

A twinge of guilt went through him at how bad a night the woman was having, and the uncertainty returned that maybe he was capturing someone who didn't deserve to be captured. As he hoisted her over his shoulder and continued down the walkway, he hoped he was doing the right thing.

"I *am*," he muttered.

Just because she was curious about things and hadn't had cinnamon before didn't mean she was a good person. Besides, if Minister Dabrowski had commed the police to come collect her, she *had* to be a bad guy—bad gal—right?

Kenji wished he wasn't deemed by many to be a bad guy himself, and that he dared to go knock on Dabrowski's door to check. Instead, he turned onto a trail that led through trees toward more classroom buildings. He needed to reunite with Kay and get off campus as quickly as possible, but his strength wasn't so vast that he could run for miles with a woman over his shoulder. He would need to find a vehicle soon. Maybe he should have kept the smoking shuttle.

Mari stirred faintly, an elbow clunking him in the spine. He ran faster, reluctant to stun her again, as more than one hit in rapid succession could damage a person's nervous system. Maybe later, he could—

Something stabbed him in the butt, and he yelped, dropping her in the bushes beside the trail. He grabbed his butt as he pointed his stunner at her, imagining that she'd stabbed him with a knife and his hand would come away bloody.

She rolled out of the bushes and lumbered to her feet, still dazed from the stun. But not so dazed that she hadn't been able to stab him. How had she even gotten out a weapon when her hands were cuffed? Wait, they *weren't* cuffed. She'd gotten free of them somehow. What the hell?

Kenji's finger tightened on the trigger of his weapon as he wrestled with the temptation to stun her again, medical side effects be damned.

He checked his free hand, but there wasn't any blood on his fingers. She lifted not a knife but her finger, showing him a gray metallic ring with a needle jutting from the bottom. Moisture on the tip caught the yellow light from a nearby lamppost.

"Is that poison?" Kenji demanded, then winced. His words came out slurred.

"A tranquilizer." Mari lifted her chin. "I am not a murderer."

"You stabbed me in the *ass.*"

"I do not know who you are or how you keep finding me, but I refuse to go with you. I have something I must retrieve, and even after I retrieve it, I will not be going back to my people."

"You." Kenji lifted a finger to point at her, but he wobbled and saw double for a moment. His legs grew rubbery, and the feeling that he had better sit down before he fell down came over him. "Didn't the police *search* you?"

"They did not search my jewelry."

Kenji's arm drooped, and his body followed, his shoulder too numb to feel pain when he thudded down on the trail.

"I'm going to have to... speak to them... about their carelessness," he mumbled, his cheek mashed against the dirt, its earthy scent filling his nostrils.

Mari stood over him, and he feared she might do more than knock him out this time. Maybe he deserved it. All of his father's training, all of the precious genetic enhancements, and Kenji couldn't catch one astroshaman girl.

8

Mari wanted to leave the university campus, having found nothing but trouble here, but she needed to get her terraformer back. Maybe it was naive, but she still believed it might be a way to prove her usefulness to the Kingdom government and get that meeting with the queen. And a diplomatic passport! Minister Dabrowski had mentioned that twice, as if it might truly be a possibility.

As uncomfortable as it had been dangling from the crusher's grip, Sato and Dabrowski had been willing to talk to her, willing to listen. If the police hadn't shown up—and if her terraformer hadn't been *stolen*—her night might have gone according to plan.

A part of her was tempted to circle back to Sato and Dabrowski's home and try again, but she had to get her terraformer first. *Then* she could make her case. The next time she approached, she would try to catch Sato without Dabrowski—or his crusher—around.

Mari found the public campus map she'd used earlier and looked for a security building. There had to be a depot where those drones went to recharge their batteries. Maybe the hoodlum who'd reprogrammed them to attack and steal from people was hunkered in there now, examining his or her loot.

A single building on the map was labeled *Campus Security.* It didn't say anything about drones, but she headed in that direction, winding along dirt trails and cement walkways between buildings and through grassy areas so she could avoid the streets.

She'd left that *man* crumpled on the trail for the police to find, and she hoped they locked him up. Her mother would call her a fool for leaving an enemy behind to try to capture her again, but she couldn't *kill* any of these people, not when she wanted to work for them. Even if that bounty hunter might be a criminal in his own right, he had a Kingdom accent, and she couldn't be positive he didn't have ties to some law-enforcement agency.

Though if he had, he wouldn't have had to stun the police to get her. What exactly had that been? A *rescue*, he'd said. How ludicrous. He'd only wanted to *rescue* her, so he could capture her himself. And collect whatever reward her family had issued for her.

A part of her wanted to message her mother and tell her to knock it off, that she was leaving, and that was that, but she'd spoken to her family of her desires in the past, and neither her mother nor siblings had been willing to accept them. One didn't leave the astroshamans, especially when one had specifically been raised to be an asset to one's people, not out of some feeling of love or a desire for children. If her mother had ever hugged her or expressed warmth, Mari couldn't remember it.

Her throat tightened with a sense of longing that she usually succeeded in pushing out of her mind. Distracted, she almost ran into a pair of students in dark clothing walking along the path in the opposite direction. She muttered an apology, tugged her hood lower over her eyes, and hurried around them.

"Focus," she muttered to herself.

Even though she hoped the police would assume she'd fled the campus, and weren't looking for her here, Mari couldn't be positive about that. Further, she'd passed several stationary cameras atop lampposts. It was possible someone was monitoring them and had been alerted to watch for a blonde woman in a cloak and hood.

She came off the trail and onto a disturbingly open grassy lawn around a three-story building. Numerous security shuttles and autoflyers were in the parking lot, and lights were on in the foyer and front offices. *Campus Security*, a sign out front read. Someone passed by a window in one of the lit offices. A night shift was working, maybe the very night shift that monitored the cameras and was looking for Mari.

Following the trees edging the lawn, she circled to the back of the building. Maybe the drones were in a less populated garage or shed.

Thwarting electronic locks and sneaking into the building shouldn't be difficult, but she didn't want to risk running into people. The police had taken her arc blaster, her destroyed backpack, and everything in her pockets. The stunner she'd grabbed and the dual-purpose rings she wore were the only meager tools she had left. It had only been luck—actually, it had been the bounty hunter's lack of foresight—that put her in a position to use one.

There was a smaller detached building in the back, with only a few vehicles parked out front, one police van and two air bikes. The police van might have made her draw back and reject the idea of entering there, but a plaque on the door read *Security Drones and Robots*.

Maybe the policemen were inside, interrogating whoever had reprogrammed the drones. Her first thought was to applaud that, but if the police confiscated all of the stolen goods that had been brought in, they would take her terraformer right along with shopping bags full of knickknacks.

She assumed that the rightful owners of the latter would be able to come claim their goods, but how could *she* walk in and do that? She had to get her device *before* it was locked up somewhere. Or, worse, taken to a government facility for study. Would the police recognize astroshaman technology when they saw it?

After checking her hood again, Mari headed for the entrance, giving the police vehicle wide berth. The front door wasn't locked, and she eased it open. With her stunner in her pocket and her hand around the grip, she paused to listen for voices. A man and a woman were talking somewhere down a hall.

Mari stepped inside and crept past closed office doors on the left and a bank of windows on the right looking into a large repair bay. A few vehicles, a couple dozen ambulatory robots, and shelves full of dormant drones were inside. The lights in the bay were off, but she found an unlocked door and stepped inside, hoping to find the bags of stolen goods on a table.

The air smelled of metal, chemicals, and lubricant, and a few indicator lights winked on equipment. Nothing stirred, and Mari didn't see her property. She thought about activating one of the drones and hacking her way into its system to look for answers, but she doubted the responsible units were in this bay.

The female voice grew louder, and for the first time, Mari could make out words.

"What do you *mean* you were playing video games?"

A new voice replied, young and squeaky. "Didn't know," were the only audible words.

Mari grimaced, fearing the drones who'd stolen her terraformer weren't here. Maybe some outside entity had taken control of them, and the owner of the young voice was a kid on staff who'd been sleeping on the job.

A man spoke, his tone conciliatory, and Mari started. That sounded like Dabrowski.

Would he have interrupted his dinner to come over here? He

was a roboticist and worked on campus, but he was also an important government official. Did such people get called in after hours to help with malfunctioning drones?

Mari reached for the door back into the hallway, thinking she might eavesdrop after all, but she paused with her hand on the knob. If Dabrowski was here, the crusher might be too, and he was convinced eavesdropping was a heinous crime.

Before she'd decided what to do, someone stepped into the hallway. The woman. She wore a police uniform and walked beside another woman in a campus-security uniform.

Mari ducked low, glimpsing weapons on both of their belts. She was stuck right in front of the door, and they were heading down the hall toward the exit. What if they paused to check the bay?

She drew her stunner. Though she hated the idea of leaving a trail of unconscious bodies behind her, she was determined to get her terraformer back, one way or another.

Fortunately, the women walked past without stopping. Mari let out a relieved breath and waited a long moment to make sure they didn't come back inside. The male voices started up again, Dabrowski and the kid.

Did she need to eavesdrop? What if she... strolled in and offered to help?

Assuming Dabrowski had been telling the truth that neither he nor Sato had commed the police, he might not be *that* perturbed if she walked in to continue their conversation. He'd seemed open to helping her, or at least listening to her story. He'd helped Mari's *mother,* after all. Of course, that might be more of a minus than a plus. If he considered her mother an ally, he might feel compelled to report her missing daughter to her.

Maybe, but Mari decided to take a shot. She needed to prove herself to these people if she was to earn asylum.

She eased down the hallway, their voices growing more distinct as she approached.

"Good," Dabrowski was saying. "Now see if you can find their locator chips. Their range is limited, so they should be within five miles."

"Yes, sir. Er, my lord. Minister." The kid sounded as flustered as he had when dealing with whichever of the women had been lecturing him. Maybe more so.

"Casmir," Dabrowski said dryly.

"You can't call a noble by his first name," the kid protested. "They flog you for that."

"I don't think that's been true for a thousand years, but even if it were, I'm mostly an honorary noble."

"Didn't they give you land? And a title?"

"And government work," Dabrowski said.

"That means you're a real noble."

"Are you sure?"

"Yes, my lord. Professor Teabottom covered it in my sociology class."

Dabrowski sighed, as if he would have preferred to be *Casmir* over anyone's lord.

"I can't find the locator chips, sir. None of them. Is it possible the drones were destroyed?"

"Probably not. And since they were in the bay this afternoon, and the security cameras suggest nobody was in here to alter them physically, the hackers likely remotely installed software to cloak their signatures as well as take over access. That sounds like the Chipfogger program. Or maybe Artarus 7. Here. You've got system-administrator privileges, right? Check for recent downloads of those programs from the underground campus servers to chips registered with the university. At this point, I'm more inclined to guess a student did this rather than some master hacker living in the city. Mugging students for what's in their backpacks isn't typical of an experienced criminal mastermind."

Mari, having been mugged, wasn't sure she agreed.

Remembering that she'd already gotten caught once for eavesdropping, and that the crusher might be standing silently in there with Dabrowski, Mari took a deep breath and knocked on the doorjamb. Since the door itself stood ajar, that was the best she could do.

The towering tarry black crusher appeared in the doorway. Mari jumped back, bumping against the wall. Not again.

Surprisingly, the crusher didn't lunge out and capture her.

"Casmir Dabrowski," it stated. "Your police authorities have failed to retain the astroshaman female. She is here eavesdropping once more. Do you wish me to apprehend her again?"

"Uh?" Dabrowski peeked around the crusher's shoulder. "Miss Mari, wasn't it?"

"Yes. I am looking for my terraformer that was stolen by security drones." She hesitated, tempted to pretend the incident with the police hadn't happened at all and see what he did, but the crusher had already brought it up. "The police were not interested in assisting me, so I had to... depart from their presence."

"I see." Dabrowski seemed more amused than annoyed or judgmental. "Yes, I've occasionally had to depart from the presence of law-enforcement authorities myself, when their mission goals deviated from mine."

"*Really,* sir?" the student asked. "I mean, my lord."

"Yes." Dabrowski crooked a finger to invite Mari into the room, then patted the crusher. "Let her come in, please, Zee. I believe someone on campus has illegally obtained astroshaman technology."

"I read the book, but I didn't know how much was, you know, fictionalized." The speaker, a shaggy-haired kid who looked like a younger version of Dabrowski, raised his eyebrows when Mari walked in. "Do you really know *astroshamans*?" He touched his chest uncertainly; a logo on his blue T-shirt proclaimed in gold that he heart-symbolled the Kingdom.

"There's only one who's deigned to talk to me."

"High Shaman Moonrazor." The student barely glanced at Mari, instead turning his worshipful eyes toward Dabrowski. "Did you really *kiss* her?"

That didn't startle Mari, since it had been mentioned in Sato's book, but Dabrowski lost his equanimity, nearly tripping over nothing and pitching sideways. The crusher reached out and steadied him.

"Kim put *that* in the book?" Dabrowski blurted. "The book that *all of the Kingdom* has read?"

"Yes, my lord. Uhm, *you* haven't read it?"

"I lived it." Dabrowski recovered enough to lift a hand and rub the appalled expression off his face, though his left eye blinked in some tic. "I hope the book explained that she kissed *me* and only to use me as a shield so Tenebris Rache, whose mercenaries were demolishing her base, wouldn't shoot her. She's at *least* twice my age and..." He looked at Mari, maybe remembering her admission that Moonrazor was her mother, and edited his words on the fly. "We were more enemies than allies at that point."

At that point. Mari couldn't help but grimace at the reminder that they were allies now and wondered if she'd made a huge mistake. What if Dabrowski had already contacted her mother, and her family was on the way to round up their wayward charge and drag her back to their isolated base?

"That's *amazing*, my lord. You've had so many stellar adventures."

"Yes." Dabrowski clasped his hands behind his back, resuming the teacherly tone he'd been using with the student earlier, and nodded toward the computer terminal the kid was parked at. "Have you found recent downloads of those files? The drones started deviating from their programming this morning, so you only need to check back a day or two. It's possible this was being planned for weeks, but students tend toward the impulsive, so I'm inclined to believe this wasn't premeditated. Someone who had more time to think about it might have realized it would be a bad idea."

"They're going to get expelled for sure. One minute, my lord." The student turned his focus back to the terminal.

Mari thought about volunteering to do the search herself, since she could likely find the culprit in seconds. For that matter, Dabrowski probably could too and was using the opportunity to teach the student. But Mari didn't care about that; she only wanted her terraformer back, ideally before a police officer sprang in to arrest her again.

"You mentioned that the device the drones absconded with is a prototype?" Dabrowski asked her, not sounding skeptical about her claims. "And for terraforming?"

"For *rapid* terraforming. It breaks down the original matter on a planet or moon within minutes and can soon start rearranging molecules into fertile soil, complete with seeds and enzymes and water."

A pensive crease appeared on Dabrowski's forehead.

"And yes, it's a prototype. That's why I risked going to the wreck to get it. I have the plans, of course." Mari waved toward the chips integrated into her brain. "But it uses a unique alloy that my people—those who settled in the forest here—can't make more of until we're able to gather more resources. Your people—nonastroshamans—would find the alloy alone extremely valuable. It's used in a great deal of our advanced technology, including ship hulls."

"Ship hulls that can be made all but invisible?"

"The invisibility is conveyed by a shield generator, but the hulls do have technology that insulates against scans."

The part of Mari that had been fully indoctrinated to be loyal to her people, and hold their secrets even in the face of death, squirmed at this openness with a near-stranger, but if she got what she wanted, to be granted asylum in exchange for working for the Kingdom, she would have to share a lot more secrets. If she did, would her family go from wanting to capture her and bring her home to perhaps trying to kill her to keep her quiet?

Maybe she could offer to work for the Kingdom without betraying any secrets, volunteering only her skills, not her knowledge. But unless her family knew she was doing that... would it matter?

Fortunately, Dabrowski looked only mildly curious, not like he was contemplating drugging her so he could extract everything she knew from her. "That technology and alloy would be very valuable then, yes. We'll try to get it back for you. Maybe the thieves don't realize what they've got, and it's currently being used as a paperweight."

"Found it, my lord!" The student opened a desk drawer and pulled out a pen and paper to scribble an address. He tore off a corner and ran it over to Dabrowski, who accepted the scrap with the same bemused expression that Mari might have had at being given information on a physical medium. "The files were accessed from that network account and at that address."

"Thank you." Casmir glanced at it, probably taking a picture with his contact camera, and handed it back.

Mari also recorded the address, experiencing the temptation to sprint away and check it before Dabrowski could send anyone.

"I had to track it through a few relay stations. They were trying to hide their location, but I found them." The student lifted his chin.

"Good work, Brodeur. Hm. This address is in faculty housing, not a dorm. Assistant Professor Donadieu lives there without a roommate. He teaches economics."

"Is the pay for faculty here insufficient?" Mari asked. "Such that someone would be tempted toward theft?"

"*I* don't think so, but I suppose it depends on what financial desires you have. One wonders if he might have been conducting some experiment for a class. An irritated student could also be framing him. This will require an in-person visit." Dabrowski considered her. "At this junction, the mature, professional thing for me to do would be to contact the police and send *them* to visit, but it will be problematic if they run into you."

"Yes. They may be somewhat distracted by the bounty hunter I left crumpled on the sidewalk, but I doubt they've forgotten me."

"Your mother sent a *bounty hunter* after you? Is she trying to get you back, or... just how forbidden *is* it to leave the family?"

"I believe my sisters may have sent him. They're as inexperienced with dealing with outsiders and outside societies as I am. That could explain why they sent someone young and inept. I think my mother would seek me out through the network and send our own people." Something that might still happen. "It's also possible she's waiting for me to realize I was foolish to leave and slink back home as a failure."

"Hm. Why don't we go check it out? Zee is a good protector if Assistant Professor Donadieu resorts to physical violence, though I'd like to think I don't have much to fear from an economics professor."

"My lord?" The student had pulled up a picture of Donadieu, a tall fit man in a martial arts gi with a black belt tied around his waist.

"Ah, maybe I *would* have something to fear. Fortunately, Zee is without peer when it comes to physical confrontations."

"Crushers are superior warriors and defenders of the helpless," the crusher—Zee—said in a flat monotone, then patted Dabrowski's head.

"That's me," Dabrowski said dryly, then gestured toward the

hallway. "Please lead the way, Zee." He bowed politely to Mari, nodding for her to go next.

Mari didn't know if she could trust him but appreciated that he hadn't treated her any differently than one of his own kind. And he didn't seem inclined to help the police find her. Too bad she didn't know if he was inclined to help her *mother* find her.

9

Kenji woke up in a brilliantly lit cell with the municipal police logo on a white wall, and he groaned. He didn't have the headache or sore muscles that he'd had after waking from being stunned, and didn't know if he should be glad Mari had used a tranquilizer on him instead. Mostly, he was embarrassed that she'd gotten the best of him. *Again.* His father would have lectured him vastly about underestimating an opponent. Not that Kenji cared about having his father's good opinion, but he couldn't help but feel like far less than the sum of his parts.

A uniformed officer stepped up to the force field at the front of his cell, her brown hair swept back in a tight bun. "You awake?"

Kenji sat up and faced her, wondering if the police had taken a blood sample while he'd been out. They would have scanned him and found the lack of an ident and banking chip. His clothing—and weapons—had been taken, and he sat in baggy blue trousers and a smock. All ready to be shipped off to a permanent detention center? He pushed his sleeves up, trying to spot a needle mark from a blood draw, though it only would have taken a tiny smudge of blood or a cheek swab for them to test his DNA.

"I'm Lieutenant Hanabusa. You'll get your one comm call, but I need some information from you." Her tone turned dry. "Like your name and why you don't have even a banking chip."

"I don't have a bank."

"What do you do? Barter for food?"

"The cheesemonger at the night market accepts chickens and cows in trade." A true fact, though Kenji had never brought either. Several of the market merchants accepted gold, silver, and old Kingdom crown coins and bills, even if they had to jump through hoops to cash physical currency these days. "My name is Kenji Backer."

"You're a Kingdom subject?" Hanabusa should have been able to tell from his accent that he was from the system, but she lifted her eyebrows.

"I was born here. I'm sort of... off the network."

She sighed and rolled her eyes. "One of those. I trust that means you don't pay taxes or contribute to society in any meaningful way?"

"Is it your job to judge me?"

"No, but it's a fun perk of my position. You helped an astroshaman spy escape. Why?"

Kenji debated on an answer that wouldn't immediately prompt her to send someone in to do a blood draw and search for his DNA in the Kingdom databases, if they hadn't done so already. It hadn't occurred to him that they might believe Mari was some kind of nefarious spy. All he'd been thinking when he *helped* her was to capture her for himself, but he might have gotten himself in far more trouble than if he'd simply stolen something. The truth might be better than a lie here.

"I'm a bounty hunter, and she has a bounty on her head."

"No, she doesn't," Hanabusa said. "Military Intelligence ran an image search and checked the bounty-hunter message boards in the Kingdom and the rest of the Twelve Systems. There wasn't a match."

"The bounty was offered to me in person by the people after her. Her sisters. Maybe astroshamans don't put bounties out to the system as a whole and just pick suitably talented people."

"And that's you? My men found you crumpled on a trail with a needle hole in your ass."

"Someone did an impressively thorough search of my anatomy to spot that."

"Sergeant Woodrow thought you were cute."

"I feel molested. Can I have my comm call now?" They'd taken his glasses along with his clothes, so he didn't have access to the network, though he suspected the detention cells were insulated to block wireless signals anyway. The police wouldn't want prisoners romping freely across the network and contacting allies to arrange jail breaks while locked up.

"Yes. Do you want recommendations for a lawyer?"

A lawyer, right. He didn't know yet *who* he would call, but a lawyer wasn't it.

Kay was his only ally. Had they collected him after finding Kenji unconscious? Or was the poor robot roaming the campus lost while wondering what had happened to Kenji? Maybe he should make Kay his one call, but Kay couldn't break him out of jail. Kenji lamented that his impulsive plan had parted him from his robot ally. Would Kay be all right by himself? He wouldn't know where to go on campus and, without an identifiable owner nearby, might end up locked up in some groundskeeper's maintenance shed.

"If you're flush with chickens," Hanabusa added, "maybe we can find one who barters in livestock."

"I'm chickenless at the moment."

She tapped a button, lowering the force field, and Kenji

walked out. Along with the rest of his clothing, they'd taken his socks and shoes, leaving him barefoot on the cold tile floor.

Hanabusa waved to a comm terminal on the wall, one that recorded all calls, no doubt. Reaching it would involve walking past other cells, some with solo occupants, some with groups of thugs that looked like the kinds of people his father had once hired to pummel Kingdom troops and create distractions while he masterminded his terrorist activities.

A man in a white lab coat walked into the cell block with a medical kit in his hand. Uh oh.

Kenji strode toward the comm terminal, hoping vainly that the doctor was there for someone else.

"While you're chatting," Hanabusa said, "Dr. Ancelotti will take a sample of your blood."

Kenji halted midstep. "Oh?"

Hanabusa was armed with a stunner and a DEW-Tek pistol, and two more policemen stood guard at the only exit from the area. No escape.

"Call us strange," Hanabusa said, "but we like to identify the people we arrest." Hanabusa's eyes narrowed, and her tone turned hard. "Especially those who help astroshaman spies, astroshaman spies who could *only* have been on campus for heinous purposes."

"You're sure that's not an invasion of people's privacy?"

"No. You better hope nothing happens to Minister Dabrowski or anyone else on campus. If your actions allow that woman to hurt someone that important, you might not survive the night."

"You're threatening my life? That seems uncalled for from a protector of the populace."

"Oh, I wouldn't kill you. But maybe we'd put you in a communal cell." Hanabusa tilted her head toward one such cell, which was full of muscular, tattooed brutes who managed to look fearsome even in the blue pajamas. They were listening to the conversation, and several brazenly met Kenji's eyes, one cracking his knuckles in the anticipation of some entertainment. "Dabrowski is pretty popular even with felons. Something about saving the entire planet from the AI supership." Hanabusa nodded for the doctor to approach Kenji.

"Must be nice to be liked." Kenji faced the terminal, debating on who, if anyone, could get him out of what was escalating into a dangerous predicament.

It was hard for him to imagine Mari, the girl who'd ask a policeman to try his latte, assassinating Minister Dabrowski, but... what did he truly know about her? Just because she'd left him alive—twice—didn't mean she wasn't on a mission. And Dabrowski *had* been integral in defeating the astroshamans scant months earlier. Maybe they were holding a grudge.

While he was debating, the doctor pushed up Kenji's sleeve. He didn't bother with a needle, simply using a tool to prick his skin and take a quick sample.

"How long does that take to analyze?" Kenji asked, aware of his heartbeat racing.

"Only a few minutes."

Great. They would throw him in the cell with the thugs as soon as they found out about his father. Kenji didn't know if that association would move them to anger as readily as the death of a beloved public figure, but he doubted the brutes had to be angry to enjoy pummeling a stranger.

"There's a selection of lawyers who work with prisoners." Hanabusa pointed at the menu on the comm screen.

Kenji ignored it and punched in the name of the only person he could think of who might be able to get him out of this—and who might be moved to help, *if* Kenji could convince him that he had information he might want. Did he?

Casmir Dabrowski had two contacts listed, a home number and an office number at the university. Given the hour, and that

Kenji had recently *seen* Dabrowski standing outside of his home, he opted for the first one.

"Uh." The doctor was close enough to see his choice and looked over at Hanabusa.

"We're old friends," Kenji said.

"That *can't* be true." Hanabusa had come to look over his shoulder.

Didn't he get any privacy for his comm? "You're right. I took one of his classes once."

Hanabusa and the doctor exchanged looks, but they didn't scoff again. Since Minister Dabrowski had formerly been *Professor* Dabrowski, they had to accept that Kenji could be telling the truth.

The comm chimed for a long time, and he feared it would drop to voicemail. What happened if nobody answered his one comm call? He was pretty sure the law dictated he get another one, but Hanabusa seemed to play loose with prisoner rights.

Someone answered the comm, a face popping up on the display. It wasn't Dabrowski but his roommate, Scholar Sato, who'd also been out on the stoop confronting Mari. Kenji stared at her, worried Dabrowski might have left the house and that his one comm would be wasted on someone who would be indifferent to helping him. Would she even pass along his message?

"You are not Captain Kucharski," Sato stated in a flat, almost robotic voice, making Kenji realize he'd never heard her speak. Unlike Dabrowski, who'd appeared in numerous interviews after the invasions and the coronation of Queen Oku, Sato was reclusive.

"Uhm, no."

"Captain Kucharski is our usual police liaison." Sato glanced to the side, probably rechecking the origin of the comm call.

Kenji didn't know why she might have a police liaison, unless people pestered the now-famous Dabrowski often, but she might only have answered because it was a familiar number.

"Sorry, ma'am. I'm a former student of Professor—Minister Dabrowski's and need a little help. Is he there?"

"He is not."

Crap. The doctor had departed to run the blood test.

"Can you give him a message for me? I'm in a bind. Actually, I'm in jail. I don't expect him to help with that—" admittedly, he hoped Dabrowski would be eager to discuss astroshamans with him and *would* bail him out of jail for the ease of discussion, "—but I have some information on the astroshaman who visited you, and I'm, ah, available here if he wants to know what I know."

Sato's expression had been as flat as her voice for most of this—she hadn't twitched even an eyebrow at his confession to being in jail—but the brows elevated slightly at the last. Less surprise and more skepticism, he guessed. Maybe she assumed that Dabrowski could get whatever information he wanted whenever he wanted.

That was possibly true. Kenji didn't know if he had any more information than Dabrowski on Mari, but if he showed he was willing to be helpful, maybe...

"What is your name?" Sato asked.

Kenji hesitated, tempted to give her the name of someone who'd legitimately been a student, but he didn't remember the names of any of the people who'd been in those lecture halls. "Kenji Backer."

"What class of his did you take?"

Why did he suspect she didn't believe him and was trying to catch him in a lie?

"It was the entry-level mechanical-engineering class two years ago. He may not remember me that well." Or *at all*, since Kenji hadn't been on the roster or ever registered at the university. "It was a big lecture hall."

"Casmir doesn't forget any of his students."

Er. Kenji groped for something that might prove he'd been there. "Please let him know that I enjoyed his T-shirt collection."

Kenji promptly wished he'd thought of something less idiotic to say.

"T-shirt collection?" Hanabusa, who lurked nearby, mouthed.

"Which one was your favorite?" was what Sato asked.

Hell, Kenji remembered that Dabrowski had worn one every day, sometimes under a blazer when he was dressing up to Zamek University faculty code standards, but he groped for a specific one. There had been several with robots on them, but that seemed such an obvious answer that someone who *hadn't* been there could have guessed it. Besides, he was fairly certain Dabrowski had been caught in robot T-shirts for some of those recent interviews.

"The one that says *I paused my game to be here*," Kenji said, plucking that out of his memory at the last moment.

Sato nodded, as if he'd answered correctly. "I will tell him."

The screen went black. As Hanabusa guided him back toward his cell, the doctor returned. He glanced warily at Kenji—that couldn't be good—then nodded to her.

"I need to talk to you, Lieutenant."

Definitely not good.

Hanabusa secured Kenji in the cell again and followed the doctor out of the area. Kenji sank to the floor with his back against the wall.

It was amazing how often desperation prompted one to make bad decisions. He wondered if he would live long enough to regret all the ones he'd made this week.

∾

A soft rain fell, mist dampening Mari's cheeks, and she tilted her face toward the sky. It wasn't her first time in the rain, but she'd spent most of her life in spaceships or climate-controlled stations or moon bases, so it was an unusual experience for her. Something about the damp air made the smell of the nearby sea more noticeable. That was also something she'd rarely experienced. What would her mother say if she admitted to finding Odin, with its amazing array of climate zones and weather options, intriguing?

To her surprise, Minister Dabrowski led her toward faculty housing on foot. Maybe nothing was that far away on campus, or maybe he couldn't drive. He appeared to have strabismus in his left eye, and Sato's book had mentioned seizures. Strange that he hadn't opted for ocular implants or even cybernetic replacements for a superior visual experience. And a responsive neurostimulation system placed under his skull could have minimized seizures.

"Assistant Professor Donadieu didn't show up for work today," Dabrowski murmured, running network searches while they walked. "We'll see if he answers his door."

Mari didn't know if he was speaking to her or only to himself. The crusher walked sturdily along beside him, gazing alertly about, not commenting on Dabrowski's mutterings.

It seemed presumptuous to start a conversation with him, though it was more his connection to her mother that made Mari uneasy than anything about his personality. She found she *wanted* to trust him, and for him to be an ally, but if he was already her mother's ally, she didn't see how that could work.

"How do you like Zamek City so far?" Dabrowski looked at her and waved toward the campus, maybe indicating the entire city. "Other than the drone attacks. And the rain. I would say that's rare, but it's not. Our maritime location leans toward dampness, but Odin also has tropical equatorial regions and deserts and a large variety of climates."

"Yes, I am more intrigued by your rural zones than your urban ones. I hope to explore and take soil samples from various agronomically productive areas. Naturally, many studies of Odin have been done, and I can find soil macronutrient analysis reports online, but it seems that when one is down on a planet, one should experience it firsthand and take samples oneself. There's so much that can be learned from natural habitats and applied to space stations and terraforming projects on other worlds."

"Your people have been here for a few months, but I suppose you've stayed in your base. I did suggest that to High Shaman Moonrazor, at least until the attacks aren't as fresh in the minds of Kingdom citizens. When you get a chance to sightsee, you might enjoy the astrophysics museum on the Southern Continent, or the botanical domes down the coast a bit from Zamek, and of course there are some great exhibits and studies ongoing at the Terraforming and Agroclimatology College on the moon. I'm sure you would find that remedial but possibly enjoyable."

"I believe so. I am eager to experience more things that normal humans experience. They need not all be related to my field of study. For instance, I have read about various types of alcohol made from crops, but I have never consumed them."

"You've never had alcohol?" Dabrowski asked.

"Mind-altering substances are frowned upon among our people. You're supposed to be able to reach a higher computational level simply by meditation and mental exercises."

"Reaching a higher computational level isn't usually the goal when drinking alcohol. I'm sure you can find a student to share some beer with you if you want the experience. This is the street." Dabrowski pointed toward a cul-de-sac not unlike the one where he lived, though it appeared to back up to a large field. Something for sporting events?

"I appreciate you helping me retrieve my terraformer," Mari said.

He gave her a lopsided smile. "Sure, but I'm actually just trying to get to the bottom of the drone mischief. I *am* the faculty advisor for the drone program."

"You have duties here even though you are now Minister of External Affairs?"

"Oh, yes. I requested it. I wasn't ready to give up teaching, which I enjoy." When they reached the house, Dabrowski started up the walk, but the crusher strode past him to take the lead.

"I will go first in case of danger, Casmir Dabrowski."

"The lights are off, so the probability of danger is likely minimal, but thank you, Zee."

A dog barked in a nearby backyard. Mari hoped they would find all of the stolen goods in a pile inside this professor's house, and that she could return to her mission. Perhaps Dabrowski could help her get an audience with the queen.

Zee rang the door chime.

"Hm," Dabrowski said. "I'm pursuing some recent network activity related to astroshaman technology. The wreck up in the Arctic Islands has been a hot topic of late, and there are people willing to pay for any technologically advanced equipment retrieved from the site. I need to see if I can find someone in Military Intelligence to clue me in on the happenings up there and elsewhere. Royal Intelligence usually keeps me in the loop, but I don't know the upper echelon of MI well, or any of the lower echelons either. And there's still a little drama going on right now that Queen Oku is trying to work out with the military heads who are giving fluffy reports to her because she's a *girl* and a *scientist*." Dabrowski lifted his eyes toward the stars. Or maybe that was what normal humans called an eye roll.

"We do not have a military per se," Mari said. "Everyone is essentially a scientist or an engineer. We use our technology to defend ourselves."

"Yes. I've noticed that. It's effective."

"Nobody is answering the door," the crusher said. "Shall I force it open in order to search the premises?"

"That would unfortunately be illegal," Dabrowski said. "We need to get a search warrant."

"Are search warrants issued to crushers?"

"In the city, they're typically issued to the police, though nobles have the right to search the premises of people living on their properties or to assign the duty to appointed representatives." Dabrowski tapped his chin. "Zamek University is public, owned by the crown, which would technically mean the queen has the power to search the campus or issue a warrant to an appointed representative. Hold one moment, please."

Mari was bemused that a high-ranking government official seemed to be hunting for loopholes, but since she wanted to look inside, she would not object.

The faint clang of a vehicle door—or maybe a hatch—shutting reached her ears. It seemed to come from the field behind the houses. A strange parking area, if that grassy land was reserved for sporting activities, but Mari had no idea what was customary here. She hoped it wasn't a police vehicle spitting out more officers to come after her, but surely it would be parked in the street nearby instead of behind the housing area.

"I am poised to enter the premises, Casmir Dabrowski." The crusher still had his hand on the door.

"Thank you, Zee. I'm debating with Oku whether this situation justifies her issuing a search warrant—and whether I, as the faculty advisor in charge of the security-drone program, qualify as a proper authority figure to *receive* such a warrant. She accused me of scheming."

"Is that not correct?"

"Oh, it is. I'm choosing to believe that her accusation was lovingly crafted with affection and does not connote disapproval."

Dabrowski lifted a hand and waved to an electronic keypad. "Let's not force the door, Zee."

A beep sounded, followed by a soft *snick*. The door unlocked. Presumably, he'd overridden the electronic lock.

It was dark inside, with no sound of voices or anything else, though Mari thought she heard an engine starting up on that field out back.

"I have obtained a warrant," Dabrowski said. "We're legally allowed to enter now."

"Was it crafted with affection?" Zee entered first.

"Of course."

Mari stepped inside after the crusher. With her implants already in night-vision mode, she had little trouble making out the details of the living area and a kitchen beyond. Stairs led to an upper level, but she paused with Dabrowski in the living room. Several of the furnishings were overturned. Numerous bags had been set on a table, all of them opened and pawed through. Stolen clothes, electronics, and knickknacks spilled out onto the table and the floor.

Mari hurried to the spot to look for her missing device.

"There is blood on the floor," Zee announced from the kitchen.

"Blood?" Dabrowski turned on lights.

Mari's implants adjusted automatically so the brightness did not overwhelm her eyes, and she continued to sort through the stolen goods. She used her built-in scanning software to search for the familiar alloys she'd used on the terraformer, but it didn't sense anything.

"It is still damp and warmer than room temperature." Zee walked to an attached laundry room. "There is a body in here. I will attempt to identify the person using the university's public network."

Dabrowski swore, joining him in the doorway. "That's

Assistant Professor Donadieu. I just looked at his face. What the hell happened?"

"Unknown," Zee said. "There are signs of a fight, and his throat was cut by what appear to have been claws. He is already dead."

"*Claws?*" Dabrowski asked. "Like... bear claws?"

"I cannot discern what animal, modded human, or mechanical construct was responsible. Perhaps a forensics study by your police services may be in order."

"Oh, I'm sure." Dabrowski pushed a hand through his hair. "This just got a lot more serious than I was expecting."

Mari slumped, both because of the daunting escalation of a simple theft to *murder* and because she'd searched the pile of stolen goods twice, and her terraformer wasn't there. If the man who'd arranged the theft was dead, how would she find—

The roar of thrusters came from the field, loud enough to penetrate the home's walls.

"Is that a ship?" Dabrowski pushed open the back door. "On the *soccer* field?"

Mari rushed out past him, wondering if whoever had parked the ship there could be linked to the stolen goods—and the murder. If that was a suspicious location to land a space craft...

"I will check, Casmir Dabrowski." Zee hurried past Mari, springing over a back fence and onto the field.

Mari ran after the crusher and vaulted over the fence, wanting a glimpse of the ship herself. Too bad she'd lost her explosives and most of her other tools. She might have been able to force it to stop.

But whatever craft was taking off was invisible—it had to have a slydar hull. Only the roar of the thrusters gave it away.

Zee sprinted across the field toward the spot, but the vessel was already airborne. He leaped upward, but it must have taken off vertically and quickly. Despite his powerful jump high into the air, he did not reach the craft. He came back down, landing with a thud on the field, the damp grass scorched by the ship's takeoff.

The ship roared as it flew to the north. Mari cycled through all of her scanners and optical options, but she did not have anything that could see a craft coated with a camouflaging material.

She slumped again, afraid that ship had her terraformer. Though she did not yet have evidence to support that notion, some human instinct—a gut feeling, the books often called it— told her she'd just missed her chance to retrieve it. And if that ship was heading into space, she might have lost her chance forever.

"Tighten security on the launch loop," Dabrowski spoke into a comm unit as he walked up to them, grass stains on the knees of his trousers. "We may have a slydar-hulled ship trying to take off tonight. Or—" he met Mari's gaze, "—could that be an astroshaman ship with one of your stealth generators?"

Mari hadn't considered that, but it didn't make sense. "Other than myself, I do not believe any of my people are seeking the terraformer. It was my project and is of most concern to me."

Granted, her knowledge of terraforming and making such devices might be the primary reason her mother wanted her back, but Mari couldn't imagine any of her people murdering someone simply to retrieve her prototype.

"Probably slydar," Dabrowski said to whomever he'd commed. "Will you please have customs tighten security and search all vessels trying to use the launch loop tonight? See if you can get one of the Fleet warships with one of our new slydar detectors down there. Thank you."

"I got close enough to the vessel to glimpse it through its camouflage before it flew out of range," Zee stated.

"Oh?" Dabrowski asked. "Did you record it? Can you send video?"

"Yes."

"Will you share it with me?" Mari asked. "There was a slydar-hulled ship searching the *Celestial Dart* in the Arctic Islands. I wonder if it's possible this was the same ship. Lured down for a chance to obtain more of our people's technology from a thief who found something more valuable than he expected?"

"That sounds plausible," Dabrowski said. "I'll see if I can find anything on the network that Donadieu might have posted announcing that he had such technology. Ah, thank you, Zee. The ship is black and shaped like a hawk or maybe a vulture. Hm, that's not a typical Kingdom design."

"I wish I'd gotten a look at the camouflaged ship in the Arctic." Mari had been riding away from the *Celestial Dart* before it arrived and only knew about it because it had bombed the shuttles. Her sisters might have seen it close up, but she would not contact them. The bounty hunter had also been on that clifftop. Would *he* have seen it? He was a more readily available resource. "I think I know someone who might have," she admitted.

The idea of asking him questions after she'd stabbed him in the butt with a tranquilizer seemed ludicrous, but he had tried to capture her first. Twice. *He* shouldn't be the one holding a grudge.

"Oh?" Dabrowski asked. "Someone who might have gotten a name or further identifying markings?"

"Maybe. He said he's a bounty hunter. I think your police may have him now." Mari waved in the direction of the trail where she'd left the man unconscious. "I'm not sure what his name is. We only tangled briefly. Twice."

"In the Arctic Islands? And here? On campus?"

"Yes. He's persistent."

"You're his target? Who's paying him to collect you?"

Mari hesitated. Dabrowski asked the questions casually, maybe curiously, and not as if he were trying to trick her into revealing information, but she still didn't know if she could trust him. It boggled her mind that she was standing here talking to her mother's ally.

"Your mother?" Dabrowski guessed. "I wouldn't have expected her to turn to outsiders to handle, ah, internal affairs."

"I think my mother sent my sisters to fetch me, and *they* might have hired him. They have their own projects and would gladly hand the job off to a stranger if it meant they didn't have to chase me across the system."

"How is this bounty hunter tracking you?"

"I don't know."

"Maybe I should have a chat with him."

Mari curled a skeptical lip.

Dabrowski's eyes glazed as he read some message on his contact display. "Hm, this bounty hunter doesn't go by Kenji Backer, does he?"

"He didn't tell me his name before he tried to capture me."

"No? That's rude."

"I thought so."

10

Two hours passed before Lieutenant Hanabusa returned to Kenji's cell, not with the doctor but with two police sergeants in blue combat armor with rifles cradled in their arms. She lowered the force field and stepped back behind them.

"Come with us, *Backer*." The way she said his surname made him certain they had figured out what his real last name was. That she'd felt compelled to return with armored men further suggested his threat level had been elevated. Or maybe she planned to take him out back to a nice firing squad.

"Right," he muttered.

Kenji trailed them into a hallway, up a set of stairs, down another hallway, and into a conference room. Mirrors lined the walls inside, the kind that people could no doubt see through from adjacent monitoring areas.

Two high-ranking police officers sat in chairs at one end of the table, but they were the least imposing of the room's occupants. Two knights with purple capes draping their silver liquid armor stood against a wall, pertundos hanging from their utility belts. As Kenji knew from the news and vids, the collapsible halberd-like weapons had telescoping handles that could extend to eight feet, and the blades could slice through the most advanced combat armor while the points fired like DEW-Tek weapons. Knights came out of the nobility and were highly trained to work for the crown as special agents, so Kenji found their presence here ominous.

The older of the two men had short gray-blond hair and a trimmed gray beard, and Kenji was fairly certain this was Sir Bjarke Asger, the new head of the knights, a recent appointment by the queen. The younger knight, who resembled Sir Bjarke but whose blond-brown hair fell to his shoulders, was closer to Kenji's age. He looked familiar, like Kenji had seen him on tubes of underwear, but he doubted knights were allowed to have modeling careers.

Sitting in the seat to the side of the head of the table was a uniformed woman in her fifties. She had a lean face, with thin lips pressed together in disapproval, and hard eyes that squinted suspiciously at him. Kenji didn't recognize her, but her insignia and rank said she was someone high up in Royal Intelligence. Maybe even the highest-ranking officer, Chief Superintendent Van Dijk, who reported directly to the queen on a daily basis.

To her side, a granite-jawed man with short, slate-gray hair wore a Kingdom fleet uniform. He had the rank of general and a Military Intelligence insignia. If he wasn't *the* head of Military Intelligence, he was certainly someone important in their command structure.

Kenji had already known he was in trouble, but with this many high-ranking people here, there could be no doubt. They had to think they'd caught a very special fish. He almost wished Hanabusa *had* dragged him out to a firing line.

It was possible the presence of an astroshaman spy in the city was the reason these people had been called together late at night, and he was only going to be questioned about her, but he doubted it.

The doctor was also in the room, sitting at the table with his medical kit. Two jet injectors rested next to that kit, and Kenji swallowed, fearing he was about to be questioned under the influence of a truth drug that would make it very difficult to lie.

What would they ask him? About his father's whereabouts? It had been years since he'd communicated with the man, so Kenji couldn't even tell them if he was in the system. Too bad. Maybe if he could have, he might have traded that information for his life. He had a feeling they would ask about far more than that, about all the crimes he'd helped his father commit when he'd been too young to say no, too young to dare stand up to the man.

Would it matter to them that he'd been a boy? That his father had punished him severely when he hadn't performed acceptably, and that he'd been too afraid to do anything but what his father wanted?

Given the severity of the crimes, probably not. Supposedly, juveniles couldn't receive a life sentence to the penal mining asteroids, but in the case of heinous crimes, they could be tried as adults. And Kenji was well aware that, even though the Kingdom supposedly didn't have a death sentence, a lot of accidents happened in those mines. A lot of criminals died horribly.

All this because he'd been dumb enough to come back to the city and get caught trying to collect a bounty when he had no experience as a bounty hunter and even *less* experience with astroshamans. What had he been thinking? He deserved to die for his stupidity.

"Sit down." One of the armored men shoved him in the direction of the seat across from Van Dijk.

Kenji managed not to stumble, though the armor gave the man more strength than typical, and the shove wasn't gentle. He sat gingerly across from her, surprised nobody had cuffed him, but with the armored officers and two knights in the room, they probably weren't worried that even the son of Kuchikukan Chisaka could kill someone. He would be suicidal to lunge across the table, grab Van Dijk by the neck, and try to use her as a shield and captive to barter his way out of here.

It was the kind of thing his father would have tried. Kenji folded his hands on the table, hoping that told them he had no such intent.

"You don't cuff terrorists around here?" the younger knight asked dryly.

Kenji slumped in his chair. There was the confirmation that they knew all about him.

Van Dijk, who might have been wondering the same thing, looked toward Lieutenant Hanabusa.

"We were asked not to, Sir Knight," she said, her tone much more respectful than it had been when she'd been teasing Kenji about chickens.

"He has *a plan*," the older knight said, looking sidelong at the younger, not saying who the *he* was.

The seat at the head of the table had been left open. Kenji couldn't imagine who else beyond the knights, Military Intelligence, and Royal Intelligence might show up. Surely not the queen. She wouldn't oversee anything to do with terrorists or questioning prisoners. She had these people to report the findings of such things to her, should it be necessary. Besides, Kenji didn't imagine that he was important enough to warrant the queen's attention, though he supposed his father was notorious enough that his name came up in royal meetings. Now that the infamous pirate Tenebris Rache was believed dead, Kenji's father had probably been elevated higher on the list of the Kingdom's most loathed enemies.

"I know *that*," the younger knight said, "but it seems wise to take precautions with terrorists and the sons of terrorists. I trust he was searched thoroughly."

"Yes, of course," Hanabusa said.

"Even my butt cheek was examined," Kenji muttered before he could think wiser of it.

"That's a notorious spot where criminals store contraband, isn't it?" a new voice asked from the doorway. A voice that Kenji recognized.

Even though Kenji had tried to comm him two hours ago, it bewildered him to see Minister Dabrowski amble into the police conference room, trailed by a hulking crusher. In part, because it didn't seem that a diplomat would have a reason to come to a meeting about a terrorist's son and in part because Kenji was far more used to seeing him in a classroom setting.

"You're thinking of the anal cavity," the older knight said. "Though I suppose implants can go anywhere."

"Versatility is important. Wait by the door, please, Zee." Dabrowski patted the crusher on the chest and headed for one of the chairs on the side of the table.

Chief Van Dijk cleared her throat and pointed to the head of the table. "Your spot, my lord. Unless you're concerned about sitting next to Chisaka. Per your request, we didn't cuff him, but that can easily be changed." She gave Kenji a hard look. "We would be happy to duct tape him to that chair mummy-style and ensure he can't so much as twitch a finger."

"Oh, I'm rarely concerned when Zee is nearby." Dabrowski veered toward the head of the table, giving Kenji a curious—and maybe faintly bewildered—look when their eyes met. "Though if I'd known you were terrorist Kuchikukan's son when you were lurking in the back of my lecture hall, I might have been concerned *then*."

Apparently, Scholar Sato had been correct. Dabrowski didn't forget any of his students. Even those who'd never registered for classes, never spoken in the lecture hall, and never presumed to turn in an assignment.

"I... I'm not dangerous, Professor. My lord." Kenji smiled self-deprecatingly, or maybe bleakly. "As evinced by my inability to capture even one slender astroshaman woman."

"The astroshamans are usually modded to the moons, have the IQs of supercomputers, and possess tech our engineers can only dream about in their beds at night. I'd be more surprised if you *could* capture one."

"Well, she's young. I thought she might be less... uhm, less."

"You're dating the beautiful and vivacious queen, Casmir," the younger knight said, "and *tech* is what you dream about in bed at night?"

The older knight elbowed him, though his eyes glinted with similar irreverence.

"You can see why I don't gravitate toward heads of tables," Dabrowski told Van Dijk. "It implies a certain level of in-charge-ness that I don't feel I possess, perhaps because the big kids still tease me mercilessly."

"Yes, but they would follow you into battle to their deaths. Whether they're supposed to do so or not." Van Dijk's eyebrows arched.

The knights exchanged looks that didn't suggest disagreement.

Dabrowski only smiled briefly and said, "On a more distressing note, I just got word that our thieves managed to get a ride on the launch loop and flee into space. We're going to have to go straight to Plan B."

Van Dijk and the general swore.

"They were supposed to get a slydar detector to the launch loop," Van Dijk said.

"They did, but the ship avoided it by landing on an automated freighter already started up the loop. They somehow grasped on and remained attached for the ride up—piggybacking essentially.

That shouldn't be possible but..." Dabrowski spread his hand, palm toward the ceiling. "One of the cameras on the pylons caught footage of the two ships as they zipped past, close enough for it to see through the camouflage."

"*Piggybacked*?" the general mouthed. "How?"

"Presumably, they've got some powerful clamps. We can figure out the how later. What matters now is how we're going to get the stolen astroshaman device back now that the thieves are off the planet." Dabrowski sat and turned his attention to Kenji. "Hello, Kenji. May I call you that?"

"Yes, my lord."

"We haven't exactly met, but I'm Casmir, and you can call me that instead of the lord thing. And that is Chief Superintendent Van Dijk, and that's General Heim in charge of Military Intelligence. The older knight there is head of the knights, Sir Bjarke Asger, and the younger fellow at his side is Sir William Asger. You've met Lieutenant Hanabusa, and her officers are Oxford and Endo."

"The older knight, Casmir?" Sir Bjarke asked. "*That's* how you describe a knight of my stature to people? I'm wounded."

"What adjectives do you prefer?" Dabrowski asked.

"Virile, cunning, and fearsome. Or, since my first name means bear, you could use that. That fearsome *bear* of a knight."

"Bonita calls him *osito*," the younger Asger said.

"What does that mean?" Dabrowski asked.

"Teddy bear."

"Oh?" Dabrowski's eyes glinted. "I could use that."

Van Dijk cleared her throat. "Gentlemen, it's getting late, and I haven't had dinner yet. Could we?"

"My apologies, Chief." Dabrowski bowed to her from his seat, then faced Kenji again. "What would you have said," he asked curiously, "if I'd been home to answer the comm?"

"I was hoping to get out of my current predicament by offering information on the astroshaman woman Mari." Kenji watched Dabrowski's face to see if he'd known the astroshaman's name or if it surprised him. "That was before the doctor analyzed my blood and sealed my fate."

"I believe your fate is somewhat ambiguous at this point, depending on what you're willing to do."

"Just about anything to avoid life—or death—in a penal asteroid mine." Kenji looked into Dabrowski's eyes, doing his best to appear earnest and trustworthy. He doubted the flinty Intelligence heads would give him a break, but Dabrowski appeared as approachable as he had when he'd been a full-time professor. "I'm also *not* loyal to my father. I ran away as soon as I thought I was old enough to take care of myself, and I haven't seen or communicated with him in eight years."

"I'd hate to say something as pompous as the crown is open to giving you a chance to *prove yourself*—" Dabrowski rolled his eyes and looked at Van Dijk, "—but if you were willing to work for the government, certain past transgressions might be forgotten."

"Not *forgotten*," the general growled, "but not punished."

Van Dijk nodded. "Work with us instead of against us. Your father is still at large, as I'm sure you know, and you could help us get him."

The feeling of bleakness returned. Kenji had spoken the truth and didn't feel any loyalty to his father, but the idea of working for the government and trying to set him up to be captured and likely killed... That held no appeal. And it might get *him* killed. As long as his father had thought he had a use for Kenji, he'd more or less taken care of him, but Kenji doubted his father felt any biological imperative to continue to watch out for him these days. He might shoot Kenji in the chest if he proved to be a thorn in his side.

"At the moment," Dabrowski said, "my interest is more in having Kenji's help to get back the stolen astroshaman tech than pitting him against a relative. It can be difficult to betray close relatives, even when their actions are criminal and you have ambiva-lent feelings toward them." Dabrowski smiled ruefully.

Kenji hid a sigh of relief.

"Besides, the elder Chisaka hasn't taken action against the new regime, right?" Dabrowski asked. "He may object less with a more progressive ruler in power."

General Heim grunted. "I wouldn't presume he has any adora-tion for Queen Oku. He tried to kill her mother once."

Kenji kept his face neutral. That defining moment in his father's career had been before he'd been born, so he couldn't be linked to that. It had been years afterward before his father had been identified as the culprit. Had Kenji's mother known exactly what kind of man she was having a relationship with back then, Kenji might never have been born.

Van Dijk waved a hand in acknowledgment of the arguments and focused on Kenji again.

"You haven't come to our awareness over the last eight years," Van Dijk said, "so you've either been very talented in carrying out crimes or you stopped assisting your father at some point and have stayed under the radar."

Hadn't Kenji already told them he'd broken ties to his father? He almost said something snarky but paused. It sounded like they might give him a chance, that they wouldn't assume he was pure evil and punish him. He had better not annoy them.

"I admit," Van Dijk went on, "*I'm* inclined to believe you just haven't gotten caught, not that you've been leading some virtuous life, but..." She extended a hand toward Dabrowski.

"Since you attended university classes," Dabrowski said, "even if you weren't enrolled and shouldn't technically have been there, *I'm* inclined to believe you wanted to better yourself and find a less criminal way to make a living. Not that mechanical engineering isn't a perfectly useful class for a criminal to take, but I seem to remember Professor Leeman mentioning you lurking in her art history class too."

"I didn't realize people were keeping track of me," Kenji murmured, wondering how Van Dijk could believe he'd been a criminal flying under the radar when he hadn't even avoided gaining the attention of the professors whose classes he'd been crashing. "I'd be willing to help the crown retrieve stolen astroshaman technology if it meant I could get a pardon." He raised his eyebrows, not positive that was what they were offering. "But I'm not sure why you think I could help with that." He turned a puzzled look on Dabrowski.

"Mari mentioned that you witnessed what might have been a black wing-shaped ship with slydar technology taking off after salvaging tech from the astroshaman wreck up north," Dabrowski said. "We encountered it down here tonight, the crew possibly responsible for murdering someone and stealing more astroshaman tech. Mari thought you might be able to identify the ship."

"You've... chatted with her? A second time since having her arrested?" Kenji shifted in his seat. Had Mari gone *back* to Dabrowski? Why had she risked that? And why did it sound like Dabrowski was on a first-name basis with her? Wouldn't astroshamans be treated with suspicion? He glanced around the table and the room, but nobody appeared surprised.

"I have. And I wasn't the one to comm the police."

"Oh."

"The ship?" Dabrowski prompted.

"I did see it, yes. Only briefly. It sent some drones into the wreck to collect items. One of Mari's, uhm, sisters destroyed one. That irked the ship owner, and it opened fire on us. We were in rented shuttles rather than anything with great defenses, so it might have blown us all up, but the astroshaman women destroyed its railgun with some little gizmo. Also, right about then, the military from the nearby outpost decided to investigate, and the ship flew off and didn't return. It had a slydar hull, so I have no idea which way it went, but it *was* black and shaped like a vulture with wings outspread. I didn't get a chance to scan its ident chip."

"Hm," Dabrowski said. "One wonders just how much astroshaman technology its crew has obtained."

"I'm surprised anything like this terraforming device you described was left in the wreck," Van Dijk said. "Military Intelligence combed over that ship weeks ago and took what it believed were choice pieces worth examining for itself. It was the only one of the wrecks that remained. The other two ships that crashed self-destructed—or were remotely detonated—soon after the battle."

"We're here because Military Intelligence reported to *us*—" Sir Bjarke pointed to the general and then to his own chest, "—that rogue drones were caught on camera sniffing around a secured warehouse on the base outside Zamek City where Intelligence stored the tech they scrounged from the astroshaman ship."

"Funny how things Casmir gets himself involved in end up tying into other troubles," the younger knight said.

"Did the drones get anything from the secured facility?" Dabrowski asked, ignoring the dig this time.

"Lasers up the ass from what I heard," Van Dijk said.

The knights nodded.

"The drones had *asses*?" Dabrowski asked. "Goodness. How inspired."

Van Dijk snorted. "They were blown up and examined. There wasn't anything sophisticated or special about the drones, but they weren't Kingdom stock. The serial numbers matched work out of a factory in System Cerberus, off-the-shelf models."

"My people took a thorough inventory," General Heim said, "and there's nothing missing from the warehouse, but there *are* pieces missing from laboratories that we've had studying the technology. Further, I'm concerned that more serious attempts will be made to get the tech in the warehouse—and that these thieves intend to sell everything to the highest bidder. Some of the missing items are believed to be weapons."

"Even the devices that weren't *intended* as weapons could be used that way. I want to speak further with Mari later, but Kim and I had a chat about how a rapid-deployment terraforming technology might work." Dabrowski grimaced. "And what the ramifications might be for anything existing when it started its work."

It took Kenji a moment to twig to what he meant. Judging by the lack of surprise from most of the people in the room, they had already considered possible repercussions.

"We want to make sure Mari's terraforming device doesn't end up in enemy hands," Dabrowski continued, "but I've spoken to Queen Oku, and she agrees that the technology would be useful to study for its original purpose, so she ideally wants it back and intact." Dabrowski nodded to Kenji. "Are you interested in helping retrieve Mari's tech? And, if possible, identifying the thieves so that our knights can lead some people in to capture them and reacquire the rest of the stolen devices?"

Kenji almost pointed out that he was more interested in retrieving *Mari*, but was that still true? He'd already been questioning whether he'd made the right choice in accepting the assignment, and if Minister Dabrowski wanted to help her instead of arresting her... He had to know more about astroshaman politics and who was an enemy and who wasn't than Kenji did. As much as Kenji could have used that money, maybe it was time to let that quest go.

"I'm not opposed," Kenji said, "especially if it gets me out of jail, but what would you want me to do?"

"That the thieves," Dabrowski said, "were not seeking one thing in particular and made off with several astroshaman items suggests they don't have a specific interest in the terraforming device and are likely collecting whatever they can to sell. I'm certain we have the resources to find out if they list it for sale on the black market—"

"There are a few illegal sites and auction networks for the exchange of such stolen items," Van Dijk said. "I've got someone watching them now to see if these devices pop up."

Dabrowski nodded. "If it shows up there, we can have someone pretend to make an offer and try to arrange a meeting for exchanging money for the goods. Practiced thieves, however, will be suspicious of an offer from someone who might be an under-cover government agent." He glanced at the knights. "We can try to cobble together a persona that *might* fool them, but if they get even the slightest bad feeling about the setup, they'll take off for the gate with plans to sell the tech in Cerberus or another system. At which point, it will become increasingly difficult for us to get anything back. It might be more plausible if a *known* buyer of stolen goods makes an offer."

Dabrowski raised his eyebrows and gazed at Kenji.

"Uhm, I only buy food, booze, and parts and lube for my robot."

"Robot?"

"Kay. A K-45 robot that I made from scrap to help me repair things when I was working as a mechanic. The poor guy is prob-ably wandering around campus, wondering what happened to me. Any chance I can get my glasses back so I can communicate with him?"

"You could communicate with him all you wanted if you got chipped," Van Dijk said.

"And be easily found by the government," Kenji said.

"Hate to break it to you, young man," Sir Bjarke said, "but the government has a pretty good idea of where you are."

"Your father has purchased some weapons and other stolen goods in the past," Van Dijk told Kenji.

"Oh." Kenji slumped in his chair, realizing where this was going. He'd hoped the gig they offered him wouldn't have anything to do with his father. "Has he purchased terraforming devices?"

"Not that we're aware of, terrorists so rarely being into farming, but as I implied, if we understand the technology correctly..." Dabrowski looked gravely at Van Dijk. "It could be used as a weapon. According to Mari, their intention was always to take it to a new system and use it on lifeless planets or moons in conjunction with technologies for melting ice caps and creating an atmosphere, but if the device was used on a planet where life already existed...." Dabrowski grimaced. "It works by rearranging raw materials at a molecular level to create the conditions to support life. It would destroy what's already there in an attempt to fulfill its programming."

"So if it was used on Odin, it could be deadly?" Kenji felt that he was in over his head. This was far more than he'd expected to be involved in.

"It's unlikely that *one* device could destroy the planet," Van Dijk said, "but it is a prototype that could be used to make more."

"So if anyone questions why a terrorist might want it, there's a plausible reason." Dabrowski eyed Kenji.

"Yeah," Kenji said bleakly. He would have liked to think that his father wouldn't traffic in anything that could kill masses of people—or all life on a planet—but he wasn't sure. He'd never fully understood the man's motivations.

"We'd like you to pretend to be a representative for your father, interested in doing some purchasing on his behalf," Dabrowski added.

"Yes, I understand," Kenji said, haunted by memories of missions he'd gone along on as a boy.

Van Dijk and Heim exchanged significant looks, making Kenji

wonder if it was truly *we* who wanted to rely on Kenji to perpetrate this ruse, or if this was all Dabrowski's idea.

"You'd have leeway," Dabrowski said, "to tell the story in your way, to make it work on the fly. You'll need a ship, of course, as the thieves won't likely agree to come back to Odin for a handoff. One that doesn't have a known link to the Kingdom."

They were going to get him a ride into space? Kenji thought about how he'd been working for so long to save up the money for a trip to another system. It would be much easier for him to leave Odin forever if he ended up halfway to the gate, thanks to this mission. Could he play his role and then disappear? He wondered how many guards Dabrowski was thinking of sending along to keep an eye on him.

Dabrowski looked toward Sir Bjarke. "I'm tempted to ask if Captain Laser is free. Thieves wouldn't find a freighter with one old railgun concerning, and the last I heard, she and the *Stellar Dragon* are visiting Odin."

"They're visiting *me*," Sir Bjarke said, a smug twinkle in his eyes.

"Both of them? I didn't know you serviced Viggo as well as Bonita."

"I'm a man of many talents."

Van Dijk cleared her throat. "Thanks to Sato's book, that freighter, and its link to the Kingdom, is now well known."

"Ah, right," Dabrowski said. "I'd forgotten Kim said she named it in there."

"All of the principal characters in that book would have a difficult time going undercover now."

"Actually," Sir Bjarke said, "Bonita got a new name and ident chip for her freighter for exactly that reason."

"She was getting in trouble because of her association with us?" Dabrowski frowned and touched his hand to his chest.

"Not exactly. She was getting requests for tours and star cruises from passengers who wanted to ride on the *Stellar Dragon* and be a part of history."

"I can see where Captain Laser Lopez might not see herself as a cruise-line operator."

"She prefers bounty hunting," Sir Bjarke said, "especially now that she has access to Qin and several of Qin's formidable sisters."

Kenji lifted his brows. Hadn't one of the two big women with pointed cat ears been named Qin?

"Her ship has also been painted," Sir Bjarke added. "I gather she still calls it the *Dragon* when she speaks about it to friends, but the ident chip and the name on the hull now proclaim it the *Espada Ancha*."

"Does that also mean teddy bear?" Dabrowski asked.

"It means wide sword in her language. I gather she and Viggo argued over an appropriate name until she put her foot down."

"Not on a robot vacuum, I hope," Dabrowski murmured.

Kenji opened his mouth, but he didn't know what to say to the odd conversation. Maybe he could find a ship of his own. Assuming he meant to help them. Did he? He wouldn't be *betraying* his father, and it was possible the old man wouldn't even hear about this. And if succeeding at this mission could get Kenji pardoned... didn't he want that? Even if he planned to leave for another system, the idea of not having to spend the rest of his life worrying about Kingdom agents finding him was appealing.

"I'll talk to Bonita. If Kenji is willing to help us with this mission." Dabrowski extended his hand toward him and raised his eyebrows. "And willing to work with Mari."

Kenji blinked. "She's going along?"

"To retrieve her belongings? Yes. She wants to."

The idea of working with someone he'd tried to capture not once but *twice* daunted him. Would she believe him if he said he'd lost interest in collecting her bounty? Would she hold a grudge? What if, at some point during the mission, he had to depend on her to watch his back? She might be tempted to get revenge for all the trouble he'd caused her by letting him get shot.

But, as Dabrowski smiled affably, waiting for his answer, Kenji couldn't imagine saying no to this opportunity. This was his chance to finally get somewhere in life, or at least get himself into a position where he could enter the races. For so long, he hadn't even been able to claw his way to the starting line.

"I can work with her if she can work with me," Kenji said.

"Think she'll be able to refrain from sticking another needle in your butt?" Lieutenant Hanabusa asked.

Eyebrows arched around the room.

"I'll try to keep my butt away from her," Kenji muttered.

"Wise," Van Dijk said.

"Excellent." Dabrowski nodded to him and stood up to leave.

"My lord?" Kenji asked.

"Casmir. And yes?"

Kenji hesitated, not wanting to ask for more favors, but if anyone would be willing to help him find Kay...

"Like I said earlier, I lost my robot on campus. If you hear of anyone finding a K-45, would you mind collecting him? He's a..." Kenji, aware of all the important officials looking on, caught himself before saying Kay was a friend. "He helps me repair things. I think he'd be useful on this mission."

"I understand." Dabrowski nodded. "I'll check."

"Thank you."

11

"Are you sure you don't mind sharing?" Mari sat at a table in Sato and Dabrowski's home, eating candies called chocolate-covered espresso beans out of a bowl while waiting to hear back from Dabrowski on his meeting with his government leaders and the bounty hunter. Kenji Backer, as Mari had since learned his name was.

"I can acquire more," Sato said.

Mari hesitated, unsure how to interpret that. She hadn't specifically said *no*.

Sato also sat at the table while reading on a tablet, as she had through the dinner Mari had consumed with her after Dabrowski dropped her off at the house with instructions to stay there until he returned. Sato hadn't appeared that comfortable with having a strange astroshaman dinner guest, and Mari wouldn't have stayed if she'd had somewhere else to go. But without a ship of her own, she couldn't chase the thieves, and Dabrowski had the political power to help her. Though she couldn't imagine why he cared, he seemed willing to do so, and she was relieved.

Kim ate a couple of the chocolates, though she'd warned Mari they contained caffeine and might not be an appropriate evening snack, especially for someone unaccustomed to the chemical. Mari was extremely unaccustomed to it. She'd had coffee only once in her life—twice now, since Sato had brewed some of the steaming liquid after their shared dinner. It had smelled wonderful, but Mari had found the taste strong and unappealing. That was when Sato had suggested the chocolate-covered version. It was *delightful*. The chocolate wrapping the beans was much smoother and more pleasing than the Moon Melters had been, and the beans were strong and sharp but somehow perfect under the layer of sweetness.

It was ridiculous, but a part of her decided it had been worth leaving her people if only to sample sweets. Though she still hoped to experience other human pleasures of the body, that would have to wait until she got her terraformer back.

"Will you require sleeping accommodations?" Sato asked without looking up from her tablet. It was full of graphs and text laden with footnotes.

"I have slept in numerous places without trouble since leaving my people. Outdoors, it is possible to find secluded spots where strangers will not stumble across me during my required rest hours."

"You've been sleeping outside?"

"Since I left, yes. I am able to regulate my body temperature sufficiently to stay comfortable outdoors in all but extreme climates." Mari knew humans had hotels and various other places where one could rent rooms, but she'd been doing her best to avoid commercial establishments. *All* establishments.

But Sato was staring at her, so maybe her choice was not considered normal or acceptable.

"I am uncertain if social conventions dictate that I offer you a pillow and blanket and the opportunity to sleep on our sofa. You are..." Sato groped in the air with her hand. "I do not know if I am required to consider you a guest."

It surprised Mari that Sato, a human who had been born into this society, would be uncertain about its social conventions. "*I do not require it.*"

"Casmir might." Sato sounded glum. "I do not like having strangers in my home, and I believe that even well-liked *guests* should stay in hotels, but Casmir believes that friends and family should be kept close, and he extends those terms to include a great many people. Last month, he invited a student he had five *years* ago to sleep on our sofa." Her lips pinched together in disapproval.

"I do not wish to make you uncomfortable." Mari didn't even know if she would *want* to sleep on these people's sofa. It seemed overly intimate and familiar. Dabrowski had dropped her off here to *stick around and enjoy some dinner*, as he'd said, while he went to the police station. She hadn't thought she would stay long. "I do not expect anyone in the Kingdom to consider me a friend or family. Or even a guest. My mother... I believe most in the Twelve Systems who are not astroshamans would believe her an enemy. She does not speak of it, but I know she has committed what would be considered crimes to your people, in addition to..."

"Leading an invasion to our doorstep?" Sato suggested.

"She was coerced by others to do that, but yes. I assumed... I kept expecting Minister Dabrowski to call the police back to get me." Mari glanced toward the window, still not entirely positive they wouldn't show up again.

"If he can't defeat them by hacking into their network or stealing their robots, Casmir prefers to befriend his enemies. Also, I believe he now considers Moonrazor an acquaintance if not an ally."

Mari noticed that Sato hadn't implied that *she* felt that way.

"If she showed up at our doorstep," Sato added, "I am certain

Casmir would offer her a blanket and pillow and our sofa, if not inviting her to use his room while *he* took the sofa. He would also offer her the use of his reading material, including his comic-book collection."

"Since they are acquaintances, if not allies, I've been a little concerned that he would tell my mother I'm here."

Sato opened her mouth but didn't answer right away. "If you asked him not to, I believe he would respect your wish, but he is also a poor liar, so if Moonrazor messages him and outright asks if you're here, that could be problematic."

"Then I will hope she believes I'm off Odin by now." Mari drew more of the chocolate beans out of the bowl and consumed them. Earlier, she had been tired, weighed down by knowing she'd come so close to reacquiring her terraformer only to have the thieves escape right in front of her, but now, she felt much perkier.

"Why have you left your people?"

Mari had placed another chocolate in her mouth, but she paused before chewing it. This was the first personal question Sato had asked, and it was the last one Mari wanted to answer. Voicing how she felt seemed almost as much a betrayal to her people—to her mother—as sharing technological secrets.

"I do not require that you answer," Sato said, "but I am trying to determine if you are yourself a threat or if your actions will bring trouble to Casmir and our people. As far as I know, he is the *only* one in the government—perhaps on the planet—who considers Moonrazor something of an ally, and he is occasionally naive in wanting to believe the best about others. As a more cynical person, I can't help but wonder if your actions, your request for *asylum*, would cause Moonrazor to use force to retrieve you—or prompt her to wish to retaliate."

"I do not believe she would blame your people for my choice," Mari said quietly. "I left because our plans were thwarted when the AI ship took the gate, and it will be much longer before we are able to settle in a new system that humanity hasn't yet touched. My work as an agronomist and terraforming expert will not be needed by my people for a long time now."

"You could not train in a new field?" Sato's flat voice made it difficult to determine if she was suspicious or not.

In truth, she spoke a lot like many of the astroshamans, with little inflection—little emotion—and Mari wondered if her mother had ever offered *her* a place among their people. She knew her mother had invited Dabrowski to join them, even offered to help him obtain a position of leadership among them. The reclusive astroshamans occasionally accepted outsiders with cybernetic parts, especially those with desirable skills to further the goals of their community, but it was rare for them to recruit outsiders.

"I could," Mari said, "but I also wished to experience... human experiences."

Sato's only reaction was a slight raising of her eyebrows.

"For as long as I can remember, I have lived in our community, usually on spaceships or in reclusive habitats with little interaction with human civilizations. There are some astroshamans who go back and forth, working and trading with people in normal human habitats, but my mother has always kept us—my siblings and me—close, not wanting us to be tainted by outside influence. Our inception was not originally her idea, but once she acquired us, she decided we would be raised to be the best scientists and engineers possible—and loyal to our people and the goals of our society."

"Your inception was not her idea?"

"For a time, she had a lover—our father—who was an intelligent and creative engineer, and who apparently admired *her* intelligence. He lived on Jotunheim Station in System Hydra and enjoyed his work there building medical equipment. He had always wished to have children, and suggested they get married, but he did not want to join the astroshaman community. Over time, my mother had been more and more drawn into it, and she'd recently taken a leadership position. She was unwilling to leave, even for him, and eventually, her duties called her away, so they ended their relationship. Unbeknownst to her, he took a sample of her genetic material and had us made—me and two sisters and three brothers. We were less than a year old when pirates attacked Jotunheim Station. My father was killed. We were found in the aftermath, and his will dictated that we be taken to our mother. I do not know what her response was, but she took us in and raised us and trained us to be assets to our community and to help further its goals to leave humanity and the Twelve Systems behind and settle elsewhere among the stars."

Mari clasped her hands on the table to refrain from eating more of the stimulating chocolates. "She has never been cruel to us or even unkind, but she is not... loving in the human sense of the word, and she has been stifling by not allowing us to leave, even for brief adventures, to experience other types of civilizations. I suspect she worries that if we ever left, we would not want to come back. It is understandable when people who were raised in human societies decide they want something else and join the astroshamans, but it is not fair to force us to choose that way of life before we've had an opportunity to try others. And especially now that our mission is on pause..." Mari shook her head. "There was no reason for her to insist we stay, other than concern that we would be seen as enemies in the Kingdom."

"You keep saying human society, as if you are not human. Many humans have replaced some of their biological parts with cybernetic ones, either to give them an advantage or to solve medical maladies. And more of us are chipped than not these days." Sato waved at her temple.

"I understand this, but a core tenet of our people is that we wish to become less and less human over time and to give up emotion and irrational feelings in order to become more like machines. Approximately half of our people have forsaken their biological forms to upload their knowledge and memories into android bodies. Some have placed themselves directly into computer systems."

"Yes, my mother is a loaded droid."

"She is?" Mari blinked, surprised since that wasn't common outside of the astroshaman society.

"Her death was imminent, and she chose that path."

"Many of our people do it even if their deaths are *not* imminent."

"Yes. I understand the differences and that there is a religious component."

Mari remembered Sato saying they were a *cult*. It wasn't entirely inaccurate, but humans put a negative connotation on that word. Mari wouldn't know if she wanted to return to her people until she'd experienced what it was like elsewhere, but she would hate to not have the option to return. She did not feel ill will toward her mother or siblings; she simply wanted the freedom to choose her fate.

The front door opened, and Mari tensed and turned, still expecting the police to come again for her.

Minister Dabrowski walked in, trailed by a clunky robot that looked like something Mari's brother would have made from spare parts as a toddler. The much sleeker and more elegant crusher followed after it.

"Hello, Kim. Mari." Dabrowski lifted a hand. "Is there any food left?" He looked toward the bowl of chocolates on the table. "Food without hidden bitter beans in the middle?"

"Mari Moonrazor likes my chocolate-covered coffee beans," Kim said.

"Probably because she's had a long day, and they're like eating caffeine pellets."

"And because they are delicious."

Mari nodded.

Dabrowski shuddered.

"That is not the bounty hunter who was seeking me out." Mari assumed Dabrowski knew that, but in case he'd somehow been confused, she pointed at the robot.

"I am a peace-loving K-45 who is willing to assist my owner in attaining his goals," the robot said, "but I would not hunt humans, astroshamans, or anyone else of my own accord. I consider such activities likely to lead to violence and to infringe on the rights and freedoms of others."

"But you're willing to help Kenji with such activities?" Dabrowski asked.

"He gave me life, building me from junkyard parts, and I am grateful to him, but I lecture him frequently about partaking in criminal activities."

"Does he like that?"

The K-45 lifted a bronze-and-tin arm toward the ceiling. "My lectures are insightful and appealing."

A bolt fell off his arm and clunked onto the carpet.

The crusher bent to pick it up. "Casmir Dabrowski, this inferior robot is falling to pieces in your domicile."

"I see that. Thank you." Dabrowski took the bolt from him. "We'll give you a tune-up tonight, Kay. You've got a mission tomorrow, assuming you're going with Kenji in the morning, and you'll want to be at your best."

"I always wish to be at my best."

"Kenji?" Sato asked.

"That is the name of my bounty hunter." Realizing she may have suggested that she *employed* him, rather than that she was hunted by him, Mari clarified. "The bounty hunter who seeks to turn me in to my family."

"Instead, they're going to go on a mission together." Dabrowski left the robots in the living room and wandered into the kitchen, sniffing liberally at the lingering scent of the tomato-based pasta Sato had served for dinner.

"A bounty hunter and the astroshaman he is hunting are going on a mission together?" Sato asked. "Casmir, that plan sounds fraught with conflict, and not only with the enemies they will oppose."

"They have a common goal. It'll be great." Dabrowski filled a bowl for himself and joined them at the table.

"How is Kenji's goal common to mine?" Mari felt the same dubiousness as Sato.

"You seek your terraforming device and asylum among our people, and he seeks not to spend the rest of his life in a penal mining asteroid."

Sato's brows rose. "The young man who commed earlier saying he liked your T-shirt collection is a heinous criminal in danger of receiving that sentence?"

"I'm not sure if a judge would condemn him to that fate, but he's the son of a terrorist who would *absolutely* receive that sentence, and Kenji apparently worked with his father to commit numerous crimes before running away from him. That's the story he told us. *I* believe it. Since he's not chipped and has done his best to have no record these past eight years—not an easy thing to achieve in our technological society—Chief Van Dijk and General Heim are skeptical that he's been innocent of further infractions. But I've talked them and the police into giving Kenji a chance to win a pardon. It's not fair to blame a kid for who his father is. That's like blaming an innocent and upstanding robotics professor for who his *brother* is."

"Not quite," Sato murmured.

"Nonetheless, we've had confirmation that the thieves' ship— make that thieves and *murderers'* ship—found a way onto the launch loop and is now in space. Mari, I trust you're adept at surfing the various public, and probably not-so-public, networks out there and can watch for signs of someone listing your device for sale."

"Yes."

"Royal Intelligence is keeping an eye out too. I've arranged for a ship to take Kenji into space so he can make a deal with the thieves to buy your device before they leave the system. Mari, it's optional, of course, but I guessed you'd want to go along to make sure we get the *right* device back and not some replica."

"The bounty hunter and I will go alone into space?" Mari took more of the chocolates, feeling the need for further bracing from caffeine. Or perhaps it was time to experiment with stronger stimulants.

"Not alone, no. Our friend Captain Laser Lopez will take you. I've already arranged payment for her time and her ship's time. And of course, Qin's time. I believe Tigress—one of Qin's sisters—may be going along too. The clan is starting up a bounty-hunting business, and most of them are busy this week, but Qin and Tigress are an army in their own right. Sir Bjarke is also sending a couple of knights to join Kingdom Fleet ships that we're readying. They'll keep a distance, but once you set up a meeting, they'll be able to get there within a few hours if you need help." Dabrowski smiled. "It should be an exciting adventure. If I didn't have so many duties here, and my stomach didn't so *much* prefer the full gravity of Odin to space, I would be tempted to join you. But you don't need a diplomat; you need the young son of a terrorist willing to partake in some subterfuge to deal with the thieves." He nodded firmly.

"Diplomatic measures can't work on thieves?" Sato asked.

"Even if I were authorized to offer the kind of money the thieves will surely ask for their stolen goods, it's unlikely they would trust that the Minister of External Affairs and queen's advisor would partake in a fair deal with them. Whoever they are.

We haven't yet figured that out. We only have a description of the ship."

Mari frowned. They'd had that *before* he'd gone off to talk to the bounty hunter. It didn't seem like his meeting had resulted in a further acquisition of knowledge. Worse, she would now have to work with a man who had tried to capture her twice—and that she'd stunned once and tranquilized once. Would he truly care about helping her retrieve her belongings or had he only agreed to go along with Dabrowski's plan so he would have another opportunity to capture her?

Mari thought of Sato's words that Dabrowski tended to be naive and eager to believe the best in people. It sounded like that might extend to the criminal son of a terrorist. Mari worried that Dabrowski might have been duped. And that if Kenji had a third chance to capture her, he would succeed.

12

Early morning found Kenji getting a ride in a police van across town toward a private walled landing area near Drachen Castle and Royal Intelligence Headquarters. He wiped his hands on his trousers, eyeing the imposing structures and the well-armed human and mechanical guards in the watchtowers.

If this freighter he was supposed to get a ride in got invitations to land across the street from the seat of the entire Kingdom government, Kenji had a hard time believing that all the thieves, smugglers, and pirates in the system weren't aware of it. That name change and new ident chip Dabrowski had mentioned had better have been recent.

"Never been here before," one of Kenji's police escorts whispered to his colleague, peering out the window as guards halted their vehicle at the gate to check it. There was an espresso cart on the sidewalk, a robot barista serving coffee to uniformed castle and Intelligence staff.

"Our prisoner moved up in the world quickly, didn't he?" the other policeman in back with Kenji said.

The two men eyed him with open rancor. The day before, the

police had regarded him with indifference—he'd been just another petty criminal—but that had changed with the revelation of his last name.

For some reason, Kenji was reminded of the hostile look the policeman had given Mari when she'd asked to taste his latte. He'd called her an astroshaman freak. Had she had an opportunity to try such a drink yet? Kenji eyed the espresso cart. Maybe he ought to bring her one as a peace offering. He knew from recent experience what a relief it was to have someone treat him like a human being when nobody else did.

After the meeting the night before, Kenji had been returned to his cell, most of the policemen he'd encountered glowering at him along the way. But the bemused lieutenant had brought him a pillow, a blanket, a bottle of grape fizzop, and a pizza with a smiling robot drawn on the box. She hadn't said so, but Kenji had known the gifts were from Dabrowski. Strange how much better that had made being stuck in a jail cell for the night.

"Your father really Kuchikukan Chisaka, kid?" one policeman said.

"Unfortunately."

"Bet that was a real loving relationship."

"He teach you how to be a good killer?" the other asked.

"He tried. I found it oddly unfulfilling."

Under the pretext of peering out the window, Kenji scooted closer to the door. There was only one person left in line at the espresso cart, but how could he get the police to let him out for a minute? Offer to buy them drinks?

"Uh huh. Sure. Bet you killed a lot of people."

"*Innocent* people."

"They should be shipping you off to a penal asteroid right now."

"And arranging for an *accident* to happen along the way."

Kenji missed having Kay to talk to, Kay who had never

condemned him, despite his dubious past and his sometimes questionable choices. Had Dabrowski been able to find him? Had he had time to look?

The police lieutenant had returned his glasses to him that morning, so Kenji had been able to check the news, but he hadn't received a reply to the message he'd sent Kay. The idea of leaving him behind on Odin, especially if Kenji found an opportunity to escape the Kingdom during this mission, was depressing. Kenji wanted to take his robot friend with him.

The door opened, a Kingdom Guard officer with a tablet peering in to check on them.

Kenji saw his opportunity. "I need to get a coffee for someone."

He darted out of the van, dodged a reflexive grasp from the officer, and jumped into line at the espresso cart, hoping his captors would realize he wasn't trying to run off and would refrain from stunning him.

"A large horchata latte, please," he hurried to tell the robot as the policemen surged out of the van after him.

The Kingdom officer dropped a hand on his shoulder. "What are you doing?"

Even though two stunners pointed at him, the robot barista repeated the order and set to making the drink.

"Just what I said." Kenji braced himself as the officer tried to pull him back to the van. "I need to get a drink for someone."

"You're a *prisoner*. You don't have coffee privileges." One of the policemen prodded him in the ribs with a stunner. He must not have been given the message that Kenji was about to go on a secret mission for the crown. "Get back in the van."

"It's not for me. It's for a friend of Minister Dabrowski's. He would *want* me to get the drink for her." Kenji pointed to the robot now steaming the milk and toward the walled compound. "I'm positive."

"Oh, I'm sure."

"Come on, prisoner."

The robot extended the completed beverage. "One horchata latte. That will be five crowns, please."

Kenji tried to dip his hand into his pocket for physical currency, but the officer, maybe worried he was going for a weapon, stopped him.

"If you're not going to let me pay, you'll have to fork over some cash for me." He smiled, though he was certain the only thing any of them would fork over was a kick in the ass.

"Get back in the van," the officer growled.

"The beverage is for Casmir Dabrowski?" the robot asked, still holding the cup aloft.

"For someone working for him," Kenji said, surprised by the question.

"Casmir Dabrowski is a friend of robots. I will provide this beverage free of charge."

"Uh, thank you." Kenji managed to grab the cup before the policemen manhandled him back into the van.

One lifted a fist to knock the drink away, but Kenji whipped his arm down, avoiding the blow. He sprang inside and settled back into his seat while cradling the drink protectively. Maybe his enhanced reflexes came in handy now and then, after all.

The men shared exasperated eye rolls and got back in without attempting to punish him—or the latte—again.

"Weirdest terrorist I've seen," one grumbled.

"Another damn freak."

Freak? Maybe Kenji had more in common with Mari than he would have guessed possible.

The van rolled through the gate and into the walled landing compound. It passed a couple of shuttles, the hulls painted purple with gold crowns on the side, and headed toward a large dome-shaped freighter with a railgun on the top. Judging by the recently painted hull, it was well cared for, but that model was older than dirt. It had to have been flying for more than a century.

A cargo-hold hatch was open, a ramp lowered to the pavement, and a gray-haired woman in a galaxy suit stood at the top with one of the knights who'd been in the conference room the night before. The older one. Sir Bjarke Asger. They were holding hands and talking and sharing smirks.

The thought that one or both knights might be coming along alarmed Kenji. Hadn't Dabrowski said they would be going with the Fleet and staying well away until after a meeting point was agreed upon? How was Kenji supposed to pass himself off as a terrorist if he had Kingdom knights looming behind him?

The van stopped, and the door opened.

"Out, freak." One of the policemen jerked his head toward the exit.

Kenji climbed out with the latte, expecting someone with a weapon to accompany him and keep an eye on him, but the police van took off. In addition to the knight, there were members of the Kingdom Guard around the private landing pad, so maybe they felt Kenji was properly secured.

The captain looked down at him, a frown replacing her earlier smile. She squinted dubiously at him, making Kenji wonder if the knight had told her all about his past. Wonderful. He could get snide comments for the whole trip.

Before Kenji took more than two steps toward the ramp, a purple shuttle flew over the walls and landed nearby. A hatch opened and a ramp unfolded. The first passenger to walk out had a familiar robot body, and Kenji cracked a smile for the first time in weeks.

"Kay!" he blurted, rushing up to grip the robot's arm.

That arm was free of dents, melt marks, and other blemishes. So was the rest of him. Even the damage he'd received recently had been hammered out. Kay was still a jumble of mismatched junkyard parts, but he gleamed and looked like he'd been intentionally crafted that way out of whimsy.

"You look good," Kenji said.

"Naturally."

Dabrowski walked out next, wearing a suit and button-down shirt, both garments out of place on him. Maybe the shuttle was taking him to some meeting of diplomats or visiting officials next.

Kenji opened his mouth to thank him for fixing up Kay—somehow, he knew Dabrowski was responsible and that he hadn't foisted it off on a repair shop—but Mari walked out next, and he forgot his words.

The last time he'd seen her had been after she'd stabbed him in the butt and then stood over him with that tranquilizer ring. Now, he tensed warily. He wanted to make peace, but *she* might not want that.

Abruptly, Kenji worried that Dabrowski might not have told her that he was part of this package. What if she kicked him or cursed him or took out that ominous tranquilizer ring again?

The look Mari gave him was as wary as the one he was giving her.

"Hi," he blurted, for some reason ridiculously nervous. "I got you this." He thrust the latte toward her.

Dabrowski raised his eyebrows but didn't say anything.

Mari frowned and looked at the drink. Suspiciously?

He feared so. Strange that he could so easily read someone who looked so different from normal humans. She still wore her cloak and hood, as if she feared being recognized even here, but he could see her pale skin, ocular implants, and a plate full of chips and circuits and who knew what else attached to the side of her head under her blonde hair.

She'd regained her pack since he'd seen her in the police van, though it appeared less filled than before, and someone had given her a stunner and a DEW-Tek pistol. That surprised Kenji. How could an astroshaman woman be trusted like that? Kenji understood why the police hadn't given *him* a weapon, but Mari had enough deadly astroshaman tech without arming her further. He couldn't help but glance at her hands and note that she still had her rings.

"What is it?" Mari asked.

"A horchata latte," Kenji said.

"Oh, horchatas are good. They're the new thing here in Zamek City, courtesy of a couple of chefs we lured in from System Diomedes." Dabrowski wrinkled his nose. "I'm not sure how or why you mix one with coffee though."

Mari's brows rose, some of the suspicion fading, or maybe being replaced by curiosity. She accepted the cup and sniffed at the opening in the lid.

"Cinnamon." The faintest hint of a smile crept across her face. "I have not tried cinnamon before," she told Dabrowski.

"I'd warn you that the coffee might ruin it, but you liked Kim's chocolate-covered espresso beans, so I can't predict your tastes. At least it will be sweet."

"I have discovered that I like sweets." Her smile turned shy, and she hefted a pink bag of colored candies. It was startlingly bright and perky in contrast to her weapons and the black-and-silver mesh clothing she wore under her cloak.

"Only recently?" Kenji asked.

The smile twisted into a wryer expression. "My mother forbade sweets."

"No wonder you ran away," Dabrowski said.

Ran away? Kenji rubbed his face. Was *that* the story? She hadn't stolen top-secret information, and she wasn't a spy, but she'd run away from an oppressive mother? If that was true, he felt like a heel.

Having finished her smell test, Mari lifted the latte for the first sip. Kenji held his breath, wanting her to like it. If she hated it, she might be less likely to believe he wanted to make amends.

She swished it around in her mouth, assessing it thoughtfully, before swallowing. He hoped she wasn't wondering if he'd poisoned it. After a few seconds, she swallowed and nodded.

"It is sweet, as you said, yes. And I believe I like cinnamon."

Kenji exhaled, relieved.

"Good," Dabrowski said. "Let me introduce you two to everyone. You've already met each other, I understand."

"Twice," Mari said.

"Briefly." Kenji resisted the urge to rub his butt. It wasn't as if it still stung, not *physically.*

"That's Captain Lopez over there," Dabrowski continued. "Bonita Lopez, though she prefers Laser. She's an expert markswoman, so don't irk her. Kenji, you met Sir Bjarke Asger yesterday, but he's just saying goodbye to Laser on his way to work. Sir William Asger and another young knight will be out with the Fleet and in the area, but as I said in the meeting, they won't get close, so they won't blow your cover. Laser also has a couple of sturdy combat specialists who should be waiting inside. You may get along with them, Mari. They're friendly. Ask them to paint your fingernails if you're into that."

"Nail-painting combat specialists?" Kenji asked.

Dabrowski grinned. "Yes. I thought about sending even *more* troops, but if things go awry, and you're boarded, a platoon of soldiers would be hard to explain."

"Yes, my father rarely employed soldiers."

Mari's eyebrows rose. Maybe nobody had told her about his dubious heritage yet. Ugh, when she found out, that might make her even less likely to trust him. Maybe he should have brought *two* lattes. She was sipping heartily from the one in her hand.

"A pilot and two combatants should be sufficient," Mari said.

"We will persevere, and you will see that I can be a valuable ally and that it's worth granting me asylum."

"I believe you," Dabrowski said.

"Do the rest of your people?"

He hesitated. "It may take some time to win them over. Sorry. It's not fair, but we're still filling in craters from the various bombings of our planet this past year."

"I understand," Mari said quietly, though the words seemed tinged with disappointment. "I came prepared to prove myself worthy of a position and your people's trust."

Dabrowski winced at the words *prove myself*, and he lifted a hand. "It's not about *proving* anything. People just have to get used to you. And enough time has to pass so they believe you're genuinely here for a job and to experience our culture. And the government needs to see that you can contribute in a meaningful way worthy of a paycheck. That's all."

"Is that not... proving myself?"

"Well, technically, maybe, but you don't have to do anything impossible. Nobody's going to threaten your friends and family if you fail." Dabrowski's mouth twisted.

"My family can take care of itself."

"I'm sure it can." He pointed her toward the freighter. "Laser will give you a cabin. You'll want to take off soon and try to make the deal with the thieves before they're halfway out of the system."

"Yes. Thank you." Mari stepped toward the freighter, but she paused to consider Kenji again.

He worried she would ask for clarification about his father.

"Candy-coated chocolate?" She lifted the bag of candy, startling him.

"Pardon?"

"You have given a gift to me. My understanding of human social conventions suggests that it would be polite for me to reciprocate." She lowered her voice and whispered to Dabrowski, "I do not truly wish to share them, because they are very good, but Scholar Sato shared *her* chocolates with me, even though I later gathered that she did not wish to."

This honesty surprised Kenji, and he didn't know what to say to it.

"Sharing is good." Dabrowski waved at the candy bag and also the latte cup. "It can help turn enemies into friends."

"Can it cause bounty hunters to be less interested in capturing you?" she asked.

Kenji winced. "Look, I'm sorry about that. I should have researched you more before accepting that assignment."

"Yes." She held out the bag toward him. "Candy?"

Kenji looked at Dabrowski, not certain he should accept, since she'd admitted she didn't truly want to share. But if he didn't, would she think he didn't trust her? That he thought they were poisoned or some such?

Dabrowski nodded encouragement to him.

"Thank you." Kenji only took one of the chocolates and promptly chewed it and smiled at her.

"You are welcome. I am pleased by the latte. Thank you for giving it to me. I had not realized cinnamon should be on the Human List."

"Pardon?"

Mari hesitated, then shook her head. Whatever the Human List was, maybe it was too private to share with enemies.

Why did it make him feel bleak that she considered him that? He had only himself to blame.

"I need a word with Laser before you guys leave." Dabrowski walked toward the freighter, leaving Kenji wondering if he was supposed to follow... or continue to stand awkwardly next to Mari, not knowing what to say next.

"Thank you for fixing my robot, Minister Dabrowski," Kenji called, realizing he hadn't said that earlier.

"Casmir," Dabrowski called back with a wave.

He hopped onto the ramp and gestured animatedly at Sir Bjarke and Captain Laser. Four robotic vacuums vroomed out of the cargo hold and started sucking up dirt around his feet. At least that was what Kenji assumed they were doing. It almost looked like a choreographed dance.

"I already thanked him for the repairs," Kay said. "He has very good hands."

"That must be why the AIs are fans." Kenji told himself not to be envious; he had good hands too. He just didn't have access to an entire robotics lab worth of parts.

"That is likely so."

Mari looked back and forth between them, as if she wanted to say something else, but she shook her head and walked toward the freighter.

"I can't tell if my peace offering worked," Kenji admitted. "She did thank me. And she didn't throw it away. That seems promising."

"Judging by what I know of human body language, you appeared stiff and uneasy with her."

"That's because she's..."

"An astroshaman?"

"No." It was because Kenji had been a dick to her. How was a guy supposed to recover from that?

"You should not allow prejudices about mechanically enhanced individuals to change how you interact with someone."

"I'm *not*. That's not it. Besides—" hoping to change the subject, Kenji clapped Kay on his metal shoulder, "—I *like* mechanically enhanced individuals."

"If you refer to me, I am not mechanically enhanced. I am merely mechanical."

"Are you sure?" Kenji pointed to a bump on the front of Kay's shoulder. "Is that a new sensor?"

"Oh, yes. I have a whole new array, front and back. Professor Dabrowski spent two hours working on repairing and improving me last night."

"He didn't reprogram you to spy on me and send back data, did he?"

"Certainly not. However, I believe that captain glowering at you with surly suspicion in her eyes may send data back on you." Kay pointed toward the open cargo hatch. Sir Bjarke was leaving, carefully stepping around and over the still-dancing vacuums, leaving Captain Laser at the top, her arms folded over her chest. She *was* glowering as she alternately eyed Kenji and the approaching Mari. Somehow, Kenji suspected she'd been fully filled in on both of them and wasn't that happy to have them coming on board. Maybe she had only agreed to this trip as a favor to Dabrowski. He was smiling and gesturing animatedly to her, unfazed by the glowers.

"Would you know it if he *had* reprogrammed you?" Kenji asked.

"Possibly not. Professor Dabrowski is rumored to have a deft touch."

"Reassuring."

Laser gestured for Kenji to come aboard. As he led Kay to the cargo ramp, he thought about how he was getting on a ship for a voyage and didn't have any luggage. He hoped the captain had a galaxy suit he could borrow—and an unused tooth sanitizer.

As Dabrowski gave parting instructions, the robotic vacuums whirring back inside, Kenji and Kay climbed the ramp to join Mari at the top. Kenji opened his mouth to introduce himself to Laser, but an armored person sailed through the cargo hold and crashed into a wall. The six-foot-plus warrior leaped up and raced back toward another equally tall person in combat armor, who sank low, meeting the charge without giving ground.

They crashed together, going down in a lightning-speed

wrestling match that left Mari and Kenji gaping. The combatants traded more blows until one hurled the other off and into another wall.

"Bonita," a male voice came from a speaker. "Your young warriors are leaving dents in my bulkheads. *Again.*"

"Please, Viggo. *Laser.* We have guests."

"If Casmir is not coming along on this mission to repair my vacuums and the dents in my bulkheads, I must insist you put an end to this unseemly roughhousing."

"They're *training*, Viggo. Qin and Tigress are the muscle. You know this. And I'm capable of hammering out your dents."

"Your touch isn't as refined as Casmir's."

"Yes, yes, nobody's is. His queen must be a lucky girl."

At the base of the ramp, Dabrowski rubbed his face. Embarrassed?

"If you don't need anything else, Laser," he called up, "I have three meetings this morning. Please apologize to Viggo that I'm not able to come along on this adventure."

"Meetings?" Laser faced him. "What a dreadfully boring life you lead now. There can't be anything in a meeting for you to repair."

"That's not true. I fixed a coffee maker last time, an act that made me a hero to nine out of ten coffee addicts in the room. The tenth had brought her own caffeinated beverage and was indifferent."

"Dreadfully boring." Laser shook her head. "It's amazing you haven't run away to space already."

"Where I could enjoy the delights of zero-g and space sickness once again?"

"Are you sure you don't want to adjust the nozzles on Viggo's vacuums while you're here?" Laser waved toward the robots. There were even *more* inside the cargo hold, maneuvering along and even *on* the walls to avoid the battle. "He's missed you terribly."

"It is an honor to be missed by such a fine being. Come by for lunch when you get back. I'll bring pizza and pot stickers aboard and make any adjustments Viggo needs."

"Who's Viggo?" Kenji whispered, wondering if Mari was as lost as he.

"The ship's AI, I believe," she said.

"Good luck on the mission, everyone. Thank you for taking it on." Dabrowski included Kenji and Mari in his bow.

"Actually," Laser said, turning back to them as Dabrowski left, "Viggo was the owner of this ship more than a hundred years ago, and when he died, he uploaded his memories and consciousness into its computer banks."

"Many of our people do that," Mari said, even as Kenji thought about how strange it was that the ship's AI had been an actual *person*.

"That right?" Laser eyed Mari. "You're my first astroshaman passenger."

"Will that be a problem?" Mari asked quietly. Warily.

"Your fare is paid for. As long as you don't make trouble or try to rewire my ship with your astroshaman computerness, we shouldn't have any problems."

"I hadn't planned on it," Mari murmured. "I'm just trying to get my stolen belongings back."

"*You.*" Laser pointed at Kenji. "You're the one who better not get us into any messes."

Given the task he'd been assigned, Kenji wasn't sure how messes wouldn't be involved, but he decided it would be unwise to point that out. "I'm only here to set up a meeting with a thief."

"Uh huh. Make sure you don't set up any meetings with terrorists. I'm not looking to have my ship commandeered."

Kenji kept himself from suggesting that the hundred-year-old freighter might not be much of a prize to terrorists. Or anyone else.

The two armored figures stopped fighting and removed their helmets and strode toward them. Kenji recognized them—and their pointed ears—and almost laughed. Now he remembered Dabrowski mentioning Qin and Tigress, whom he'd last seen at the shuttle rental shop.

"This is Qin, and that's Tigress," Laser said. "Sisters. You probably noticed the resemblance."

"We've met." Qin nodded to him.

"We had a *brief* flirtation." Tigress smiled, showing off her fangs, and gave him that long once-over again. "Perhaps we can make a more extended and intimate acquaintance on this trip."

"Uh." Kenji didn't know how to respond to that. Would a simple *no, thanks* offend her? It seemed unwise to offend tall, fanged, muscular women in combat armor.

Laser watched him closely for his reaction. Something told him she would shoot him if he called either of the women freaks —the typical Kingdom term for anyone who'd been genetically engineered—or was anything but polite, but it wasn't their pointed ears that concerned him. More that this Tigress looked like she wanted to shove him up against the nearest wall and have her way with him.

Qin elbowed her sister. "You're supposed to talk to a man and see if he's interested first before propositioning him."

"Please, if I waited for men to realize they were interested, I'd be forever bereft of company. You have to take action and *cultivate* interest." She slid a hand over her chest, which might have been more intriguing if she hadn't been in combat armor. It was hard to even tell a person's sex in the hard-shelled gear.

"It'll be good to work with you," Kenji told them neutrally, hoping the words neither annoyed anyone nor suggested he would be available for sex. He didn't think he was as stodgy and stuck in the past as a lot of Kingdom men, but he wasn't ready for fangs and fur in bed.

Mari nodded polite agreement. If she was surprised by the women's feline attributes, she didn't show it.

"They're our fighters," Laser said. "Be nice to them. If you manage to arrange a meeting with these thieves, they'll go in with you to take them down and get the stolen goods back."

"Yes, I've seen them fight." Kenji looked toward the fresh dents in the bulkhead. "I'm sure they'll be effective."

"I'm Mari," she told the big women and held out her bag, not mentioning this time that she was sharing to be polite and didn't truly want to lose any of her precious candies. "Chocolate?"

Qin removed one of her gauntlets, revealing strong elegant hands with retractable claws that sported a different shade of nail polish from the day before. She dipped her fingers into the bag and withdrew a few candies. "Thank you."

"And what's your name?" Tigress asked Kenji. "We didn't get a formal introduction before. Last I saw, you and your robot were hiding behind a fake tree."

"I'm Kenji, and Kay here was hiding behind the counter."

"Right. Now I remember."

"He's the son of an infamous terrorist," Laser said. "You might not want to stand close to him in public places."

"I was mostly thinking of lying next to him—or on top of him —in bed." Tigress winked.

"On top?" Kenji mouthed.

Mari looked over at them, her expression curious or maybe puzzled. For some reason, his cheeks warmed.

"I'm a take-charge girl." Tigress put a hand on Kenji's shoulder. She still wore her gauntlets, which was good, since that kept him from feeling her claws.

"Your sister is horny, Qin," Laser said.

"I know. And fearless. She had no qualms about propositioning Tenebris Rache's mercenaries when we were on his ship."

Tigress grinned, her fangs on full display. "I do like a nicely firm soldier."

"Who doesn't?" Laser waved for everyone to come inside, so she could raise the ramp and close the hatch.

"I am not overly enticed by such things," Kay said.

"Yeah, me either." Kenji scooted to the side, wanting to extract himself from Tigress's grip without offending a person he might have to rely on in a fight later.

"This way." Laser headed across the cargo hold toward a short corridor and a ladder on the far side. "I'll grab you two galaxy suits and show you the kitchen, lounge, and your cabins."

It occurred to Kenji, as she took them on a brief tour, that unless one counted Kay and the ship's intelligence, he was the only man on the freighter. The women were capable in a fight, but Kenji wondered if this little crew would be enough if the thieves had a lot of troops at their disposal. Nobody had even given him a weapon.

He couldn't help but think the Kingdom, or at least the people who'd arranged this mission, might still consider him a prisoner. An expendable prisoner?

Somehow, he doubted Minister Dabrowski would see anyone that way, but he was only one person. The knights and the Intelligence officers were likely the ones overseeing the mission. And Kenji seriously doubted they cared one way or another if he lived or died.

13

Mari sat in a pod in the freighter's lounge and looked out a porthole as the craft flew along the coast north of Zamek City toward the planet's sole launch loop. Astroshaman ships had the fuel and thruster power to break orbit by themselves, even on planets with strong gravity such as Odin, but she'd learned that most human vessels in the Twelve Systems relied on launch assistance for a boost into space.

The hatch clanged open, and she swiveled her pod from the porthole to face the newcomer, the high-walled seat already cupping her like an egg, though they were not accelerating as rapidly as they would for takeoff.

Kenji walked in, but he paused when he saw her and glanced back, as if he might leave. Because she was in the room?

Mari didn't know what to think of him. After his two attempts to capture her, she should have considered him an enemy, but he'd apologized and given her a tasty beverage. Unfortunately, she deemed it highly probable he was trying to get her to lower her guard, so he could capture her and complete his original bounty-hunting mission.

The more time Mari spent away from her people, and the more interesting human experiences she had, the less she wanted to return. She rubbed the back of her ring with the spring-loaded needle, its tiny reservoir again filled with a tranquilizer. She would work with Kenji to retrieve her terraformer, but she would not let herself trust him.

His clunky K-45 robot trundled in after him, almost bumping him. Kenji plucked at the form-fitting black galaxy suit that he'd borrowed from the captain—Mari had been given one too—then nodded to himself and continued into the lounge.

"Hi." He lifted a hand as he headed for the kitchen built into the wall at one end of the lounge. "I came to see if there's anything to drink."

"The refrigerator contains water, fizzop, two juice-based beverages, and coffee bulbs. I took an inventory earlier." Mari had been looking for alcohol, wondering if she might check it off her Human List one evening while she was aboard, but if the freighter contained the substance, it was not stored in the refrigerator.

"Oh? That's, uhm, efficient."

The way he said it made her think he meant *odd*. Well, what could he expect? She wasn't yet familiar with human habits pertaining to food and beverage inventorying.

"Perhaps Mari the astroshaman could resolve our issue." The K-45 robot pointed at her.

"I don't think she wants us to bother her."

"As someone who lives among robots and computers, perhaps she would consider it a simple and unobtrusive matter."

"Or perhaps she would consider you a pest."

"This is a matter of mission security, and I am a robot, not a pest. Mari the astroshaman—"

"*Kay.*" Kenji made a cutting motion with his hand.

Even with her limited familiarity with normal humans, Mari

could tell what that gesture meant. Still, the robot had roused her curiosity.

"You can just call me Mari. What's your issue?"

"Nothing." Kenji pulled a coffee bulb out of the refrigerator and shook his head at the robot.

"You may call me Kay," the robot continued, ignoring Kenji. "I have recently had repairs done by the renowned roboticist Casmir Dabrowski. Kenji is concerned that he may have installed monitoring software within me that will, unbeknownst to me, send back reports about his activities on this mission."

"Isn't the captain Minister Dabrowski's friend, and wouldn't *she* just send back reports?" Mari asked.

"Exactly what I suggested," Kay said as Kenji tilted his eyes toward the ceiling. "But since astroshamans are known to be excellent with computers, and presumably robots, perhaps you could examine me and check for monitoring devices."

Kenji lifted an apologetic hand toward Mari. "Sorry, please ignore him. You don't have to *examine* him."

"Would it not set your mind at ease to know I haven't been bugged?" Kay asked.

"She's not a gastroenterologist. She doesn't want to scrutinize your insides."

"That is an inaccurate analogy, as I do not have an intestinal system."

"I know. It was a joke. Never mind."

"I can take a look if you wish," Mari offered them.

Maybe if she made an overture of friendship, Kenji would be less likely to attempt to capture her again. Besides, it would give her something to do besides look out the porthole and worry about how they might fail to retrieve her terraformer and how she would be inadequate at proving herself to the Kingdom government. If that happened, they would not grant her asylum.

"You don't have to," Kenji said, but Kay was already ambling over to her pod.

"I can get you a toolbox if you wish, Mari," Kay said.

Kenji rolled his eyes upward again, then sighed and sat in a deck-locked seat at the table. Once they reached the launch loop, he would have to find a pod, or he would end up plastered against a wall, but they should have some time.

"I have a few tools." Mari patted one of her pockets.

"Does a wrench come out of one of those rings?" Kenji muttered.

"That would be impressive, but no."

"Sorry." He glanced at her face. "I'm a little bitter because you bested me twice."

"I have no wish to best you at all." Mari opened the robot's housing. "I was only defending myself. I do not wish to return to my family."

"I know. I get that now. Are your parents, uhm, mean?"

"My mother is restrictive. My father is no longer alive."

"That's tough. My mother died when I was younger too. I really miss her sometimes."

"That is unfortunate. I was very young when my father was killed by pirates. I do not remember him."

"I wish I didn't remember *my* father," Kenji said wistfully.

Mari did not know how to respond to that. Since learning his full name, she had looked him up and was aware of his past and of the crimes he had committed with his terrorist father. She did not wish to judge him for what he had done as a boy, especially since he no longer seemed associated with his father, but that past did make her more inclined to believe that she shouldn't trust him.

"Sorry," Kenji said. "It's not like you asked. Uhm, what do you mean restrictive?"

Mari hesitated. If she opened up about herself, and he found her story sympathetic, was it possible he would no longer wish to collect her bounty? Was that wishful thinking?

Still, she found herself answering. "My mother does not want any of her children to leave the community. We're close-knit and rely upon each other not only to achieve our goals but for protection as well. Astroshamans have beliefs that aren't popular among humans in the rest of the Twelve Systems, and we are often targeted by those who allow themselves to be guided by their prejudices. I am not certain if my mother is more concerned that I will be in danger out here, or that I might develop *other* beliefs if I experience more of the universe, but she has always forbidden us to leave."

"She forbids it?"

"Yes."

"How old are you?"

"Twenty-four."

"Huh. We're the same age. An age at which humans are supposed to be grownups and allowed to do what they want."

"*I* thought so." Mari ran her fingers over Kay's circuit boards and servomechanisms, cycling through her ocular implants' various ways to see so she could check for anomalies.

Kenji fell silent, merely watching for several minutes. Before, he'd been avoiding looking at her. Now he wore a pensive expression as she worked.

"I needed the money," he said abruptly, startling her after the silence.

"What?"

"That's why I took the bounty-hunting gig. It's been a rough few years, and I needed the money, but I should have asked for more details before accepting the assignment."

She resisted the urge to emphatically say *yes*. Instead, she said only, "Ah," and tried to make it nonjudgmental.

"I feel like I should apologize for tackling you. Twice."

"It is what my mother told me to expect if I left our enclave and went out among regular humans."

"Being tackled by men? You are kind of cute, other than the weird eyes, and, er—" He waved to the side of her head.

Mari had been about to correct his assumption, but the comment derailed her. She was cute but *weird*? She didn't know how to respond.

"Never mind. That was a dumb thing to say." Kenji frowned down at the table. Maybe he realized it had been rude to call her weird. Or did he regret admitting he thought she was cute?

Better to ignore it all. "My mother told me to expect regular humans to believe me to be a spy and to judge me unfairly, and that they might shoot or incarcerate me."

"I wasn't judging you, just trying to capture you. And *your* people put the bounty out, not any *regular* humans."

"They likely won't be the only ones. The police came to arrest me simply because someone reported an astroshaman on the university campus."

"Well." Kenji prodded the table. "It's not a good time to be an astroshaman on Odin. Last year, you might have gotten stared at instead of arrested."

"Enormously more pleasant."

"As someone who spent the night in a jail cell, I can say that I'd prefer stares to arrests."

"If it matters to you, I was not among those who attacked your military ships and bombed your planet. I can't deny that my mother was heavily involved in that, but even she was a reluctant participant and coerced by two other high shamans."

"Oh." He didn't look like he had intended to ask. Maybe he didn't care. Maybe it was only about the money for him.

Was it odd that Casmir Dabrowski hadn't asked her about the battle? Hadn't asked if she was innocent or if she had any Kingdom blood on her hands?

Kenji plucked at his galaxy suit again. Mari couldn't tell if it was because he was nervous, because it didn't fit, or because he'd never worn one before. Even if the latter was true, they were generally comfortable without much need for adjustment. Even though the Kingdom version wasn't as advanced as what Mari was accustomed to, she trusted it did its job of insulating against g-forces during acceleration and deceleration and had the trademark sturdy fabric that would protect its wearer from temperature extremes, should a spacewalk be necessary. The suits could also deflect everything from pieces of space junk to weapons fire. They weren't as indestructible as combat armor, but they were much easier to wear on long trips, with a pouch below the back of the neck containing a flexible helmet that could fold out if self-contained operation was needed. There were attachments on the back for an oxygen tank.

"Thanks for checking out Kay," Kenji said.

"You are welcome."

Mari glanced at him, appreciating the little social niceties, even if she was resolved to remain wary of him. She let herself study his face for the first time, for some reason thinking of Tigress's flirtation with him. Presumably, she considered him desirable. He *was* handsome, with dark intent eyes, tousled black hair, and a jaw defined by a couple days' worth of beard growth, but she did not know if he could stir libidinous thoughts within her. Perhaps if he had not *attacked* her the first time they'd met. And the second.

"I don't really think he's bugged," Kenji said. "It was just a... Well, he *could* be. I doubt Minister Dabrowski and all those knights and department heads really trust me."

"Not being trusted is disconcerting," she said blandly.

He snorted. "I guess you'd know."

"Yes."

"Anyway, Minister Dabrowski probably *didn't* do anything, but he had the opportunity. Last night, he fixed Kay up, improved his wiring, gave him some higher-quality parts, and smoothed the dents out of everything else."

"He also lubed my joints," Kay said, "cleaned some odious gunk out of my foot and ankle creases, and gave me an all-over alignment. My panel gaps are no longer uneven. I am not ungrateful to Kenji for bringing me to life, but I do feel much better now."

"I'm glad," Kenji said dryly. "Anyway, I'm not planning on doing anything shifty, but I'd like to know if my every move is being transmitted back. Especially since I'm sharing a cabin with Kay."

"The captain said that robots don't get their own cabins," Kay said. "I either have to share with Kenji or find room in the closet where the vacuum robots are stored when they're charging."

"I don't see any physical monitoring devices." Mari closed most of the robot's panels.

"That's a relief," Kay said.

"I should check your operating system to see if any new software has been installed."

"Ah, of course."

A faint ding sounded in her mind, and she paused in her inspection. It was an alert from the program she'd created to monitor the black-market sites in the system. She scanned through the results, then smiled fiercely at Kenji.

He seemed taken aback. "Are you okay?"

"My terraformer has been listed on a private site favored by black-market buyers of goods—the Dark Comet Nexus—as has other astroshaman technology that I recognize as having been scrounged from the *Celestial Dart*. Surprisingly, the descriptions of what the devices are and what they do are reasonably accurate. The thieves must have already had familiarity with our technology. May I have permission to contact you via your chip—" Mari waved at his glasses, "—to send you the details?"

Kenji hesitated, and she wondered if he would find it unpalatable if an astroshaman had permission to contact him chip-to-chip. She recalled that she had contacted him in the police van without asking first. Normally, she would not do that, but that had been a mitigating circumstance. This time, she wanted his permission.

"It's a private site?" he asked. "How were you able to get in? And how will I?"

"One moment." Mari broke into the back end of the site and created an account with the necessary permissions for making purchases. She explained what she was doing as she worked. "I hope this isn't presumptuous, but I'm making this in your name—your *real* name, as I understand our ruse may hinge on the thieves believing you are your father's son. Even though it's a reasonably large database, and it's *possible* the thief wouldn't be suspicious about a new buyer with a name he or she doesn't recognize, it sounds like the Kingdom government believes it will be more plausible to the thieves if they can openly connect you to a terrorist."

"Openly connect," Kenji mouthed.

"Yes. Ah, I've found an existing account that your father made years ago on the Nexus. That means he's already known there. It's not under his name, but under a code name linked to him, but if I could find the connection easily, then it's likely many people who operate in this area know it's his account." She kept working as she spoke. "I'm taking the liberty of establishing a purchasing history for you and linking your account to his with some light social connections. It's *possible* that if he's monitoring things closely, he'll notice your account popping into existence and making links to his, but he hasn't made a purchase on the Nexus for two years, so he's likely busy elsewhere. Your father may not be in this system at all. That would be ideal for this ruse."

"You're doing all that *now*? In like, thirty seconds?"

"It's been closer to three minutes."

He stared at her, and she once again sensed he believed her odd.

"I have numerous chips integrated with my brain," she explained, though it might not change his opinion of her. "I can perform many mental processes at once."

"Even while you're examining Kay's innards?"

"Yes." Mari shrugged. "I've completed the setup. If you're ready, I'll send the auction site and account information to you."

She pinged Kenji's chip, sending the contact request. Her mother, who'd been a talented computer engineer, programmer, and occasional hacker before she'd become an astroshaman, had taught Mari and her siblings much about getting into secured places, but she wouldn't force her way into Kenji's inbox.

"Okay." He still looked a little stunned—and had that been horror that flashed in his eyes when she said his father might notice the link?—but he accepted the contact request.

It worried her that this mission hinged on him. He had so little at stake. Did he care if the terraformer went into enemy hands? Dabrowski had said he could earn a pardon for his crimes if he performed adequately, but did he even want that? He might plan to collect her bounty and disappear back into the ether.

As she sent the information along, Captain Laser spoke over the speaker. "Come to navigation for take-off, Backer. We need to have a chat about our course once we get out of Odin's atmosphere. Casmir said there would be a rendezvous point but not where."

"Guess I better figure that out." Kenji touched his glasses, then nodded to Mari and rose. "Are you coming, Kay, or are you still being examined?"

"My software has yet to be scanned," Kay said.

"Yes, sorry. I got distracted." Mari blushed, realizing she'd said she could do numerous tasks at once—which was true—but had allowed herself to forget this one while talking to Kenji.

"Understandable, yet distressing, that I am not engaging enough to command full attention."

"I think my robot is flirting with you," Kenji said.

Mari blinked. "Is that a joke?"

"Yeah." Kenji waved and walked out.

"Humans have quirky senses of humor," Kay said.

"Yes," Mari agreed and installed a program to scan his software.

"Since you and my maker will be working together to perpetrate this ruse, I feel compelled to tell you something about him."

"Oh?"

"Kenji has no wish to be a bounty hunter. Nor a thief nor criminal of any kind. In the years I have known him, he has worked hard to accumulate funds legitimately. His goal has been to make enough to pay for passage out of the Kingdom and start a new life elsewhere.

"He had been very close to achieving his goal when the invasion fleet came. His apartment building in town made it through the first bombing unscathed, but then your people came and dropped more bombs. The city's defenses were down—an astroshaman hacker knocked them offline through the network—and a bomb took out our home, the entire apartment building. Many people died.

"We were fortunate to react quickly and spring out before the building completely collapsed, but Kenji had no time to grab his belongings or any of his money. You see, he doesn't have a banking chip, because of his need to stay off the grid, so he's had to work for people willing to pay in physical currency or other physical valuables. He lost everything. He was also injured by the bombing, and I helped him to a lady we know who treats people who aren't in the system and can't use the hospital and other public services. She was treating a lot of people that night.

"By the time he could return to the remains of the apartment building, human scavengers had been all over the place. We spent a couple of days digging in the rubble and looking for his belongings, but everything was inaccessible or gone. And there is no insurance for those who don't officially exist in the system. That, I believe, is what has forced him to take less desirable work."

"It sounds like he has a reason to harbor ill will toward me." Mari didn't know why Kay had told her all that, but she didn't know if it changed anything about her determination not to let herself trust him. If anything, he had more reasons than she'd realized to dislike and work against her.

"I do not know if he does, but perhaps you understand now why he didn't research you before accepting the bounty. He had no reason to believe astroshamans might be good people."

"I gather most of his kind feel that way," Mari said bleakly, then read the results of her scanning program. "There aren't any anomalies that I can detect in your hardware or software, other than that your wiring upgrades are higher quality than one expects in a K-45. Minister Dabrowski must have choice materials lying around his house."

"One would assume a robotics professor would have access to the best. I am pleased to now have *high-quality* parts."

"Let me run the software scan again to double-check. The first time I heard Minister Dabrowski's name was because he was infiltrating our moon base, and my mother was cursing him for getting onto our network."

"Is that difficult to do?"

"For someone who's not an astroshaman, very difficult. You're clean." Mari uninstalled her scanning program.

"Good. I was disinclined to believe that Minister Dabrowski

would have installed spy equipment inside of me, but Kenji is distrustful of people. Even though I have only worked with him for two years, I've seen that he's rarely been helped by anyone and is suspicious of others in general."

"Are you supposed to talk about him to strangers?"

"There's nothing in my programming that forbids that. Do you think he wouldn't approve?"

"I don't know, but you're a very open robot."

"I *am* open." Kay lifted a finger and closed a panel on his torso. "I have few secrets."

"I see that. I believe if Minister Dabrowski wanted to use you for spying, all he'd have to do is ask you for information."

"That is possible. I do hope that my sharing has convinced you not to hold Kenji's actions against him. He has had a hard life."

"I wasn't going to hold anything against him anyway. I expected to face challenges when I left my people. It's why I've been carrying stunners *and* tranquilizers around."

"I am pleased that you did not kill him for his presumptuousness."

"I assumed it would be harder to gain asylum if I killed Kingdom subjects."

"Possibly so."

14

Despite calling him up to navigation, Captain Laser didn't say much to Kenji until she'd slid her freighter onto the launch loop and they were accelerating along tracks that left the coast and angled upward and outward over the Arashi Sea. She'd directed him into the copilot's pod, and it cupped his body, making their rapid acceleration less noticeable. The robot vacuums that had been sucking up dust when he'd entered disappeared into their charging cubby.

"You been into space before, kid?" Laser asked.

"A few times when I was younger." Kenji didn't explain the handful of missions his father had taken him on to bomb or otherwise sabotage Kingdom bases and government transport ships. Instead, he poked around the auction site with the account Mari had sent him, somewhat bemused that she'd not only created it but also given it a history of purchases. According to the Nexus, Kenji was the owner of a first-generation star hopper, several rare paintings, and a trio of nukes. It seemed terrorists were supposed to have eclectic tastes. "The farthest out I've been is Forseti Station."

"I know it well, and I'm not getting paid enough to take you that far. You better arrange a meeting point that's on one of the moons or at least within a few days' travel. I'm supposed to be back on Odin to pick up a cargo next week. It was just luck that I had this opening. I've been accusing Viggo of rearranging my calendar to make *sure* I had this opening. He'll jump through hoops to do favors for Casmir."

"Really, Bonita," the ship's computer said. "It's not *my* fault you can't remember what's in your own calendar."

"My own calendar that I foolishly store in your memory banks instead of on my chip."

"It's important that I know the route and expectations for our freighter in case you are incapacitated during one of our runs. Naturally, I am capable of landing or docking and even picking up a new cargo on my own."

"Or delaying a cargo pickup to help a friend."

"Friendships are more important than freight."

"Uh huh."

"Do you work often for the crown?" Kenji wasn't familiar with her accent but could tell she wasn't from the Kingdom, and if the computer voice could be judged as a fair reflection of its previous owner, Viggo hadn't originated here either.

"Way more often than is wise," Laser grumbled.

"Working for the Kingdom now is much less fraught than it was six months ago," Viggo said.

"True. I hardly know what to do now that I'm not getting screwed left and right. And it's been handy trotting out that I know the queen when anyone questions me. I hardly ever get searched anymore."

"You know the queen?" Viggo asked. "I thought it was more that you know Casmir who knows the queen."

"She came by the ship once, remember? To pick up Casmir on their way to that hoity-toity luxury transport that's painted purple inside *and* outside. What a ridiculous thing to fly on. Do you think the toilets are purple?"

"As an ambulatory person capable of stepping into other ships, you would have to confirm that." Viggo sniffed, sounding exactly like a human being. "Not that I know why you'd want to."

"Anyway, kid. I called you up to see if you have a course for me." Laser peered around the high side of her pod to look over at Kenji. "Don't take this the wrong way, but I have concerns about you calling the shots for this trip."

"Because of who my father is?"

"Because you're twenty."

"I'm twenty-four."

"That's *so* much better. Worldly and wise." She squinted at him. "Do you get space sick?"

"Not unless the piloting is particularly slipshod."

"That will *not* be the case, unless someone starts shooting at us. Even then, the piloting will be exquisite. Just vigorous."

Vigorous piloting sounded more alarming than slipshod piloting.

So far, Kenji's stomach was fine. Outside, the pale blue sky had shifted to a dark blue. Soon, they would be off the track and shooting into space. And then where?

He adjusted his glasses and shifted from examining his own account on the Nexus to looking for the listing. He needed to find the terraforming device and offer to buy it before a meeting point could be determined.

"Maybe just head to whatever moon base or habitat is close? I need a few minutes to find... Ah, I think this is the right spot." Kenji skimmed through the listings of astroshaman devices. They were all by one person, or perhaps one group, that went by Lupus.

"What site are you on? The Dark Comet Nexus?"

"Yes."

"Have you got an account?" Laser asked. "A way to bid? It's invite-only. They try to keep out the law-abiding citizens."

"Mari made me what will appear to others to be an established account with a convincing history."

"Nobody's supposed to be able to do that, but I suppose astroshamans have hacking in their blood. Or their circuitry."

"I think so," Kenji murmured, then frowned. There were a *lot* of astroshaman gizmos listed, far more than Mari's terraforming device, and more than he would have guessed those drones could have scrounged from the wreck.

He lamented that *he* hadn't gotten an opportunity to take a few items from there himself, especially now that he saw how much one could get for them. Or at least what the thieves were asking for them. It was possible nobody would pay that much, but damn. "For the terraformer, our guy has it listed for two hundred and fifty thousand crowns."

Laser let out a low whistle. "You could buy a whole spaceship for that."

"I spent years of my life trying to scrounge up *five* thousand for a ticket to another system." Kenji shook his head. "According to the site rules and the listing, items like this are exchanged in person—that's what we were hoping—and most of the money is paid at the time of the transfer, but I need to be able to put down... let's see here... ten percent to secure the item."

"Yeah, that's how it works. Normal *legal* sales on big-ticket items involve going through a third party that holds the money, but the Nexus doesn't work like that. When you show up for the handoff, it's expected that both parties will bring guards to make sure everything goes smoothly. If you don't have suitable protection, you can expect to get the snot beaten out of you and your money or object taken by the other side." Laser looked over at him. "We've got Qin and Tigress for that, but do you have ten percent for the down payment?"

"I don't have anything."

"How are you going to pose as a buyer then?"

"Ask Minister Dabrowski to put some money into our new made-up account." Kenji had assumed proof of funds would be required before the trade could be made and had expected someone in the government to give him money to use, but he hadn't guessed he would need so *much* money to set this up. What if Dabrowski thought he would take it and run? That general from Military Intelligence would absolutely think that.

"You're going to ask *Casmir* for money?" Laser asked. "You know he pays in patents, right?"

"What?"

"The kid isn't rich."

"I assume he'll have access to military or government funds... Whatever they use for covert missions and setting up thieves to be captured."

Laser grunted skeptically.

"Besides, he's a noble now," Kenji said. "He should have *some* money. Didn't he pay you to take Mari and me up for this mission?"

"He schmoozed someone in Military Intelligence to send us some money, but it wasn't twenty-five thousand crowns. From what he's said, being a noble means he got some land, not piles of money. They don't even pay him to be a Minister Whatsit. It's his honor to serve supposedly. I think he's still living on his university pay."

"What's *on* the land?" Kenji well knew that most noble families ran all manner of industries on their expansive properties, everything from manufacturing plants to wineries to timber mills. He'd grown up among orchards, his mother's family using the fruit for jams, juice, candies, alcohol, and more.

"Trees, I think. It's some remote swath out in your Kingdom

Forest. I'm guessing all the good land was given out a long time ago."

"Lumber has value."

"Good point. Offer a few thousand trees to the thieves. I'm sure they'll accept that."

"Probably... not. Will you comm the professor for me? I need to arrange something." It occurred to Kenji that he hadn't asked for permission to contact Dabrowski chip to chip. Maybe he should have. "Uhm, do you know how to reach him?"

"*Of course* I know how to reach him. At the university, at home, and I've even got a direct line to your Drachen Castle." Laser shot him a dirty look and tapped the comm panel. "Don't you think I have a way to rat you out if you go astray on this mission?"

Yes, Kay had suggested just that, and it didn't surprise Kenji. Laser was a near stranger, so it shouldn't have stung, but all the glares, glowers, and dark comments he'd received since people found out who his father was—who *he* was—were starting to weigh him down.

Some need to be tough, or at least not let Laser know her comment mattered to him, made him flippant. "You have the comm code to the castle? Impressive."

"Viggo and I are valued." She waved a hand as if it were no big deal.

"That's good," Kenji said and looked away, ignoring the longing pang he felt as he tried to remember the last time anyone had valued *him*.

It had been his mother, his mother who had been gone a long time. Funny how spending one's life in hiding made it hard to develop relationships. He'd spent the last few years working toward some nebulous future where things would be better, but it hadn't left time for much else, for becoming someone others valued.

He pushed a hand through his hair, annoyed with his maudlin

mood. Maybe he should have taken more of Mari's candies. Didn't women swear by chocolate for repairing one's emotional state?

Kenji hoped Laser and her ship truly were valued. It had crossed his mind that he and Mari had been given the clunky old freighter for this ruse, not because it would be more believable but because nobody had been willing to invest that much in them. The knights in their Kingdom Fleet warships might be cruising around the system right now, well-trained Intelligence officers also poking around on the Nexus and determining where the thieves were. Maybe Kenji was even the distraction to occupy the thieves' attention while the experts homed in on them.

The comm display activated, and a dark-haired woman with elegant features and thoughtful brown eyes appeared. Sunlight streamed through walls of windows in the background, with vining plants rising on trellises behind her. For a bewildered moment, Kenji thought Laser had mistakenly commed some gardening center, but it dawned on him that he was looking at Queen Oku. Did the castle have a greenhouse? It must.

His cheeks heated as he remembered his misadventure in trying to help thieves rob her greenhouses in the park.

"Good afternoon, Captain Lopez. Casmir is indisposed but will be here shortly." Oku smiled—or was that a smirk?—and looked off to the side at something not visible on the display.

"Good. Tell him to bring some trees. His secret agent left the planet without any money to make a deal."

The flush to Kenji's cheeks increased.

"Trees?" Oku asked.

"Never mind, Your Majesty." Kenji tried to bow from his pod, but the ship was still accelerating away from the planet, and the seat's sides gripped him protectively, so all he managed was a head bob.

Barking sounded in the background, and Oku glanced away

again. Still smirking, she looked back. Since she was in a good mood, maybe she was the one to ask for that ten percent.

"I commed to hopefully arrange some funds for our mission," Kenji said.

"That is Casmir's project, so I'll let you talk to him about that. Here he is."

She stepped aside as Dabrowski slid into view, grease on his cheek and short blades of grass dusting his shoulders. There were even a few green strands in his hair. More barking sounded in the background, as if a dog was having a fantastic time chasing a squirrel.

Kenji decided he didn't know the professor well enough to make jokes or ask what he'd been doing to acquire such hair decorations. Laser felt differently.

"Looking good, El Mago," she crooned. "No wonder world leaders can't keep their hands off you."

Dabrowski blinked. "Uhm, I believe there's only one world leader moderately interested in putting hands on me."

"You sure? Didn't that astroshaman leader kiss you?"

Dabrowski sighed, his eyes rolling heavenward. "Why does everyone keep bringing that up?" he mumbled.

"And I *know* that sultan at Stardust Palace enjoys your company. I heard a rumor that he was putting you in his will."

"You're in fine form today, Laser," Dabrowski said. "After four *hours* of meetings, I felt the urge to put my hands to work, so I made some adjustments to the castle's lawn-mowing robots. They now mow more optimally and are programmed to play with Queen Oku's dog."

"And spit their clippings at their maker?" Laser asked.

"Hm?"

The queen had stepped out of view, but she reached over and brushed the grass out of Dabrowski's hair and off his shoulders.

"Oh, yes. I happened to be nearby when Chasca—that's her

dog—took a shortcut to head off the robot she was chasing and ran through the compost pile." He lifted his arms expansively, demonstrating an explosion of grass flying everywhere, then nodded to the queen. "Thank you for striving to make me presentable."

"You're welcome. I believe you're about to ask General Heim to allocate funds for your special project, so it may help to look like a respectable diplomat instead of one of the gardeners."

"Ah. Yes. He is a crown pincher when it comes to funds allocation, especially for projects that aren't his idea." Dabrowski faced the camera again. "Does that mean you've already made progress, Kenji?"

"Yes, my lord. Mari found the listing for her terraforming device and numerous other astroshaman trinkets—*expensive* trinkets—for sale on the Dark Comet Nexus."

"Good. Send the information, please. It'll help if I show it to him."

Kenji transmitted the data to Laser's comm, so it would show on the display for Dabrowski, then braced himself to say, "It looks like I need ten percent of two hundred and fifty thousand crowns."

"Actually, it looks like you need ten percent of two hundred and fifty thousand Union dollars," Dabrowski said dryly.

"Oh, hell." Kenji hadn't checked the exchange rate lately, but he knew Union dollars were worth substantially more than crowns.

"Is the terraforming device worth that much?" the queen asked skeptically.

Worried that his mission—his chance to get that pardon and avoid the asteroid penal mines—might be scrapped, Kenji looked for something to say that would convince them of its importance.

"It's worth a lot to keep it from going to someone who could use it as a weapon." Dabrowski sighed and tapped a control on their comm unit. "I'm seeing if we can get General Heim on the line. He enjoys being kept in the loop."

"He enjoys yelling at you about how diplomats aren't supposed to meddle in military affairs," the queen said.

"He *enjoys* it? That's not the impression I've gotten from the throbbing vein at his temple that comes out when we discuss that."

"Funny how many people show off that vein when they talk to you, El Mago," Laser said.

"Isn't it? It's why I was a natural fit for a diplomatic position."

The queen snorted.

"You sure there just weren't any other openings available?" Laser asked. "And that they had to stick you somewhere?"

"Somewhere we could keep an eye on him," the queen agreed and found another piece of grass to brush out of Dabrowski's hair. Since her eyes twinkled when she said that, Kenji assumed it wasn't heartfelt.

The display split in half, and a second face appeared, General Heim in a drab office with beige walls, a liquid whiteboard on the wall behind him. He was scowling.

"Two hundred and fifty thousand Union *dollars*?" were the first words out of his mouth.

"Kenji only needs twenty-five to set up the meeting and lure in the thief," Dabrowski said.

"*Only* twenty-five. An amount I'd be *delighted* to give to the son of a terrorist."

"We've already discussed why he's the perfect person to carry out our ruse."

"Or the perfect person to take the money and flee to another system," Heim growled, every bit as suspicious as Kenji had feared he would be.

"Even if we believed that was true, which we don't—"

Dabrowski smiled and nodded at Kenji, "—Captain Laser and her fearsome crew would put a stop to it."

"Yes, the seventy-year-old freighter captain and her cat women," Heim said.

"I'm a *bounty hunter*, and I'm sitting right here." Laser didn't lower her voice much when she added, "Asshole."

Heim's jaw clenched.

"Her charming irreverence makes her perfect for dealing with thieves," Dabrowski hurried to inform the general.

"And abysmal at dealing with the military," Heim growled.

"Hence why the thieves won't suspect she's aligned with you. I'll arrange the transfer of the funds, Kenji."

Heim started to sputter a protest, but Dabrowski continued on.

"If at all possible, Kenji and his team will recover *all* of the stolen astroshaman devices. So we get our money's worth, eh? And I'll ask Mari to see if she can find a way to mark the thieves' ship so the Fleet can give chase after they leave the meeting area, even if they have a slydar hull."

"An astroshaman," Heim said. "Someone else I'm eager to put faith in."

"Together, they will achieve great things," Dabrowski assured him.

Heim did not appear convinced. Even Kenji was skeptical that he and Mari could achieve *great things*.

"We'll try," he felt compelled to say when the men looked at him.

Dabrowski waved. "Keep us updated."

"Yes, my lord."

Dabrowski closed his side of the comm down before the general, leaving Heim's glowering face filling the display.

Kenji waved his fingers toward Laser, hoping she would hang up on him.

But Heim had time to say, "If you screw us over, boy, my people *will* find you." He hung up first.

"Asshole," Laser repeated.

Kenji agreed.

"I never would have returned to this benighted system if Casmir and Oku hadn't ended up in charge," Laser said. "I bet they're counting the days until the gnarled fossils reigning over their military and senate keel over and die."

Kenji didn't point out that the gray-haired Laser might be older than General Heim.

"Was it not your *osito* who was the reason for your return, Bonita?" Viggo asked. "Such a shame that his duties precluded him from coming along on this little mission and keeping your toes warm."

"Yeah, yeah, he's a perk too. But if any black-market thief got a whiff of a knight, this deal would be off." Laser looked at Kenji. "You better buy that doohickey as soon as you get the money, kid. And pick a rendezvous spot that isn't all the way out by the worm-hole gate. The sooner we can meet with these thieves, the less time they'll have to poke around and figure out you're lying to them and setting them up. They don't like that."

"I imagine not." Kenji wondered what the odds were of everything working out—and what they were of everything exploding in his face like the queen's compost pile.

15

After Kay left the lounge and Mari was done adding finishing touches to the account Kenji would use to make an offer on her terraformer, she rose from her pod to investigate the lounge. They had broken Odin's orbit, and she was alone in the room without a task to occupy her mind.

Curious about the captain and the crew, she poked into the cabinets. What did they do for mental stimulation while on prolonged travels? Did they read and research? Study astronomy from among the stars? Or—more likely from what she'd seen of them—train at combat maneuvers?

She wondered if any of them would have a birthday while they were on this mission. *Birthday party* was on her Human List. Her people did not celebrate such things, nor holidays of any kind, there being no logical reason for people to get together and consume cake and hurl confetti into the air, at least according to her mother and the other senior astroshamans. When Mari had asked for a party for her tenth birthday, after reading about such events in a book, her mother had dismissed the idea as wasteful frivolity and suggested she start a new science project if she felt the urge to do something recreational. As she recalled, she'd given sugar to yeast to create enough carbon dioxide to fill a balloon. It had been... somewhat festive.

Two large cubbies held treadmills that could be pulled out for exercise sessions. Mari was contemplating using one when the hatch opened, startling her.

She spun, feeling guilty at being caught snooping around. The captain had said, "Make yourself at home," but that might not have included peering into cabinets.

Qin and Tigress walked in, appearing nearly identical in their matching galaxy suits—and almost-matching faces. Tigress's features were a little softer, her cheeks a touch plumper, and she looked like she favored indulgences in life. They were both, however, in excellent physical shape, the galaxy suits fitted enough to show off muscular arms, backs, and legs.

"Hello, Mari," Qin said. "We came to pump you for information."

"I... am not familiar with that term." Mari closed the cabinet door. "Do you mean to interrogate me?"

"Yes, but without torture or any other implied nastiness. We could even bribe you. We know you like chocolate." Qin smiled.

"Who doesn't?" Tigress asked. "Though I prefer licking melted chocolate off a lover's warm flesh."

"That doesn't sound sanitary," Qin said.

"Men don't usually mind. They like being licked."

Qin crinkled her nose. "I should have brought Pounce along on this mission."

"You should have brought more men."

Mari didn't know what to think of the conversation. Having sex was on her Human List, but she didn't recall licking being discussed that often in the books she'd read.

"Maybe I'll lick your knight when we get back," Tigress said, eyeing Qin sidelong. It seemed more like teasing than a serious suggestion.

Since Mari had read novels and seen vids starring knights, she could understand the appeal. At one point, her list had said *have sex with a knight*. After later deeming that unrealistic and overly specific, she'd shortened it to simply *have sex*.

"If you put your tongue on Asger," Qin said, "I'll hurl you into the wall. Again."

"You're so singular, Squirt. Why don't you share your men? I'd happily share mine."

"You don't have a man currently."

"I might. Our new passenger has a nice ass. I'd have plastered him against a wall already, but with Kingdom men, you never know if they'll flip out over modded women." Tigress lifted a finger, a claw extended, and pointed it down her body.

"I think even progressive men might be alarmed by you plastering them against a wall," Qin said.

"Only those with a poor sense of adventure."

"Most," Qin mouthed to Mari.

"Do you find it difficult," Mari asked slowly, "to find mates who accept your differences from the human norm?"

That was something she'd long wondered, having read about the various prejudices and stereotypes common among humanity, and Kenji's comment that she would be cute if not for her implants sprang to mind. In some of the systems, cybernetic implants and genetic modifications were common, but she'd always gotten the feeling anything *too* different from the norm could lead to people being ostracized. They ended up in communities of like-minded—like-modded—individuals.

"You just have to know how to work your assets." Tigress wriggled her hips, then slapped her butt.

Qin rolled her eyes. "*Yes.* We find it difficult. Especially if you want a nice man who cares about you and doesn't just want to have sex with you to see what it's like to sleep with a freak."

Tigress lowered her arms, her expression growing a touch wistful. "There's some truth to that. I've had no trouble finding those types, and there's fun to be had with them, but I am a little envious of Squirt and her knight."

"His name is William Asger, and he's not *my* knight."

"I know." Tigress smiled at her, then nodded at Mari. "Do you have trouble? You're pretty and shapely and all, but you know." She waved at the implant on the side of her head. "Not everyone wants to sleep with a computer."

Mari combed her fingers through her hair, as she often did, to make the implant less noticeable.

Qin elbowed her sister. "Don't call her that. It's like someone calling *us* freaks."

"Is it? Computer doesn't seem as derogatory."

Mari shrugged, having expected such comments, and Tigress hadn't intended to be mean. She did wonder if she would have to cross *kisses* and *sex* off her Human List. They might be more difficult to obtain than chocolate and alcohol.

"I'm not sure yet if it's difficult to find someone," Mari said.

"You've got all of the rest of your people, right?" Tigress asked. "Astroshamans? I assume if someone is modded themselves, they're not as uppity about implants."

"They aren't, and it's traditional to choose implants that are blatantly computer-like rather than subtle and less noticeable, but our people aren't encouraged to seek out biological pleasures of the flesh."

Tigress looked blankly at her.

"Most of us don't have sex," Mari clarified. "My mother, I've heard from other elders, was somewhat libidinous before she came fully into the fold and became a high shaman, but she doesn't think her children should be that way. We're supposed to be perfect representations of astroshaman culture with the goal of one day leaving behind our human bodies and taking android bodies or simply uploading our consciousnesses into computer systems."

Qin's mouth formed an, "Oh," but she didn't say anything else. Was she repulsed?

"That would make sex difficult," Tigress said.

"Yes. It's why I left."

"To have sex?"

Mari blushed. "Not *only* that, but I wish to experience... what it is to be human. Mostly human." She waved at her implants. "What did you want to *pump* me about?"

"Oh," Qin said. "We wondered if you know anything about our mission. The captain has only said we're flying out to rendezvous with some thieves to get back something they stole. She said we'd probably have to be Kenji's protection."

Mari looked at their muscular arms. "You seem ideal for that."

"We *are* ideal." Tigress lifted her chin and smiled, flashing her fangs. "But we like to know what we're getting into."

Mari saw no reason to keep them in the dark and explained the terraforming device and the plan, as far as she knew it.

"So he's up in navigation with the captain pretending to buy some gizmo you made?" Tigress asked. "Can't you just make another one?"

"I could, but it would be easier for me to replicate the work if I had the prototype back." She didn't go into where her people were staying and how they no longer had easy access to some of the expensive and rare materials that had gone into the device.

"I need my powerful fighters up in navigation to look fierce," Captain Laser said over the comm. "We're about to make contact with the target."

"That's us." Qin headed for the hatch, Tigress right behind her.

Mari doubted she qualified as a powerful fighter, especially compared to those two, but curiosity prompted her to follow them. Maybe they were about to find out who'd stolen her device.

Digital currency wasn't as impressive as money piled up on a table or stashed away in a secret vault, but Kenji still admired the digits in the bank account that Military Intelligence had given him access to. A neat twenty-five thousand Union dollars were waiting to be transferred to the Nexus.

A part of him was dumbfounded that the Kingdom was trusting him to do it. If it had been up to that General Heim, Kenji knew he wouldn't have seen a single dollar. For whatever reason, Dabrowski had faith in him.

Even though he appreciated that faith, after so many years of being broke, he couldn't deny he was tempted to make another account, transfer the money into it, and figure out how to sneak away from Laser and her ship. Twenty-five thousand was five times as much as he'd been trying to save up, more than enough to get passage to another system and start over. In addition, he still had some of the money the astroshamans had given him as a down payment on Mari.

He felt guilty about that and worried they would hunt him down if he didn't bring Mari back to them, but that was something he no longer planned to do. It would be a good idea to figure out how to return their money to them.

But this twenty-five thousand from the military...

Kenji sighed. No, he couldn't make off with it either. The thought of disappointing the only person willing to trust him kept him from contemplating the theft further. It was silly, given that Kenji had never actually been his student—never even talked to him until this week—but he hated the idea of Dabrowski being yelled at by Heim. And of the important people who'd been in that meeting having a reason to tell Dabrowski *I told you so.*

Kenji muttered the commands to his glasses chip to transfer the money to the Nexus account so he could pay the deposit on the terraforming device. The display on his lenses showed the money whisking away. A soft ping of confirmation vibrated through the frame of his glasses as the Nexus accepted his offer. He leaned back in his pod.

"It's done?" Laser asked.

"Yes."

The hatch opened, and Tigress and Qin walked in, Qin moving to stand behind Laser's pod and Tigress standing behind Kenji's. Navigation wasn't that large, and the presence of the big women made it claustrophobic. Mari stopped in the hatchway, standing back a few feet, a hesitant expression on her face.

Laser hadn't called for her. Maybe she didn't know if she was welcome. Kenji waved for her to come in if she wanted.

"Is the mastermind putting things into place?" Tigress rested a hand on Kenji's head and eyed him over the back of his pod, a smile curving her lips.

"Is that me?" Normally, Kenji didn't mind interest from the opposite sex—he cheerfully invited it—but he found himself groping for a way to politely let her know that she wasn't his type. He supposed sex with a warrior woman with cat genes could be an intriguing and educational experience, but he didn't know if his ego could take sleeping with someone who had more muscle mass than he had. *Furry* muscle mass.

"You got it, cutie." Tigress patted his head, then rested her hand on the back of his pod.

He felt like a pet.

"I just put in the offer. Your intimidating presence in the background may be premature." Kenji waved at Qin and Tigress. "The seller may wait before comming to see if there are more and better offers. Or he may spend a few hours researching me."

No sooner had the words come out than another faint ping vibrated his glasses. His offer had been accepted.

"Or not," he said.

"Is it concerning that it happened so quickly?" Laser asked.

"I... don't know." This was Kenji's first time scheming against thieves.

"I manipulated the search data on the Nexus to make the listing for my terraformer less visible to bots and human viewers than it might otherwise be," Mari admitted. "I assumed the Kingdom coffers would prefer it if we not get into a bidding war."

"I know about the Nexus," Laser said. "It's supposed to be hacker proof. There are all kinds of security protocols so that unscrupulous types can't fiddle with things."

Kenji peered past Tigress to Mari.

She shrugged, looking more embarrassed than pleased with herself. "I'm used to sophisticated networks. It's what my people have. It wasn't that difficult to figure out how to get in or how to tinker without leaving signs."

Kenji remembered Dabrowski's comment about the abilities of astroshamans and how he hadn't been surprised that Mari had gotten the best of him—twice. He was beginning to realize how foolish he'd been to accept that bounty-hunting gig and felt lucky that Mari wasn't the vengeful sort. What if he'd gone after an astroshaman who thought nothing of slaying enemies that pestered her? Like the ones who'd led the raid to the Arctic Islands? A lot more Kingdom warships had been wrecked up there than astroshaman vessels.

"We've got someone comming us," Laser said. "An unfamiliar contact."

Nervous, Kenji nodded for her to put the message on the display. "Wait, we better hide you, Mari." He glanced back.

"They're going to be suspicious about us wanting to buy astroshaman tech when we have our very own astroshaman."

"I understand." She started to back away.

He lifted a hand. "Is there room for you to duck down? It would be good to get your opinions on these people."

Qin stepped aside so Mari could squeeze into navigation. She hesitated, looked around, then crouched between the two pods so her head was below the console.

Kenji patted her on the shoulder. Sometime between her sharing encyclopedia entries on cinnamon and her offering to examine Kay for bugs, she'd stopped seeming so... weird. Maybe it was silly, since he'd been adding to her torment until recently, but he had the urge to include her and make her feel welcome.

"Getting cozy in here." Laser reached for the comm panel.

"Try to pinpoint where they're comming from, will you?" Kenji asked.

"I am already working on it," Viggo said.

"As am I," Mari said quietly.

The display came to life, showing someone sitting in a pod in a dimly lit cabin with computer instrumentation blinking in the background. A hood and heavy shadows obscured the person, offering only the hint of lumpy features, with a jaw jutting too far forward. Kenji resisted glancing at Qin and Tigress for comparison. *Their* jaws were fine. This person looked to have features more canine than human. It could be a mask, but they were likely dealing with another genetically modified individual.

"You're the son of the Kuchikukan?" The rough voice was hard to understand, the jaw mangling the formation of words, but he spoke slowly enough that Kenji could decipher them. "I wasn't expecting someone so young."

"My father started training me at eight. I'm a crack shooter, a fighter, and can thread a needle with any aircraft." He half-expected Laser, who hadn't seen him do any of those things, to make a snarky comment, but she was leaning out of the video pickup, staying silent and making it clear this was his mission.

Nerves fluttered in Kenji's belly. Even though Dabrowski hadn't said Laser would be in command, he hadn't quite realized *he* was in charge of the whole thing. Such strange trust to be given to an unproven operative who'd been in jail two days ago.

Mari looked up at him and gave him an encouraging nod. Nobody else did, so he appreciated it.

"I'm Lupus Zhor." The man pushed his hood back, revealing more canine features, including prodigious fangs and alert pointed and furred ears. "I can do all those things *and* tear your throat out with my teeth."

Laser rolled her eyes. It had to be killing her not to make snarky comments.

"Do you always threaten the people you sell your goods to?" Kenji asked.

"I just like them to know what they can expect if they betray me." Zhor looked at Tigress and Qin, who stood with their arms crossed, their muscles on display. "You'll bring some kitties to play with me when we meet? An unexpected treat in Kingdom space."

"They'll be with me when we make the trade," Kenji said. "I trust you'll leave them be if I bring the agreed-upon amount."

"As long as you don't cross me. If you *do* cross me, there'll be ramifications." Zhor smiled—inasmuch as someone with a canine snout could smile—and waved to someone off the camera.

No, *six* someones. Six hulking men, their torsos devoid of clothing but covered in fur, walked into view carrying pistols and cutlasses. They lined up behind Zhor's pod, making it easy to see how similar they all were. The same faces, fangs, and ears.

"I've got more puppies than you've got kitties," Zhor said, still smiling. Unlike Qin and Tigress, *all* of his teeth were pointed, not only the human canines.

"Since we're just making a trade, and presumably not battling each other, I fail to see how that matters," Kenji said. "Should things go smoothly, I'll be in the market to purchase more astroshaman tech in the future."

"Good. I trust you'll want to see a demonstration before the exchange to make sure it works."

Uh, that *was* a good idea, though he was surprised Zhor would volunteer. What if the device had broken and no longer worked? Would he be willing to let a buyer back out of a trade?

"I would like that, yes, but what are you going to do?" Kenji arched his brows. "Terraform a planet for me?"

Beside him, Mari lifted a hand and rested it on the console, careful not to move it into range of the vid pickup. She was gazing at the paneling ahead of her, a vacant expression on her face. Laser frowned, maybe thinking she was interfacing with her ship's computer—was she?—but didn't do or say anything with Zhor looking on.

"Perhaps a smaller environment," Zhor said. "I propose the asteroid base atop Sif's space elevator. There's a station with hollowed-out tunnels inside that we can use. I see that you and your rusty freighter are not overly far from my current position." Zhor's eyes narrowed. In suspicion?

"*Rusty?*" came a protest from Viggo. "This vessel is freshly painted and completely free of corrosion."

Laser glared at a speaker on the wall and raised a finger to her lips.

"As I'm sure you're aware," Zhor continued, ignoring the protest, "long-term terraforming efforts have been ongoing on the planet's surface for some centuries. Once you see how rapidly the astroshaman technology can work, you'll be eager to give me your money—and more."

"You've already tested it? Was your cabin in need of new soil and nutrients?"

"I know it will work. This isn't the first astroshaman technology I've acquired." There was that fanged smile again. Very similar to a wolf anticipating a meal.

Even though Mari couldn't see the smile from her spot, the words made her scowl. And why wouldn't they? He'd admitted to stealing—frequently—from her people.

"Good," Kenji made himself say. "It wouldn't be worth anything to us if it didn't work."

"We'll meet at the space elevator in two days at 1300 Odin Zamek time. If more ships than that one arrive, or if you step out of your airlock with an army, I'll assume you mean to betray me, and the deal will be off." Several of his canine bodyguards, or whatever they were, growled. "And you will be dead."

"I'm just looking for the device, not a fight."

"Excellent. We wouldn't want anything to happen to your kitties."

This time, *Tigress* growled.

Zhor cut the comm.

"Does anyone else want to tear his *puppies* limb from limb?" Tigress asked.

Qin lifted her chin. "I am not afraid to battle them."

"I'm a little concerned about it," Kenji muttered. "Especially since *he* picked the place, he's volunteering to demonstrate the tech, and he's got more people than we do."

"You should have picked a different place," Laser critiqued. "It sounds like he's setting a trap for you."

"I got that impression, too, but I don't know why he would. If he's a thief, he should want my money. Why would he betray me?"

"Because you immediately looked shifty to him, and he didn't think he could trust you?"

"*I* don't look shifty. He may have recognized your non-rusty freighter, despite its name change."

"I doubt it," Laser said. "He doesn't look like he's from this system. I don't know if you noticed this, but your Kingdom isn't very friendly to modded humans."

"*I've* noticed," Qin murmured.

Kenji thought of the way Qin and Tigress had been attacked at that rental shop, simply for showing an interest in opening up a business in the neighborhood.

Mari gazed sadly back at them before rising to her feet and removing her hand from the console. "I have acquired some information about Zhor and, by tracing his transmission through the comm network, about the location of his ship. He attempted to route his signal through relay stations to hide his position, but I was able to track it back to him. He's about six hours ahead of us and flying toward Sif."

"You want me to change course to meet him there?" Laser asked. "Or are we going to be smart and back away from this mission?"

"No," Mari said with soft determination.

"What information did you gather?" Kenji didn't point out that Mari wasn't in charge, because he didn't want to quit either, not when he'd already sent off General Heim's twenty-five thousand Union dollars. If the Kingdom didn't get something out of that, Kenji would *definitely* end up on a penal asteroid, working for the rest of his life to pay the money back.

"Zhor is a well-known thief originally from System Cerberus," Mari said. "He is an opportunist and works—steals—from people all over the Twelve Systems. He doesn't come to the Kingdom frequently, but he *often* steals from the astroshamans." Mari scowled. "Not only from wrecks but from my people who choose to live among humans and go back and forth between their communities and astroshaman bases. He's robbed their apartments and taken small items. It is likely the wreck of the *Celestial Dart* offered him an opportunity to gain more significant and recent tech. Though he did some other heists earlier in his career, acquiring astroshaman devices has been his specialty for the last five years. It's surprising my people haven't chosen to deal with him, but most of his thefts, at least from our point of view, have been petty. If the terraformer were not my personal project, one I intend to share with the Kingdom, nobody would have bothered going after him." Mari looked at Laser. "He's wanted by several planetary and station governments, and there are bounties out for him in numerous systems. If you could capture him, the Kingdom could recoup its twenty-five thousand and more."

"Or *we*—" Laser rested a hand on her chest, then pointed at Qin and Tigress, "—could keep it for ourselves, and the Kingdom could find another way to recoup its money. We ought to get a bonus for flying into a trap."

"*Is* it a trap?" Kenji asked. "Or are you still speculating?"

"Judging by the position that his communication came from," Mari said, "he was already en route to Sif. It's possible he planned to test the device there himself even before you put in an offer on it."

"Is a tunnel in an asteroid a legitimate place to test a terraforming gizmo?" Kenji asked.

"It could be. We originally tested it in enclosed domes, both because there's a limit to how much one device can terraform, and so our molecular modifications wouldn't escape and alter more than we wished. There's a chain-reaction effect that radiates outward from its deployment spot."

"That's why Dabrowski and the others are worried about it being used as a weapon," Kenji said. "If it was unleashed in the wild... or in a city..."

"Yes. It works by changing the molecular structure of what exists and shifting it into a more desirable matrix."

"Even if what exists is a city full of people?" Laser asked.

Mari hesitated. "Yes." She glanced at Kenji and Laser. "That was never our intent, of course. We were—we still are—planning to terraform planets in the new system our people will one day travel to, using it to alter a world that is devoid of life."

"You just *accidentally* made something that could also be used as a super weapon?" Laser arched her eyebrows.

"We would never do such a thing. We cannot be held responsible for thieves stealing our equipment."

"No? You sure?"

Mari grimaced, her face more concerned—even haunted—than indignant or defiant.

Kenji bristled, tempted to defend her from the unfair sarcasm, even if he also found the possible ramifications unsettling.

"I am certain," Mari said, though it sounded like she was trying to convince herself. "Pardon me. I was asked to find a way to remotely mark his ship so that the Kingdom Fleet can find it. I will work on that now." Mari nodded curtly and walked out of navigation.

"Think we offended her?" Qin asked.

"Given what she's made," Laser said, "I don't care."

"We once carried a terrible bioweapon around the system."

Laser scowled at her. "Not *knowingly*."

Qin opened her mouth, but Laser cut her off with a chop of her hand.

"Set a course, Viggo," Laser said. "And keep an eye out for other ships or anything suspicious. I've still got a niggling hunch this Zhor knows we're setting him up—and that he wants to set *us* up."

Kenji eyed the stars on the display ahead. He hoped that wasn't the case, but he worried she was right.

16

Mari sat cross-legged with her back to the wall in the cargo hold, the constant acceleration of the freighter keeping her in place as effectively as gravity. It wasn't quite the same as being on a large vessel that spun and created artificial gravity, but it was enough so that they didn't have to spend the whole trip locked in their pods or walking around with the magnetic soles of their galaxy-suit boots activated.

Voices drifted to her from the ladder well. Since Qin and Tigress had been in the lounge, Mari had come down here to work, to study the layout of the Sif space elevator station and to see if she could dig up more information on Zhor and his genetically modified army before their meeting. It sounded like her private spot was about to become less private. That was all right. She could have worked in her cabin if she'd truly wanted to be alone.

As strange as it was, given that she'd voluntarily left, she'd found herself missing her siblings and those among the astroshamans that she considered friends. In addition to her other research, she'd been checking the news back on Odin to see if her mother or any of her people had been mentioned.

"If I go onto the station with a bunch of firearms," came Kenji's voice, "they'll be suspicious that I don't intend to deal fairly."

"If you go onto the station without *any* firearms," Laser's voice followed, "they'll think you're an idiot."

"Maybe that'll be good. Maybe they'll underestimate me."

"Or maybe they like to shoot idiots on sight. Cleaning up the gene pool." Laser walked out of the short hallway and into the hold with Kenji coming after her. "Besides, I want to see if you can actually shoot, and if you'll have the girls' back, or if you're going to be a liability in there."

"I can shoot." Kenji noticed Mari and paused. "Hi."

"Hi," she said.

"Come on." Laser had also noticed Mari, but she kept walking across the hold and toward a small armory next to engineering. "No time for flirting."

Kenji stumbled. "How was that *flirting*?"

"You seem shy. I figured that's how you did it." Laser disappeared into the armory.

Mari decided it had been a joke, and she didn't need to point out that Kenji found her cute but weird, a feeling that would likely preclude flirting.

"We'll give you a pistol," Laser called out. "No thief is going to raise an eyebrow at a contact meeting him with a pistol. If you know what to do with a grenade, I can give you a couple of those too, as long as you promise not to blow your own balls off."

Kenji halted. "It's a good thing I'm *not* trying to flirt, because you assuming I'm inept and talking about my balls being blown off would not impress a woman." He looked over at Mari, his eyebrows up, as if to ask for confirmation.

"I am uncertain how much genitalia factor into relationship decisions for normal humans, but since my people produce offspring through the mingling and manipulation of DNA in a laboratory setting, with artificial wombs employed for gestation, damage to sexual organs would not affect reproduction and might not prompt a dismissal of a person as a potential mate."

"Look at that. There's someone for everyone." Laser walked back out with three armored hover targets and a pistol. "I put this on the lowest setting. I don't want you shooting holes in my walls."

"*Thank* you, Bonita," Viggo's voice came from a speaker. "I am still waiting for someone to repair the dents left by Qin and Tigress's vigorous battle practice."

"Yeah, yeah, Casmir can do it when we get back. He'll owe me for flying into a trap with a couple of rubes."

Kenji scowled and accepted the pistol. "The kind words you offer your passengers must ensure people line up to fly with you again."

As Laser stepped back, activating one of the spherical targets, Mari wondered if she should leave the area. Despite Laser's razzing, Mari doubted Kenji was inept with a weapon. He'd had no trouble stunning those police officers—and *her*, for that matter. She was, however, interested to see how this practice session would go. And if the pistol was on the lowest setting, she shouldn't feel more than a buzz of discomfort on the off chance that a stray bolt *did* hit her.

Laser tossed the sphere into the air, its hover jets keeping it aloft, and it started zipping around in a random pattern near the high ceiling of the hold. "All right, kid. I've programmed it so it won't fire back at first. Just try to hit the thing."

Kenji gave her an exasperated look, glanced at the sphere, and fired. The DEW-Tek bolt streaked up and nailed the target. It paused and dinged softly, acknowledging an acceptable hit, before darting away.

"Not bad." Laser tossed the other two targets in the air. "They'll start moving faster and getting harder to hit with every shot you land."

"I'm familiar with them."

"After ten successful hits, they'll start shooting back."

"Got it."

The first few shots didn't challenge Kenji, but as the spheres started zipping around faster and firing back, he took cover behind crates fastened to the deck and gave his full attention to the task. They beeped in warning a half second before firing, so if he was fast enough, he could hit them first and disrupt their shot. Kenji managed to do that often, though with three in the air, the devices working together to spread themselves apart and make it hard to focus on them all at once, he was challenged. Overall, he proved skilled, darting in and out from behind cover to keep from taking hits.

Since the targets, either through chance or Laser's programming, didn't fly near Mari, she stayed in her spot. As she watched the show, she kept up her research. Laser yelled insults about how slow and clumsy Kenji was, which wasn't even remotely true, but she nodded and looked pleased by his display, so Mari decided it was her way of encouraging him to greater heights.

On a whim, Mari looked up Assistant Professor Donadieu back on Odin. The last she'd heard, Minister Dabrowski hadn't figured out why he'd been using drones to steal from students on the university campus. It was unlikely it had anything to do with Zhor, beyond the fact that Zhor might have been the one who murdered him to steal the stolen technology himself, but it was also possible there was more of a tie-in than that, and that further information would be valuable in facing off against Zhor.

She did find a few articles that mentioned Donadieu, including one by an investigative journalist who'd dug up an off-planet bank account of his with more funds in it than a simple professor should have had. They'd also found a listing he'd put up on one of the black-market sites for a *mysterious device of astroshaman origins*. The time stamp meant he'd done it almost immediately after the drones had robbed Mari.

If Zhor had been in the area, perhaps investigating the military warehouses near Zamek City that contained astroshaman technology taken from the wreck, he could have gotten an alert for the posting. And, instead of *paying* what Donadieu asked, perhaps he'd decided to kill the man and take the device for free. Or maybe Donadieu had been home and had put up a fight, and that was why he'd been killed.

Either way, Mari didn't see that it would affect Kenji's upcoming confrontation with Zhor. Other than to suggest that Zhor didn't play fair. But she gathered that Kenji already suspected that. It concerned her that Zhor had more fighters to take to the meeting than Kenji, but Mari believed she could help out with that, not by fighting but with her skills at navigating secured systems.

She brought up the blueprints for the space elevator station again, as well as everything she could find on its computer systems.

Clangs and clunks came from the ladder well, and a minute later, Kay walked out of the corridor. "What a dreadful system for navigating a spaceship. *Ladders.* They are *not* robot friendly."

"The little vacuums seem to navigate them adequately," Mari said, though she had no trouble seeing why the bipedal robot had difficulties. A K-45 did not have the flexibility of a human or an android.

"*They* have suction systems that allow them to climb walls and stick to the ceiling. My maker did not see a need to outfit me with such."

"There weren't any... suction cups... in the junkyard... where I got... your parts," Kenji called between dodges and rolls and pants for breath. The three targets were moving so quickly now that an android would have been hard-pressed to keep up with them. "Laser, turn those... off. My robot... needs me."

"I do not need you," Kay said. "I merely came to ask if you have a role for me in the upcoming meeting."

"Hm, where'd I leave the remote?" Laser ambled toward the armory.

"*Laser!*" Kenji dove behind the crates, hitting the deck with a thump.

Mari could no longer see him from her spot, but two of the spheres sped behind the crates after him. Assuming he was exhausted after the lengthy workout and would appreciate a break, she located the targets on the ship's wireless network and deactivated them.

"*Thank you,*" Kenji said. It came out as more of a groan.

"Huh?" Laser stepped out of the armory, waving the remote, but noticed the targets had settled to the deck. "How'd you turn them off?"

"I thought... you did." Kenji crawled out from behind the crates on hands and knees, looked warily at the targets, and pushed himself to his feet. His chest rose and fell with each deep breath, and sweat dampened his black hair.

"Nope. Let me guess." Laser frowned at Mari from across the hold.

"I believed that Kenji wished a break." Mari hadn't realized Laser might be upset.

"My network is *secured.*"

"With a simple encryption. I can set you up something more difficult for outsiders to hack into."

"Or you can keep your nosy astroshaman self off it."

"Bonita," Viggo said in mild censure, "you do not object when Casmir hacks into your network."

"That's because I *know* him."

"I believe a double standard is in effect," Viggo said.

"Yeah," Laser said. "A double standard of *knowing*."

"*I* appreciate your intervention, Mari." Kenji had caught his breath enough to say it without gasping, and he managed a wave for her.

She smiled back at him.

"That's because you were on the deck in the fetal position being pummeled by DEW-Tek bolts," Laser said.

"That's precisely the reason, yes."

"Uh huh. Go rest and talk to your robot." Laser pointed at Mari. "Your turn, kid. Do you know what to do with a pistol, or have you spent your whole life plugged into computers? And strangers' networks?"

Mari blinked. "I cannot accompany Kenji, Tigress, and Qin to the meeting. Since I am obviously astroshaman, Zhor would immediately suspect treachery."

"He suspects that anyway, I'm sure, but I just want to know if you're an asset or a liability in a fight. Ships get *boarded*, you know."

"That is a valid point." Mari rose to her feet.

It would not take long to demonstrate that she was capable with a firearm, thanks to targeting software that integrated with her ocular implants and could also, with her permission, control her body's movements. Since astroshamans were not infrequently targeted by humans with malevolent intent, they also practiced self-defense with and without weapons. Not as much as Qin and Tigress, certainly, but enough to remain sufficiently fit and agile, so they were not injured when they allowed their chips to guide them.

"Good luck." Kenji handed her the pistol as he passed her on the way over to talk to Kay. "I'd suggest that you take that remote from her, but I guess you don't need it."

"I do not. Thank you."

"Are you going to cheat by reprogramming them?" Laser asked.

"Because if they all lie down in a row on the deck at your feet, I'm going to start shooting you myself."

"No, it is advisable for me to practice and allow you to see that I should not be a liability."

"All right. Good." Laser clicked her remote, and the three spheres rose into the air again.

As the targets whirred to life, zipping in and out of view around the crates and streaking across near the ceiling, Mari let her software take over and guide her movements. The shooting was rhythmic and somewhat meditative, so she also returned to researching the space elevator station.

Only when the targets started firing back did the need to dodge, jump, and run make it difficult to multitask. Also, it was quite tiring. She soon found that the optimal way to handle the training was to shoot the targets before they fired at her, so she concentrated on doing that. That allowed her to simply stand in the hold with a wall at her back and move her upper body and arms.

She was aware of Kenji talking to Kay about how robots who struggled with ladders probably shouldn't come along to meetings that could turn into battles, while inviting suggestions on how he might gain the upper hand when facing off against Zhor. After a while, they fell silent. Watching Mari, she realized. All three of them were. That made her feel self-conscious, and she was glad that her chips and software were incapable of poor performance due to nervousness caused by fear of spectator judgment.

Even though she was able to perfect her system and didn't need to run and duck, she still found herself starting to breathe heavily and sweat after twenty minutes. She was debating turning off the targets via the network, but Laser clicked the remote first.

"Well, shit," she said.

Mari lowered her pistol, confused by the response. She believed she had performed adequately.

"Maybe we'll just send you over there by yourself," Laser added.

Oh. She *had* performed adequately. That was a relief.

"That was amazing," Kenji said, staring at her, what seemed like genuine reverence in his voice.

For some reason, Mari blushed.

"You're like an android." Laser's tone was less reverent, and Mari suspected it held the implication that she was a freak. A computer.

She grimaced and wiped her brow.

"A sweaty android," Laser added.

"Internal fans, heat sinks, and liquid immersion cooling keep androids from overheating, so they have no need to sweat. I am human."

"I guess."

"Don't pay attention to her." Kenji came over and patted Mari on the shoulder. "I don't know if you've noticed, but she's surly and grumpy as hell."

"I did notice," Mari said quietly.

"Well, at least you two are observant," Laser said. "Maybe that will keep snipers from taking you out. Viggo, see if Qin and Tigress want to come down and join me. I'm going to get some shooting practice in too, assuming Mari didn't overheat the hover targets with all that."

"They should have fans and heat sinks too," Mari offered.

"Good to know." Laser headed into the armory to get more targets.

"It is difficult to find acceptance among normal humans," Mari said.

"You shoot a few of her enemies, and I bet she'll warm up to you." Kenji smiled at her, then seemed to realize he still had a hand on her shoulder. He drew it back and stepped away. "I know *I'd* walk into battle with you at my back."

He was still smiling, so she wasn't positive that he wasn't joking. Even if he meant it, she reminded herself that she shouldn't lower her guard and let herself *appreciate* any praise coming from him. It was still possible that he was being nice as part of a ruse and that he would, if she let him, capture her to drag back to her family.

She wished that weren't a possibility. So few *normal* humans were accepting of her people—of her—that it would be nice to count him as one.

"And I'm starting to feel less bad about not having been able to capture you," he added. "The Kingdom would be pretty dumb not to give you asylum if that's what you want. Nobody would dare break into the laboratory where you're working."

Laser returned to the cargo hold with more weapons and more targets. Clangs on the ladder rungs announced Qin and Tigress coming down. Kenji took another step away from Mari and clasped his hands behind his back.

She didn't know how to interpret that. Did it mean he hadn't intended to get close or touch her? That it had been a mistake?

"I'm not any more capable than an android," Mari said quietly. "And I was easily captured by Minister Dabrowski's crusher."

"I think everyone is easily captured by those crushers. That's not a failing."

"I'm glad you think so."

Even if he didn't want to be close, he was being pleasant. It was nice.

"What's going on?" Qin asked, walking in with Tigress.

"Flirting." Laser waved at Mari and Kenji.

The women looked at them, and for some reason, Mari's cheeks flushed again.

"Are you sure?" Tigress asked. "They're stiff, awkward, five feet apart, and not even looking at each other."

"That's how they do it," Laser said. "They're shy."

Mari shook her head, and Kenji rolled his eyes.

Laser smirked and waved for Qin and Tigress to join her for target practice.

Kenji roamed the bottom level of the freighter, eyeing crates and poking into tool chests, seeking inspiration for his upcoming meeting with Zhor. He'd seen six fighters in the captain's navigation cabin; that probably meant the man would bring twelve or eighteen. If Kenji didn't come up with a way to gain an advantage, he wouldn't walk off that station alive.

But as he'd told Laser, he couldn't come out of the airlock riding a tank—even if he found one lurking in a corner of her cargo hold—or Zhor would know Kenji meant to deceive him straight away. Zhor wouldn't bring the terraforming device if he suspected betrayal, and if it remained locked away on his ship, Kenji would never be able to get it. It was a foregone conclusion that Laser's old freighter couldn't win in a firefight against a sleek new ship with a slydar hull and who knew how many weapons.

"Are you certain there is nothing I can do to be of assistance?" Kay was trailing him around, avoiding being smashed in the cargo hold. The target practice had turned into hand-to-hand combat between Tigress and Qin again.

"I don't think so, buddy, but thanks. You can stay on the ship and assist Mari with whatever hacking she has planned."

After seeing her shoot, Kenji was half tempted to suggest Mari come to the meeting with them. If she wore the helmet on her galaxy suit, their enemies might not be able to tell she was an astroshaman. But she could probably do more from the safety of the ship. Even if her chips let her do a bunch of things at once, Kenji had to assume that being shot at would make it hard to focus on infiltrating enemy networks.

"I am programmed for tutoring, not hacking," Kay said. "You should know this since you selected my operating system."

"You've never felt the urge to teach students how to slip seamlessly into secured databases?"

"My specialties are Old Earth history, mathematics, and string instruments."

"String instruments?" Kenji paused in front of a display in the wall of the compact engineering room. "Like musical instruments?"

"Indeed. I do not have lungs or lips, so wind instruments are difficult, but I am adept with lutes, harps, and zithers."

"Zithers? I had no idea. All this time, I could have made money by having you perform on Zamek's street corners." Kenji tapped the display. "Viggo? Are you able to hear me? If the captain recorded my message with Zhor, I'd like to watch the replay, please."

"Certainly," Viggo said. "And have no fear. Bonita is recording everything you do."

"I'll assume it's because I'm handsome and sexy, and she doesn't want to forget a moment of my passage, not because she's suspicious about my intentions."

"That is your prerogative, though I don't believe those are the adjectives she's used to describe you."

"Does she actually like anyone? Besides Qin and Tigress? And her knight boyfriend?" Kenji hadn't missed that Laser was giving Mari as hard a time as she was him, and her only crime was being an astroshaman.

Admittedly, that was enough for most people in the Kingdom. As it had been for him. He still regretted that he'd assumed the worst of her. His comment that he would gladly go into battle with her at his back had surprised him when it came out, but he decided it hadn't been inaccurate. Not only could she shoot like a targeting computer, but she'd been dead calm and completely unflustered as the hover targets fired back. If her mechanical bits kept her from panicking in scary situations, he was envious.

"A select few people," Viggo said. "She has been betrayed many times in her life and does not easily give trust to strangers."

"I get that."

The recording played, and Kenji gripped his chin as he watched and listened for something he could exploit, either with Zhor, his people, or the ship in the background. Thumps came from the nearby cargo hold as Qin and Tigress threw each other around.

Laser had done some target practice of her own—he'd been almost as impressed by her speed and accuracy as Mari's—before handing the area over to her *girls*, as she called them. Kenji was glad he had a couple of strong allies to go in with, but he feared Zhor's fighters with their canine attributes would be at least as fast and strong as Qin and Tigress. Kenji needed something else, something Zhor wouldn't see coming.

On this third time through the video, he noticed one of the guard's pointed canine ears rotating, presumably at some noise elsewhere in their ship. Kenji paused the playback, held a finger up to Kay, and stepped into the cargo hold again.

Mari, who'd resumed sitting on the deck by the wall, looked over at him. Laser was cleaning combat armor that presumably belonged to her—Qin and Tigress were wearing theirs. Kenji couldn't imagine that a seventy-year-old woman would go into battle with them, but she had mentioned wanting to be ready if her freighter was boarded.

"Qin? Tigress?" Kenji asked when they broke apart. "I have a quick question."

Tigress draped an elbow on Qin's shoulder and looked at him like she would say something libidinous—probably a demonstration of how *she* handled flirting—but Qin slapped a hand over her mouth.

"What is it, Kenji?" she asked.

"Is your hearing enhanced? Like much more sensitive than a normal human's?"

They both nodded.

"Hearing, eyesight, and scent," Qin said.

"Would a loud noise hurt your ears?"

"Yes. Crowds, loud music, and sirens are all things that I don't care for. Why do you ask?"

"Maybe it's goofy, but I noticed the dog ears of Zhor's people and thought... if I took some kind of whistle to blow, and it was loud enough, maybe it would make them falter a little if we have to fight them."

"It would make *us* falter too," Tigress pointed out.

Qin grimaced.

"Maybe we could give you cotton balls ahead of time," Kenji said.

"Very high tech and sophisticated. I *do* have ear plugs." Laser tilted her thumb toward engineering. "The thrusters whine like a cranky baby when Viggo is in need of a tune-up."

"*Really*, Bonita," Viggo said with impressive indignity.

"You know it's true. Look, kid. I don't think a dog whistle is going to stop your enemies in their tracks."

"Wait." Qin held up a hand. "I don't know about a whistle, especially since we should go onto the station with full armor and our helmets up, but we *are* sensitive to extremely loud noises. It can be genuinely painful, and I would find it difficult to fight in such circumstances. Perhaps some kind of sound generator?"

"With a few tools and some basic materials, I could help make something like that." Mari rose to her feet.

"Could it be small enough that it wouldn't draw attention?" Kenji asked.

"Easily. Captain, may I check your parts cabinet?"

"Take whatever you need," Laser said. "Just promise me that if it works, you'll record footage of Zhor's *puppies* rolling around on the floor and grabbing their ears."

"I gladly will," Kenji said.

"We better find those ear plugs," Tigress muttered to Qin.

"Thanks for the help," Kenji said as Mari joined him in engineering. "Let me know if I can get you anything."

"Just my terraformer."

"That's the plan."

"I know. Thanks."

17

Mari gazed out the porthole in the freighter's lounge as she tried to find sign of Zhor's ship on the route she'd earlier determined it was on. Thanks to what was likely a slydar hull, no scanners in the system could see it. When Zhor had been speaking to Kenji, she'd been able to locate his vessel through its comm signal, and she'd attempted to subtly mark it with a virtual tracker, but it had failed to stick. That was strange, since she'd done such things before, and she'd thought she had successfully done so again. It was possible Zhor, or his ship's computer, had found it and erased it. She had the uneasy suspicion that Zhor not only sold astroshaman technology but might have incorporated some of it into his ship.

A part of her was tempted to contact her people and ask if they cared one way or another if Zhor was captured. If they did, and if she assisted with the arrest, perhaps her mother would be more inclined to let her stay out here. Maybe Mari could help her people in ways that went beyond laboratory research and engineering, and they would appreciate her for it.

That was wishful thinking. Her mother and the other

astroshaman leaders cared far more about their plans to leave for another system than petty thieves.

"Focus on one problem at a time," she murmured, though that was always hard, since she had the computing capacity to dwell on numerous problems simultaneously. A blessing and a curse. "First, we get the terraformer back."

She'd spent a couple of hours helping Kenji make a compact sound generator and hoped that would assist with their mission. Qin and Tigress had let them test it on them once and only once. They'd promised it was effective and had threatened dismemberment if Kenji pressed the button again.

It had hurt Mari's ears, as well, so she did not doubt that it would irritate their enemies. Whether it would be enough to keep them from firing, she didn't know. At the least, it could prove an opportune distraction. They'd designed it to hang on Kenji's belt and look like little more than a key fob.

She marveled a bit that Kenji genuinely seemed prepared to go out and confront Zhor and his people over Mari's device. Even though she knew that a pardon hung in the balance for him, she wouldn't have been surprised if he'd chosen not to risk his life over this. After all, the terraformer didn't mean anything to *him*.

It was possible that he intended to disappear on the station and leave Mari to deal with this with only Laser's crew for assistance, but if that were his plan, would he have bothered coming up with the sound generator?

For his sake, as well as hers, Mari hoped they made this work. She worried not only about the possibility of death but also what would happen if she and Kenji survived but failed, if they lost the terraformer and also the money the Kingdom had invested into this mission. She wouldn't receive asylum, and he might end up back in jail.

She thought of her Human List and how many items were left on it. Maybe she should have spent less time seeking the terraformer and put more effort into checking off items. By the time she returned to Odin, her mother might have learned where she was and be in the capital, waiting to drag her back.

The hatch opened, and Kenji stepped in.

"Hi," he said, waving at her.

"Hi." She remembered Laser's comments about flirting and smiled, even though it was silly.

He couldn't know what she was thinking about, but he smiled back. "What are you up to? Hacking networks?"

She thought about bringing up her concerns, but she didn't want to worry him.

"Trying unsuccessfully to locate Zhor's ship," she said, "and going over the items on my Human List."

"You mentioned that before. What's a *Human List*?"

"A list of items that I have wished for several years to experience. As I mentioned, I have led a secluded life, and many of the things that normal humans take for granted, I have not experienced. I have only read about them in books."

"Like cinnamon and chocolate?"

"Yes. Sweets were something I was eager to try. They did not disappoint."

"Astroshamans aren't allowed to have sweets?"

"My mother has not wanted me or my siblings to be influenced by the temptations of the biological body, as she calls them."

"So no potato chips, bacon, or ice cream, either?"

"In our ships and bases, we usually grow strains of algae and fungi that contain all the nutrients necessary for the human body and brain to thrive and interact optimally with our cybernetic upgrades. They are flavored and formed into various bars, patties, and loaves for variety."

"No wonder you left your people."

Mari wasn't sure if it was a joke, but she smiled in case it was. "They are not entirely unappealing, but I did wish to try other foods. I also wished to have a less rigid and structured life, at least for a time. I suspect that my mother will retrieve me eventually, even if you speak the truth and no longer plan to capture me, and then I'll have to go back."

Something flashed in his dark eyes—guilt? Maybe she shouldn't have mentioned his previous attempts to capture her. They had been getting along well on the voyage thus far.

"Well, you should try things now then. What's on your list that you haven't gotten to try yet? Maybe we can raid Laser's cupboards." He glanced toward the kitchen side of the lounge.

"I have not yet consumed alcohol. I also have not leaped from tall heights with artificial wings so that I can experience adrenaline and exhilaration and the sense of soaring like a bird."

"There probably won't be any hang-gliding on this mission." Kenji headed for the cabinets, probably to look for alcohol rather than artificial wings.

"I have also not experienced kissing or sex."

He tripped, though the deck was flat and should not have prompted such an action.

"You haven't had *sex*?" He gaped at her for a moment before recovering.

"Is that more typical an activity than hang-gliding?"

"I suppose it depends on the person. I just assumed—well, I guess you talked about test tubes and artificial wombs, so maybe it's not that shocking that your people don't have sex."

"We have no biological need to engage in coitus for procreation, but I find the notion of recreational sex fascinating."

"Yeah. That's what it is. Fascinating." Were Kenji's cheeks a touch pinker than usual? With his darker skin tone, it was difficult to tell.

"It is believed that all mammals descended from Old Earth stock have the physiological capacity for orgasm, but not all engage in mating activities outside of the breeding season."

His cheeks were definitely pink. Perhaps she had brought up a taboo subject. According to her reading, some human cultures were more comfortable speaking about sex than others. The Kingdom, as she recalled, was a bit stuffy and repressed.

Kenji took a long moment to investigate the contents of the kitchen cabinets before clearing his throat and speaking again. "Here we are. I think I'm only up to helping you with one item on your list, but hopefully, it'll live up to expectations."

Even before he pulled out two bottles of liquid, one amber and one a richer brown, Mari assumed he did not mean sex. Though it did make her ponder again whether she was physically appealing enough to attract a human mate. Or would her visible implants cause a response of repulsion from all unaltered men? She'd read about establishments where one could purchase sexual encounters but found the idea of such intimacy with a stranger unnerving. It would be better to engage in sex with someone who considered her cute. Perhaps not, however, cute but weird.

"Looks like Laser's options are tequila and Stellar Comfort." Kenji opened the bottle of darker liquid, sniffed it, and wrinkled his nose. "This is a traditional spacers' drink. As the label says, it tastes like stardust, moon regolith, and bad decisions."

"That doesn't sound that appealing."

"I agree. We'll try the tequila. But we better mix it with something if you don't want to get very drunk very quickly. I can imagine Laser taking shots, but she's not your typical lady."

"I am also not a typical lady. Should I consume *shots*?" Mari ran a quick search to make sure shots were what she thought they were and also to check the ingredients of tequila. Fermented cactus hearts? That seemed an odd base ingredient. Why would humans find fungi and algae strange when they drank liquids made from cactus?

"Probably not. We're meeting Zhor tomorrow. I assume you're

still planning to stay on the ship for that, but you may not want to be smashed in case there's trouble."

"That's correct. I do not wish to be a liability to Laser or anyone else."

"Me either." Kenji pulled out a couple of tumblers, found lime fizzop in the refrigerator, and proceeded to mix alcohol with the carbonated beverage. "Under no circumstances would I want to be hung over when meeting someone who thinks nothing of calling Qin and Tigress *kitties*."

"I will remain on the freighter and attempt to hack into his ship's network, mark it so the Kingdom Fleet can find it, and ideally sabotage Zhor's systems so that he and his forces are distracted during a crucial time."

"I like that idea. Do you think you can do it?"

"Certainly." Even though Mari was struggling to find the thief ship now, she trusted she would be able to gain access once they were docked at the same asteroid. "I have also downloaded everything about the station. It is all automated, with robots unloading any cargo that arrives and sending it down to the planet where other robots set it up. It is likely I can get on the station's network and take over some of the automation and further cause distractions for Zhor's people."

"Good."

Mari shifted from her pod to one of the chairs around the lounge's dining table. "This may matter little for your meeting, but I've learned that Zhor, and likely his bodyguards, were made in a lab in Sayona Station in System Cerberus for the Miners' Union Prince Hawkstar some thirty-five years ago. Zhor served the prince for a time, then stole a ship, and escaped to live life as a free person."

"So the prince raised him to be a good little minion and kick his enemies' asses, but then he ran away?" Kenji's mouth twisted as he brought over the drinks. "That sounds familiar."

"Do you refer to your origins? Or mine?"

"That's my story, except insert my father for the prince. And my genes are just a normal mix of his and my mother's, but he did engage in some gene editing during a time when that was illegal in the Kingdom." He handed her one of the tumblers and sat across from her at the table. "It's always great to know you were birthed —or created—to further your parents' ambitions."

"Yes." As she eyed the drink, it occurred to her that he could have put a tranquilizer in it, with the plan of taking her gear and locking her up until they got back to Odin.

But she'd consumed that latte he'd given her and suffered no ill effects. And Kenji *should* want her help for this mission. As unlikely as it might be, he seemed committed to it.

She studied him, not noticing fidgeting, sweating, tension in his face, or any other signs of being nervous. He'd been more flustered by the orgasm discussion. Now he sat comfortably, as if they were simply friends having a drink together.

Her heart ached as she realized how badly she wanted that. Friends, drinking, normal human experiences.

"Your parents also made you to be a good little minion and kick enemy asses?" Kenji sipped from his tumbler, not pointing at hers or doing anything to suggest he cared one way or another if she took a drink.

She decided she could trust him, at least until their mission was over. Maybe... she could even trust him after that.

"I believe the father I do not remember may have wished for children for the usual reasons, but he was killed, and my mother, who took in my siblings and me, did indeed raise us to be good little minions. Ass-kicking was not required, though we learned rudimentary self-defense skills, but we *were* required to study engineering and science in order to create that which our people will need when we one day settle a new system."

"So the unintentionally deadly terraforming device was your mother's idea?"

"She chose my field of study when I was young." Mari couldn't lie and say she'd been forced to make that specific device—it had simply been the logical way to create what her people desired—but would she have become an agricultural engineer if she'd been free to choose her own path? She didn't know. When she'd been little, she'd enjoyed music and the arts and had dreamed of being able to create beautiful things for a living. But the astroshamans, while not opposed to aesthetically pleasing cultural creations, had little use for frivolity and would not encourage careers in such fields.

"Huh." Kenji grunted. "So, we're all kind of the same. You, me, and this Zhor guy."

Mari sniffed her beverage, the sweet lime soda a far more dominant scent than the fermented cactus liquid, and sipped from it. "Will that make you hesitate to shoot Zhor if it's required?"

"No." Kenji drank again from his tumbler.

It took a moment for her taste buds to register the harsher bite of what had to be the alcohol.

"I do regret that I tried to shoot *you*," Kenji said after a few moments. He gave her a sad lopsided smile.

"Because you do not believe I deserve to be dragged back against my will to my people? Or because you are imbibing an alcoholic beverage, and it is altering your usual neurochemical state?"

"I haven't had enough to have altered anything yet," he said. "But I figured out a while ago that you don't deserve to be dragged anywhere."

"How long a while ago?"

"When you were asking the policeman for a drink of his latte."

"You still attempted to apprehend me after that."

"I know. I'm not that smart of a guy." There was the sad half-smile again.

"Perhaps you should consider an implant with extra computing power."

He stared at her, then threw back his head and laughed.

It startled her, as she hadn't meant the comment as a joke, but she decided the laugh was nice. It was the first time he'd done it around her.

He wiped a tear from the corner of his eye. "I'll keep that suggestion in mind."

After a few more sips, Mari asked, "How much of this beverage do we need to consume before we experience mild euphoria, relaxation, decreased social inhibition, and joy?"

"Probably not much for you, especially if you never drink. As for the rest, I usually get mellow and melancholy."

"Increased verbosity is another side effect." Mari took a longer drink, the cool fizzy bubbles from the soda tickling the roof of her mouth.

"So I've heard."

"You are already speaking to me more than you have in the past." She took another sip.

"That's not because of the alcohol. That's because I've been—like I said—regretting blaming you for things that it doesn't sound like you had anything to do with—or any choice in even if you did."

"If you're speaking of the invasion, those who spearheaded and eventually took control of that mission did not survive. The rest of us are not without blame, but it is unlikely that any astroshamans who are hiding out on Odin will bother your people. I know that I may never be able to walk openly in your cities without being arrested and shunned, but..." Mari lifted a shoulder. Was *she* feeling melancholy? If the alcohol had that effect on her, it would be disappointing. She had looked forward to joy and euphoria.

"You're probably right," Kenji said. "Sorry about that. Another system might feel less irritated with astroshamans right now."

"Perhaps, but traveling from System Lion would mean leaving my family behind. While I have wanted to leave them and experiment, I am not certain I wish to irrevocably cut ties with them and move to another system. I have never lived on my own, and even though I am reasonably intelligent and capable of researching how to do most things via the network, I am intimidated by the idea of existing in solitude. That is what I envision happening, since my people have traditionally been ostracized. It is why those of like minds originally banded together and formed the astroshamans."

"Enforced solitude *is* unappealing." Kenji finished his drink. "That's why I built Kay."

Half of Mari's drink remained, and she was debating if she could feel effects of inebriation. Perhaps she was slightly more mellow? Could that be construed as euphoria? "Robots can be good company."

"Yes."

"I forgot to mention it earlier, but when I examined your unit, I was impressed."

"My... unit?" Kenji glanced down at his lap.

"The K-45 robot."

"Oh, of course." His cheeks grew pink again. What had he *thought* she meant? Perhaps he was feeling inebriated.

"Not at Minister Dabrowski's upgrades, though those were impeccable, but at the fact that you created your Kay from what appeared to be scrap parts. I assume you do not have a foundation in mechanical engineering?" She raised her eyebrows.

"No. My father wasn't interested in giving me *that* kind of education. Knowing how to fight and fly were what he considered important, but I worked as a mechanic and taught myself things."

"It was good work."

"Thanks." He shrugged and looked down at the table, as if the praise made him uncomfortable.

That was not her intent.

"I'm not sure I can remember anyone complimenting me," he said, dryness in his tone. And... bitterness? "Not since my mother died." He lowered his voice. "I miss her sometimes."

"I regret that I lost my father before I got to know him," she said. "I think I would have liked him."

"More than your mother?"

"I shouldn't admit that, but from what I've read about him... yes."

"Your mother sounds like a dick."

"A dick?"

"Yeah, it's like a unit." He winked and took his empty tumbler to the sink and sanitized it. "I think you're a good person, Mari. I'm glad I didn't succeed in either of my attempts to capture you."

He sounded sincere. Maybe she truly could trust him, even beyond the mission. If so, that was heartening, because she wouldn't need to worry about betrayal. They would just need to survive the mission itself. She hoped that was possible. If Kenji died because he'd been helping recover her terraformer, she would deeply regret that.

"I'm sorry you had to come on my retrieval mission." Mari lowered her gaze to the table as he returned. "It's my fault. I mentioned to Minister Dabrowski that you might be able to describe the thief's ship since you got a better look at it in the Arctic. I had no idea that would end with the government compelling you to travel to another planet and risk your life arranging a meeting with a thief and a murderer."

"Given that I was already in jail at the time, and that's the only reason I was offered a chance to get out, I think I have to thank you rather than blame you."

"I do not wish you to die because of me."

"Let's both do our best to live then." Instead of sitting in his chair, Kenji knelt on the deck beside hers and gazed at her. "How's the alcohol? Do you feel relaxed and euphoric yet?" His brows rose, and he smiled faintly. "Joyful?"

A strange urge to touch his face came over her, but she resisted it, doubting he would appreciate physical contact from her. From cute but weird.

"I feel a little warm and flushed. From what I've read, this may be due to the buildup of acetaldehyde as my body attempts to metabolize the alcohol. It's possible I have an aldehyde dehydrogenase 2 deficiency."

"Probably." His smile grew less faint, and his eyes crinkled at the corners. "See if this helps."

He leaned in and placed his mouth on her mouth. A kiss.

It startled her, and it took her a moment to remember that a response was required, at least if she wished to show sexual interest in him. Did she? She'd stopped thinking of him as an enemy, but was he a suitable romantic partner? That might not be what he wanted. Perhaps he was only helping her with her list.

As her mind whirred, debating the wisdom of responding to his kiss in a positive way, her body made the decision for her, and she found her lips mirroring what his did, exploring the sensation of touching him and being touched by him.

He drew back, making her wonder if that had been the correct response. He looked a little surprised, then recovered, and smiled again before patting her on the shoulder and standing up.

"Goodnight, Mari."

As he turned toward the hatch, she asked, "Kenji?"

"Yes?" He sounded wary.

She *had* done the wrong thing. She assumed his swift withdrawal indicated he was not interested in pursuing further physical intimacy. "Why did you kiss me?"

"It was on your list, wasn't it?"

Ah. That *had* been all it was.

"Yes," she said.

"There you go. You help me build a dog-ear-attacking sound generator, and I help you with your list." His smile was fleeting, and he hurried out of the lounge without looking back.

That was unfortunate. She had enjoyed the kiss, though her body was now even more flushed. Maybe the alcoholic experiment had not been wise. She *clearly* had an aldehyde dehydrogenase 2 deficiency.

18

The space elevator was a fancy name for a thick cable that rose up from Sif's anchor station on its rocky red surface to a base carved into a huge asteroid that acted as a counterweight at the top. Sif didn't have as much gravity as Odin, but it still required a great deal of fuel burn for ships taking off from its surface, so most that came to deliver equipment and raw materials for the terraforming project used the elevator to save energy.

Kenji had never been to Sif or the asteroid base and watched curiously from the hatchway into navigation as Laser guided the freighter closer. They would have to fly through a huge cave-like entrance to reach the station inside, including its docks, manufacturing facility, and the tunnels where Zhor supposedly would show off what the terraforming device could do. Kenji hoped they could make the exchange before that happened.

He slid into the empty copilot's pod beside Laser, hoping she wouldn't mind. From what he'd seen, Qin and Tigress were more likely to be sparring or exercising in the cargo hold than hanging out up here, and Mari never presumed to enter without an invitation.

Kenji hadn't seen her since the night before and couldn't decide if he was disappointed or relieved. Somehow, he'd gone from regretting treating her unfairly to feeling kinship to her to finding her Human List amusing to kissing her. That had *not* been his plan when he'd walked into the lounge. It hadn't even been his plan when he'd gotten up to wash out his tumbler.

But she'd looked miserable sitting there, apologizing to him for getting him stuck on this mission, and he'd wanted to let her know it wasn't her fault and to make her feel better. Why he'd thought he should do that with a kiss, he didn't know. Other than that her list had put it in his mind. He wasn't even attracted to her. At least, he hadn't *thought* he was, not with the weird chips and implants, but there was nothing unappealing about the rest of her body, and one could probably get used to the cybernetic stuff.

Not that he *wanted* to get used to it. He was looking to escape the Kingdom, not pick up a girlfriend. Especially not a girlfriend from a whacky cult that looked down their cybernetic noses at normal humans.

Of course, *she* didn't do that. She seemed more curious than judgmental about normal humans. There had even been wistfulness and longing on her face when she'd spoken of her list. And vulnerability. He hadn't expected that from the woman who'd knocked him on his ass not once but twice. He also hadn't expected her to kiss him back like a normal woman. Why, he didn't know—it wasn't like she was an *android*—but what he'd intended as something of a pity kiss had turned out to be far more... intriguing than he would have imagined.

But it had been a mistake. He hoped his impulsive move hadn't led her to expect more. He already had Tigress leering at him; he didn't need anyone else undressing him with her eyes.

"I'm not reading any ships inside," Laser said from her pod, oblivious to his thoughts. The tip of the navigation arm touched her temple as she piloted the freighter closer to the asteroid.

The yawning entrance appeared even larger now, wide enough for a fleet of ships to fly through together. It was dark inside, a contrast to the stark sunlight brightening the top of the asteroid and glinting off banks of solar panels. Sif orbited not much farther out than Odin, so days out here were almost as bright as back home.

"Not even any automated ones belonging to the station?" Kenji shifted from musings about kisses to mulling over the coming confrontation.

He didn't have another two hundred and twenty-five thousand Union dollars, but Laser had dug him up a case that *looked* like it could hold thousands in physical currency. The plan was to make Zhor believe it did, at least long enough to get close. At which point, Kenji, Qin, and Tigress would have to fight. Against at least seven men with enhancements. Maybe more. It would be foolish to assume Zhor had shown his entire hand during that comm call.

But Kenji's team hadn't shown all of its cards either. They had Mari. He didn't doubt that she could remotely take over some of the station's automation to distract the thieves, and maybe even their ship.

"There are ships at the anchor point on the planet's surface," Laser said, "but not up here. Looks like nobody is expecting a cargo today."

"Zhor's ship may already be inside. Hidden."

"That's what I'm thinking. Wish I could get one of those fancy new slydar detectors, but they're only for Kingdom Fleet ships."

"Had I known you desired such a device, Bonita," Viggo said, "I would have asked Casmir to install one."

"His people just started manufacturing them, and they're all going to their military ships. Trust me, I asked."

"You should have had *me* ask. I am, after all, closer to Casmir than you are."

"Is that so?"

"Certainly. I've shown him appreciation since he first came aboard, whereas you were short with him."

"He likes my shortness. It's endearing." Laser looked over at Kenji. "Right, kid?"

"*I'm* charmed."

"I thought so. So, what's the plan? All I'm supposed to do is give you a ride and lend you the use of my combat forces." Laser waved vaguely toward the cargo hold to indicate Qin and Tigress. "But I'm partial to my combat forces, and I want to make sure they survive this. You walking in there with nothing but hope and a pretend case of money doesn't inspire my faith in your success."

"Don't forget my sound generator."

"Right, the dog whistle is sure to turn the tide." She eyed the fob clipped to his belt.

"It might," he said, though he admitted it looked more like something one would use to open a garage door.

Still, they'd tested it, and it put out an ear-splitting wallop. He also intended to wear ear plugs for the incursion.

"The plan is to go out and face them while Mari diddles with their ship and whatever computers are on the station that can cause distractions." Kenji expected Laser to scoff at the idea of computer diddling as a plan, but she leaned back thoughtfully in her pod.

"Tell her to take over the station's *robots* instead of just the computers," Laser said. "That's what Casmir would do. Robots that can beat up enemies."

"I don't know if there are robots." Kenji smiled, wishing Kay were up here with them, for he would have commentary on robots beating up enemies. But Kay was struggling to climb up and down the old freighter's ladders. The lounge and the crew cabins were on the middle level of the ship, so he'd opted to stay there today.

"You better hope there are," Laser said. "Robots are deadlier than computers. Even if they don't have weapons, they can stomp on your foot, and if they're heavy, that hurts. A lot."

Mari stepped into the hatchway, raising her eyebrows as she heard the last couple of sentences.

"Captain Laser has suggestions for your infiltration of the station's network," Kenji told her, his gaze snagging on her lips, his mind flashing back to their kiss.

Hell. He turned away. His wayward mind had better knock that off.

"I've gained access to the station network already." Mari's face was hard to read, and she didn't hold his gaze for long or comment on the kiss.

The freighter flew deeper into the unlit interior of the cave, and the flat gray wall of the station with six airlock docks came into view ahead. Their running lights played across them and the uneven rock of the rest of the hollowed-out interior. Here and there, more caves—or were those the tunnels Zhor had mentioned?—opened up to the sides.

"I will look for robots," Mari added.

"*Heavy* robots," Laser said.

"Yes, Captain," Mari said politely.

Laser navigated toward one of the docks; they were all open. As Viggo had said, there didn't appear to be any other vessels there. They were getting close enough now that they should have been able to see even a slydar-hulled ship.

Kenji found it odd that the thieves hadn't arrived first to set up the meeting spot to their liking, with Zhor placing his combat troops where they would have the advantage.

A proximity alarm went off on the navigation panel.

"I was afraid of that." Laser peered at her scanner display.

"We are now detecting another ship docked here," Viggo said.

"No kidding."

As the freighter glided toward one of the docks, that other ship came into view on the display, seeming to materialize out of the shadows. It was the same black-winged ship that Kenji had seen in the Arctic Islands.

"It is not training weapons on us," Viggo said, "or otherwise making aggressive moves."

"It's hard to be aggressive when you're attached to a station via an airlock tube," Laser said.

"I presume its copious weapons would work fine even in such circumstances."

"True."

"What about people on the station?" Kenji wanted to know how many of Zhor's bodyguards were waiting for them. "If they're already set up and waiting for us, your scanners should be able to see them, right?"

"It is difficult to detect people in combat armor," Viggo said, "since most of it is designed to give off no heat or energy signature."

"Meaning there could be an army waiting for us." Kenji grimaced.

"An army in combat armor, yes."

"Better hope our astroshaman is *really* good at diddling things." Laser eyed Mari.

Mari didn't respond or even seem to notice. She was gazing toward the ceiling, probably so busy with her network probing that she didn't hear.

"I have faith in her abilities," Kenji said.

He hadn't thought she'd been paying attention, but that earned him a quick smile. Good. Even if he'd made a mistake the night before, he didn't want her irked or disappointed in him. Although, as he considered her profile, he realized that he believed she would do her best to keep him alive and protect him even if she *was* irked with him. Lucky for him, she didn't seem to have a vengeful nature. He hoped she believed that he truly had no interest in trying to capture her for that bounty anymore and that he would also do his best to protect *her* on this mission.

As the freighter eased closer to the docking spot, the chip in Kenji's glasses alerted him to a local network, that of the station, but it was secured, so he couldn't access anything. If the thieves' ship had a network of its own, he couldn't detect it. He would trust that Mari and her more sophisticated hardware would find a way in.

The comm dinged.

"I think that's for you, kid." Laser waved for Mari to get out of sight.

She crouched low, her head below the console again.

When Kenji answered, the hooded Zhor appeared on the display in the same dim navigation cabin as last time. His army might be waiting inside, but he wasn't. Maybe he was the kind of leader who sent his people in to do the fighting while he remained in his cushy captain's chair.

"I'm ready for the demonstration and handoff when you are, Chisaka," Zhor said without preamble. "Don't forget to bring the money."

"I won't," Kenji said.

"Meet us at Experiment Tunnel Number Three in twenty minutes." Zhor smiled, showing off his rows of sharp teeth, and closed the comm without waiting for a response.

"Still smelling like a trap to me," Laser said.

"What does a trap smell like?" Viggo asked.

"What do you care? You haven't got a nose anymore."

"I'm mildly curious," Mari said, still crouching.

"Guns, burning hair, and despair," Laser said.

"Unappealing," Viggo said.

"You got that right. You do what you need to do inside to get the gizmo, kid." Laser pointed at Kenji. "I'll be here with the engine on, but we're not a match for them, so if their ship starts firing at us, we're going to be in trouble."

Yes. He could see railguns, cannons, and were those sun destroyers? And that was only on the side of the ship that was visible to them.

"More than trouble," Viggo said. "Should we get in a firefight with them, they will obliterate us in seconds."

"I will attempt to disable their weapons remotely," Mari said.

Laser eyed her. "I'm not sure I've even seen Casmir do that."

Mari shrugged.

Kenji wished she'd proclaimed with confidence that it would be a simple matter. He had faith in her taking over the network of an automated space station with nobody home; hacking into the weapons system of an advanced enemy ship was another matter.

Qin and Tigress clomped into navigation in their full combat armor, including magnetic boots that kept them firmly affixed to the deck. Now that the freighter had entered Sif's orbit, weightlessness acted upon everything in the cabin, and Laser's gray braid floated behind her head. Qin and Tigress had rifles strapped to their backs, carried space-rated grenades in bandoliers, and Qin also cradled a Brockinger anti-tank gun lovingly in her arms.

"We're ready to protect you, Kenji," Qin said.

"Here's your pretend money case." Tigress handed him a black box with metal hinges and decorative metal trim. It had an electronic lock pad.

"Thank you." Kenji tapped the button to order his pod to release him, and Mari stepped back to make room for him, but she bumped into Tigress's armored chest. Kenji reached out a hand to steady her. "Uhm, Captain Laser? Can I borrow one of the pistols in your armory?"

She'd suggested he take weapons, but he didn't want to assume, and be accused of theft, especially since Viggo had bluntly said Laser was reporting back to Dabrowski or Military

Intelligence or whomever on him. Kenji wished he could ask to borrow a full suit of combat armor too, but such gear was expensive, and it was unlikely Laser had extras. He already wore a galaxy suit he'd borrowed from her. At least the material was sturdy and would offer some protection in a firefight.

"Yes, of course. Help my girls if you can." Laser waved toward the hatch.

"I will, Captain."

Mari slid into Kenji's pod after he exited it. "The station's network is simple, as I believed it would be. I am working on getting into the ship's systems now." She tilted her head. "Interesting."

Kenji had been trailing Qin and Tigress out, but he paused in the hatchway to listen.

"They do *not* have a slydar hull," Mari said. "They are using astroshaman cloaking technology, which relies upon a generator and energy manipulation. It is not a paint application."

Kenji almost snorted at the idea of slydar simply being *paint,* as he'd seen the cost of outfitting ships with the special hull plating that fooled the eye as well as most scanner technology.

"I take it that's why they were able to sneak off Odin, even past their slydar detector?" Laser asked.

"Yes, and they have other technology from my people incorporated into their ship. I've thus far found it difficult to get into their network. I wasn't even able to verify its existence until a moment ago."

Kenji hesitated. "Meaning no diddling?"

"Not necessarily," Mari said, "but it could be more difficult than I anticipated."

Kenji blew out a slow breath, eyeing the other ship uneasily. Qin and Tigress had disappeared into the ladder well that led down to the cargo hold and the airlock hatch, and he had to follow, but this new revelation increased his unease. If Mari couldn't do anything to their ship and couldn't even the odds—or, ideally, tilt the odds in their favor—this could go very badly very quickly. Even if Zhor didn't mean to betray them, Kenji meant to betray *him*. As soon as the thief found out he didn't have the rest of the money for the device, this would turn into a firefight.

"I'll find a way to take that ship out of the equation." Mari looked back at him and must have interpreted his daunted expression correctly. She gave him a reassuring smile—or was that a *determined* smile? "Just because they have astroshaman technology doesn't mean they have an *astroshaman*."

"Yeah," Laser said. "I hear they're hard to pick up at seedy space bars."

"Unless you wander in with a bag of chocolates in hand," Kenji murmured.

The determined smile turned into more of a grin. "I cannot speak for the rest of my people, but that would indeed work to *pick me up*."

She said the words as if she was unfamiliar with the term, and Kenji found himself grinning too.

"I was wasting my time with a stunner," he said. "I should have dangled some Cosmos Crunchers at you when we first met."

"If those have chocolate, caramel, cinnamon, nougat, or nibs, it is possible you might have managed to kidnap me right then."

"Then we never could have come on this adventure together."

"How *horrible* that would have been." Laser made a shooing motion. "Get your ass over to that station before Zhor notices you're not showing up for his date and gets cranky."

"I suppose Cosmos Crunchers wouldn't work on him," Kenji said.

"Try a raw steak. And kid?" Laser looked back at him.

"Yes?"

"Don't screw this up."

Kenji's first thought was to give a snarky retort, but something in her eyes made him believe it was a sincere warning and that she maybe even cared. Because of the danger to her freighter? She'd probably only come along as a favor to a friend, not believing she'd be in any real trouble, but with the thief ship and all its weapons looming nearby, she had to be concerned. Possibly *more* concerned because this relied so much on him.

"I won't," he said seriously.

He nodded to Laser, nodded to Mari, and headed for the ladder.

Thank you, Kenji, Mari messaged him as he descended. *I appreciate you taking this risk to help me.*

He almost replied that he was only here for his pardon, but he realized that wasn't true, not anymore.

19

Mari sat in the copilot's pod, splitting her attention between locating resources on the station's network that she could take over and gaining access to the computer system on Zhor's ship. Not only was the ship's network well secured, but she had learned that a sentient intelligence controlled it, something similar to Viggo, but the astroshaman version. It blocked her every time she thought she'd found a way to burrow in. It was like playing chess with a master.

She clenched her jaw, irritated that this Zhor had been stealing from her people for a long time and was using her own technology against her. It might even go beyond theft. Some of the hardware and software now installed on his ship wouldn't have been easily acquired. He might have killed more than the Kingdom professor for it.

"I suppose some overly alert comm officer on that ship," Laser said, "would notice if we sent a message to the Kingdom Fleet and asked for help."

"When we're this close to the enemy craft, that is particularly likely," Viggo said.

"The Kingdom Fleet knows where we are," Mari said. "I told Minister Dabrowski our destination earlier, as soon as Zhor stated the meeting place. He said he would relay it to the knights that are stationed on Kingdom ships in the area. Some of them are waiting to help us, but they didn't want to spring their trap prematurely and scare off the thieves, so they've been keeping their distance."

"In the area?" Laser eyed her scanners. "I don't see any of their big warships closer than... eight hours away."

"Is that not *in the area*?"

"Not close enough to help when these guys could pummel us into space dust in seconds."

"I'm attempting to make sure they can't do that," Mari said.

"Is it working?"

"We'll see."

"I'm not reassured. Viggo, are you reassured?"

"I trust our astroshaman ally can navigate enemy networks at least as effectively as Casmir," Viggo said.

"I guess Viggo is reassured," Laser said.

"I'll try not to disappoint him." Mari took another stab at bypassing the other ship's security measures. The station's network was fully under her control now, but she needed to ensure Zhor couldn't fire upon their freighter.

Laser glanced at a display. "Our team is about to exit our airlock and head onto the station. The hatch leading into the arrival area is locked, so they're going to have to force it. I assume Zhor doesn't have a key and is doing the same thing right now. We're still not detecting any sign of people on the station."

"We can barely detect that there's a ship docked next to us, breathing its exhaust fumes all over my hull," Viggo pointed out. "I do detest astroshaman technology."

Mari smiled bleakly. She detested it when it was in the hands of people other than her own.

A message came in on her chip from Odin. Minister Dabrowski.

Greetings, Mari. Our stalwart knights asked me to check in on you, see if your team has acquired the terraforming device yet, and ask if you're ready for them to swoop in to pulverize Zhor's ship into stardust. I suspect not, since Captain Laser just sent me a message complaining about all the armament on said ship and pointing out that the Stellar Dragon, *er, the* Espada Ancha *doesn't have shielding sufficient to defend against it. She attached close-up imagery of that armament, including some state-of-the-art astroshaman weapons that we weren't anticipating. I admit when I asked her to help out with this, I wasn't expecting a thief's ship to have more than a modest amount of firepower. Thieves aren't traditionally known for picking fights.*

I was also not expecting it to have so much technology stolen from my people, Mari replied. *So far, I'm having difficulty hacking into the ship's network and gaining access to its computer systems. I'd hoped to be able to nullify its weapons. I haven't given up hope of doing so yet, but it is proving challenging. As for the terraformer, we don't have it yet. The team is about to board the station and meet with Zhor.*

There was a pause before Dabrowski's answer came in, reminding her that he was back on Odin. He was on Odin, and the Kingdom ships with the knights were eight hours away. When they'd been coming up with this plan, she'd imagined help being closer.

Mari bit her lip, tempted to ask him to give the order to send the Kingdom ships in immediately, but Zhor had to be aware of them. He would have someone at a scanner station keeping an eye on the space around the station, and if several warships abruptly headed this way at top speed...

Keep working on it, came Dabrowski's reply. *If anyone can deal with astroshaman technology, it's you, right?*

She was tempted to reply that she was an agronomist, not a computer-hacking specialist, but that wasn't entirely true. She had the knowledge and experience to do this. And she *would* do it. *That is correct. I will find a way to deal with the ship, but please be prepared to send in the knights.*

Excellent. They're ready. Just give the word.

As they'd been conversing, Mari had been inventorying what the station had that she could use now that she controlled its computer system. She noticed internal security cameras. If she could grab the feeds and display them in here, she and Laser could keep an eye on their team's progress—and they might be able to see what their freighter's scanners couldn't. Armored enemies lying in wait inside.

"May I take over your forward display?" Mari asked.

"Have at it," Laser said. "The view of fifty weapons pointing at us isn't that inspiring. Maybe you could replace it with tropical fish in an aquarium."

Mari replaced it with a grid of camera displays. Few lights were on in the station, and she could barely make out the open arrival area that all six airlock docks emptied into. Beyond it, cavernous bay after cavernous bay extended deeper into the asteroid. Most of those bays were filled with manufacturing equipment except for aisles wide enough for automated vehicles to drive down on tracks. Giant robotic arms worked in sync, building and wiring frames for solar panels for use on the planet below.

Beyond the bays, a corridor led to smaller laboratories and supply rooms, but none of the cameras showed views of them. Zhor's men might be hiding back there. Aside from the robots, she didn't see a sign of anyone moving in the bays.

"Wait." Mari pointed at huge metal double doors barely visible in the dim lighting. They were one of several sets of them along the walls in the bays. "I bet those are the experiment tunnels."

"Zhor said for our people to meet them at Tunnel Three," Laser said. "Is there a camera that shows what's behind those doors?"

Mari double-checked, but most of the cameras focused on the manufacturing bays and the arrival area. "No."

"What about Zhor's dock? See if there's a camera pointing at it and if his hatch is open."

"I am now detecting a small energy signature somewhere deep in the station," Viggo said as Mari cycled through the video feeds.

"Not a bomb, I hope," Laser grumbled.

"I do not believe so. One moment."

"Here." Mari zoomed in with one of the cameras in the arrival area. "That should be the airlock his ship is attached to."

"The hatch is open." Laser sighed. "I'm messaging Qin to warn them. His people are already inside."

"I have isolated the energy signature and will put it on the forward display." Viggo bumped one of the camera feeds off to show them the readout from his scan.

Mari pressed her lips together as she recognized the energy signature. "That's my terraformer."

Laser's eyebrows flew up. "They've activated it? The part of it that can destroy every living thing all around it?"

"No. That would be a much more significant signature. It's just on, not doing anything." Not yet, Mari amended silently.

The idea that her terraformer, a device designed to help create life where life could not otherwise exist, could be used as a weapon disturbed her greatly. It wasn't as if she hadn't known about the possibility when she'd been building it, but it hadn't concerned her when she'd believed nobody but her own people would have access to it. *Her* people would never use it as a weapon.

"But it *could* do something?" Laser asked.

"It could. But Zhor mentioned wanting to demonstrate it, right? It is possible he only intends to show that it could be used for its intended purpose. If his goal is to sell it and be paid for it, then that is all he *should* want to do."

"What happens when he finds out the kid doesn't have the money for it?" Laser grumbled.

"They will likely have to fight to acquire it and escape, but that was always the plan." Mari nodded to the camera feeds. "And I am prepared to assist them, thus to swing the odds in their favor."

She used the station's network to reach out to the terraformer. Earlier, when it had been off, she hadn't been able to do so or even locate it, but now she ought to be able to give it commands remotely. Assuming Zhor hadn't changed the passcode or figured out another way to lock her out.

"I hope so," Laser said. "I don't think the kid's dog whistle is going to cut it."

Mari wasn't so dismissive—she'd seen Tigress and Qin react to the sound generator by gasping and flinging their hands over their ears—and thought Kenji had come up with a good idea, but she agreed that he would need more help than that.

Fortunately, the robot arms building solar panels weren't the only robots inside. There were also numerous mobile security constructs. She surfed along the network, flicking power switches on.

Laser looked over at a smaller display that still showed the enemy ship—and all of its weaponry. "You figure out how to assist with *that* yet?"

Mari hesitated. "I'm still working on gaining access to their ship's computer."

"As soon as our team starts a fight with theirs, that ship is going to start blasting us."

"I'll get in," Mari said.

"I hope it's soon enough to matter."

"It will be."

Laser looked darkly at her—or did that expression convey skepticism that she could do what she'd promised?—but didn't speak further.

Mari *could* gain access to the ship, and she *would* do it in time to help.

It took plasma cutters to force open the locked hatch leading onto the station, an act of vandalism that made Kenji uneasy. Zhor, he had no doubt, wouldn't mind and was likely doing the same thing over in his airlock, but what if, after all this was done, Military Intelligence sent Kenji a bill for any damage his team did to the station during their mission?

"We're in," Qin said, her voice muted to Kenji's ears.

All three of them had put in ear plugs for this. They could still hear each other over their helmet comms, but hopefully, the noise from the sound generator wouldn't be as debilitating for them as for their enemies.

Qin traded the plasma cutters for her big gun and pushed open the hatch.

Kenji let her and Tigress go first, then stepped out of the airlock tube that attached their freighter to the station. Since they wore combat armor and had more weapons, letting them lead made sense, even if it felt cowardly. He'd grabbed a DEW-Tek pistol and a stunner from the armory, but he had to carry the money case and look like a businessman prepared to make a trade, not a supersoldier about to lay waste to the enemy.

Few lights were on in the station as they crept out, their helmets up and oxygen tanks secured. Viggo had detected a breathable atmosphere over here, no doubt for the sake of the human visitors who regularly brought cargo, but it didn't hurt to be safe. There was no gravity to speak of, so they had to step carefully, relying on the magnetic soles of their boots to keep them from floating off and getting stuck without anything within reach to grab.

As they walked into the spacious arrival area, high ceilings disappearing into shadow above, Kenji eyed the airlock where Zhor's ship was docked. The hatch was open. Interestingly, it didn't appear that it had been forced open. Maybe Zhor had an astroshaman lock-picking device.

"This room is all clear," Tigress said quietly.

"We've got rats in the station though." Qin pointed her Brockinger at the open hatch.

"I like rats." Tigress patted her rifle.

The women led the way into an attached bay filled with automated manufacturing equipment, robotic arms taller than Kenji assembling solar panels. He activated the night vision in his helmet so he could more effectively peer down the narrow aisles between the rows of equipment. There were a lot of places for people to hide. Tigress and Qin also looked left and right—and up —as they continued forward.

They reached a row of unmoving security robots on treads, each with two articulating arms with graspers and two arms that ended in cannons. They had boxy heads with the vague semblances of faces, power indicators glowing a soft red and reminding Kenji of eyes.

"The station's security forces," Qin said.

"I've fought robots like that before." Tigress pointed her weapons at them. "I'm surprised we haven't triggered them yet."

The robotic heads swiveled to track them as they passed. That made Kenji uneasy until a message came in from Mari.

I have control of the security robots. I will have them assist you if there is a fight. We are monitoring your progress and looking for the thieves with the station's cameras. If I spot them, I will try to warn you ahead of time.

Thank you.

"Mari says she's controlling those robots and that they'll help us if there's a fight," Kenji said.

"Just like Casmir," Qin said.

"What?" Tigress asked, not having been there for the robot-take-over discussion in navigation.

"By the end of our travels, he'd gotten good at hacking into enemy networks. And he was *always* good at taking over people's robots and making them his own. It's probably why the astroshamans wanted him."

Kenji blinked at the new information. "Wanted him... dead? Or wanted him for themselves?"

"High Shaman Moonrazor attempted to recruit him." Qin kept scanning their surroundings intently as she spoke. "He was in the middle of helping Tenebris Rache infiltrate her base at the time, so it might not have been the most sincere offer, but I heard she made it again later."

Kenji had a hard time imagining the affable—and extremely human—professor signing up for the cult, even if he enjoyed building and interacting with robots.

"I'm glad you're working with Mari," Qin said softly, glancing at Kenji. "And have been talking to her on the trip."

Not just *talking*, he thought, but he doubted Qin knew about the kiss.

"I was wary of her at first," Qin added, "because she's an astroshaman, and a lot of astroshamans have tried to kill me and my friends, but... I think she's more like us than them. And she seems lonely. I know how that feels. It's hard being different. I was fortunate to reunite with my sisters. Mari's siblings don't sound that great."

"Yeah." Kenji hadn't realized Qin had spoken to Mari that much during the trip. It made him wish he'd spent more time in the lounge with all of them. Especially since he agreed with Qin that Mari was different. And worth talking to. "They hired me to capture her."

"Oh." Qin looked over at him. "She didn't mention that."

He wouldn't have blamed Mari if she had. It seemed like the kind of thing that might come up during a girl chat. *You know that guy riding along with us? He's a dick who's been trying to collect my bounty for the last week...*

"I hope you're not planning to capture her anymore," Qin said.

"No."

Tigress was eyeing another manufacturing area, then turned abruptly, pointing her rifle toward shadows up ahead. Kenji hadn't seen any movement but tensed, his finger tight on the trigger of his pistol.

The outline of the first of several sets of double doors had come into view. They looked like they were made from solid metal and were tall enough that massive vehicles could drive through them.

"Checking something." Tigress prowled farther ahead of them. "For a second, I thought I caught something on my helmet's scanners."

Have you seen anything on the cameras yet? Kenji messaged Mari.

Not yet, she answered promptly, *but they don't show what's behind those doors. Also, you should know that Viggo detected the energy signature of my terraforming device. It appears to be ahead of you and to your left.*

That was the direction Tigress was heading.

Thanks. Kenji's palms were damp inside his gloves, his nerves kicking into overdrive as the moment he would meet Zhor, or at least his people, grew closer. He was glad Mari was watching over them and would find a way to help.

As he and Qin advanced together, trailing a dozen yards behind Tigress, they passed the first set of closed doors. The words *Experiment Tunnel Number One* were printed in large letters above them. More sets of doors were visible ahead, all on the left side of the linked bays they were walking through. The larger right side of the bays was reserved for manufacturing equipment.

Tigress paused at the second set of doors but only for a moment before continuing on.

"I think I detected movement at the ones up there." She pointed her rifle toward what had to be Tunnel Number Three, though Kenji couldn't yet read the lettering. What he *could* see was that, unlike the other doors, these were open.

"That's supposed to be our meeting place," Kenji whispered.

He and Qin quickened their pace as much as they could. Jogging in zero-g with nothing but magnetic soles to keep them on the floor was difficult.

Tigress crept up to the open doors and leaned around the corner, pointing her rifle inside as she examined a lightless room or—if the labels were to be believed—a tunnel.

"Your kitty is leering at us," came a gruff voice from inside. Zhor.

"He's in there with those six warriors," Tigress said quietly. "They're armed, and they're looking at me like I'm lunch, but I can handle them. A few of them anyway. I'll leave some for Qin."

"Generous," Kenji murmured.

"I enjoy a rousing battle," Qin said.

Kenji wouldn't mind skipping the battle, but he doubted that was an option. He glanced back the way they'd come.

We might need those robots soon, he messaged Mari.

This time, she didn't answer right away. Hopefully, she was only distracted for a moment and not by something as ominous as the enemy ship attacking their freighter.

"Do be a good boy and bring the money for the exchange," Zhor called.

"He's holding a metal sphere," Tigress added. "Is that what you're expecting? Or is it a bomb?"

"It should be the terraforming device." Kenji leaned past Tigress to peer inside.

The spacious tunnel went back farther than he could see, with no lights inside helping with visibility, but it looked like these doors might be the only way out. That made sense if the area was for experiments. It would be designed to be sealed off so whatever was unleashed in there couldn't escape.

As promised, Zhor stood inside, about twenty feet back from the doors, with his six fighters. He held up the sphere.

Kenji hadn't yet seen the terraforming device in person, but it matched the picture that had been on the Nexus site, as well as what Mari had described.

And Zhor had come with the exact number of guards who'd been with him when they made contact. Was it possible he *didn't* mean to betray Kenji?

It didn't matter, since the plan had always been for Kenji to betray *him*, but he would have preferred it if the thief were the one to go back on the deal first. Even though Zhor was wanted by numerous governments, and might be a murderer, Kenji had first encountered him doing exactly what *Kenji* had been trying to do— scavenging goods to make ends meet. That made it hard for him to condemn the man.

"Let's see the box, boy," Zhor said. "Throw it in here, and then I'll toss the device to you."

"I don't trust this guy," Tigress murmured.

"Nor do I," Qin said.

The warriors were shifting and flexing in their armor, eyes gleaming with eagerness while Zhor stood quietly among them. They were all armed with guns, grenades, smoke bombs, and other projectiles Kenji couldn't name on their bandoliers. It was probably only in his imagination that he could hear them growling and slavering behind their faceplates.

As Kenji lifted the case to show it to Zhor, he eyed the

hinges on the doors, wondering if they could be operated manually. Maybe as soon as they did the trade, he could lock Zhor's people inside, and his team could retreat. How strange that Zhor had chosen this spot. Maybe it wasn't the dead end that it appeared.

"I'm tossing it in now." Kenji drew his arm back to propel the case inside.

"Excellent." Zhor's tone turned wry. "Your father would be so pleased."

Kenji had been about to let go, but he halted, his suspicions roused. "You know him?"

"We've crossed paths."

If Kenji hadn't truly been his father's son, he would have worried more, but even if Zhor had looked him up, all he should have found was the truth. Still, something about his tone made Kenji hesitate longer.

"Send in the money, boy," Zhor said coolly and hefted the sphere like a ball he meant to throw.

Reminded that there wasn't anything in the case for him to lose, Kenji pushed it inside. It floated through the air until it reached the men and one of Zhor's warriors lifted a hand to stop it.

Kenji was surprised when Zhor threw the terraformer before checking the contents of the case. It was a poor throw, and it sailed too high for Kenji to reach.

Qin crouched, as if she might spring up to catch it, but that would have meant releasing her anti-tank gun. She and Tigress let the sphere sail over their heads in favor of keeping their weapons trained on the men.

Afraid it would be damaged if it struck a wall or manufacturing equipment, Kenji spun and raced after the sphere as well as he could in zero-g. With the lack of gravity, the sphere didn't arc downward, instead continuing to sail through the bay. It outpaced

Kenji, and he realized he couldn't catch up. He would have to hope it could take a hit.

Then he noticed a yellow indicator blinking on its spinning surface. Alarm flashed through him. What did *that* mean?

Abruptly worried that letting it hit something could be very bad, he redoubled his efforts to catch it. As he passed a manufacturing robot bolted to the floor, he used it to push off from with both feet and dove after the sphere.

Certain Zhor had thrown it over his head on purpose, Kenji hoped the women could protect his back as he flew across the bay, manufacturing equipment speeding by under his belly. He gained on the sphere, but he didn't know if it would be quickly enough, since the far wall was coming up fast. He wished he had jet boots.

As Kenji reached out toward the device, fingers stretching, someone opened fire behind him. *Several* someones.

Crimson and orange DEW-Tek bolts shot out of the tunnel.

Kenji caught the sphere scant feet before it struck the wall. He pulled it close to his chest, cradling it and twisting so his back hit first. The galaxy suit protected him from injury, but the jarring thud didn't feel good. An instant later, something like a lance slammed into his shoulder. He yelped in pain, almost losing his grip on the sphere. One of the DEW-Tek bolts had found him.

"Get behind the equipment," Qin ordered.

She and Tigress were holding their position and firing back at Zhor's people, using the doors for cover as much as they could. They growled with determination, not giving ground.

"No kidding." Kenji winced and glanced at his shoulder.

Again, the suit had protected him, but smoke wafted from the material, and he would have a grapefruit-sized bruise later.

Still gripping the sphere, he groped for a way to pull himself behind cover. He'd bounced off the wall and couldn't reach it. He patted at his belt for the sound generator but feared he was too far away for it to be as effective as he needed it to be.

While he hung becalmed, more energy bolts ricocheted through the bay, pinging off walls and equipment. To his side, a solar panel blew up, shards flying in dozens of directions. Kenji grunted as several struck him, though they were like the patter of rain against his suit compared to the DEW-Tek bolt.

While twisting and trying to protect himself, he spotted one of the robotic arms working below him, happily affixing silicon wafers to its panel and oblivious to the threats. Kenji hooked it with his boot and pulled himself down to the floor.

The yellow indicator light on the sphere was still flashing. Maybe it was his imagination, but it seemed to be flashing *faster* now.

Mari, what does this flashing light mean? Kenji messaged, though he still hadn't received a reply to the last message. *Any chance you can turn this off remotely?*

The firefight stopped, and that worried Kenji almost as much as when it had started. Unable to see Qin and Tigress through all the equipment, he hurried back through the maze of robotic arms and solar panels.

"That was unexpected," Tigress said, her voice puzzled.

Kenji finally made it back to them and found them looking at the doors—the *closed* doors.

Qin glanced back at him. "They shut themselves inside."

"They never even opened the case," Tigress said. "It was just hanging there while they opened fire on us."

"You mean Zhor doesn't know that we didn't bring him any more money?" Kenji crept closer, confused.

"Uh, is that supposed to be blinking like that?" Qin still had her rifle pointed at the doors, but she was staring at the device.

Kenji still had it in his arms, and it vibrated faintly against his chest.

"It's blinking faster and faster," Tigress said, alarm replacing her puzzlement.

"Like a *bomb*." Qin looked like she wanted to shoot it.

Zhor's voice sounded from a wall speaker. "Kenji Chisaka, perhaps you should have checked with your father before pretending to make a purchase on his behalf. Oh, and next time you intend to pull one over on an experienced businessman, don't come to the meeting in a ship known to be allied with the Kingdom government."

Horror thundered into Kenji as he realized exactly how he'd been set up.

"Shit!" Kenji gawked at the blinking indicator—it *was* flashing faster. All he could think was that it was counting down to destruction.

Or *life*, as the thing was meant to give. Life through destruction.

Mari, he messaged again. *I really need you! How do I turn this thing off?*

"Ah, but you won't get a next time, I'm afraid," Zhor continued on, supreme boredom lacing his voice. "If I read the specs correctly, that is now going to terraform the entire station—with you and your kitties in it."

"The hell it is." Kenji set it down and shouted, "Let's get out of here," to his allies.

He raced toward the arrival area as fast as he could, waving for the women to follow him.

The terraforming device? came Mari's reply. *My apologies for the delay. I was deflecting an attack on my personal chips by the enemy ship's sentient computer. And now that sentience is on the station network with me. I will work through this. One moment.*

We don't have a moment!

Before Kenji, Tigress, and Qin made it halfway back to the docks, a huge firewall door slammed down between one bay and the next. It landed right in front of them, blocking the route back to the arrival area.

They were trapped in the same part of the station as the sphere.

"Qin, your big gun!" Kenji pointed, having no idea if even an anti-tank weapon would work on the giant firewall door, and worried they didn't have enough time anyway.

Once that device started spitting out whatever technology scrambled molecules, would they be instantly killed? Or would it take hours for everything to unravel? If they hadn't already run through two bays and lost sight of it, he would have ordered her to shoot *it*.

"Stand back." Qin pointed her weapon at the firewall door.

Tigress grabbed Kenji, pulling him behind the nearest manufacturing equipment. Qin fired, and an explosion ripped through the bay, blinding light flashing. Kenji lifted an arm to shield his eyes as the tinkle of broken glass—broken solar panels—came from all around them.

Someone attempted to arm my terraforming device, Mari's reply scrolled across Kenji's glasses—he almost missed it.

Yeah, we noticed. Zhor did it, and then he threw it at us, and locked his people inside a tunnel. Has it gone off yet? How much time do we have?

"This is a heavy-duty door," Qin called. "It's going to take another round. Stay there."

I have deactivated it, Mari said. *Please bring it to me, and—*

And what? It won't turn us into dirt? It's safe to pick up?

It is safe. As I said, Zhor has stolen astroshaman technology, but you *have an astroshaman.*

Words he never in his life would have thought he would find comforting. But he did.

Thank you, he replied.

You are welcome, but be careful. For the moment, the enemy ship's sentience is on the station network with me. It also has access to the cameras. Zhor will soon know—

Another boom sounded, Qin firing again. The wrenching of metal echoed through the bay.

Kenji peered back the way they'd come. The doors to Tunnel Three were still closed, Zhor and his men hiding inside. But they would figure out soon that the sphere had been deactivated. Kenji had to get it now or risk losing it again.

"That should do it." Qin had successfully blown a hole in the door large enough for them to pull themselves through. "I do enjoy brute force now and then."

"Hang on." Kenji ran from his hiding spot and toward the sphere. "I'll be right back."

Something rocked the station, and he almost misstepped and ended up floating helplessly in the air again. Qin hadn't fired again. Who had?

Mari, did something new happen? I'm getting your device.

Distant clangs came from the direction of the docks. Something else was definitely going on.

Mari?

The device was where he'd left it and no longer flashing. Kenji bit his lip, swooped in, and picked it up.

Two more ships have arrived, Mari replied. *They were also camouflaged, so we didn't see them until they were on top of us. They are identical to Zhor's ship, and they have us trapped.*

Kenji swore and turned to run back toward the others, but the doors of Experiment Tunnel Three flew open. Zhor and all of his troops charged out, firing straight at him.

DEW-Tek bolts slammed into his torso, the galaxy suit not enough to keep pain from pummeling him. Kenji twisted, diving for the manufacturing equipment and reaching for the sound generator even as he tried to keep his attackers from blowing up Mari's device. Why the hell he worried about *that* right now, he didn't know.

"Need some help!" Kenji cried as solar panels and robotic arms blew into hundreds of pieces under the assault.

He scrambled behind equipment, his body throbbing with agony from at least four places where he'd been hit. With shaking fingers, he found the button on the fob. He pressed it and pointed the end in the direction of his foes. The high-pitched squeal blasted his eardrums even through the plugs, and it was all he could do not to drop it.

Alarmed shouts of rage and pain echoed from the walls, and Zhor's men stopped firing.

Kenji shifted the sound generator to his other hand and tucked Mari's device under his arm so he could draw his pistol. As he leaned out from behind the equipment to fire, a furious armored figure charged straight at him.

The other men were grabbing their helmets and writhing in the air, half having lost their footholds on the floor, but Zhor launched himself at Kenji. Behind his faceplate, his canine features were contorted with pain, but that didn't keep murder from blazing in his eyes.

Kenji fired, holding down a sustained blast as he targeted the seam between his enemy's helmet and torso plate. His aim was true, but his blast only burrowed into the spot for a second before Zhor reached him and tackled him, gauntleted hands scrabbling for the sound generator.

While Zhor was focused on that, Kenji grabbed the man's rifle. He tore it out of Zhor's grip, hurling it toward the ceiling. Unfortunately, Zhor latched onto the sound generator. He yanked it out of Kenji's hand and crushed it in his grip. Zhor roared as it broke, the squeal ending with a plaintive bleat.

Though agony assaulted his entire body, Kenji twisted and kicked out, slamming his boot into Zhor's armored hip. Pain and fear lent him strength, and the blow hurled his foe a dozen feet. Zhor crashed into a solar panel, knocking it from its mount.

Panting, Kenji fired, again holding down the trigger for a sustained blast. It was his only shot at getting through the armor and hurting the big man.

As Zhor struggled to right himself and find a way to push off toward him again, Kenji kept firing. This time, he aimed for the seam between arm and shoulder, tracking it even as Zhor whirled about, looking for his rifle. Zhor spotted it, but it floated far above them. Kenji's pistol fire bit through his seam, and Zhor yelled in pain, jerking around to hide the vulnerable spot from view. Kenji aimed at another seam.

Crashes and thumps came from the doors by the tunnel. Fearing the rest of Zhor's men would spring on him now that the noise had stopped, Kenji risked glancing in that direction.

But Tigress and Qin had come back to help him. Not only were they engaging the six fighters, but the station's security robots had come with them. They fired at and grabbed the men, trying to force them back into the tunnel.

Kenji was about to send a *thank you* to Mari, but Zhor got his feet behind him and shoved off one of the robotic arms. Once again, he arrowed toward Kenji with murder in his eyes.

Kenji fired, aiming at his faceplate, but there wasn't time for his blast to melt through. Zhor reached out, resorting to using his hands, but he didn't look like he would have any problem tearing Kenji's head from his neck.

Kenji ducked low and shoved off another piece of equipment to dive out of the way. Zhor lunged for him, but Kenji jerked away, and the gauntleted fingers missed him by inches. Bracing his back against the floor, Kenji kicked upward. He caught Zhor in the crotch—too bad it was as armored as everything else.

As Zhor flew upward, Kenji realized he'd made a mistake. The man's trajectory would take him close enough to his rifle to grab it.

But before he got close, something slammed into Zhor's chest. "Duck, Kenji!" Qin yelled.

The round from her anti-tank weapon blew with a boom and a flash of light. The shockwave struck Kenji, knocking him back against the floor. He already hurt all over, so it hardly made a difference. Through the smoke, Kenji saw Zhor fly backward across the bay. Relief surged through him. He didn't know if that would kill Zhor, but at least it would take him time to get back into the fight.

Tigress clanked over to grab Kenji. "Come on. The rest of his team is locked inside again, but Laser said there are more ships, and that's going to mean more men.

"Right." Kenji hadn't forgotten.

Realizing he'd lost hold of Mari's device during the skirmish, he whirled and searched for it. If after all this, some inadvertent blow had destroyed it...

No, there it was. He pushed himself into the air and grabbed it.

Tigress caught him by the ankle and pulled him back down. "Your suit looks like hell," she said. "Are you all right?"

Throbbing pain pulsed through his body as Kenji shook his head. "No, but I can run."

He might collapse and die later, but he was determined to get the device back to Mari first.

"Good." Tigress pulled him back into the aisle, where Qin gave him a thumbs-up.

"Let's get out of here," she said.

As their little team maneuvered toward the hole in the firewall door as fast as they could, the station's security robots following on magnetic treads, another clank sounded. Kenji groaned, fearing some new obstacle, but as Qin had been about to crawl through the hole she'd made in the door, it rose back into the ceiling.

I am battling the enemy ship's sentience for control of the station's network, Mari messaged, *but I have managed to command the firewall doors to release you. Unfortunately, we're in a bind. Captain Laser says to hurry back, so we can leave, but I fear these other ships might object to our freighter departing.*

Kenji, his injuries making it hard to keep up with the others, waved Qin and Tigress to sprint back to the arrival area ahead of him. Just as the airlocks came into sight, the two hatches to either side of the freighter's dock flew open. Men—more of the canine troops—in combat armor rushed out, blocking the escape for Kenji and his team.

"Back, back," Kenji ordered.

He shot twice at Zhor's men, hoping to catch them before they were prepared to fight, but they returned fire promptly. Once again, Kenji dove for cover behind manufacturing equipment. They were outnumbered, so there was little more that he could do. Besides, he doubted his galaxy suit could take any more hits. A warning was flashing on his helmet's heads-up display, letting him know that it had lost integrity. No kidding.

Qin and Tigress swore as they opened fire, but they were also forced to run for cover as crimson blasts pinged off their armor. Even the hardened warrior women knew when they were outmatched.

Kenji opened his mouth to suggest they run back to one of the tunnels so they could fight where they could limit how many enemies came at them at once, but more clangs and a wrenching noise echoed from the other direction.

The doors to Experiment Tunnel Three opened again, and four of Zhor's men walked out. Their armor was dented and blackened, and one had a crack in his faceplate, but that didn't keep them from striding back into the station.

Kenji and his team were surrounded.

20

"*La madre que te parió!*" Laser swore, lunging to her feet.

Mari didn't know what that meant, but she agreed with the sentiment.

Kenji's team was in trouble, the freighter was now surrounded by three enemy vessels, and it was only a matter of time before they all opened fire. Mari was keeping Zhor's ship busy by fencing with the intelligent computer, but she still hadn't been able to get past it, and she worried the two newcomers would also have astroshaman technology.

She was in the middle of investigating their network defenses when Laser slapped her on the shoulder.

"We have to help them." Laser pointed at the camera feeds on the forward display, several showing the men streaming through the arrival area, firing on Kenji's little team. "Those are my girls over there."

Not waiting for an answer, Laser lunged out of navigation and raced to the ladder. Mari hesitated, thinking she could do more from there, but she ought to be able to watch Laser's back at the same time as she battled virtual enemies.

As she followed Laser, Mari sent a quick message to Minister Dabrowski to let him know Kenji had acquired her terraformer. If only the Kingdom ships weren't so far away. She and the others would have to get out of this mess by themselves.

As she descended toward the hold, Mari also rechecked the station's network. She had been on the verge of finally slipping into the enemy ship's computer when all the backup had arrived, distracting her. She scowled, aware of the intelligence over there spotting her and driving her away from its virtual borders again. For now, she had to focus on the station, on making sure she maintained control of the security robots and directing them to help their people.

When she reached the cargo hold, Laser was already halfway into her combat armor, growling and cursing as she donned the cumbersome gear. She tossed a rifle over to Mari.

Busy maneuvering the robots, and investigating the new ships, Mari almost missed catching it. "I've got ten of the station's robots circling our people and deflecting fire. Give me a second, and I'll get them shooting at their enemies."

"Good. We *need* a female El Mago right now." Laser headed for the airlock hatch, affixing her helmet as she went.

Mari didn't know what that meant either, but she nodded as she groped for more that she could do. Ah, the firewall doors. If she could lower another one, she might be able to cut the remains of Zhor's original team off from Kenji, Tigress, and Qin. Then they would only have to shoot their way past the newcomers to escape.

Since Kenji had the terraformer, all they had to do was get out of the station and figure out a way to escape the asteroid without being obliterated.

"Come on!" Laser ran through the airlock tube, fast and spry for someone Mari had assumed would be beyond her fighting years. She carried two rifles and a netted bag that held grenades.

With her new rifle in hand, Mari hurried after her. But the firewall door—she needed to drop that. She checked the cameras to make sure there was still time.

Watching the videos on her tiny lenses wasn't ideal, and she had to cycle through the feeds to find Zhor's men. They'd almost caught up with Kenji, Tigress, Qin, and the cluster of robots, all of whom were busy defending themselves, firing at enemies to both sides. There was one firewall door left between her allies and Zhor's team.

Mari flicked a software switch, and the door slammed down, almost squashing one of the dog men. Zhor's people would find a way through eventually, but Kenji's team ought to be able to make progress toward the airlock now that they had a reprieve from behind. And they did. Tigress and Qin led a charge toward the enemies in the arrival area.

Kenji followed more slowly, his gait uneven. Had he been wounded?

Mari commanded the robots to roll along at the team's sides, firing to help clear the way.

"Hah," she whispered as she trailed Laser into the airlock chamber on the station. She felt triumphant at their team's progress.

Laser glanced back at her.

"We're evening the odds," Mari promised, wanting the captain to know she was being useful.

"You keep doing that." Laser had reached the open hatch into the station but paused there.

Shouts echoed throughout the arrival area, and DEW-Tek bolts streaked about, bouncing off the walls. Shrapnel floating all over the place promised some of them had found more vulnerable targets. A robot head tumbled slowly through the air not ten feet from the hatch.

More than a dozen armored men were either in the arrival area or firing from the protection of their airlocks. Tigress, Qin, and Kenji came into view, the security robots helping deflect fire as they advanced, but the team was still more than fifty yards away. Too many people were firing at them, and the women's armor was charred and smoking. The heads and arms of several security robots had been blown off.

Fortunately, the firewall door that Mari had lowered was still intact, keeping Zhor's original team from firing at their backs. But booms and clangs echoed from it, promising they were trying to get through.

Qin fired her anti-tank gun, the round slamming into the armored torso of a man leading a charge toward them. It exploded, smoke clouding the area as he flew backward, crashing into two of his allies. *That* weapon had the necessary heft to do damage to armor, but how many rounds did Qin have left?

"These are not good odds, kid," Laser muttered.

She didn't run out into the bay, instead dropping to one knee with her rifle pressed into the crook of her shoulder as she took aim from the partial cover of the hatchway. Mari activated her targeting software and leaned out beside Laser. She fired at enemies in the arrival area as she focused the rest of her computing power on finishing her investigation of the two new ships. She hadn't yet detected sentient computers on them. Maybe, unlike Zhor's ship, they didn't have astroshaman technology. That would make them easier to hack.

As she worked on sneaking into their systems, Mari kept firing at enemies and guiding the robots that were helping Kenji's team. She was glad she had enough chips and power for the multitasking, because her allies needed all the assistance they could get.

Laser kept firing as well, trying to drive people out of the way and clear a route for their team to reach them. By using sustained blasts, she burrowed into seams in their enemies' armor. One man yelped, spun, and fired at them.

Laser calmly ducked back into the airlock as crimson bolts

bounced off the hatch beside her. Mari was less experienced with firefights and sprang back into the airlock tube with a startled squawk, tripping over her own boots. One of the enemy bolts ricocheted back, missing her faceplate by inches.

"We've got their attention now." Laser leaned out and fired again, then grabbed one of her grenades to throw.

Mari had lost her focus on the robots, but she hurried to regain control. Their team was only twenty-five yards away now. She sent the robots ahead of them, their big cannon arms booming.

One of the robots bumped into one of Zhor's men, knocking his magnetic soles from the floor and sending him tumbling into the air. He could still shoot, but he struggled to control his body or find anything to hang on to.

Thanks for the help, a message came in from Kenji.

You're welcome, Mari distractedly sent back as she directed more robots to knock enemies from their feet. Though she was busy concentrating, she felt a burst of gratitude that Kenji had noticed and appreciated her help.

She managed to take control of the weapons systems on the two new vessels and clenched her fist. That had been *much* easier than with the other ship.

But she couldn't yet order them to open fire on their leader. Laser's freighter was in the way.

Mari needed to take command of their navigation computers and maneuver them all to one side of the docking area. "One step at a time," she breathed to herself.

The floor quaked as an explosive went off. It wasn't one of Laser's.

We're going to try to make a rush and reach you, Kenji messaged, *but— Look out! Some men are coming your way.*

Laser swore, threw another grenade, then backed into the

airlock tube with Mari. "We might have to retreat into the cargo hold and make a stand there."

Several armored men stormed into view in front of the hatchway, one snatching a floating colleague out of the air and pulling him back down to the floor. They pointed rifles straight into the tube at Laser and Mari, barely noticing that Laser was firing at them, hitting their seams and faceplates with pinpoint accuracy.

Mari ordered several of the robots toward this new group of attackers, hoping to ram them so they couldn't rush into the airlock tube. But the men were too fast. Shots hit Mari and Laser, forcing them farther back.

A bolt struck like a hammer blow to Mari's galaxy suit. It wasn't as painful—or deadly—as it would have been had she only been wearing clothing, but it made her cry out and brought tears to her eyes. She scrambled back, wanting to get out of there.

One man lunged into their airlock tube, swinging his rifle at Laser, who wasn't retreating as quickly. She ducked and tried to ram into him. Her armor gave her extra strength, but he was young, enhanced, and fast. He had the advantage. When he grabbed Laser, and they grappled, her knee buckled. She swore with pain as he forced her down and tried to tear her rifle out of her hands.

Though Mari wanted to keep retreating, she rushed back in, drawing even with the fight. She braced herself on the side of the tube for support and side-kicked Laser's enemy in the hip.

It startled him and knocked him back, his boots coming off the bottom of the tube. Laser yanked her weapon back from him and fired at his faceplate, holding down the trigger. As he struggled to right himself in zero gravity, she kept firing. The sustained blast melted through his faceplate and burned into his skull.

He screamed and tried to whirl away, but it was too late for him. Laser shoved him out of the way and rushed forward to face the next challenge, but Kenji, Qin, and Tigress had reached their airlock and were clearing it of enemies.

As Mari was about to let out an elated cheer, Viggo spoke.

"Bonita," his voice came over their helmet speakers, "we have a problem."

"*Another* one?" Laser growled, waving their allies into the tube.

"Yes, a large one. *More* ships have arrived."

"We've got more company!" came Laser's warning over Kenji's helmet comm, and he couldn't stifle a groan.

He had the terraforming device, Qin and Tigress were still with him, and with the help of all those robots, they'd made it to the airlock. He'd started to believe they could actually get away, but now...

"More ships, Viggo says," Laser added. "That bastard must have brought an entire armada. Hurry inside. If there's any way we can get out of here, we'll take it."

Kenji had thought Qin's blast had put Zhor out of commission, if not killed him outright, but maybe he had survived. Maybe he was still back there giving orders to his legions of men.

"You go in first, Kenji," Qin said, standing shoulder to shoulder with Tigress and firing into the arrival area, keeping the remaining troops from getting close. They nudged him back into the airlock.

He hesitated, reluctant to leave them to fight while he ran.

"We'll be right behind you," Tigress said, glancing back.

"Okay." Kenji spun and rushed through the airlock tube, his hip, shoulder, and back pulsing with pain with every step.

Mari and Laser had already disappeared into the cargo hold. He hoped Laser could do something from navigation. He was *sure* Mari could. She seemed able to help from *anywhere*. He'd seen her firing at their enemies with the steady mechanical mien of an android even as she controlled a dozen security robots, directing them to fire as well.

When Kenji reached the cargo hold, he found Mari waiting inside, though she wore a distracted I'm-diddling-with-the-enemy's-networks expression, and he knew she wasn't simply standing there. Laser had already climbed up to navigation.

"I've got something for you." Kenji pressed the terraforming device into her hands, making sure she had it before letting go, then turned to check on the others.

"Thank you." Though clearly still distracted, Mari smiled at him.

Something struck the freighter, making the deck quake and her smile drop.

Kenji swore. He'd been afraid of that. The other ships had to be firing on them.

Tigress and Qin charged into the hold. They slammed the exterior and interior airlock hatches shut, and Qin pressed a button to retract the tube.

Qin shook her head. "There's a rip in the tube. The captain won't be happy about that."

"If the entire ship gets blown up," Tigress said, "I doubt the rip is going to bother her overmuch."

"Possibly true."

"Whoever has convinced Zhor's two ally ships to fire at *his* ship," came Laser's voice over a speaker, "I appreciate that."

Mari smiled tightly.

Before Kenji could ask about the newest arrivals, something else struck the freighter. A jolt almost knocked his boots off the deck. Mari might be helping with the battle, but they weren't out of trouble yet.

Qin and Tigress sprinted past him, hurrying toward the ladder.

"Are we going to have to fight more, Captain?" Qin called up. "Do you think they'll board us?"

Kenji didn't hear the answer, but he wanted to know what was going on, so he hurried after them. When he was halfway up the ladder, Mari laughed, startling him.

He peered down at her.

"The new ships belong to the Kingdom Fleet," Mari said, her voice light with relief. "They're not firing on Laser's freighter but on Zhor's three ships."

A clunk sounded as something else struck the hull.

"Are you sure?" Kenji asked.

"We're being hit with debris from Zhor's ships. I managed to maneuver them all to one side of the docking area, but we're still very close to them."

She'd managed to maneuver them? He would ask about that later.

"A big enough piece could damage us as much as weapons fire." Kenji, wanting to see the scanner display in navigation for himself, continued up the ladder. "How many Fleet ships are there?"

"Three warships." Mari climbed after him. "I believe... Yes, they have slydar hulls. That is a new development and why we didn't realize we had allies so close. When my people battled the Kingdom warships a few months ago, they did not have that technology themselves."

"Times change."

"Indeed."

Kenji and Mari squeezed into navigation behind Tigress. Laser and Qin had already taken the pods, Laser's fingers flying over the controls so they could leave—or at least get out of the way and take less damage as the Kingdom ships fired on the other three vessels.

"One of those is the *Osprey*," Qin said as the freighter eased away from the dock—and from the battle.

"I saw," Laser said. "Never thought I'd be so glad to see that pompous Captain Ishii. His big butt is making it crowded in here, but I'm going to forgive him, as long as he doesn't misfire and pulverize us."

Railgun and cannon blasts lit up the dark cave outside of the station, slamming into the hulls of the enemy ships. Interestingly, Zhor's two ally ships weren't firing back. Mari's doing? Zhor's ship, with all the advanced weaponry, *was* launching attacks, but the warships had excellent armor and shields. It didn't take long for the signs of battle to dwindle.

"I am monitoring the comms," Viggo said as the freighter headed for the asteroid's exit. "The warships have disabled Zhor's vessels and are demanding they surrender and prepare to be boarded. The Kingdom intends to take back all of the stolen goods they find and arrest the thieves."

"Good." Mari held her terraformer to her chest, as if she'd recovered a lost baby.

Kenji, who'd been positive the thing would kill him ten minutes earlier, had no desire to touch it ever again. He did touch *her*, resting a hand on her shoulder. "We would have been scragged without your help. Thanks, again."

She smiled warmly at him and inclined her head.

"*We* helped a little bit too." Tigress tapped a finger on her armored chest, dents and scorch marks covering it.

"Yes, you did." Kenji nodded at her and Qin. "Thank you too."

"No problem." Tigress thumped him on the shoulder.

Between her strength and her armor's enhancements, it almost sent him smashing against the wall. Thankfully, his galaxy suit offered some protection, but Kenji couldn't keep from gritting his teeth in pain from his earlier wounds. He hoped the freighter's sickbay had some powerful drugs.

"If you don't mind," Tigress added, "I'll take a testimonial from you for our new business."

"From me?" Who would want a testimonial from him?

"Yes. We helped you stay alive in there, right? Once we've satisfied a few clients, we'll have less trouble picking up new work. *And we'll be reputable enough to be able to lease a location for our office anywhere in Zamek City.*" Tigress sniffed. "No need to deal with uptight business owners who don't want superior genetically engineered neighbors."

"Are you hoping to get more work like this?" Kenji looked toward the battered ships on the display and raised his brows; he couldn't imagine anyone voluntarily signing up for gigs like this. It had almost killed all three of them.

"Sure," Tigress said. "It's what we do."

"Challenging work is rewarding," Qin said.

Rewarding, right.

I am glad I'm not a bounty hunter, Mari messaged Kenji directly.

I'm glad that I've retired from the business, he replied.

A wise decision.

I thought so. After all, I failed to capture even one astroshaman woman.

Because you didn't bring the Cosmos Crunchers you spoke of.

That is obvious in hindsight.

As more things are. Mari rested a hand on his shoulder. *Do you need help getting to sickbay?*

Probably.

Do you want me to bring the tequila?

He managed a lopsided smile for her. *Probably.*

Mari sat in a pod in the freighter's small sickbay cabin, watching Kenji as he slept on the combination bed and exam table.

He'd taken several hits from DEW-Tek bolts during the battle, and despite Laser's promise that she had skills and expertise as a medic, Mari had been concerned ever since she'd learned how wounded he'd been. Qin and Tigress had also been injured through their armor, but they'd said they had genetic enhancements to ensure rapid healing and hadn't stayed in sickbay longer than it took to grab some painkillers.

Since then, they had been in and out to check on Kenji, but there were some lengthy comm messages going on between Laser and the knights on the warships, so they had mostly been up in navigation. His last visitor had been Kay, who'd stayed for an hour, until Viggo had suggested a robot with a mechanic's skills would be useful in assisting with repairs to the damage the freighter had received in the battle.

Mari was glad they hadn't taken a lot *more* damage. If the knights and other Kingdom leaders determined that she and Kenji had performed adequately and had done all that had been asked of them, she would consider the mission victorious. She hoped they wouldn't be held accountable for the destruction inside the station.

"I don't think they'll blame us for that," she murmured.

Kenji, his eyes still closed, did not respond.

Laser had injected him with strong painkillers, as well as several sets of nanites programmed to mend his injuries, and he'd been sleeping—or was he unconscious?—for several hours. Mari had brought the bottle of tequila as well as her dwindling bag of candy-coated chocolates to sickbay in case Kenji would like to enjoy either of them. A few days earlier, she hadn't had much interest in sharing the delicious chocolates with anyone, but she would gladly offer them to him now.

They had worked together—and *trusted* each other. Unfortunately, she had no idea if she would ever see him again once they returned to Odin.

Greetings, Mari, a message from Minister Dabrowski came in. *I understand from Captain Ishii, Sir Asger, and Captain Laser that you successfully retrieved your terraformer, that Kenji worked with you all instead of against you, and that a great deal of astroshaman technology is currently being recovered from Zhor's ship.*

Mari zeroed in on only one of those statements. *You doubted that Kenji would help us?*

I personally believed that he would help, but as my colleagues have pointed out numerous times, in addition to his upbringing being less than stellar, we basically coerced him into going on our mission. Even I was holding my breath to see what he would do after we sent the money to him. There's a reason I asked Laser to be the one to fly you out there.

Besides keeping an eye on him?

Because I knew she, Viggo, Qin, and Tigress would be able to thwart Kenji if he tried to take over the ship and sneak off to some nearby station to disappear.

He's an honorable ally. Mari leaned over and rested a hand on Kenji's arm. *He would not have done that.*

I'm pleased to hear that. Do you need anything else? We'll all have a thorough debriefing when you get back to Odin.

Mari thought about asking about her own status. She had little doubt that this had been a test for her as well as for Kenji. But maybe that was something that wouldn't be determined until the debriefing.

I am curious why you didn't tell us that camouflaged Kingdom warships were so close. We all would have been bolstered if we'd known. And less scared. Mari was fairly certain that even Laser hadn't known.

My apologies for withholding that information, but Captain Ishii insisted. By that point, we suspected Zhor had quite a bit of astroshaman technology, and Military Intelligence worried he might intercept and decrypt any communications going to the freighter.

I don't think he did. But I do wonder... Because she'd been on the station's network at the time, Mari had heard Zhor's words over the speakers. *I don't think he ever fell for the ruse. At the least, he knew Kenji wasn't working as his father's representative.*

No? One wonders why he came to the meeting then.

Zhor tried hard to kill Kenji.

I'll ask Military Intelligence to do some digging, Dabrowski said. *It's possible Kuchikukan Chisaka is holding a grudge against his son for running away—or for some other reason.*

You think he might want Kenji dead? That he might be willing to pay an acquaintance to kill him?

If so, we'll find out. And we'll let Kenji know.

Dabrowski said goodbye, and Mari leaned back in her pod. She didn't know what Kenji planned to do in the future, but if his father was gunning for him, he might have a hard time even if he moved to another system.

"How's our patient?" Laser stepped gingerly into sickbay, favoring one leg. She'd also grabbed painkillers earlier. Maybe she should have programmed some nanites for herself.

"He hasn't woken yet."

"Not even for candy and tequila? What a weird kid. You might have to wake him with a kiss."

Mari fumbled her bag of chocolates, and it fell on the deck. "What?"

"Like in Qin's fairy tales. The beautiful princess wakes the handsome prince from the sorceress's evil spell with a kiss. Though I've got to admit, you two aren't exactly prince and princess material." Laser eyed them both dubiously.

"My mother is a high shaman. And I believe Kenji's mother was a noble."

"Sorry, I don't think that would get you into anybody's fairy tales."

"It sounds like they suffer from a paucity of variety."

"That's not a lie." Laser stepped up to the side of the exam table to check on Kenji.

Mari, realizing Laser wasn't truly suggesting that she kiss him, picked up her bag of candy and scooped up several pieces that had fallen out. She debated whether the time spent on the deck would have contaminated them with germs.

"Go ahead and eat those. Viggo's vacuums keep this place better sterilized than a clean room. Has he had them demonstrate the new incineration mode for you yet?" After eyeing the medical scanner display, Laser swatted Kenji on the chest. "Wake up, kid. I've got news."

Mari stood up and would have protested Laser's treatment, but it proved effective. Kenji emitted a faint groan and opened his eyes, blinking blearily at them.

"I think he would have preferred being woken with a kiss," Mari muttered.

"You took too long."

"News?" Kenji mumbled, focusing on them.

"I thought you might like to know that Zhor is alive but that the knights captured him when they went in to mop up the station. He was pretty badly injured, but he was hiding out in some office in the back, hoping he wouldn't be noticed. They've got him in the brig of one of the warships now."

"I hope he ends up in a penal asteroid mine," Kenji said.

"That's a possibility. Or maybe they'll make him clean up the mess his people made *here*." Laser waved in the direction of the station. "Anyway, our work is done. We're heading back to Odin. I guess there's going to be a big meeting, and the government will figure out what to do with you two."

"Should we be worried?" Kenji asked Mari.

Mari thought of all the things still up in the air, such as whether her mother had found out yet where she was, and could only say, "I don't know."

"I was hoping for something more comforting."

Laser touched her chest. "*I* thought you did all right. Both of you. Now, give him some tequila." She swatted Kenji again before walking out.

"I think that was a compliment," Kenji said, "though her bedside manner is somewhat lacking."

"I noticed." Mari thought about mentioning the suggestion of a kiss but decided this wouldn't be the appropriate time, and she doubted Kenji wanted to do that again with her anyway. He'd only been helping her check an item off her list. "Chocolate?"

She offered him the ones from the bag, not the deck.

"Thank you." He accepted and nodded to the bottle. "Have you been testing your, ah, what deficiency was it you thought you had?"

"Aldehyde dehydrogenase 2."

"Yeah, that. Maybe we should share a drink together again and see how it goes. Scientists have to replicate their experiments before writing up papers on the outcome, don't they?"

"It's a good idea, yes."

"I thought so."

21

When Captain Laser's freighter came down once again onto the landing pad across from Drachen Castle, it was morning on Odin, and no fewer than twenty uniformed people waited outside.

From the copilot's pod in navigation, Kenji eyed them on the display, trying to tell if they were all Kingdom Guard and Fleet uniforms, or if local policemen were among them. He didn't see Minister Dabrowski, or any of the leaders who'd been at the late-night meeting at the police station, and he worried that didn't bode well.

He and Mari had done all Dabrowski asked, but they'd also been a part of completely trashing a Kingdom space station, and he had no idea if the military would be able to get that twenty-five thousand Union dollars back from Zhor. They'd captured him, but that didn't mean Zhor hadn't already whisked the funds off to who knew where in another system.

Grimacing, Kenji rose slowly from his pod. The nanites had done their job on the return trip, so he couldn't complain about his recovery, but he worried that the queen, or whoever would ultimately determine his fate, had decided he hadn't helped enough and that the mission hadn't been worth it. Or what if the Kingdom government had always intended to use him for this one mission, then dump him back in a jail cell?

He would like to think Dabrowski wouldn't do that, but it wasn't as if the robotics professor owed him anything. Kenji hadn't even been a legitimate student of his.

Kay and Mari were waiting in the cargo hold, prepared to depart. She held her terraforming device and her backpack and had changed from Laser's borrowed galaxy suit back into her regular clothing.

The hatch was already open with the ramp lowered, and some of the uniformed men were visible outside. Kenji was tempted to stay where he was until they came in to drag him out, but Laser had followed him down the ladder. Even though she hadn't insulted him as frequently on the return voyage, Kenji doubted she would offer him a spot among her crew.

"It is good to be back in the full gravity of my home world," Kay proclaimed. "And look at all of those armed men waiting outside to greet the returning victorious heroes."

Kenji arched his eyebrows. "Is that us?"

"I consider myself a victorious hero."

"All you did was hang out in my cabin while we battled the bad guys," Kenji said.

"I assisted the freighter's intelligence with repairs on the voyage home. Victoriously and heroically."

"In that case, maybe those troops are here to pin a medal to your chest."

"A pin would scratch my paneling. A magnet would be more appropriate."

"I'll be sure to put in a request."

Since Mari was already standing in the hatchway, Kenji took a bracing breath and joined her.

"Do you think all of those people are here for us?" Mari sounded a little trepidatious too.

That quiet uncertainty seemed odd coming from the powerful ally who'd saved all of their butts on that station. The memory of her fighting and holding her own against armored combat troops, all while controlling the station's robots and taking over the enemy ships, was... inspiring. If the Kingdom higher-ups weren't idiots, they would give her the asylum she sought. Promptly. In addition, they should put her on the payroll with fat bonuses every month.

Kenji wished *he'd* been even half as impressive out there. The fact that his father's name had once again been a bane rather than a boon didn't surprise him that much, but it made him wonder if he would ever escape that dreadful legacy.

"I assume they're here for me," Viggo said, "to honor my magnificent presence. And perhaps they'll buff and paint the copious dents and scratches in my hull that I received during this mission."

"Oh, I'm sure. That *has* to be what they're here for." Laser checked a display, indifferent to the uniformed guards waiting outside. "Your ride is here, kids."

A purple shuttle landed within sight of the ramp.

"That could be Queen Oku herself, Viggo," Laser added. "Do you think she enjoys buffing and painting freighters?"

A human-like sniff issued from Viggo's speakers. "I am able to detect your sarcasm, Bonita."

"Good."

"We'll go face them together," Kenji told Mari.

Before they could start down the ramp, thumps sounded behind them, Qin and Tigress jumping out of the ladder well. They trotted across the hold toward the hatch.

"Are you leaving the ship with us?" Mari asked them curiously.

"No," Qin said. "We just wanted to see you off and wish you

luck in dealing with the Kingdom authorities. They can be... difficult, but it's *much* better than when their old king was in charge."

"Yup. It was good flying with you, even if we didn't get time to have sex." Tigress winked at Kenji.

"We?" Qin rolled her eyes. "*We* were never interested in that."

"You're so staid, sis."

Qin and Tigress waved and bid them good luck as two Kingdom guards walked up the ramp. They bowed to Laser, then gestured for Kenji and Mari to follow them to the purple shuttle. Kay ambled along after them.

"Sit inside," one man said. "It's just a short hop."

"Are we going to Royal Intelligence Headquarters?" Kenji guessed, glancing at Mari.

"I am not certain where the debriefing is," she said.

They could easily have walked to the headquarters building, but the guard pointed them to seats without comment.

Despite Laser's joke about the queen, nobody royal or more interesting than the castle guard and a pilot waited inside the shuttle. As soon as Kenji and Mari sat, with Kay grasping a hand grip for support, it took off. The pilot flew them over the intervening street, castle wall, and past guard towers to land on a small pad on Drachen Castle's grounds.

"Oh, how wonderful," Kay said. "As a student of history, I've read about Drachen Castle, but I've never been permitted inside. Do you think there will be a tour?"

"Hopefully not of the dungeon," Kenji muttered.

He didn't know if this was better or worse than Royal Intelligence Headquarters. Would they meet Queen Oku? And if so, why?

It had been unnerving enough talking to Minister Dabrowski when the queen had been with him in the background. If Kenji met her in person, he would feel the need to apologize for everything he'd ever done at his father's side, especially since she was probably *aware* of everything he'd ever done at his father's side. Though she wasn't much older than he, Kenji trusted her chief superintendent of Royal Intelligence had briefed her thoroughly on him.

More guards waited to lead them into the rambling castle, its stone walls originally laid nearly two thousand years earlier, shortly after humans had first colonized Odin. The interior had been remodeled to modern tastes, and amenities like force fields, wall displays, and robotic butlers were apparent as the group strode through several halls and up marble stairs to a large conference room that overlooked the ocean.

A guard who stood outside raised a hand to halt them and ran a scanner over Kenji and Mari.

"You will find that my parts are sublimely assembled and that there is no hidden monitoring equipment within me," Kay informed the guard.

"Uh huh. You'll have to wait outside anyway. This is a top-secret meeting, and you and your memory chip aren't cleared for recording."

Kenji expected Kay to protest.

Instead, he asked, "May I have a tour of the castle while I wait?"

"You can stand next to the door and study that wall over there." The guard pointed across the hallway at a plain stone wall decorated with a couple of bland landscape paintings.

"Is it historically significant?" Kay asked.

"Very."

"Hm."

"Maybe Minister Dabrowski will give you a tour after the meeting," Mari told Kay.

"Oh, yes. *He* knows how to treat robots well."

The guard rolled his eyes and waved for Kenji and Mari to go inside.

Queen Oku was indeed sitting at the table within, bodyguards lining the wall behind her, as well as two six-and-a-half-foot-tall black crushers. Oh, sure, *they* were cleared to watch the top-secret meeting.

A guard near the door cleared his throat, and Kenji remembered one was supposed to bow, if not grovel on the floor, before royalty. In the vid dramas, the knights always dropped to a knee with their heads lowered. Kenji opted for a deep bow. Mari paused uncertainly, then emulated him. He was fairly certain women were supposed to curtsy, but Oku smiled and didn't point that out.

General Heim and Chief Superintendent Van Dijk were also present. This time, there weren't any police officers in the room, and Kenji hoped that was promising.

He smiled encouragingly at Mari, but she was looking warily toward a glass door leading to a balcony outside the room. Someone in a brown cloak with the hood pulled up, the wind whipping at its hem, stood at the railing, her back toward them as she gazed at the sea.

Kenji supposed it could have been a man, but the figure wasn't large, and the pointed shoes were feminine.

Mari sighed, her shoulder bumping his as they were directed to seats. "I regret that I didn't get to do all the things on my list," she whispered.

"Oh?" He wondered why she was worried when things seemed to be looking up. "You should have come to my cabin on the freighter last night."

"Did you have a hang-gliding apparatus in the closet?"

He snorted, having forgotten that was also on her list. "Something like that."

Her face grew curious, as if she were piecing together what he'd meant. Kenji decided not to explain further. Besides, it had been a joke. He didn't truly think it would be a good idea for them to sleep together anytime soon. He didn't even know if she'd liked their kiss.

As they sat, Minister Dabrowski walked in, another crusher trailing after him. He wore a suit jacket over a T-shirt, the lapels not quite hiding the cartoon robot underneath, and carried a tool satchel, as if he'd hurried here after instructing students in a university lab. Most of the faces around the table were grave, or at least masked with practiced professionalism, but Dabrowski smiled and waved at Mari and Kenji. He plopped down next to Chief Van Dijk, his tools clattering.

Mari perched uneasily on the edge of her chair, glancing again at the balcony, though the woman hadn't turned around. Kenji sat next to her, feeling the protective urge to stay close.

"Good morning, Kenji and Mari," Queen Oku said. "We thank you for helping us to retrieve the astroshaman technology that had been stolen from Odin—admittedly, after it was stolen from your people." She nodded at Mari, who had rested the terraforming device on the table in front of her.

General Heim eyed it like it was a snake.

Kenji noticed Oku hadn't taken credit for ordering the military to collect astroshaman technology from the wreck; maybe she hadn't been the one to do it. Queen Oku had only been coronated a couple of months earlier.

"You're welcome, Your Majesty," Kenji murmured, though almost everyone was looking at Mari. His thought that he might end up in jail and that *she* was the jewel that they might put their efforts into claiming came to mind again.

"We are also pleased that you returned to us, Kenji," Oku told him, meeting his eyes. "Some people believed it a certainty." She glanced at Dabrowski. "But there were others who doubted." Her next glances went toward Heim and Van Dijk.

"You can hardly blame us, given his background, Your Majesty," Van Dijk said. "It's not as if he is an innocent boy who only happened to be born to a terrorist; he *assisted* his father for years. We couldn't be sure he isn't even now his father's servant."

Kenji curled a lip at that.

"*Most* of us couldn't." Van Dijk gave Dabrowski a puzzled frown. "I'm still not sure how Minister Dabrowski was so certain. The fact that Chisaka had crashed some of his lectures hardly seemed an unassailable endorsement."

"Only good people with a genuine love for learning come to my lectures." Dabrowski winked at Kenji. "And don't forget the DNA."

"Blood is hardly conclusive." Van Dijk lowered her voice and muttered, "We know who shares *your* DNA."

General Heim's bushy brows drew together, suggesting *he* didn't know. Kenji didn't know either, but he was far more interested in what in his own DNA had drawn their attention. All it should have proven was that he was his father's son and had been genetically enhanced. Unless his father had ordered the scientists to splice in something odd to give him his faster reflexes. He would snort if he ended up sharing some of Tigress's cat DNA—or Zhor's canine DNA.

That seemed unlikely though. All he had was an edge in a race or a fight with a normal person. He wasn't blatantly superior.

"Tell us about your mother, please, Kenji." Dabrowski extended a hand toward him. "I'm curious. I'm sure you know that you share your parents' genes, but do you know the rest?"

Mari looked curiously at him. Everyone in the room did.

"I... don't, Professor. Er, Minister."

"Casmir," Dabrowski offered. "Your mother was Johanna Wyss, correct? Of the nobility?"

"Yes. She raised me while my father was off doing—" Kenji curled his lip again to let them know he didn't approve, "—his terrorist things, but she died in an auto-flyer accident when I was eight. I... always hoped that was all it was. An accident. Later, I sometimes wondered if he'd arranged it. I remember them fighting about custody over me—by then, he was notorious, and she'd gotten a powerful security system to keep him away, but it didn't work. Once she was gone, he took me. I would have had nowhere else to go anyway."

"Took you and trained you, correct?" Van Dijk asked.

"To be useful to him, yes."

"Johanna Wyss is in your DNA, as is your father," Dabrowski said, "but they're only part of the mix."

"I know he did some enhancements."

"To make you stronger and faster than a normal human, yes. We saw evidence of that."

Kenji nodded. That part he knew, and he couldn't imagine why it would have shaped Dabrowski's opinion of him in any good way.

"But do you know about the pacifist-poet?" Dabrowski smiled.

"The what?"

"Lord Akito Okawa. A copy of his DNA was checked out from the Zamek Royal Seed Bank. You'd be surprised how many frozen bits of interesting living and dead people are in there." Dabrowski quirked his lips, the expression hard to read, and glanced at Oku. "The poet would have been a strange choice for a terrorist looking to raise a supersoldier to help him. I can't know what happened, of course, but your mother was the one to check out the DNA."

"She was a scientist." Kenji knew that much. "The one who mixed me up at my father's behest. I'd thought... Well, I thought I was mostly made from *his* DNA and that they'd been lovers, but that she was mostly my mother in name, not blood, that I was more of a clone of him with some other stuff added for, ah, improvement."

"Stuff being the scientific term," Oku murmured.

"There's a lot of your mother in you," Dabrowski said. "And quite a bit of Lord Okawa. Some of your father, but more like a quarter than a half."

"That's... not what he believed."

"I imagine it was your mother's little secret. Maybe she didn't *want* a terrorist for a son."

Her secret or her rebellion? Kenji stared at the table, floored by this revelation about his blood—about *him*. Was this why he'd never developed the taste for killing and violence and destruction that his father had possessed? That he'd tried so hard to inculcate in his son? Kenji had assumed it had been his mother's influence —her nurturing influence—rather than anything in his DNA. Could tendencies toward violence and aggression truly be all genetic? He didn't know.

Kenji lifted his head, meeting Dabrowski's friendly eyes. "That's why you had faith that I wouldn't take your money and run?"

Did Dabrowski have any idea how tempted he'd been? How much he'd wanted to get out of the Kingdom? And for that matter, how tempted he'd been to turn in Mari in the beginning? He looked at her, distressed to think about what might have happened if he'd succeeded at capturing her either time he'd tried.

"It was part of the equation," Dabrowski said.

"And why he succeeded in talking *us* into going along with this scheme," Van Dijk said, pointing her thumb at General Heim. "*I* wanted to send trained agents."

"*I* wanted to send the Fleet with slydar detectors to guard the gate," Heim grumbled.

"That might not have been sufficient since Zhor's ship had an astroshaman camouflage generator," Dabrowski said.

"At least *we* now have an astroshaman camouflage generator," Heim said.

Dabrowski glanced at Mari and then out to the balcony, where the cloaked woman was still looking toward the sea instead of paying attention to the meeting. "If the astroshamans let us keep them," he said.

Heim lifted his chin. "They are in no position to take them."

"I wouldn't bet on that," Dabrowski said.

"I sure wouldn't want to cross them," Kenji said, seeing a chance to put in a good word for Mari. "You should have seen Mari fight. While taking over three spaceships *and* the asteroid station. She flung a herd of manufacturing robots at our enemies."

"You defeated your enemies with robots?" Dabrowski beamed a smile at Mari, then told Oku, "I knew I liked her."

"And now we all see the reason why." Oku's smile was more wry.

"She's really good," Kenji said, aware of Mari blushing beside him, her eyes toward the table. She was too shy and polite to point out her own attributes. Someone had to do it for her. "You better give her asylum and hire her. And give her everything on her list."

"List?" Oku asked.

"That's not necessary," Mari murmured.

"I'm *sure* you can get hang-gliding lessons worked into a signing bonus," Kenji whispered to her.

"Pending the results of an upcoming private meeting," Oku said, looking at Mari, Dabrowski, and then the woman outside, "we *are* prepared to offer you work and the asylum you seek, Mari Moonrazor."

Mari lifted hopeful eyes. "Truly?"

"Yes." Oku nodded firmly, then looked to Heim and Van Dijk.

They sighed, and their nods were more grudging, but they *did* give them.

"We would value you as a scientist working for the crown," Oku said, "but you also seem to have some aptitude for... field work." She looked at Kenji. "If Royal Intelligence doesn't mind—"

Van Dijk groaned. "Your Majesty. *Must* you put them in *my* division?"

"Neither are soldiers, so it seems appropriate."

Them? Kenji looked back and forth between Oku and Van Dijk. They weren't including *him* in whatever this was... were they?

"Can't Dabrowski start a division of his own and find things for them to do?" Van Dijk asked.

Dabrowski blinked and touched his chest. "What kind of division would the Minister of External Affairs have? I'm only cleared to send diplomats around the Twelve Systems, and I don't think diplomacy is what anyone has in mind for these two."

"Please." Van Dijk's glare was exasperated. "You've got your fingers in everything. You shouldn't be involved in any of this other than to talk to *her*." She waved at the cloaked figure.

"I believe this is what the senate had in mind when they appointed him as my advisor," Oku said dryly, though the look she gave Dabrowski was more fond than exasperated.

"To the delight of all of us over fifty." Van Dijk shook her head.

"And over sixty," Heim said, though he didn't sound exasperated. He'd folded his hands on the table and looked quite pleased. Because Mari—and Kenji?—wasn't being assigned to *his* division?

"Uhm." Kenji lifted a finger, hoping for clarification about his role.

Oku met his eyes and nodded. "If you're willing, we would like to have you work with Mari as a special agent. We will pardon you for the crimes you committed as a juvenile, and it is possible that at some future date, we would consider having your family name and your mother's lands returned to you."

Kenji opened his mouth, but he was too stunned to speak. The best he'd thought he could hope for was not to be thrown in jail.

For so long, he'd planned to leave the Kingdom, but if he could stay here and work with Mari, did he truly want to flee to another system? Another system where his father might be waiting to hunt him down? He'd chatted with Mari on the way back about that possibility, and it chilled him and made him a lot less interested in venturing out.

"I accept, Your Majesty," Kenji said.

"Excellent." Oku looked to Mari. "And are you willing to work with Kenji?"

Kenji watched her, afraid she might object, given how their relationship had begun. He also worried she might hold that kiss against him. What if she'd considered it unprofessional and had doubts about teaming up with him because of it?

"Kenji is agreeable to work with, and to trade my services for asylum is what I hoped for when I came here. But..." Again, Mari looked to the balcony. "I'm not sure if it'll be permitted."

The woman finally turned around, the wind having knocked her hood down around her shoulders. It revealed short white hair, milky white-blue eyes, and a vague alienness that suggested she was an astroshaman. Was this... Mari's mother? The high shaman who'd forbidden her to leave her people?

Dabrowski stood up and gestured toward the door. "Let's go find out, shall we, Mari?"

Judging by her glum expression, Mari had no wish to speak with her mother or find out anything. Maybe she already knew what the answer would be.

Kenji patted her hand, hoping the gesture reassured her. She only looked sadly at him before walking outside with Dabrowski.

Kenji would have watched the encounter, trying to read lips, but Van Dijk came over to speak with him.

"We'll get you quarters in the high-security building where many of our agents stay," Van Dijk said. "It's more for your safety than because we don't trust you, but I'll admit some of us trust you less than others."

She didn't have to look at Dabrowski. Kenji already knew Dabrowski had been responsible for all of this and was the only reason he wasn't moldering in a jail cell. Kenji hoped he could prove himself worthy of that faith and that Dabrowski never had a reason to regret his decisions.

"You'll be watched these first years of your new career," Van Dijk continued, "but you're not a prisoner. You'll have pay commensurate with your position as a new agent, and there will be mission-completion bonuses."

"Thank you, ma'am." Kenji stood up and bowed to her. He had a feeling they were mostly offering him the job because they thought they could use him to get to his father one day, but he would cross that bridge when he came to it. He hadn't envisioned a future for himself in the Kingdom, but the promise of a regular paycheck, a full belly, and not having to hide his identity and live off the grid any longer was appealing. "Is there any chance my quarters will have a window?"

Her description of a safe, high-security building had him envisioning something similar to a jail cell—or a dungeon.

"I believe the apartments there have three or four," Van Dijk said.

"Oh? That sounds posh."

"I hope it'll suit you." She waved to the door. "Come along. I'll have one of my people get you settled in and issue you gear."

"What about Mari?" Kenji didn't mind the idea of being an agent, since it would be a significant upgrade to his old life, but he *really* liked the idea of being an agent who teamed up with Mari.

"If things work out, she might get an apartment in the same building."

"And... if things don't work out?" he asked.

Van Dijk hitched a shoulder. "She'll be back living with her people. Maybe you two can be pen pals."

Kenji couldn't manage a smile. She'd wanted asylum from the beginning. It wouldn't be fair if he got it, and she didn't.

~

Mari took a bracing breath before walking out onto the balcony, the gray sky thick with mist. Seagulls squawked over the waves far below.

She'd known right away who waited for her out here, and was glad that Minister Dabrowski was coming out with her. Though maybe she shouldn't be. Had he been the one to alert her mother to her presence here?

Maybe it had been foolish from the beginning to seek him out. Mari had known they knew each other—after all, Mother's *crusher* had been a gift, or something thrown into a negotiation, from Dabrowski. Technically, it had been Scholar Sato whom Mari had sought out, but she'd read the novel, and she'd known Sato and Dabrowski were friends. Admittedly, she hadn't known they were *roommates* and that she wouldn't be able to find one without the other.

Mother turned to face them, and her mouth twisted with familiar wryness, perhaps because they were coming out together. Allies facing a threat.

No, Mother wasn't a threat, neither to the Kingdom nor to Mari. Not *physically*. Just... emotionally.

"Hello, Mother. I hope you're well and that your projects and research have continued without hitches in my absence."

"Not the *terraforming* research."

"Will you be needing that soon?" Dabrowski put in with a bright smile. "I trust your current focus is on building a wormhole gate. How's that going? Did you have time to study the ancient one sufficiently before the AI ship came and slurped up all the pieces?"

Mother shifted her gaze to him. "Slurped? I don't believe advanced machine civilizations imbue their physical representatives with the parotid, submandibular, and sublingual salivary glands necessary to produce saliva and *slurp*."

Mari barely resisted the urge to groan at this precision.

Unfazed, Dabrowski said, "You're right. It was figurative slurping. As I recall, there was *grinding* as the pieces were dragged across the ice."

"Our studies are progressing," Mother told him. "*Some* of them."

"Perhaps after a break of a few years, Mari will be ready to return to her portion of them. She requested asylum from us, though I assure you, we wouldn't be so foolish as to attempt to keep you from one of your own people."

Mari winced. It wasn't that she'd expected the Kingdom to go to war to protect her from being kidnapped by her own kind, but she'd hoped... She wasn't sure what. That they were a formidable enough people that her mother wouldn't want to irk them, especially now that they were neighbors.

"But what it sounds like she *really* wants," Dabrowski continued, "is a sabbatical. A little break to explore the delightful quirks and foibles of humanity at large."

"She wants to eat blood-sugar-spiking foods devoid of nutritional value and have sex with panting young knights excreting pheromones."

Mari rocked back, horrified that Mother was bringing up the Human List with Minister Dabrowski. A crude and derogatory version of it. Mari couldn't even remember sharing that second desire with her mother; her sisters must have tattled on her.

"As many young women do." Dabrowski smiled easily. "I can personally attest to the delight of blood-sugar-spiking foods devoid of nutritional value. I'm less moved by panting knights, but I can see their appeal for others. Isn't it wonderful that Mari is interested in citizens of the Kingdom? That means she'll stay in the area during her sabbatical, and it'll be easy for her to visit you and vice versa. Just imagine if she wanted to have sex with pirates in System Cerberus or mercenaries in System Hind. It would take you *weeks* to visit each other. And those pirates are dangerous, unscrupulous, and terribly flagitious. You wouldn't want such partners for your daughter, would you?"

"I see what you're doing," Mother said.

"Oh?" Dabrowski raised his eyebrows in innocent inquiry. "Is it working?"

Mari raised her own eyebrows, skeptical but hopeful. She felt that she should be saying more on her own behalf, but was it possible a stranger could accomplish what she hadn't been able to with her mother? No, not a stranger, she supposed. A neutral third party. A *diplomat*.

"Better than arguments that she's a grown woman and not *owned* by the astroshamans, even though we raised her, cared for her, and educated her." Mother turned a flat look on Mari, who'd made precisely those arguments. Numerous times.

"Such as all parents do with their children." Dabrowski extended an open palm. "Until the time comes to set them free to choose their own destiny."

"You just want her because she's trying to win her asylum with astroshaman technology—*more* astroshaman technology—that your people want."

Dabrowski smiled at her. "I would be happy to offer refuge to any person or robot willing to work and provide value to our community, whether they come with technology or not."

"Even the flagitious types?"

"Certainly. I have such an acquaintance right now who is working for the good of the Kingdom and seeking atonement for past wrongs."

"What if I said she wouldn't be permitted to share any existing technology or proprietary astroshaman secrets?" Mother walked up and took the terraformer from Mari's hands, though she was talking to Dabrowski. "While I doubt *you* would chain her in a laboratory and force her to use her knowledge to make dangerous weapons, you are not your entire government. Your King Jager may be dead now, but he left a bad taste in all of our mouths, and the fact that you still have a monarchy with one of his children in charge doesn't inspire trust and adoration in us."

"I have no objection to that stipulation," Dabrowski said, not commenting on the rest. "Your daughter has many talents and abilities useful in their own right, as she demonstrated by assisting us with our mission." Dabrowski surprised Mari by bowing to her.

"I thought your people were assisting *her*." Mother held up the terraformer.

Mari was tempted to snatch it back, but if it was what she needed to trade for her freedom...

"We mutually assisted each other," Dabrowski said. "She got her device back, we retrieved others that had been stolen, and we captured numerous thieves who had been plaguing not only our system but others. The Kingdom will likely never have the reach it once did, but we wish to make the Twelve Systems a better place whenever possible. It is not only *people* who sometimes need to seek atonement for past wrongs."

Mother snorted. "At one point, I thought you might end up in charge of this morass of a government, but I see now that they picked the perfect job for you."

"Diplomacy?"

"Sucking up to people and making promises that they want to hear."

"Yes, diplomacy." Dabrowski nodded firmly and smirked. "The Chief Superintendent of Royal Intelligence has offered to pay Mari and give her an apartment in the city, so you needn't worry about her having trouble thriving in our society. And I'll be happy to arrange accommodations for you if you wish to enjoy the rest of the day here with your daughter and spend the night before returning. My roommate *loves* when we have guests stay over."

Mari almost choked on that, remembering Scholar Sato's

comment to the opposite, but Mari was positive her mother had no interest in sleeping on some former enemy's sofa.

"I will return today," Mother said, "and I suppose I will thank you for letting me know my wayward charge was in your city, since *she* failed to inform me of her plans. Though I noticed you only mentioned it after I asked you if you'd seen her."

"You're welcome," Dabrowski said. "I'll leave you two alone so you can have a private chat if you wish. Enjoy the balcony and the view, though you may want to watch out for that squall at sea that's threatening to roll in. Also stray seagulls dropping, er, droppings. They do *not* respect the sanctity of ancient architecture." He waved cheerfully to Mother, gave Mari a thumbs-up, and walked inside.

Mari didn't feel as cheerful or optimistic when she was left alone with her mother. Despite Dabrowski burbling on as if Mother were agreeing to everything he said, she hadn't truly agreed to any of it.

"I'm sorry I didn't tell you where I was going," Mari said, "but then you would have caught up with me sooner and dragged me back. As it was, I had to tinker with our base's security system so it wouldn't take note of me leaving."

"I noticed."

"Are you going to let me stay? For a while?" Mari had originally planned to leave forever if need be, but she realized that suggesting she would return might help Mother loosen her grip. And it was possible that Mari would eventually check off all the items on her list and decide that normal human life wasn't for her. At which point, it would be nice to have the option to return.

Mother sighed. "I suppose. As *Diplomat* Dabrowski pointed out, you're more accessible here than if you felt compelled to flee to another system."

Mari didn't know if she wanted to be accessible to her people, but since it sounded like she would be permitted to stay without further struggle, she wouldn't object. "Thank you, Mother." She forced herself to make an overture of kinship. "Do you wish to obtain something to eat together?"

"Do you believe there's a place where we could eat without being shunned, mocked, and possibly shot at?"

"I don't know the city that well yet."

Mother shook her head. "I can't believe you want to live among these people."

Undaunted, Mari offered, "Perhaps Qin could recommend something. I understand that she and her sisters have similar problems fitting in with the locals."

"Wonderful."

Though Mother was as sarcastic and dry as ever, and had claimed Mari's hard-won terraformer for herself, Mari smiled as they walked out together. She would be allowed to stay for a time. It was enough.

EPILOGUE

The apartment had not three, not four, but *five* windows. It was late, but Kenji couldn't stop walking from window to window, looking out on the city lights. The highest towers of Drachen Castle were visible over the stone wall that surrounded the sprawling structure, with the unwalled but more ominous Royal Intelligence Headquarters beside it. In the other direction, the skyscrapers of downtown rose up, the magtracks snaking between them, and auto flyers and shuttles banking around them on their way across the city.

The apartment featured two bedrooms, a bathroom, a living room, a kitchen, *and* a dining room. An entire dining room, not just a corner of another room with a table in it.

Given that Kenji had been born into the nobility and had lived the first eight years of his life on a sprawling estate on the Southern Continent, it shouldn't have felt so strange—so luxurious—to have so much room to himself, but it had been a *long* time since he'd had a place of his own. One that he had the right to inhabit and wasn't some temporary and illegal shelter.

His temple throbbed, and he touched it before he caught

himself. A small bandage was the only outward sign that he'd had a chip surgically implanted and linked to his brain so he could communicate directly with it. All he had to do was think commands, and he could read the results on a contact display that took the place of the glasses he'd always worn, glasses that could be removed and tossed aside if someone was trying to track him.

Supposedly, the government didn't care about tracking people through their chips—and it was forbidden for corporations to do it via software—but his father had always warned him that wasn't the case. If one didn't want to be found, one couldn't ever get chipped.

Kenji lowered his hand. If this didn't work out, he could get it removed later. For now, he'd spent the last few hours tinkering with the novelty of it, and it had given him a headache. Or maybe that was from the surgery. Or poking himself in the eye countless times trying to figure out how to put in the contact. At least, since his vision was fine without correction, he'd only had to get one.

"This apartment is quite lovely," Kay said. "It has a fabulous view. Even my limited optical receptors find it agreeable."

"I'm glad. You can have your own bedroom."

"I do not require sleep, but I usually power down to recharge in a quiet corner or, as you know, occasionally a closet."

"Well, now you can use the closet in your very own bedroom."

"Sublime. Will you take me on your new secret-agent missions?"

"Did you enjoy going to an asteroid station where we were horribly outnumbered and threatened from all sides by angry dog men?"

"Since I did not leave the ship, the dog men did not trouble me."

"Lucky you."

The control panel by the door chimed. Mari?

When he'd left the castle, she'd still been out on the balcony with Dabrowski and her mother. Negotiating her fate. For all he knew, Mari might already have been dragged back to wherever her people lived.

Since Chief Van Dijk had promised the building was secure, Kenji didn't take the new stunner or DEW-Tek pistol he'd been issued with him to the door. Hoping it was Mari, he opened it without checking to see who it was.

Then sprang back in shock, trying to slam the door shut on the man in full black combat armor standing in the hallway. A black gauntleted hand caught the door before it shut, but the man didn't storm inside the apartment as Kenji expected.

Though surprised he had the time, he grabbed the DEW-Tek pistol off the table and pointed it at the apartment entrance. Was this the damn Main Event again? Kenji hadn't looked long enough to see the letters ME emblazoned on his helmet, but who else stalked around Zamek City in black combat armor and a mask?

The man pushed the door open, but he remained on the threshold. Kenji pointed the pistol at his chest, though it was only symbolic. The firepower wouldn't be sufficient to damage that armor and reach the man underneath.

"Look," Kenji said. "I'm here *legally*. I mean, I got a job. I have to be in the city. I'm working for Royal Intelligence now."

"So I heard," came the dry response.

"How did you get *in* here?"

Did Chief Van Dijk know that random thugs in armor could breach her supposedly secure building?

"I go where I wish. I came to inform you that since you have been pardoned and will presumably not commit further crimes in my city, you need not hide behind counters or potted plants when I am in the area."

Hell, that meant he'd known Kenji was in that rental shop all along. Why hadn't he grabbed Kenji to turn him in? Or rough him up? Whatever the self-proclaimed superhero did?

"I'm relieved," Kenji said warily, expecting him to threaten to tell Royal Intelligence about his heinous crime at the park. But surely, Chief Van Dijk knew all about everything Kenji had been up to in his life—and more.

"I thought you might be. Stay out of trouble, Chisaka." The man turned and disappeared into the hallway.

Kenji swallowed. That was his father's surname, not the name he'd gone by for the last eight years. How could the *Main Event* know about it? And who could he know in Royal Intelligence who'd blabbed about Kenji and his new assignment?

"Perhaps shutting the door would be wise," Kay, who'd watched the exchange from the window, said.

"Uh, yeah. Good idea."

First, Kenji stuck his head into the hallway, looking in both directions. The Main Event was gone.

He was about to close—and bolt—the door, but he spotted someone else stepping out of the elevator. His heart lifted.

"Mari!" he blurted, waving at her.

Given that it had only been hours since he'd seen her and not days or weeks, the wave was possibly more vigorous than convention dictated, but he didn't care. He'd been afraid her mother would drag her back to her people.

Mari smiled when she met his eyes, though he couldn't tell from her expression if she was only coming to say goodbye or if she would be allowed to stay.

"Hello, Kenji." She stepped into the apartment with him. "This is your new home?"

"Yes, included with the job, I understand. Are you... getting one yourself?"

Maybe he shouldn't have jumped right to that question, but he had to know.

Mari took a deep breath, and he braced himself, expecting the worst.

"Yes. I'm being allowed to stay for a while and work as an agent alongside you. I'll also be permitted to do some scientific research and experiments, but Minister Dabrowski and my mother came to an arrangement regarding that. I'm not allowed to work on building new terraforming devices or share any of our advanced technology with your people. I do hope I'll be able to be useful without that."

"You *will*. Trust me. And that's great that you can stay. You're an adult woman. You should be able to choose your life and where you lead it."

"I agree. I have something for you."

Mari withdrew two Royal Intelligence identification cards, one with his picture on it and one with hers. There was a brown smudge that might have been chocolate on one of her fingers, but he only smiled and didn't point it out.

"There will be versions that get linked to our chips, too, but we can show these if we're ever stuck in trouble somewhere with people who don't have chip scanners. In addition, I'll be receiving a diplomatic passport." Mari smiled wryly as she handed him his ident card. "I'm also thinking of purchasing clothing that proclaims that I *heart* the Kingdom."

Kenji could imagine idiots in Zamek City making trouble for her simply because she was an astroshaman. Hopefully, the ident card would convince people to back off. In general, nobody wanted to garner the attention of Royal Intelligence.

"That might not be a bad idea, but I'm pretty sure we'll be issued uniforms. You could wear that on the weekends." Kenji lifted his card. "I wonder when they got the pictures." He eyed his, guessing it had been taken as he'd walked into the conference room. "I'm an I-1," he said, reading his pay rating, description, and name—they'd gone with Backer instead of Chisaka. "Entry level. Given my complete lack of experience in this field, I suppose that makes sense."

Whatever I-is made, it would be a lot more than he'd made scrounging odd jobs as an off-the-grid mechanic, though he was a tiny bit wistful that he wouldn't see twenty-five thousand Union dollars again anytime soon.

"I assume that with the satisfactory completion of assignments, one gains in pay and rank over time," Mari said.

"Let's hope." Kenji checked out her card, expecting she had been given the same rank, since she didn't have experience in the field either, but he ended up gawking. "You're an I-4?"

"It does say that. I am unfamiliar with the scale. Is that a lesser or greater rank?"

"Greater. You probably get *six* windows." Kenji didn't resent that—not exactly—but he found it puzzling, since they were the same age and they were starting the job at the same time.

"Windows?" She tilted her head.

"Never mind." He pointed at her card. "It means you're my boss and get better pay."

"Oh. Odd."

He was tempted to agree, but he supposed she was being given credit for however many years of experience she had as a scientist —or maybe the fact that she could hack her way into systems that were supposed to be unhackable. Grudgingly, he admitted that she had a lot more useful expertise than he did.

"It also means I should kiss your ass on a regular basis." Kenji found a smile, or maybe a wry smirk, though a hint of sadness touched him as he realized... "But probably not other things."

"My ass?" Mari touched said ass and looked down. "That is not on my list."

"Having your ass kissed isn't on the Human List? You should add it. It's quite a delightful experience, or so I've heard." He waved his ident card. "I'm going to have to work hard for a long time to get to the point where people feel compelled to kiss *my* ass."

Strangely, he found that he didn't mind the idea. He'd worked hard for a long time just to stay alive and not be noticed. It would be nice to work toward becoming a more capable, more *respected* person. Maybe he could even sign up for one of Minister Dabrowski's lectures. Legitimately this time.

"I shall consider your advice," Mari said. "I understand that you are likely a wiser and more contemplative and sensitive soul than I'd realized."

Was that a reference to his poetical genes? "Yes. I'm sure my DNA imparts wisdom and sensitivity, along with the ability to rhyme on the fly."

"I am not surprised. You didn't seem to have the heart of a bounty hunter."

"Because I failed to capture you?"

"Because you opened with *I want to talk to you* instead of simply shooting me."

"Which denotes wisdom and sensitivity rather than incompetence? I guess I'm pleased."

"Good." Mari smiled, lifted a hand as if she might grip his arm —or touch his cheek?—then dropped it in favor of a Kingdom bow. Maybe she'd also gotten the gist that if they were going to work together, and she was going to be his boss, they should keep their relationship professional. "I will see you in the morning for work."

"Yes." He returned her smile a little sadly as she walked back toward the elevator. "Goodnight, Mari."

THE END

Made in the USA
Monee, IL
20 August 2023